GIFT FROM THE WING

SOURCE OF ELEMENTRA BOOK 4

WILLA RAE

Gift from the Wing

Source of Elementra Book 4

Edited by Lawrence Editing

Gift from the Wing/Willa Rae-1st ed.

ISBN-979-8-9898968-7-5

To those that always had to choose the path of "kill them with kindness"
I hope you get a sense of satisfaction after this.

Content Warning

You will find dark content within the pages of this book that may be triggering to some readers.
Including but not limited to: Conversations and flashbacks of abuse, both mental and physical including rape, torture, and violence. Parental death. Murder/violence, gritty language, steamy situations, sexual situations, and other adult content is in this book!
Read at your own discretion. Intended for individuals 18+.

One

Willow

I've been struck by lightning.

That's the only explanation for the ruthless attack happening to my body right now.

The bolt of electricity rips through my mind and travels to my chest, searing every nerve with a flare of unbearable heat and light. Every heartbeat is a painful aftershock that leaves me stunned, breathless, and shaking so violently I'm surprised I don't burst out of my skin.

My ears ring with piercing static and my thoughts—memories—scatter like sparks in a storm. The intensity of the strike tears them apart left and right, and they're battling to figure out where in my mind they're supposed to be.

Everything's spinning.

I search Aurora's kind eyes for some semblance of grounding. The calm, gentle nature seeps from her, beckoning me to latch onto the lifeline, but whatever's going on with me is acting like a shield, blocking out her attempts to protect me.

My back bows as my mind fractures—I swear the force splits my skull in half. For a fleeting, blissful blip in time, there's nothing. I see nothing, hear nothing, feel nothing, taste, smell, you name it.

Nothing.

The reprieve is over far too fast. The life I was beginning to know and grow accustomed to comes crashing down around me.

Barrier after barrier in my mind crumbles like poorly constructed buildings after a cataclysmic earthquake. There's no stopping it as memories splinter in from all angles, yet I haven't the slightest clue why they're bringing me such devastation.

But that's all I feel.

My heart is shattering beneath my tightly clenched fist as though it's me who's reaching in and carving it out. The fingers that're running soothing circles on my cheek flinch as an anguished scream rips from my throat and glass pelts the floor as it explodes all around me.

"Guys...Tillman...Someone please make it stop. Make it stop," I beg, but there's no answer.

Nothing can penetrate the havoc.

Elementra, please.

If this is the peril the memories bring forth, I don't want them.

I don't...

"I don't want a shot. No, please, please," I shout at the top of my lungs as my father wraps his arms and legs around my trembling body.

"Enough, Willow. If you can't stay still, I will hold you down. Do you understand me?"

"P-please. I don't need a shot," I beg quietly as the tremors course through me, fierce enough to make my teeth chatter.

My current subconscious shoves its way to the forefront of my mind, and I glance through the blurry eyes that I know to be mine.

Only, they're twenty years younger.

I try but fail to rip myself free of this moment. I want to rip six-year-old me out of the arms of that monster, but I can't break away from the lock on my mind. Restraints I can't see trap me in this particular memory, and I don't want to relive this.

This day will forever haunt me despite the growth I've had.

"Enough," my father commands, shaking me slightly and silencing any more of my begging.

A man standing above the chair my father and I are sitting on grips my wrist so hard I gasp. That inhale swiftly turns into a scream at the piercing pain of a needle shoved into the crook of my elbow, and my body naturally reacts to the fear pulsing through me.

Hot liquid runs down my legs at the first sight of red pouring through the tubing connected to my arm, and I sob harder as my father grips my arms painfully.

"You vile child," he barks, causing me to flinch and tense, but my bladder won't stop. I can't make it stop. "One bag will be enough for today. My daughter has a lesson she needs to learn here and now."

The man nods to my father, not bothering to spare me a glance as he flicks the sight of where the needle is protruding from as if that will make my blood flow faster.

I sit, petrified, shaking in my father's lap, transfixed on the bright red that fills the clear bag to the rim, and the tears that won't stop pouring from my eyes taste metallic on my tongue.

My small chest rises and falls faster and faster when the needle is pulled carelessly from my arm and a pitiful whimper passes through my lips as I fixate on the little droplet of blood that pools at the exit site.

It's the first time in my life I can recall ever seeing my own blood and it turns my stomach inside out. The confusion and fear warring inside of younger me intensifies the turmoil rolling inside of my current self.

Fuck, I was so scared, so confused.

He'd given me no warning of what was to come when he sent a house staff to retrieve me from the sunroom where I was eating my breakfast. I had just sat down. Taken one bite of scrambled eggs and was doing a happy shimmy to the taste when my blissful moment was broken.

My disassociation breaks when the color is smeared down my arm as my father yanks me off his lap and drags me out of his study, muttering something to the man who just did his bidding. I try to dig my heels in, but all that gets me is a deadly glare. No command needs to leave his mouth because that look has fear skittering through my body.

"I-I'm sorry," I hiccup through my sobs.

"Not yet, you aren't, but you will learn today what your defiance and disgusting mannerisms bring you, Willow. I have instilled enough in you by this point that you should know better than to fight me," he says back so gently, my little heart pounds with naïve and childlike hope that he's not truly angry.

The house staff we pass pause whatever they're doing, bowing their heads low as I'm marched through the estate and out the back door that leads to the forest.

My gaze stares through the tall trees until it becomes too thick to see any farther and I swallow roughly, scared to death that he's about to force me in there. There's no telling what monsters hide inside.

"Put her in," my father's command startles me out of my staring, and I scream as I'm lifted off my feet.

The noise continues to rip from my throat as I'm dropped just a few inches from the bottom. The movement is so sudden and jarring, I tumble to the ground and take in a mouthful of dirt. My arms tremble as I try to push myself up on all fours, but shock has taken hold, zapping all my strength, and I roll onto my back.

"If you want to behave like a filthy child, I will treat you like one. You will stay out here until I deem you've learned your lesson."

Getting my first glance around at where I am sends fright burning through my body. I jump up from the ground and claw my hands down the side of the dirt wall, screaming and begging as I search for a way to get a grip and climb out. It's useless as I continue to fall on my butt, pulling more and more dirt down on me with each attempt.

"I'll be good. I'll listen. I promise," I scream, cry, gag, and the sobs ripping through me are so hard they drag the contents of my stomach up with each desperate inhale.

"I find that hard to believe, Willow. It's in your blood to defy me, but rest assured, I will break you of the habit." He swears before stomping away, leaving me there breathless, petrified, and begging for his forgiveness.

Eventually, my stomach does revolt against me and somewhere along the way, I lost my shoes, so my bare toes get buried in both the contents of my breakfast and dirt. Exhaustion weighs my little body down. I just can't fight any longer and with swaying staggers, I sink to the ground and pass out into the darkness.

I cry to myself where I'm still trapped in the dungeons of my mind with this memory that won't release me. Using all the mental strength I have, I push at the barrier surrounding me, but it doesn't relent. It doesn't loosen up. If anything, it latches onto me tighter, and I'm forced to continue to endure this. Endure the first of many days to come that warped me into the person I am today.

"Wake up, Miss Abott."

My crusted eyes flutter open and the pounding in my heart starts immediately as I'm roused from what I thought was a horrific night terror. As I take in the dark dirt walls and the cool temperature of the earth, my tears instantly start flowing down my cheeks and my breathing quickens. My tiny fingers uncoil from the fistful of mud I was clinging to for dear life as I swiftly push myself up and look above me.

"You may come out now, Miss Abott. Your father had business to attend to," my nanny, Ms. Johnson, says as she lies on the ground with her arms outstretched toward me.

Reaching down, she grabs me by my hands and pulls me out, then sets me on my feet and stands to clean herself off. I can't stop staring at the long rectangular hole. From above, it doesn't look so big, but in there...it seemed gigantic, never-ending.

"Now, you need to go get cleaned up. Your father will be away for the night and I'm to report to him any bad behavior, so keep that in mind," she says so sternly, it feels like she slapped me.

Why is she being mean to me too?

My heart splinters open.

To feel now the confusion that was warring through my mind then is heartbreaking. Overwhelming. I was only six. I was still a baby, and I had no clue what was going on. I couldn't understand why the lady who laid my clothes out for me every day and brushed and braided my hair was suddenly treating me as though I'd done something wrong.

When she reaches out to grip my arm, panic takes hold.

Pulling away from her, my chest heaves as I backpedal, glaring as if she's the biggest monster in my life. The crunching of leaves underneath my feet has me turning my head and peering at the forest behind me.

The monsters in there or the one in front of me.

The forest wins.

I force my legs to propel me forward, away from the sound of her calling my name, away from that hole, away from that house. Away from it all.

"Run," I quietly whimper to myself repeatedly as my bare feet pound across the forest foliage.

Tripping, I cry out in pain as my chin lands on a pinecone and my palms split open from the briars I grip while trying to push myself up on wobbling arms. I sit on my heels and bawl my eyes out, wiping the blood from my hands and the trickle running down my neck.

The sobs tear through my confused and flustered heart as I furiously rub at the dried and crusted mud between my thighs. All I do is spread the red from my hands all over myself and I continue to freak out to the point I throw up once again.

I breathe a sigh of relief, thinking this is over because, in my tortured mind, this is all I remember. I recall passing out after getting sick for the second time, but this memory never fades. This is a different version of the truth I've known for the past twenty years.

My current mental denial shoves once again at the lock keeping me caged in my mind, but a wave of calm rushes over younger me strong enough I feel it in my subconscious.

The persistent need to go farther, to keep traveling through the forest overwhelms me and my shaky legs finally gain some strength as I stagger along, holding on to the trees for support.

What is going on?

The more steps I take, the more my fear blossoms into my first taste of anger as I aggressively wipe the tears from my eyes. With each stomp, I feel something else. Something unexplainable for my age. It festers like a virus, spreading through my veins. Taking over completely.

Sure, I'm certain six-year-olds have big emotions and can throw quite a tantrum at times, but this is something completely different brewing in me.

It's desperation, longing.

The farther into the forest I get, the more it intensifies.

The more at home I feel.

My steps falter as I snap my head up at the quiet sound of humming. It's a sweet melody that draws me closer, but I take two steps back as a man, with hair the color of fluffy clouds, smiles warmly at me. He's sitting with his back to the weirdest tree I've ever seen. It doesn't look like any of the trees around me.

My body freezes like a deer in headlights when his kind eyes that match the sky pin me in place. The deeper I sink into his stare, the more familiar he feels. I don't want to move away from him but toward him.

"My, my, you've wandered quite a ways away from your house, Willow," he says, standing up.

He pauses in a half hunch, holding his hands up as I stumble backward, falling to my butt and crab-walking away from him as fast as I can.

"Whoa, whoa, it's okay. Everything's all right. I'm not going to hurt you."

My retreat stills, but my breathing quickens, and my eyes track his every move as he lowers himself back to the ground. There's a warmth about him that spreads throughout my body and despite my fright, my limbs relax until I'm sitting on the ground, mimicking him.

"I'm not supposed to talk to strangers," I mumble quietly after a minute of him just smiling at me softly.

"You shouldn't. It's very dangerous to do that."

"But you're a stranger," I say, cocking my head to the side.

His laugh fills the space between the two of us and like a fishing line with candy on the end, I crawl toward the sound as though he's luring me in until I'm merely a foot away from him.

"To you, yes, I am for now, but I've known you nearly my entire life. My name is CC," he says with a small smile on his lips, reaching his hand out for me to grasp.

Staring at its clean, golden shade, then at my pale skin that's covered in dried mud, I try to wipe my fingers on my shirt, to no avail. I shrink in on myself, quickly pulling my hand back and tucking it under my leg. My face grows hot from both embarrassment and fear that he's going to punish me for being dirty.

"It's okay, Willow. I don't mind a little dirt. I'm used to it," he whispers softly, stretching his arm toward me a little more.

After another long, silent stare off, with trembling fingers and a clipped nod, I lay my hand into his warm palm.

A surprised gasp comes from me as my brain grows dizzy.

All fear flees my body as a voice fills my head, along with pictures of this man and me. He's running with me through the forest, singing to me, fixing my booboos, rocking me to sleep. My heart triples in size as the lady in my head promises me all these things will come true along with a love like I've never known.

Before she tells me goodbye, she promises I'm safe with him and he'll never hurt me.

Although I'm dizzy, as though I went on the merry-go-round too many times, I can't stop from flinging myself at him in a fit of tears, clinging with my arms around his neck.

"There, there, it's okay. I'm here now," he says as he smooths his hand down my hair, shushing me quietly as I cry.

Time seems to stand still as I continue to let the heartache and confusion of the day pour out of me and into him. All my young, puzzled mind wants is to feel this affection and soak in this feeling that I've never felt before.

"You're CC." I hiccup as I finally release him and lay my head on his chest as though I've known him forever, not minutes.

"I am."

"That's not the name the lady called you in my head."

"Oh really? When did a lady speak to you?" he asks.

"Just now."

"Can you tell me what she said?"

"She called me a funny name and said she sent you here to look after me. Then she called you a different name. It was long."

"I see. Did she give you her name?"

"Yeah, it's...Elma...Elma..." I grunt, growing upset with myself as my stuttered, tear-drenched speech can't get the word out.

"That's okay. I know who spoke to you. Her name is Elementra," he says softly, washing away the frustration.

"So it's true? You're going to take care of me from now on?" I pop up excitedly, smiling from ear to ear.

His eyes soften as he smiles down at me, but it's not as full as my own and I immediately feel his restraint. "Yes and no. I'll be here every single day, right in this spot, but you still must live in your house, and no one can know about me."

My lip trembles and my eyes water as heartbreak spreads throughout my chest. "I-I don't want to go back there."

"I know, and I wish more than anything you didn't have to, but for now, it's the only way. It'll be our secret and an adventure you get to go on every day," he murmurs.

"Adventures? Like playing games and make-believe?" I ask with a new-found childlike excitement at the opportunity to do things I hear all the other girls talk about at school.

"Just like that. It'll be like we live in a whole other world," he says.

"I'd like that. Very much."

"Me too, Willow, me too." He sighs softly as he traces my face. Reaching up with his thumb, he wipes away the blood still dotting my chin, then looks up at the sky. "It's time for you to get back."

"No, not yet," I beg.

"They're out looking for you, my girl, and I have somewhere I must be, but I promise I'll be back tomorrow."

"Where do you have to be?"

He laughs lightly, wiping the tears pouring down my cheeks. "Today is a special day. My oldest nephew turns fourteen."

"Fourteen?" I gasp. "That's so old."

His laughter echoes through the forest and he tilts his head back against the trunk of the weird tree. It's so warm and comforting, I giggle right along with him.

"One day, you're going to find that hilarious, sweet Willow," he says gently, with a small smile. "Come on now."

Again, I cling to him like my life depends on it, refusing to allow him to put me down. Without a complaint, he stands, holding me cradled in his arms, and makes it back through the trek that I practically crashed through to get here.

My tears flow down my face faster the farther away from that tree we get and the closer my house grows. The entire walk, he hums his quiet song and eventually, I mimic the music. With perfect timing, our song ends just as he stops his steps.

When he gently sets me on my feet, I hold his hand in a death grip as we stare at the back lawn from where we're concealed from sight. My nanny and a few other house staff members are running around, hollering my name, but for the life of me, I don't want to leave him.

"I don't want to go home," I whisper.

"This isn't your home, Willow. You'll go home one day," he mumbles as he crouches down in front of me. "Remember what I said. You can't tell anyone about me. Can you do that for me?"

"I can. I'm good at keeping secrets. I have a lot of them."

His smile makes me want to tell him all the secrets I keep locked away in my little mind. I want to tell him everything about myself, although it feels like I've never gone a day without him in my life. My heart has known him forever.

"There are so many more to come, my sweet girl. I'm so sorry you have to be so strong for your age, but I'm so proud of you and I'm here now to help you," he whispers as he brings me in close for a hug that I melt into.

I don't want to let him go.

"I'll see you tomorrow," he promises again as he releases me and turns me toward the estate, then gives me a small push to get my feet moving.

I look back every few steps.

By the time I'm surrounded by the house staff who's fussing over the condition I'm in, more fearful over their jobs than how I truly am, I no longer see him standing at the tree line and my mind finally starts to release me.

"Oh, CC..."

"Welcome home, filia mea."

The peaceful silence that welcomes me as my subconscious gains back control is shattered the second my eyes fly open, and a blood-curdling scream leaves my chest.

Heartbreak. Grief. Pain.

The concoction of the three of those emotions creates a type of torture I've never experienced in my life. It ripples through my body like a sonic boom, and I sob in agony as it all rushes back to me.

"How could you?" I scream.

The infuriatingly soft, plush blanket that someone laid over me tangles around my legs, and instead of standing, I roll to the floor off the couch and that sets me off.

I can't hold in my anger, my rage at the unfairness of this feeling, and I let it all out.

Bashing my fist into the ground, I scream bloody murder as I lay waste to nothing but the ebony hardwood beneath me.

"How could you leave me?" I sob.

Tears flow down my face like wild rapids and I fight mercilessly against the arms that wrap themselves around me. I don't want anyone to touch me. I don't want to calm down. I don't...

"Primary, stop before you hurt yourself. Look around, we've got you. We're here." Caspian's cold but calm tone cuts through the madness that's slicing me to pieces. But it's not enough.

My own darkness has taken hold.

My men. They're here.

Stay with them.

"That's right, little warrior, we're here."

It's not enough.

"Take me to the South Wing," I demand through my sobs.

"Princess, we need—"

"Take me," I scream, surprising even Caspian as his arms flinch around me.

Corentin nods over my head, and a different kind of darkness swallows me whole as we move through the fabric of Elementra and are spat out in what seems to be a place frozen in time.

The second Caspian sets my feet on the floor, I run.

I've never seen this foyer with my own eyes, but my heart knows where to go. This is the only area that's not blocked off and as I cross through the arch, I slam to a stop as my gaze takes in the shimmering ward.

I hear their footsteps, more than my men's, running toward me, but I couldn't give a fuck as my body vibrates with pent-up hurt, trauma, sorrow, mourning.

"We can't go any farther, little wanderer," Draken says softly from somewhere behind me.

No.

With a guttural screech, I pound on the barrier with everything I got and when it pushes back, I push harder. I give myself over fully to the darkness that's always lurked below my surface. The void built up by the horrors I've lived through. Those that I remember and those that were hidden from me. Yes, to protect me, but hidden from me, nonetheless.

I pour my heart, soul, and body into every punch. Every strike, every scream has the ward trembling beneath my fist.

"How could you leave me? How the fuck could you do this?" I shriek until my throat is raw.

"Child, please. Please, calm down."

I whip around on my heels at the sound of that voice.

Standing a few feet in front of my men, who look as though they're preparing to declare war on someone, Gaster's holding out a shaking hand for me to take.

My Gaster.

My *Guardria*.

He's suffered just as much.

My chest heaves heavily as I clench my fist so tightly, my partially shifted nails slice through my skin. My heart seems to splinter apart even more as I fall into the depths of his baby blue eyes that portray the same grief as mine.

"He left us, Gaster. How could he leave us?"

His gaze fills to the brim with water and his entire body shudders. When the pierce of his pain hits me, I lose the tight hold I had on my elements and the entire structure rumbles, sending my Patera-Nexus, mother-in-law, and Keeper to the ground.

But not my men.

Not Gaster.

"Please, Willow, step away from the ward. Come talk to us," he says softly, taking a step toward me.

I immediately take a step back. I can't trust myself or my emotions in this moment and I don't want him so close to me. I'd never forgive myself if I hurt him, hurt any of them.

My bloody palm lands against the ward, sending a violent tremor through the floors of this wing, inhibiting anyone from getting any closer to me.

Then time seems to slow.

Everything, everyone falls unnaturally sluggish as though they're walking through tar.

My erratic heartbeat thuds in my ears, blocking out all noise, although I clearly see my men shouting something at me. They're taking steps toward me, more like attempting to run, but they make no progress. It's all in slow motion.

A vine wraps around my wrist, and my head tilts down to look at it, then back up at its caster. We're the only two who can move.

"Step out of the ward, child, please. It's imploding."

Imploding.

His warning finally cuts through the rage-filled haze and panic immediately sets in. Trying but failing to jerk my arm free, the pull of the ward continues to drag me back, refusing to release me.

"Guys..." I tremble, staring at them with wide, shocked eyes.

I'm not getting out of wherever this is about to take me.

"I'm so sorry."

Their bodies vibrate with the effort it's taking them to try to break through whatever this stasis is that's keeping them from moving, but it's a useless feat.

Slicing through the vine tied around my wrist, I shoot a watery smile to Gaster, apologizing with my eyes for not being strong like he was. I apologize for letting my grief take control when a piece of my soul splintered off.

"He loved us both. So, so much," I murmur in his mind.

His frantic gaze searches for a way out for me. He scours every nook and cranny he can see in the ward before letting his eyes settle on mine.

"Gaster, no!" I shout, but it's too late.

The explosion is outwardly massive, but it sucks my body backward through a swirling void of rainbow to whatever awaits me on the other side.

But I'm not alone.

I'm wrapped in the arms of my only living *Guardria*.

Two

Willow

Time seems meaningless as Gaster and I get thrown around every which way through the fabric of this ward.

Realistically, seconds have passed, but the way we're slamming into the sides of this deadly rainbow repeatedly as we fall through existence makes it seem like an eon's gone by.

The fibers of this void are connected to Elementra, that much is clear as her presence swarms me, but it doesn't bring me any comfort.

The queasiness brought on by a transport is a cakewalk compared to this. My stomach flips mercilessly as our bodies are tossed around like nothing more than rag dolls and I wish, pray, for a transport at this moment. Hell, ten simultaneous ones if it means getting me out of this never-ending vortex.

"Hold on, Willow," Gaster orders and he wraps his arms around me tighter. Too tight.

A scream gets lodged in my throat as the unyielding pressure surrounding us begins to squeeze to the point it's painful, unbearable.

It's smothering.

Suddenly, we stop tumbling head over heels and plummet through a now colorless void. My stomach lurches even more as gravity seems to reassert itself in this new level of our descent.

With a forceful shove, Gaster and I are ejected through the final layer of the ward and the noise that's been building up in my throat roars out of me as we hit the solid ground with a bone-jarring thud. The impact sends a shockwave through my body, causing me to cry out and Gaster to huff a harsh breath of air, but we have no time for any other reactions.

We soar across the floor like we've been shot from a cannon until my senses come rumbling back and I send out a burst of air that blocks us from crashing into a wall.

Holy shit.

I roll off Gaster unceremoniously, hitting the floor with a bone-deep groan, and I let my heavy, shaking limbs fall beside me as I squeeze my eyes shut tight. The spinning from the ward has only intensified the dizziness I felt before getting sucked through and I'm seconds away from losing my breakfast.

"Here, sit up and drink," Gaster commands gently, wrapping his hand around my elbow to pull me up.

"How in the realm did a healing vial survive that, Gaster? And how do you not feel like you've been tossed in a dryer?" I groan and my world spins as I struggle to push myself up.

"Why would being dried toss you around?"

"Never mind," I mumble, washing down the saliva collecting in my mouth with the healing vial.

I whisper a breathy thank you as I let my head fall back against the wall behind me and my lungs burn with each deep breath I take.

Fuck, that was absolutely awful. I hope I never...

Gasping, my eyes fly open as the clarity of the situation returns to me tenfold. It's an ambush of emotions all at once and I search the room for someone I know I'm not going to find.

"Oh, CC," I say mournfully, using the wall as leverage to push myself up on wobbly legs.

Taking a few unsure steps, I let my gaze devour the sight around me.

"Willow..."

Tears flow freely as I stare up at a light gray stone vaulted ceiling and I allow myself to fall into the master craftsmanship of the architecture above me rather than answer Gaster's plea of my name.

The soaring ceiling is decorated with complex but delicate carvings, and stone ribs that spread out across the surface are like dragon's wings splayed out in flight. The tall, crisscross arches that lead you from one area to the next are sharp, commanding, and off to the side is a massive window that's shedding enough light to breathe life into the whole room. It's all crafted to precise, careful perfection.

The walls are a beautiful light lavender, that's almost white when you first look at it. Ivy plants, flowers, and vines breathe fresh air into the space and add just enough of a pop of color to bring the area to life. Everything about this room gives me a sense of peace. Of home. It's so familiar as if I've seen it a million times, but I've never stepped foot in here.

I choke on a sob as I turn around and my eyes find the center of the room.

There, surrounded by a wall of bookshelves, behind a sectional couch large enough to fit multiple Nexuses, is a willow tree.

A willow tree that matches mine to perfection.

With slow, measured steps, I walk around the couch until I'm standing in front of the tree and gently rub a leaf between my finger and thumb. A harsh exhale falls from my lips as the texture brings forth so many memories at once, it's hard to stay standing on my feet as I sway.

"Gaster, where are we?" I ask through the wave of nausea.

"If you had asked me that while we were traveling through the ward, I would've said we were entering the south wing, but this is not at all what it was the last time I entered," he says from somewhere behind me.

"How long has it been since you've entered?"

"My, it's been—"

"I'm so glad you both are here."

Whipping around, searching for the voice although it was said in my mind, my gaze collides with Gaster's, who's as pale as a ghost. His gaze has doubled in size, and even though the sight of him tells me my answer, I still ask.

"You heard him? Didn't you?"

"That's not the voice you've always heard," he croaks out.

"No. Not until the memories unlocked."

"This...this is impossible. He's...gone."

The heavy tears that fall from Gaster's eyes nearly slice my heart from my chest. His grief is as potent as my own and the confusion warring within both of us is palpable.

"I'm sorry to both of you for the rough journey to get here. The ward and everything else. But I promise, it'll all make sense soon."

"CC, what does that—"

Suddenly, my mental voice is stolen from me as Gaster and I are lifted from our feet and suspended in the air in the middle of the room. I lose all control over my limbs, my movements, my thoughts, everything as we're brought closer to one another by the bond that tethers us together.

Blinding light flashes between the two of us and an ear-piercing scream leaves my chest as pain splices through every inch of my body. Like a pair of scissors has been taken to the cord connecting us, Gaster's bond is cut from me, and I bellow out in agony.

My soul attempts to shed off yet another piece, but I hold on to it for dear life. I refuse to let it tear completely. Every ounce of love, strength, devotion I have within me, I use it to fight against the hold over me.

I can't lose him too.

Scalding tears burn a trail down my face, and I command every gift, every element free, begging them to do something, to fix this. Protect us. Put us back together again. There's a slight crack in the pressure surrounding me before my powers are shoved back down.

"Bear with me, Ultima unum. It is almost over."

"Elementra, please don't do this. Please give him back to me."

"I vowed to you before, and I will vow it once more. Your bonds will never break. None of them."

Every ounce of air in my lungs is sucked out and my back bows as power pours from my chest. I faintly hear Gaster's grunt as the force of Elementra explodes between the two of us.

The arch in my back corrects itself and I'm left gasping, staring at the bright luminescent cords connecting my chest to Gaster's. Not two but three purple threads of fabric braid themselves together, weaving tightly as one.

Starting from the middle point between us, the strands work themselves until they reach our hearts. The second they penetrate, they latch on to our souls, and our awakenings blossom.

Just like the moment at my willow tree when I shook Gaster's hand for the first time, my mind begins to play a picture of the past.

Gaster bops a tiny little swaddled baby on the nose. A baby whose face I now get to see. Even as an infant, his features alone tell me exactly who that is. He has the lightest sky blue eyes. They're almost clear. Even his pupil is a fairer shade of black. His hair...it's as white as snow.

"Your mother has bestowed on me the privilege of gifting you a middle name. Under the stipulation, I couldn't name you after myself," Gaster says gently, to which the baby, I swear, narrows his eyes.

Gaster chuckles and the soft sound has the baby's face morphing into a smile before a small, sweet little laugh falls from his lips.

"I believe we can work our way around that a little. There're ways to spin Gaster Ducere Cato. Let us think..." Gaster hums, continuing to grin down at the baby as if he's his whole world. "How about Caduceus? CC for short, when you're behaving."

As the baby coos and reaches his little hand up, Gaster sighs deeply, falling into his eyes, and I continue to fall through time.

Watching, reliving, experiencing our awakening in a whole new light.

CC is no longer hidden from me, and I get to watch the true growth of their time. Their bond together grows and flourishes from one that started as a father-son relationship, one CC desperately needed, to a beautiful, impenetrable friendship.

Coming back to the present, Gaster's soft eyes are on me, and as the new threads of our bond slink their way deeper into our hearts, we're lowered to the ground. When my feet touch the floor, I throw myself into his arms and cry in relief.

"There, there, child. Everything's okay," he murmurs repeatedly, patting my back and holding me close.

"Do you...I..." I stutter through my tears. The question, maybe comment, I don't know, is stuck in my throat and my whirling mind.

I know what Elementra just did. My soul sings out in elation at the feeling of being whole once more, but I'm so confused. How is any of this possible? What is going on?

"I'm so sorry for the things I've put you both through," CC softly mumbles, and Gaster and I twitch, startled by the sound.

"How is this possible? Please explain this to us," I beg.

"I will. It will take some time for all your memories to settle down, and the ones that are still locked away will be revealed with time. There's so much at play, but it will all continue to make sense."

Gaster and I huff, rolling our eyes, causing not just us but CC to chuckle as well.

"After two hundred and fifty-two years, I didn't believe you could surprise me anymore, Orien Caduceus Vito. Is this communication here to stay?" Gaster asks timidly, sniffling even in our minds.

"Not exactly. You can hear me now because of the contact and bond with Willow. Her Memoria stone is the conduct for many, many possibilities."

"So the original severing..." Gaster trails off.

There's a long, tense moment of silence where I feel his hope rising like a tide. We hold our breaths, waiting for the true verdict, although my heart knows the truth. I just don't want to be the one to tell him. CC needs to. I don't know how he's doing what he's doing or all the whys yet, but he's gone.

He's in the beyond.

"Truly happened. I asked, begged really, Elementra for many, many things over the years. Some of my requests were granted while others were not. This situation we're in now is one of those requests she allowed."

Gaster squeezes his lids shut, blocking the tears that are gathering again. His pain isn't nearly as harsh as it was earlier. Having the severed bond restored has helped ease that burden, but it doesn't truly take away the grief we both feel. The pain now is just emotional, no longer physical as well.

"Where are we?" I ask, trying to change the subject to distract Gaster's mind for a moment.

"You're in the south wing."

"Gaster said this looks like nothing what he remembers it as, though."

"About that..." CC trails off.

"Orien Caduceus Vito," Gaster warns, narrowing his eyes.

An unexpected chuckle slips free despite me trying to hold it in. The gentle scolding coming from Gaster makes me feel like I'm witnessing my grandparent reprimanding my parent.

That sudden thought makes my entire body shudder and my eyes widen in shock, although it makes perfect sense.

"Our Guardria bond manifested as a father-daughter tie. That's why Gaster's formed as a familial one as well," I whisper.

"Very good, filia mea."

"What does that mean?" I ask.

"That memory will come forth soon. If it's okay with you, I'd rather you recall that conversation on your own than me tell you, although I believe if you searched your heart and soul, you'd know its meaning."

I want to reject his request instantly, but I force myself to pause. I crave to know everything now, but that's just my impatience. The more I think about it, the more I'd rather let my memories emerge naturally. Even without remembering them all, my heart knows there are moments—special ones—that should stay just between us. Moments that shaped our bond.

My heart also has a feeling about the meaning of *filia mea*, but that makes no sense in my mind.

"That's okay with me."

"Good. Now, there's a lot I need to tell you, all of you, but it would probably be best if you allowed the boys in before they tear down your home."

Why would they...

The thought of my Nexus immediately pushes everything else to the side. It's not like I forgot about them or anything like that, but I was so overcome with grief, followed by everything else going on since we entered this wing. It seems my senses were blocking the rest of the realm out to protect the thin shred of sanity I'm clinging to.

Their emotions, thoughts, everything bombards me, and my feet move faster than my mind does. I cross the room as if my ass is on fire and lay my forehead against the ward. I don't need any instructions or guidance.

"Allow them to enter," I command, pushing my magic out of my palms.

I hold my breath and take a step back as the ward shivers. Its tremors aren't nearly as vicious as earlier, and my men won't have to fall down the pit of pain like I did to get to this side.

They don't give me a chance to fully lay my eyes on them as their silhouettes become visible to me. Instead, they ambush me from every angle.

A ball of air whisks me off my feet as a vine latches itself around my waist. A calming purr permeates the space, soothing my tense muscles as we're shrouded in a thin veil of darkness.

No words pass from any of us as they close in so tightly around me, all I feel is them. I roam my hands over each of them chaotically, without restraint, and feeling their relief pulls tears from my eyes.

Fuck, they were so worried for me.

"Princess," Corentin says, strained.

"I'm so sorry."

"Hey, you have nothing to be sorry for," he whispers, kissing my forehead and pulling me into his chest.

I soak in the feeling of him deflating with my touch, and I try to pull all the worry from his heart by pushing as much love and reassurance as I can from my soul to his.

He gives me a sweet kiss that's over far faster than I'd wish for, and I chase after his touch. He smiles down at me, running his thumb across my bottom lip, then turns me around to face my dark protector.

His eyes are so soft, it takes me by surprise. The emotions pouring off him scream he's figured it all out. Well, most of it.

"Primary." Cas sighs, reaching his fingers up and running them down my tear streaks.

"I'm back," I say when I see his eyes searching.

"I know. Even the darkest part of yourself can't smother out the light."

Leaning forward, he lays his forehead to mine and takes slow breaths until our hearts beat as one. He sits like that for a long moment before gently gripping my throat and tilting my head up until our lips touch.

"Don't leave me behind again, Primary," he warns darkly, completely opposite to the tender kiss he just gave me, and a smile pulls at the corners of my mouth.

"Never."

"Little warrior," Tillman whispers, almost cautiously, like he's afraid he won't get an answer.

"My gentle giant."

His coiled shoulders sag and he pulls me from Caspian's hands, then lifts me until my feet no longer touch the ground.

"Your mind is a mess right now, Will."

I snort, because well, what can I say to that when it's the truth.

"A mess I never want to be shoved out of again. Are you okay?"

"Yeah, I believe so. There's so much I need to explain."

His understanding eyes douse the rising panic in me about how they're going to feel hearing everything I need to tell them. The calm and patience that always surround him ground me in a way nothing else can.

Reaching out, gripping his cheeks in my palms, I pull his face to mine. Each swipe of his tongue eases every burning anxiety I have, and I fall as deeply as I can into his protection and unwavering belief in me.

"The dragon is gonna go feral if he doesn't get his hands on you." He chuckles lightly in my head.

"I love it when he goes feral."

With another chuckle, he spins me around and Draken pulls me into his chest as if he knew we were talking about him. Unlike the others, he doesn't take the sweet and soft approach. It's all heat and passion from him as he captures my mouth in a consuming feast.

His flames lick across my skin and I allow mine to merge with his as soon as they begin boiling my blood. I let them roam his body completely until I feel his dragon back off from the surface.

"Little wanderer," he breathes, burying his face into my neck.

"Hey, you."

"Fuck, my dragon was ready to burn this palace to the ground."

"Well, I'm glad he didn't. It's far too beautiful to be turned to ash." I giggle, running my fingers down the back of his neck.

"Let me see your hand," he orders.

I honestly forgot I'd punctured myself with my claws. That sting of pain couldn't come close to comparing to what I felt in that moment.

"Gaster gave me a healing vial," I say when they all gather closer to look at my already healed palm.

"The old man's always prepared," Caspian says.

"I don't know if I'd say always." I sigh. "Will you pull your shadows back in, please? There's something you all should see."

His throat bobs as he swallows, and again, I find myself surprised. I've seen many sides of Caspian. Sides the rest of the realm—hell, maybe even his brothers—hasn't seen. But not this side.

There isn't a time that I've known him that I ever recall seeing him nervous. Sure, there have been times when maybe a shred of the emotion may have poked through, but right now, that's all he is. A ball of nervous energy.

"I don't know what all is in this wing waiting for us yet, but I can promise you, it's going to be okay. One way or another," I whisper, wrapping my own shadows around his wrist. All their wrists.

I need solidarity as much as they do.

With a clipped nod, his shadows slowly retreat into his skin.

The apprehension and anticipation in each of them grow to substantial heights. This is a moment they've been waiting their entire lives for. The burning curiosity would've driven me mad years ago if I were in their shoes. That's probably a top reason why they call this beautiful wing a curse.

As soon as the veil of darkness completely fades away, my eyes immediately seek out Gaster, just to make sure he's okay. I find him observing my tree with a faint smile on his face, gently caressing the leaves just as I had.

My tree...

Possessiveness rises in me quickly. Not over the fact Gaster's touching a random tree that I've suddenly declared mine, but the fact that in my mind, in my heart, this whole space is mine. Ours.

Obsessive much, Willow?

"Is talking to yourself going to become a thing, little warrior?" Tillman picks mindlessly as he looks around the space with keen fascination. His eyes trace the architecture, the craftsmanship with an appreciative glint that shows a lot of respect for the person who built all this.

"Maybe. Sometimes I get answers back."

"This space is yours. All of yours," CC says as if he was waiting for his cue.

My guys freeze in their spots. Their bodies shiver as if they've been covered in ice and it breaks my heart to literally see the color fade from each of their faces. Dissecting their emotions is difficult, but I get a sense they'd worked out their uncle was involved in my life, but not to this extent.

I don't know what to say as they each turn to face me slowly.

The immediate tension in the room is so thick, I could slice through it with my claw.

"That was..." Draken whispers, unable to finish his sentence.

"He's your stranger," Corentin mumbles. The hurt and the confusion coloring his tone are loud and clear despite the soft delivery.

With a small, sad smile, I lead us over to the couch to sit before my legs give out. My body is so jittery and the way my mind is still doing somersaults, I need a minute to sit or I'm going to pass out.

"There's so much I—we, need to tell you."

"We? As in you and our dead uncle who can apparently still speak?" Caspian asks skeptically.

"Don't sound so discouraged, nephew. Weirder things have happened in Elementra," CC says and Caspian's body trembles before he closes his eyes and sinks down onto the armrest of the couch. *"I need to show you all some things that'll hopefully make this easier to understand."*

"How will you—"

My echoing gasp interrupts Draken's question as my Memoria stone blazes against my chest. Their minds, including Gaster's, latch on to mine without my command. This isn't something I've caused, nor is the Memoria stone doing this on its own.

"Everyone, hold on. I don't know what's happening."

That's the only warning I get to give them before we're sucked into my mind, with no control or any idea at all about what's to be seen.

Three

CC

Eight years ago

"I try not to question you, Elementra. You've never led me astray, but I simply can't understand this."

Her whimsical, powerful laugh vibrates my entire body and I close my eyes at both the comfort and annoyance of the sound. I may have chosen my words poorly just now.

I tend to question everything.

"Yes, you do, in fact, question it all, but questions are allowed and encouraged. Just remember, you may not like the answers you seek, Seer."

Sighing, I run my fingers through my hair, gripping the roots as I look around the grand room.

My subconscious always brings me here when I request her guidance. A marveling library with more knowledge and information than I could consume in a lifetime, yet anytime I touch the books, they fade to nothing.

Nothing more than figments of my own imagination.

My own desires.

Life would be simpler if I could lock myself away here and read to my heart's fulfillment rather than travel the realm playing fates maker.

"The girl, the one you keep showing me. She's just a child. What use could she possibly be in this war?" I ask.

It's rich that I call her a child when I, myself, am barely an adult. By our standard of living, that is. Merely thirty and I've already assisted, many times, in shifting the fate of this realm. My most recent adventure to the cave's portal proves that the growth of adolescence is sure to change. The beaten and bloodied sight of Iris was evidence enough that the days of remaining irresponsible into our hundreds are over. Really, the day I watched her emerge should've solidified that belief for me. I was holding out hope, I suppose.

Neither of us will be allowed that privilege.

Many will sacrifice that opportunity.

Nonetheless, I can't shake the child's sad silver eyes that haunt my dreams. The first time I saw them, I swore I was seeing Iris's past. A glimpse in time before I led her to her future, but no, these eyes are slightly different. They're tinged with a lavender hue that you can only see if you look closely. If you can manipulate time and the sight, you can catch the undertone. And unlike Iris, the child's eyes are veiled in deep fear and sadness as though she has no clue what is going on.

"Girls do grow up to be women, Caduceus. That child has yet to even become. Her spirit still sits with me in the beyond, but she will be the end of this war. The last one of the line. One way or another," Elementra says cryptically as always.

"What is that supposed to mean? And what does she have to do with me?" I ask frustratedly.

Again, Elementra's laugh permeates the entire space, rattling my imaginary books and making my legs shake.

"Much must come to light before you get to know who she is, but when she does come, she will mean more to you than any other that walks this realm. She will mean more to you than even me. Have no fear, Seer, I will prepare you for her arrival."

Blinking my eyes open, I stare up at the makeshift crystal stars that decorate the amplifier room and wrap my hand tightly around the Memoria stone that's clutched in my fingers.

"I no longer need that memory, *filia mea*, you may have it," I whisper to the stone, laying my lips to it gently as the encounter with Elementra leaves my mind and enters its new home.

Standing, I brush my hands down the wrinkles in my pants and stretch my body out. Jumping back into my own memories like that, hundreds of years ago, always takes a lot out of me, but that's okay. I soon will have all the time in the realm to laze around, but for now, for a few more moments, there is much I must do.

Today is the day.

The wing is almost complete and Gaster is due to meet me here in just a few. Although he has no idea what for.

Making my way down the halls, I run my air over the light-colored walls, cleaning off any possible speck of dust. I smile at every fond memory that surfaces as I pass by each room. I let my heart fill with the feeling of love for each of my boys. The nephews my sister's blessed me with, the rough and rowdy dragon that brings me more laughter in minutes than many get in lifetimes.

The boys who have become more of pseudo sons.

Passing by the room that Tillman will one day occupy when he feels like it, I allow the ivy to wrap around my wrist, and a boisterous laugh leaves me as I sink into my mind.

Staring up at the gargantuan tree, I shake my head. Why in the realm Tillman decided four hundred feet in the air was the perfect spot for a hideaway, I haven't a clue, but if it brings him peace, so be it, I guess.

Fuck. Here goes nothing.

Swallowing down my fear of heights, I command my air beneath my feet and propel myself to the top. The second I hit the landing, I step as close to the door as possible and refuse to allow myself to look down.

It's ridiculous I can travel through the fabric of realms without a second thought, but being this high up has me on the verge of keeling over.

Raising my hand to knock, ivy wraps around my arms and legs, inhibiting me from pounding on the door to wake Tillman, and a laugh bursts out of me.

"Come on, nephew, allow me entry."

"Uncle Orien, surprised to see you up here before the sun. Haven't pissed yourself yet, have you?" Tillman asks with a teasing smile as he opens the door.

"Har-har, hilarious. Please allow me in before I faint. I need a favor from you."

His face grows serious, as expected. Tillman will never be one to turn away from helping his family, but he must let go of the quiet, rigid persona, though. It won't be tolerated.

Internally, I laugh at what's to come and allow him to hear the sound, only to tease him with a little peek inside my mind. My poor nephews have been trying their entire lives to get a glimpse of everything I do.

"It's not that serious of a request if you're laughing," he says, arching his brow at me.

My, how he looks like Tilly when he does that.

"On the contrary, my boy, it's very important," I say, pulling out Corentin's shirt from my back pocket.

Whistling low, grabbing the shirt from my outstretched hand, Tillman holds it in front of him before handing it back to me.

"You have a death wish, Uncle? Touching Corentin's clothes without his permission."

"He doesn't even wear this shirt. Since you originally made it, when has he ever put it on?"

"Never, but that's beside the point. For whatever reason, he asked for a light purple shirt. It doesn't matter that it sits in the back of his closet. He asked for it," Tillman says, trying again to hand it back to me, but I push it into his chest.

"And trust me, he will ask for another once he gets over being pissy that it's gone. But I need you to do something with it."

"Do something with Corentin's stolen clothes?"

Chuckling, I shake my head as I look down at my feet.

These boys, I swear.

"Yes. I need you to make a dress out of this shirt."

"A dress? Seriously?" he asks, incredulous.

"Yes, seriously," I say, handing over a piece of parchment with Willow's size written down. There's plenty enough fabric to make it perfectly if he'll just do as I ask. I hold my hand up when he opens his mouth and he halts his next question. "I'm sorry, Tillman, this is just one of those times when I can't give you much. The dress is a present for a girl who needs it. That's the most I can say."

He looks at me contemplatively for a long moment, then glares down at the measurements. With a sigh and a clipped nod, he hands me the parchment back and his element coats the space. I sit in silence with a small smile on my lips as he gets to work molding the small purple sun dress and my heart thunders in my chest with happiness.

One day, he will know who he made this for.

"Is this good enough?" he asks as he holds it up.

"Perfect, my boy. One more thing, if you don't mind. Will you wrap it for me?"

With an eye roll, he twists his hands around, creating a small box with a purple bow to match that I didn't even ask for, and I have no doubt he's wondering to himself why he did that, but I just stay quiet and smile.

"There. Anything else?"

"That'll be all. Thank you, Tillman."

"Yeah, yeah, don't mention it. I'm going back to bed now if you don't mind," he grunts with a smirk on his lips as he turns from me.

Guilt quickly rises in my chest, but I swallow it down, whispering, "Of course. Sleep well, nephew."

Muttering the spell, a small beam of light flashes from the Memoria stone around my neck to Tillman's mind. He's none the wiser as his body falls still as the last few minutes slink from his memory.

As our time together just now fades, I quietly backpedal out the door, then close it silently behind me. He's hard and fast back to sleep as the light returns to the stone and I drift down the tree on a current of air as if I was never there.

One day, he will understand. They all will.

My feet touch the soil for a second as I envision the willow tree in the nonmagical realm, then open the transport. Moving from Elementra to the nonmagical used to take so much of my energy, but over the years, it's become as easy as breathing.

In the span of a blink, the sight in front of me changes from the lively colors of Elementra's landscape to the crowded forest that surrounds the willow that was once an oak.

Time sure changes a lot.

Well, as does Elementra's interference, but I digress.

"You know it's rude to tell the birthday girl to be out here before the sun comes up, then you show up late." Willow's voice sasses from behind me and I laugh as I spin on my heels to her.

"My sincerest apologies, Miss Priss." I chuckle, pulling her in for a tight hug, and my finger gets caught in the knots of her curly hair. "Willow, did you not even brush this out before coming out here?" I tease, untangling the knot before I rip a chunk out.

"Well..." Her gaze leaves mine, and I follow the sight to the small pallet under the tree.

"Why did you camp out here?"

"Father had a business party last night, so I snuck out my window. It's safer out here than in there," she whispers and I pull her back into my chest.

"I'm sorry, filia mea."

"Don't be, it's okay. Is that for me?" she asks with a forced smile that slowly becomes more earnest.

"It is, but my present first," I say, pulling out the purple journal from my bag.

She squeals in delight as she opens it and my heart hurts at how excited she gets over the smallest of things. She refuses to talk about it, but the timidness she always had with the first few gifts I ever gave her showed that she'd never received anything in her life and didn't know how to accept it. Now she's like a child in a sweets shop every time she's given something.

"The pages are enchanted and concealed from view. Only you and I can see it, but you only see what you write," I tell her as she sticks her nose to the binding.

"This is perfect. Thank you so much," she exclaims, giving me another firm hug.

"Now this present is from my nephews. The older two," I say, handing her the box. Her face blushes a bright red as she tentatively brings the box to her chest.

"Oh my..." she says, carefully running her hands down the soft material before jerking her hand back. "I'm going to get it dirty."

"That's what washing machines are for, Willow."

"Very funny..." She cuts her eye to me with a sly smirk, then looks back down at it. "I'd like to wear it today."

"Today would be a perfect day for it. Go change behind a tree," I tell her, turning around.

My gaze looks out over the vast, thick forest. The forest we've basically memorized over the last eight years since we first met and had our awakening. I imprint as much of it as possible on my memory, knowing it's all about to change in just a few moments. It'll be years and years to come before she remembers this as it was.

"So how do I look? It fits perfectly. The one with an earth element must be the one who made it, but I don't know which is the other one..." she says lightly, spinning around, and the dress flares out. She brings one of the frilly layers up to her nose and takes a deep breath.

When her eyes open in shock and she takes a staggering step back, gripping her chest, my gaze softens as I send out a huge blast of air to barricade us in a dome.

"CC...what's happening?" she asks, swaying.

"It's okay, filia mea, don't fight it," I say gently.

Reaching into my bag, I pull out a rope made of vine and quickly tie myself to the willow tree while simultaneously whispering reassurances to Willow as she continues to sway and gasps for breath.

"CC, please. I can't breathe. Wh-What's going on?" she asks as her panic fully sets in.

Loosening my rope enough that I can reach her, I cup her cheeks in my hands and shush her quietly. "Everything's okay, filia mea. You're emerging. Don't fight it. I have us protected. I promise. Let it out, my sweet girl," I tell her, and when she gives me a small, scared nod, I step back as close to the tree as I can.

I tried my best to prepare her for this. She knew one day it would come and it would be painful, but I was never allowed to tell her exactly what to expect. Fuck, I'm not even sure I know exactly what to expect. Elementra loves to give me crumbs of information.

Her first scream is like a knife to the gut. It pierces straight through me, but I hold strong, for her. If she sees me crumble, it'll make this so much harder for her.

"You've got this, Willow, it's okay. Embrace the pain. Become one with it," I coach as her limbs shake from her restraint.

She can barely nod in acknowledgment, but she does manage to take a deep breath. A breath that sucks every bit of air out of the space. The trees bend to her will and on her exhale, they're forcefully released as though they were strapped down to a catapult. Branches, roots, whole trees crack and some are pulled from the ground as swirling vortexes of air fall from her fingertips.

"Everything's okay. Don't try to stop it. It's okay, filia mea," I yell repeatedly over the wild winds as she becomes frantic, screaming for it to stop.

Her petrified, watery eyes meet and hold mine, searching, begging for instructions.

"Close your eyes. Close your eyes and picture your ideal home. Everything you've ever wanted, think about it. Think about it so strongly, that's all you can see in your mind. Let the rest go, my girl. Don't worry about what is happening around you. Do it, Willow," I order as agonizing sobs tear from her throat. I want nothing more than to release myself and hold her through this, but I can't. It would be far too dangerous, and she needs to do this on her own.

Holding my breath, I clutch the rope tighter as her shoulders relax and her breathing levels out. The sudden change doesn't fool me. If there's one thing certain about my little girl, she can conquer anything. Everything. Even herself. She was a force to be reckoned with before these elements emerged, and she'll be an even greater force afterward.

This is just her calm before her storm.

"It's large, but so homey. There's so much natural light, there's no need for electricity or chandeliers. The rays of the sun warm my skin as I laze around, reading until my eyes hurt and my heart's content. There's always something to learn or an escape, or an adventure in the books. The walls are purple, of course they're purple. Not bright like my favorite color, though. That might be too much, but a light purple. And there's a willow tree in the middle of the room with books surrounding it. That's only one room, but it'll be my favorite. Aside from my bedroom. I'd like a big bedroom with a magical bathroom...There's no pain. No hate. No fear. Just home...Yeah, I'd like that a lot," she says softly with a smile on her face as the pain escapes her for a blissful minute.

When her eyes flash open to meet mine once again, they're as violet as the Willowrrie flower her mother named her after and I see the beast begging to break free, but it's not her time yet and she knows it. She'll be here for her, though.

With a thundering roar, her knees hit the ground and mine do as well as the earth beneath me shakes and trembles violently. The air pouring off her shoves me back until I'm plastered to the tree, barely able to draw in any breaths, and together, the two elements decimate our surroundings. For hundreds of yards around us, the trees crumble as none are strong enough to withstand her power.

Her back bows and her arms stretch out beside her as a flood of water rushes from her palms, burying the fallen trees, bushes, all the foliage in a pond of her own making.

The wild rapids swallow everything whole before settling and sinking back into the earth. The water's retreat causes a scream, piercing enough to bring tears to my eyes, to belt from her chest.

She rubs furiously at her skin as her blood begins to boil beneath the surface. I hold in my own sobs as her skin begins to bubble, but I refuse to take my eyes off her. I pray, beg, plead with Elementra to let her get through this.

This last one.

Let it free, filia mea.

Flames finally shoot from her fingertips and circle her body as she falls to all fours. When her palms slam into the ground, the fire spreads, drying the land completely until nothing remains but sand. The heat from the fire causes sweat to drip down my back and in seconds, my shirt is drenched, but I don't dare budge or make any sudden moves toward her just yet.

As the last of the flames crawl back into her hands, with a grunt, she collapses to the ground, and the hold that her power had over the land snaps. It's an eerie silence. The only noise to be heard right now is our labored breathing, but the sight is breathtaking. Scarily so.

If I hadn't cast the dome, there's no telling how far her powers would've flowed. There's no doubt in my mind, Elementra herself bolstered my block.

My sweet girl is far, far more powerful than me.

Pride like no other swells in my chest as with a cough and a muttered 'shit, that hurt,' Willow rolls to her back, groaning and covering her eyes with her arm.

After quickly untying myself, I pull two healing vials out of my bag and race to her side.

"Here, filia mea. Drink," I command lightly, smiling down at her.

"Worst birthday surprise ever," she groans as I make her sit up.

Guilt nearly rips my heart out at her words because unfortunately, this will be a better remembered birthday surprise one day.

"You did amazing, Willow. I'm so proud of you," I murmur, choking down my own emotions.

"You have a lot of explaining to do, CC."

"Yes, yes, I do. But first, I'll teach you how to grow some grass. I can't stand the way sand feels when it gets stuck in my shoes."

With a snort then a gasp, Willow gets her first glimpse at the clearing she created around her willow tree.

Gently unraveling the ivy from around my wrist, I lay my palm on Tillman's door and smile. One day, he and Corentin will know their creation with that shirt triggered not only her emerging but her bonds' realization that her Nexus was somewhere out there. It'd protect her, at least emotionally, in a way she could never understand.

Continuing my way down the halls, I allow the surfaces to bring forth my most treasured memories and I command each of them, those I can part with at this time, to filter from me into the Memoria stone.

Entering the lounge, I look around the open space and massive windows that for now only allow me the opportunity to see out and no one else to see in. This wing has become somewhat of a legend amongst the palace. No one's allowed in but me, and my, does that drive my sister and the boys absolutely nuts.

Little do they know, this isn't even my space, contrary to their popular belief.

Smirking, finding a semblance of joy in my secrecy, I turn around to glance at the grand bookshelf. There isn't a row or spot empty. It's overflowing with my most treasured reads and research, but this space is only a touch of the information I'm leaving behind for them. Everything else they will need can be found behind other doors of this wing and my own room in the central wing. A room believed to be long forgotten.

A tearful laugh falls from my lips as I recount a vision yet to come to fruition. My sweet, sweet Aurora. She's going to have a field day to find out I was hiding in plain sight, just down the hall from her for years and years.

Checking my timekeeper, I only have ten more minutes before Gaster arrives, so I busy myself with straightening the already straight books and cleaning the already spotless surface of the shelves.

What else is there to do in your last few moments in this realm?

Running my fingers along the spines of the books appreciatively, I stop on the book that has the darkest of bindings and I swallow roughly.

Oh, my boy. Elementra has not allowed me to see much of your future. It's far too murky and changes as rapidly as the tides, but I hope, pray, by the point in time you see this, Willow's helped guide your way.

I beg you to find forgiveness in me.

Grabbing the copy of the Book of Shadows, I flip through the pages, letting the memory of how it came into my possession surface.

"I figured I'd find you here," I say quietly as I enter the lounge of the mansion.

"Yes, where else should I be?" Caspian says, never taking his eyes off his book that he's furiously scribbling in.

Once he finishes the sentence he was writing, he picks up his glass of whiskey, tosses it back as though it's water, and my throat closes as guilt, regret, and so many other emotions try to take over.

"May I ask a favor of you, Cas? It's important."

His eyes shoot up to meet mine and I hold in a breath of relief to find him sober...for now. That relief is short-lived when I spot the resentment in his glare. It tears my heart in two.

Although I understand it.

I understand he feels betrayed, forgotten, and I wish more than anything I could take those emotions from him. But I can't. It's not time for him to know what comes yet and even if I did tell him the truth, right now, he'd only hate her more. Not love her as he should.

Therefore, I will endure his bitterness and love him through it.

"You can ask all you want." He chuffs. His way of saying whether he grants said favor is debatable.

"I need to copy your Book of Shadows, as is," I say, getting straight to the point. He doesn't tolerate roundabout ways of things, so might as well get it over with.

"Yeah, not happening."

"Caspian, please. It's important."

He leans back, crossing his arms over his chest, staring me down. I already know what he's going to ask.

"Tell me why it's important and I'll consider it."

Releasing a deep breath, it's frustrating all the same even if I knew the question was coming. I wish I could tell him every single secret I hold in my mind. If I could, I would in a heartbeat so it would heal this pain, this hatred within him. That's not my job, though. I'm not allowed to.

"There is a teenager who recently emerged. They're having a very rough go. They...they've experienced much of the same things you have, and they need some guidance, not just books written based on facts, but experience."

"What do you mean they've experienced much of the same things?" he asks darkly, sitting up a little straighter.

"You know what I mean, Cas, but that's as much as I will speak on it. It's not my story to tell," I say firmly.

He may grit his teeth, but there's a hint of respect in his eyes. It bothers him not knowing the whole story, but he appreciates me not gossiping as others do to him.

"There're things in my book that no teenager has business reading," he says, slamming said book shut.

"There's nothing written in there that will surprise said teenager. I can assure you. Unfortunately."

His eyes shut down as his darkness descends. It's a place he goes to often when he needs to be protected. A place he is slowly but surely making his home. Just as she is and if she's not pulled back soon, it'll swallow her whole.

Unlike my nephew, all she has is me, and sadly, I can't be with her twenty-four seven.

"I'll allow you to make a copy if you vow no one will see inside but this random teenager, and they can't know it's mine," he says, clipped.

"I can vow that no one will see inside but them and me. I've already seen, hence why I'm asking for a copy. I wouldn't have known to ask you without the sight showing me," I tell him honestly. It's as close to the full truth as I can give him.

"Fine," he grits out angrily, "but I'll be with you when you make the copy. The old man, not Tillman."

He stands from his seat forcefully and stomps past me out the doors of the lounge. I tilt my head back, blowing out a breath, begging Elementra for some patience.

By the time I make it down the stairs in the mansion, he's already gone, so I transport to Gaster's front steps and find the two of them standing there, waiting for me.

"Let me see it then," Gaster says quietly, no doubt sensing the tension surrounding us. Caspian hands his book off with a huff and in just a few seconds, there's an exact replica made.

Passing both versions over to Caspian, he flips through them quickly, checking for accuracy. He hesitates only for a moment—his brief show of vulnerability—then hands me the copied version.

"Thank you, Cas, and I'm sorry."

"For what?" he asks as I lay my hand on his shoulder, as well as Gaster's.

Muttering the memory spell, the concealed Memoria stone lights up, and the two of them fall unnaturally still as the last few moments in time get stolen away from them, replaced with new ones. I forcefully swallow down the bile and tears clogging my eyes.

This never gets easier.

Every memory taken without permission slices away at me and the only thing that keeps me pushing through is the knowledge of what's to come from all of this.

"As I said, you can't tell your mother that Gaster and I are teaching you how to use your shadows to pass through her detection and tracking spells. It'll be our heads if she finds out. You'll have to take full blame once she does."

Caspian crosses his arms, looking between Gaster and me with disbelief coloring his features. He's been asking for her to remove the detection and tracking spells she has on him for years. For the first few years, he tolerated it. But it's been nine years since his kidnapping and knowing she is monitoring his every move is only making him angrier, more resentful toward every adult in his life.

I've known for some time now, we were going to teach him this. I've already explained to Aurora that it had to happen, but he doesn't need to know that yet. He needs to relearn how to have conversations with his mother.

"You're really going to teach me? What if she flips out? I don't want to deal with that shit."

"She isn't going to flip out, but it will spark a conversation that needs to be had between the two of you. It's time you talk to her about your boundaries, and you need to understand her concern isn't stemming from controlling you but wanting you safe. Regardless, yes, it's time for you to know how to utilize your shadows in situations such as this, so we will teach you."

A mischievous smile, one I haven't seen in years, takes over his face as he rubs his hands together with the thrill of having his full freedom so close to his grasp. I already know I won't regret this decision, so Gaster and I waste no time jumping right into teaching him.

Closing the book, I release another deep breath as I allow that memory to escape me as well.

I, of course, will always hold a sliver of regret about the memories I've taken from the ones I love, but this situation really and truly paid off. Cas grew to be able to speak openly to Aurora, sometimes too bluntly if I'm being honest, and Willow...

Willow memorized that book in a matter of days. She was approaching her seventeenth birthday when I gave it to her, and Franklin's sessions of blood draining had picked up increasingly. It was to the point she stayed in a disassociated state. Reality was too much for her to bear sometimes.

Reading the things Cas had written in his book opened her eyes to many things. Firstly, and no dig at Caspian whatsoever, she said she felt like she was becoming this person, and she didn't want to become jaded. She wanted to stay happy in the moments that mattered. She swore that if she ever met the owner of that book, she'd pull them from their darkness if it was the last thing she did.

It was so hard not to share his secrets, but I never did. I always just hoped and prayed she would be right one day.

A subtle vibration across my skin lets me know that Gaster just entered the foyer of the south wing, so gently, I return the Book of Shadows back to its rightful place on the bookshelf and exit the ward to meet him.

"What in the realm could you need of me this early in the morning, Caduceus? Today is a day of celebration. Waking before the sun is punishment," Gaster gripes teasingly, but his curious eyes observe the ward that he desperately wants to see behind.

Poor thing.

"I need your help in the wing for a minute if you have time for me, old man." I smirk as his eyes widen, then narrow.

"I'm in my prime, thank you very much, and is this some twisted joke of yours? You haven't allowed anyone to enter this ward in—"

"Over two hundred years. Yeah, yeah, I get it."

Again, he looks surprised, but in a few moments, he'll understand how it is I knew he was going to say that. "Well, do you care to help or not?"

"Of course I want to help. What kind of question is that?"

Chuckling at his enthusiasm, I lay my hand on his shoulder and walk us back through the ward. As we pass, I also release the memories of his that I'm holding hostage in the Memoria stone.

Gripping his elbow to steady him as he sways, I pass over one of his own healing vials to ease the sickness that comes every time this happens, and I wait for the tongue-lashing that's to come.

"Orien Caduceus Vito, I should have your neck. Countless times you've done this to me."

"Yes, and I'm sorry, for the millionth time, but it will all make sense soon. I swear. Plus, as you most certainly remember, you agreed to help me in here and knew you'd be giving away your memories until the time was right for them to be returned."

"Fine, yes, yes, I remember," he says, waving me off as he looks around at all the work we've put into this wing.

He knows, at least for the moment, that I've never lived here. I do work and use the amplifier room in this wing, but I've reserved, decorated, and redefined this space for Willow and the boys. They'll need a space that is theirs without the dark cloudy memories that the east, west, and central wings carry with them.

I haven't even allowed my sister entry here.

"So what's the finishing touch?" Gaster asks.

"A willow tree. Right here," I say, pointing to the empty spot between the bookshelves.

"A willow tree? Really?"

"Yes. It'll make sense soon enough."

I describe in detail exactly what I want, need, the tree to look like. Down to the texture of the bark. I leave nothing out and by the third time I ask him if he can picture what I'm describing, he gives me a warning glare and I shut up.

With a huff and an eye roll that cause me to laugh through the tears that want to fall, I watch silently as he gets to work.

My entire life, Gaster has amazed me. The millennia he's been alive have taught him so much, and it's fascinating, an honor to be able to witness it up close and personal.

Fuck, I'm going to miss him so much. So fucking much it hurts.

As a single tear finally falls, I quickly wipe it away before he turns around and sees. Over the years, I've mastered blocking my aura from him, but with the knowledge of what's to come in the next few hours, I have no confidence in my ability to hide my emotions from him.

Like the unreal expert craftsman he is, an exact replica of Willow's tree in her forest begins to grow. It's absolute perfection and I beam as it flourishes before my eyes.

"To your liking, CC?" he asks sarcastically and rubs his hands together.

"It's more than I could've expected, Gaster," I say, choking back the emotion clogging my throat.

"What's wrong, my boy?" he asks, immediately sensing an issue.

"Everything's fine. Just as it's supposed to be. Thank you so much for helping me with this, with all of this. It's perfect."

He stares at me, unconvinced, but I don't waver. I don't allow my heartache and grief to shine through. Instead, I smile brighter, relishing the memories of him and all he's done for me. All the stages of love he's shown me and will continue to show my Willow.

"Well then, what are you up to for the rest of the day?" he finally asks.

"I have some errands to run, but I'll be by your cottage in a little while if that's okay?"

"Of course it is. I'll be there with the tea ready." The smile on his face stabs me right through my heart, but I suck it up and allow the pain to sink beneath my skin. "I guess this is the part where you steal my memories back?"

"Yeah, this is the part," I whisper softly.

I want to laugh at his sigh, but I can't bring myself to do it. It's taking every bit of mental strength I have to shove down the urge to spit the truth out, tell him today is my last day in this realm with him, but I can't do that, for it'll ruin the last two hundred years of work.

So instead, with a heavy heart and soft touch, I lead him back through the ward, taking his memories with every step. I transport us to his cottage while the Memoria stone continues to do its thing and I walk us until we're in his kitchen.

Mindlessly, he begins preparing his kettle for his morning coffee, followed by his tea fix. As the light between the stone and him grows dimmer, I step back until I'm out his door, where I lean my forehead to the old wood and collect myself as the light fully fades out.

This is the way it must go, Orien.

Go see the boys.

Pushing away from his door, I take the steps down two at a time and hurriedly make my way before he notices me and comes outside.

Taking a moment for myself, rather than transport, I glance around. I gaze at the trees that've changed so much over the last couple hundred years, the grounds that are greener, trimmed to perfection. The boys have come here their whole lives, but now that this is their permanent residence, their energies alone have already started shaping the land. They don't even recognize the changes yet, but their solidarity, their love for one another, has made the bond in the land blossom right alongside their own.

I'm so proud of them. They haven't the slightest clue.

As my eyes take in the shimmering surface of the pool, my gaze grows hazy, and I pause my steps, allowing the vision to surface for me. I wasn't expecting one last vision on my last day, but it's a welcome distraction. Sometimes the sight gives me gifts rather than disappointment.

"Corentin, my boy, may I have a moment with you? Maybe some breakfast. I need to talk to you about some things."

I sit silently in my mind as my heart races and bile collects in my mouth. Playing out before me is a vision that can go one of two ways.

One we have the conversation and everything changes.

Not for the better.

If he accepts my invitation, I must tell him all my plans. Everything that's to come. He'll rally his brothers together and instead of my life being the one to end today, he'll lose both Tillman and Draken in battle. That starts the chain reaction of Caspian's and his downfall. Willow will make it to Elementra but as a slave, and she'll never have her true Nexus. Her soul will rot away until she's nothing more than a weapon.

The fate of the realm will be decided.

Or the second scenario, he declines, and everything stays how it is. The carefully laid out plans, my acceptance of my death, Willow's future. Their future. It all stays guaranteed as long as he rejects me.

As the vision releases my mind, my body shakes uncontrollably with a pent-up rage that burns hotter than the sun. How? Why?

"Answer me, Elementra," I demand.

"Today is the day of days. Many have a choice to make. Every choice will change the path. This is Corentin's. His decision will warp every choice made from this moment forward. Much will be determined today, Seer. Stay on the path you've planned for now."

She shoves me out of my mind when I attempt to push for more. She doesn't allow it. For the first time in many, many times I've called on her, she doesn't answer, leaving me to make the decision on my own.

Closing my eyes, I breathe through the turmoil waging war within me. It's a brutal battle that I'm not confident I'll win. The walls are closing in around me. The deep regret I've felt over the years lying to my family, how I've had to keep the boys in the dark, how Willow only gets the partial truth of everything.

My poor sister. How last night at dinner, I had to pretend everything was fine. I unlocked their memories for a short time so we could talk freely. Then when I took them back again, I spent hours laughing with her and my Brethren-Nexus because I knew it was our last moments together.

It's too much to sacrifice now. I've come to terms with what must happen. I've accepted I will have to love them all from the beyond.

The last two-hundred-plus years can't be for nothing.

"Uncle Orien, you good?"

Turning on my heel, I force a small smile on my face as I take in Tillman. Dressed from head to toe in E.F. gear, it's obvious he's preparing to start his morning workout then hit the academy.

I take him in from head to toe and let a genuine smile creep out. He's truly the much, much larger version and well, male version of my late sister. Fuck, how she'd be so proud of him.

"Oh yes, I'm fine. Just stuck in my head, that's all," I say with a chuckle as I tap my temple.

"Uh, I know how that is. You're here early today."

"Duty of the realm calls, so I'll be gone for...a while. I wanted to come see you all before I left."

"A mission? Where? Do you need backup? Me and Cas can join," he says sternly but also enthusiastically.

He's going to make a killer leader.

"It's a solo trip, I'm afraid," I say as I tap my head again. He knows all too well that means I've seen something they can't know and of all my nephews, he accepts that quicker than any other.

"Well, be careful. Debrief when you get back?"

"We'll have our time for a debrief. May I ask a favor before I go?"

He snorts, shaking his head as if it's mental that I still ask permission from him for favors. "Of course. What can I make for you?"

"A couple things if you will. I need a wooden box with yellowish-brown coloring. Like a jewelry box. With a surface as fine, as smooth as you can get it and a bronze hinge that locks it together. A block of silver. And a fireproof stone bowl."

A booming laugh bursts free of him, one joyous, humorous enough the ground beneath my feet shakes and I can't help but join in. It's a wondrous sound when my burly nephew lets it ring free.

"That's quite the concoction. One I didn't expect."

"You never know when all three of those things can come in handy, nephew."

He runs his hands down his face, wiping away the small laughter still pouring from his lips, and gives me an easy smile.

First, he whips up the block of silver and tosses it in the air a few times before handing it over. Followed by the stone bowl. He's had to get proficient at making everything fireproof with Draken around and in no time, he passes me a bowl that I have no doubt could survive being dropped in Pyra's mouth.

Finally...the box. He takes his time with this creation. Mapping it out in his mind before molding the item in front of him. Countless times, he gently runs his hands over the surface, smoothing it out until it's flawless.

He unhooks and hooks the hinge repeatedly, verifying its durability. And lastly, he holds it up to his face and blows away the dust covering it.

Flawless.

"Thank you so much," I say with a smile.

She's going to love it.

"No problem, Uncle. I got to hit this trail, then get to the academy, but I'll see you after this secret mission," he says, smiling proudly as he hands me the box and turns to take off.

"Yeah, I'll see you, Tillme," I whisper.

Tilly and Tillme.

Exhaling, I pull the last few moments from his mind. Only the bits of him making these three items for me. I replace those moments with me telling him how I know he's going to be a great leader, just like his mom and dads were. Hell, even better.

Turning, heading toward the mansion whilst wiping my watering eyes, I put the items he just made me on the patio table and check my time-keeper. *Shit.* I'm running out of time, so I don't waste another emotional second and head straight for the boys' hallway.

I don't push my way in, but I do lay my hand on the door that I know will be Willow's. One day, they'll make that room just for her. Perfect to her liking.

Passing by Draken's room, I smother a laugh as his loud, unpitched singing filters through his door, and I decide to come back to him when he's done taking his shower. Wild one that boy is. His carefree craziness calls to you like a beacon. What joy he's brought into my life.

When I round the corner, I choose to go to Caspian first before making my way to Corentin. Taking a deep breath, I knock. Then wait. Then knock again. As the silence stretches and no answer comes, a lump forms in my throat and my heart splits open.

I'm too late to see him. He's already left.

Leaning my forehead to his door, I send him my love, my apologies, my pride. Everything I feel for him, I send into his room.

Elementra, one day, let him understand.

I use my air to dry my face and hide the evidence of my sorrow. Corentin will be able to see right through me if I don't. I've never met someone who's so finely tuned to everyone and everything around him.

Approaching his door, I choke my fear down. It's now or never.

Time for your decision, nephew.

Exhaling, I knock at the same time to hide the harsh sound of my breath falling from my lungs and wait patiently.

"Come in," he calls out, less patiently.

"Corentin, my boy, may I have a moment with you? Maybe some breakfast. I need to talk to you about some things," I ask somewhat cheerily.

"Is it important, Uncle Orien? I'm in the middle of Advanced Enchantments," he says, not bothering to take his eyes off the books.

"Advanced Enchantments? You still have two years until you need that class," I say as I tuck my hands in my pockets and lean against the doorframe.

"Yes, well, I've decided I won't be waiting until I'm fifty to take the Headmaster role. Headmaster Rux is doing well enough, been a family friend of Mom and my dad's for years, but I don't like the direction he's moving the academy. So I'll complete my studies early, begin my apprenticeship, finish it in two years, then take over in the role at thirty. That's four years from now. Plenty of time."

Pride bursts from my heart as I stare down at him where he mindlessly continues to flip pages, write notes, shake his head, grunt. He just throws one hundred percent of himself into the books. Fully dedicated. Once his mind is made up, that's that.

I've seen this. There are two ways it will go.

Good luck with this argument, sister.

"I'm so very proud of you, Corentin, and I love you so much."

His insistent scribbling stops as he finally looks up at me and I mask everything I'm feeling. I slow my breathing and regulate my pounding heart as his gaze tracks me from head to toe.

"Everything okay?" he asks, arching a brow.

"Everything's fine. As I said, I just wanted to see if you had a moment for breakfast and a chat."

He sighs deeply, laying his pencil down, and my ears ring. Everything inside of me screams.

Pick the pencil back up. Pick it up.

Send me on my way.

Please, my boy.

"I don't mean to be rude, Uncle Orien, but I need to finish this. I don't really have time. I'm sorry."

"Don't be. It's okay. Don't let me distract you from your studies. You're going to do amazing things, Corentin," I say softly, standing back up straight, preparing to leave before he changes his mind.

"Thanks, Uncle. I'll see you later. Please shut the door on your way out," he says as his eyes find the words on the pages once more.

Smiling warmly at him, I back out and shut the door as he asked.

Thank you, Core.

Hastily pushing from his door, I lay my hand to Cas's once more as I pass by, knowing it's still empty inside, and I jog down the hall to catch Draken before I miss him as well. The moment I approach his room, there's nothing but silence on the other side, and I pull at the roots of my hair.

Fuck, I can't have missed him too.

Transporting to the back patio, I quickly grab the box, silver, and bowl off the table where I left them, then turn to check the back lawn. Air whooshes from my lungs as I spot Draken walking out across the green grass and the relief that washes over me makes my body slump.

"Draken, wait up," I call out, jogging toward him.

"Uncle Oreo. Thought I heard you talking to Corentin," he says happily, wrapping his arms around me in a hug, lifting me off my feet.

I can't help but laugh. That nickname has stuck since I slipped up once and spoke about an Oreo cookie. I convinced him it was a delicacy that's long been forgotten but I'd try to make it for him one day.

That day never came, sadly.

"Yeah. Trying to track down all of you this morning. Busy boys you are. You headed to the academy?"

"I need to fly first. My dragon's a little worked up this morning. Hate to scare any of the pups in class today so..." He laughs it off, but I see the shame shining through and I bite my tongue. This boy just doesn't understand how spectacular he is.

"Don't worry about the wolves. They're just jealous they can't fly," I say with a wink.

"Exactly. Bitches. Anyways, you want to come up with me? Promise no flips this time," he says with an unconvincing smirk that I know is a lie.

"Wish I could, nephew, but there's business I need to attend."

"Damn. Next time then," he says disappointedly as he squeezes my shoulder.

"Next time...May I ask a favor of you before you go, Draken?"

"Sure, Oreo. Whatcha got?"

"I need you to melt this silver down for me."

He snorts, shaking his head, looking over the block that I pass to him. "My fire isn't hot enough to melt silver. You know that." He chuckles, tossing the brick at me.

"Your fire may not be...yet. But your dragon's will. Give it a go for me, yeah?"

If only he knew what that majestic beast inside of him is truly capable of. One day he will.

"You really think so?" he asks with wide eyes.

"I know so. Go on, shift and give it a go. The worst that'll happen is it won't melt. No harm."

With a cocky smirk, he runs off farther into the lawn and I hold my breath, mesmerized. I'll never grow tired of watching his dragon break the skin. How amazing it is to see a blessing from multiple realms take form.

Auburn scales and blazing blue eyes flicker in existence before me, and I smile at the wonder of Draken. He's truly breathtaking.

"All right, my boy, listen to me carefully. Start building in your chest. Grow your flame to the point you feel like you can't hold it in any longer. Once you feel the tingle in the back of your throat, let it flow. Directly at this bowl now. It's fireproof, so it will hold," I yell up to his massive twenty-foot size.

At his nod, I backpedal out of the way so I don't end up burned to bits. When he notices I'm far enough away, he shakes his wings out, steadying his feet, and takes a deep breath.

I watch, infatuated, as his enormous chest begins to expand and if I listen closely enough, I can hear the crackling of his fire gathering. Lowering his head, he aims his snout right for the bowl, and fiery red flames pour from his throat with a screech. The heat forces me to cover my face with my forearm and I stumble back another step.

As the temperature starts to fade, I drop my arm and rush over to the bowl. Staring down, there's a soup of mercury floating in it, and I jump up and down laughing before ambushing him.

"Fantastic, dragon. I told you, you could. Never doubt yourself, Draken." I cheer as I hug and pat his face.

With a chuff and a nudge, he tilts his head to the sky and lets out a victorious roar. The sound travels for miles through the air and my heart triples in size with my pride for him.

"Take to the sky, dragon," I whisper to him and lay my forehead on his scales. Slowly, I pull this moment from his mind and replace it with a happy, joyous conversation. One where I tell him how proud I am and how I believe his dragon is the greatest blessing in Elementra.

His massive wings beat three times when I step back, and his claws leave the earth.

One day, dragon, you won't fly alone.

You'll never be lonely again.

Bending down to the bowl, I wrap a small, controlled air bubble around it so I can carry it to Gaster without searing my skin. This will be the perfect amount, and he'll know exactly what to do.

I don't even make it to his steps before his door opens and he greets me with a warm, loving smile.

"CC, my boy. What's got you out here so early?"

I plaster on the fake, happy smile I've had to wear so many times. "Came to ask for your creative assistance if you don't mind," I say, lifting my hands to show him everything I have.

"My, my, melted silver. How in the realm did you melt it?" he asks as he creates mittens for his hands and takes the bowl from my bubble.

"Not me. Draken." I beam.

"You continue to encourage him, and he's going to burn the forest down. Tillman will have a field day."

"He needs encouragement. He shouldn't fear what he is capable of but embrace it fully. You have books on the dragons of Essemist Keep, yes?"

"Of course I do."

"Allow him to read some. It'll do him good. It'll give him something to enjoy learning," I say.

Gaster snorts, shaking his head while he lays out everything I've brought with me across his dining table. "The boy hates to read, but I will offer them to him if you insist. Now, tell me, what is it we're doing?"

Pulling the Memoria stone from around my neck, I reveal its appearance and slyly smirk at his audible gasp. Tracing my finger over it, I carefully remove it from the leather wrap I've always carried it in.

"By your astonishment, you know what this stone is, yes, old man?"

"Where in the realm did you procure a Memoria stone, Orien Caduceus Vito? You know the dangers that come with this stone," he harshly whispers, looking out his window as if someone is spying on us.

"I do, but it won't be in my possession for much longer. It's going to be put somewhere safe, but I need you to do something for me before then."

He looks at me warily before giving me a clipped nod. I could laugh at how many times I've received that look in my lifetime. It'll never get old. If only he remembered all the shit I've asked him to do.

"I need you to wrap the stone in the silver. Make it into a necklace. I need it to be intricately knotted and barricaded in the casing of a willow tree. Use your imagination on the design," I say softly, passing the stone over to him. I hold in my chuckle as he holds it in the palm of both hands as if it's a newborn.

"That's all?" he asks quietly.

"No, but that is step one. Take your time. Whilst you do that, I need to borrow some parchment," I say, gently clapping his shoulder as I walk by him, to which he glares at me.

Leaving him be in his living room, I make my way to his small, crammed full of shit office, and sit at his desk. Staring around the space, I think about all the things he's taught me in here. I mourn the thought that after today, he will move all of this out and spread it across his cottage. But I take comfort in the fact he'll make this area a guest room that Willow will one day use when my boys act like fools.

Laughing to myself, I pick up the pen and stare down at the parchment in front of me. I write one small letter, a joke if you will, then my laughter slowly turns to sobs as the words flow freely on the next parchment.

Knowing Caspian, he's away in his pocket dimension or eliminating the wrong that walks this realm. I don't want to admit it, but it's probably for the best we do not see each other today. Caspian has a sixth sense of when death is in the air, and he would stalk me if he knew my time has come.

So I pour my love into the parchment. I let what I can of the truth flow out so he understands the decisions I made. I let him know just how much I love him and how proud I am of him. Not many are made the way he and Willow are. They will find strength and balance in one another that no other will understand.

She will find the missing parts of herself in each of them.

Together, the five of them will make each other whole.

Sealing his letter up, I mutter to it quietly, "Conceal the sight from his prying eyes, only reveal my words when his heart accepts the ties."

Opening a transport, I send the letter to a place he will only find once the time is right. Not a moment before, not a moment after. When he needs it the most, it will reveal itself.

Blowing out a steady breath, I move to the next piece of parchment and smile down.

Willow,

Happy birthday, filia mea.

Wear the necklace and don't take it off, no matter what.

It will all make sense soon.

CC, xoxo

After folding her letter up, I bring it to my lips gently. This will accompany both the worst and best birthday present I could ever give her.

Standing, I grab an envelope and hold on to the pen as I make my way back out of Gaster's office and into his living room. As I step into the room, he lets out a great sigh, and I watch as he slowly lowers the necklace down on the table. I don't have to see it to know whatever he did is going to be perfect, but still, I grow nervous with every step I take.

I hum happily as my eyes catch sight of it.

Laid out perfectly on the table, the purple Memoria stone shines brighter than any star in the night sky in its new casing. The silver is delicately woven together at the base, creating the trunk of the tree, as thinner cords spread out, forming its branches. Around and around the rim the silver tangles to establish a protective shell that will no doubt hold it in place no matter what comes out of my girl at any given time.

A thin but indestructible chain slips through the anchor at the top, completing the masterpiece.

"It's everything and more, Gaster. Truly beautiful. Brilliant," I murmur, running my hand across it.

"Are you going to tell me who it's for?" he asks, arching a brow.

"Her name is Willow. Would you mind, actually, engraving that on this box, please?"

"Willow, you say. Is she a special lady?" he asks and I visibly gag.

He's going to understand why that is so vile once his memories are returned and I hope it embarrasses him.

"An important lady," I grumble, and he laughs mischievously as though he's caught me.

"Well, let me get busy then."

With unwavering concentration, he scripts her name across the lid of her box. His cursive writing is one he rarely uses nowadays because most of the younger generation can't read it, but her name is clear as day. Perfect.

"Aht, aht. You can't just lay that necklace in a wooden box. You're going to damage it, careless boy." He fusses at me as I attempt to do just that.

Pushing my hands away, he calls forth his element once more and creates a bed of silver silks that cover the bottom of the box in soft layers. Just right for the necklace to lie on top of.

"Thank you," I say.

"Is today her birthday?" he asks.

"It is." I smile.

"What a magical, wonderful, wonderful day. Off you go then. Don't leave the birthday girl waiting, and you two enjoy yourselves. Please tell her happy birthday from me."

"Will you seal this for me?" I ask, passing him her letter.

His element glides across the parchment, pouring a glob of wax on the fold, imprinting it with an impression of a willow tree.

"Gaster, I can't even begin to thank you for all you've done for me. You've been my father, my mentor, my best friend. The realm's most amazing *Guardria*. You're my greatest blessing and I only hope I've made you proud." I breathe as I pull him in for a tight hug.

"Oh, CC, my boy. That means more to me than you will ever know. You're a blessing. Every day. I couldn't thank Elementra enough for bringing you into my life."

My tears slowly track down my face and when he attempts to pull away from me, I hold on harder as I command these past few moments from his mind. I replace them with us enjoying a nice cup of coffee in the rocking chairs out front. I tell him that the sight is sending me away, but I'll return in due time. All in all, I give him a blissful, uninterrupted hour of time together. Laughing, joking, teasing, and teaching. Everything that over hundreds of years have brought us closer.

Grabbing the box off the table, I back away from him slowly, letting my heartache pour out of me before he comes to and senses it.

It's a strange feeling mourning when you're still alive. Knowing you're going to die in just a short time but you can't tell everyone you love. In my two hundred and fifty-two years of life, I've known for two hundred and thirty-seven of those that this was the day I'd die. I just didn't know the adventure I'd be sent on in the meantime.

Closing my eyes as my feet hit the porch, I transport out.

There're a couple more stops until my final destination.

Opening my eyes, groaning, my insides feel like they're shrinking to nothing, and I use my shaky hands to pull some cloth from my pocket to clean some of the blood off me before Willow arrives. She's going to go into full panic mode when her eyes land on me, but I do my best to conceal the worst of the worst.

Leaning my head back against her willow tree, I use what energy I have left to reach around me and pull her present through the pocket dimension in the trunk. I'm careful not to sully her box with my blood, and I lay it gently on the ground beside me as I close my eyes again and breathe through the pain.

"Elementra?"

"Yes, Seer."

"I ask one more favor of you. Please."

"You've succeeded in all that I have asked, plus more. Ask what you please, Orien Caduceus Vito."

"I'm not ready to leave her, not completely. I want to see what she grows to be. What she and the boys become. The small bits I've been fortunate to see are not enough. I want to be a part of their lives. I ask for more," I say, sobbing as the pain spreads through every part of me and of my reality. I'm truly dying. I will have to leave them all.

I thought I'd prepared myself better, but that was a naïve assumption.

Elementra's power washes over me, only to calm me because even she can't stop what has already begun and I relish her feeling of home, comfort.

"Your request comes with a decision. Whichever choice you make, I will honor."

Her otherworldly essence flows across my mind, and the options available to me become clear.

In either option, my Willow must endure horrors I can't bear to watch, but I force myself to so she is not alone. Neither choice will alleviate that for her, but one choice gives me time with her. Forever with her. With them all.

Picking up her box from beside me, I open the lid and move her envelope over so I can see her stone.

"CC! Oh my God, oh fuck. Are you okay?"

As if my thoughts alone summoned her, my greatest blessing falls to her knees, dropping the box in her hand, shrieking beside me. With shaky fingers, she traces the markings of the beating I took.

"Wh-What happened?"

"Everything's going to be okay, *filia mea*."

Looking down at her stone again, I gently run my fingers across it.

"Tell me, Seer. Is this a present for today or another?"

"Another."

Four

Willow

The connection in my mind snaps and I suck in a sharp gasp as I clutch my head.

Standing too fast, I sway harshly as the room spins around me. My face would've met the floor if shadows didn't wrap around me to catch my fall while a vine wraps around my waist, gently pulling me back down to my seat.

Still, the room doesn't stop its rotation as my mushy brain tries to solidify itself again and everything I see doubles.

"I...I still don't understand. You skipped parts. We didn't get to see what happened to you and I don't understand your choice. CC, what did you do?" I ask out loud as I start to hyperventilate.

Although we just watched the memory from his perspective, that day tries to come to the forefront of my mind. What came after that is still blocked from me, but those emotions in that moment aren't. The helplessness, the petrified way I felt seeing him lying against my tree, rushes me, and I don't know if I want to scream or throw up. If he hadn't shown us that just now, the entire occurrence would still be shielded from me.

"Take a deep breath for me, princess. I've got you," Corentin whispers in my ear and his air fills my lungs.

Simultaneously, a healing vial is pressed to my lips, and I lock on to the watery whiskey orbs of Caspian. His body shakes violently, but his hands stay steady as he pours the liquid miracle down my throat. As soon as the last drop touches my tongue, he trails his fingers down my neck as if he's following the liquid's path to make sure I got it all.

"He was your first *Guardria* bond, wasn't he, Primary?" he asks softly, just to confirm what he heard, and at my nod, he turns to Gaster. "And yours as well?"

"Yes," Gaster answers, wiping the tears from his eyes with a cloth.

Cas doesn't comment further, and his features give me nothing. They're a cloud of confusion, understanding, and anticipation. Any other time, I'd swear the chaos of this situation would have him giddy, but right now, he's so...subdued.

Understandably.

"I can't put it all together. The pieces that are still missing..." I trail off, hissing as the sharp pain in my mind sends a zap through my entire body.

"Stop trying to force it, little warrior. It'll just hurt more. Everything will settle and come when it's supposed to. For now, we have more answers than before," Tillman says.

Ever the understanding. Ever the patient.

"Yes, he is, and he's right. All the times I've told you, it'll all make sense soon. Well, soon is sooner than it's ever been. Allow it to come as it's supposed to, filia mea," CC murmurs and I shudder at the sound.

"If you can't give me the answer of how this is possible, will you at least tell me is this permanent? Will I hear you forever like you asked for?"

"Yes and no. There are rules for the request Elementra granted me. Such as, I will always come to you in times of importance or need if my presence doesn't interfere with your path. I'll always know what is being said and can respond in time like a conversation, but most times, I won't be able to speak to you freely, give you all the answers you seek, or have everyday moments. There must be a purpose for my presence. As there is now. For now."

"And the guys? Gaster? Will they always hear you?"

I ask because none of them have flinched or moved whatsoever since he spoke. I can't tell if they can hear him, or they just know I'm having a conversation in my mind, so they don't interrupt. One way or another, I'd like for them to have a warning. The effect this is having on all of them today is obvious and they're only holding it together because I'm crumbling.

"Gaster and I will have conversations in your presence but none on our own. And the boys...not really. Few and far between will situations arise where they'll hear me as you do. Today is an exception to that. Your freshly completed bond is at its peak of unsettledness, which allows the Memoria stone easier access to them, but that will not be the case for long. In the future, if you choose so, you may allow them in to hear or replay what I've said."

"And what about—"

CC's laugh ricochets through my mind, silencing my next question, and the sound makes the corner of my mouth twitch. That's a melody I've long since forgotten, but now that I hear it clearly, remember it completely, I can recall the millions of times I've caused it. Me and my never-ending questions. Or my foul mouth.

"You get it all honestly, Willow. Never change. For now, though, take some time with the boys. Allow your mind a break. If you can." His teasing tone pulls a choked laugh from my chest as I wipe beneath my eyes.

He's never discouraged my questions, my curiosity. Even if he couldn't tell me the truth, he found humor in the seriousness, and a teaching opportunity at every turn. He never made me feel like a burden for my always racing mind.

Turning my attention to my men and Gaster, I inform them of what I was just told, and the guys' shoulders relax while Gaster's almost perk up. There's a stark difference between how my Nexus and my *Guardria* feel about having conversations with someone in the beyond.

"Corentin..." I whisper, gaining his attention from where he's staring off into nothingness.

"Yeah, princess."

"Are you okay?" I ask quietly.

This is a huge reality check for all of us, so I'm attempting not to invade their deeper emotions. The ones they're trying to bury, but he's completely blocked off. He's giving me nothing.

"I'm not sure honestly," he grits out.

"I'm sorry," I mumble. I don't know what else to say.

What he discovered is only one surprising truth that we just uncovered. Multiple things, big things were just revealed to all of us.

"Gaster, are all your memories back?" Tillman asks.

"Yes, they've all returned now from what I can tell," he says quietly, with a small smile on his lip.

"This is how you knew he was gone. You were the only one. Mom gave us no choice but to listen, believe he was gone although there was no proof. Did she know about the bond? Why did you keep it a secret from us?" Caspian asks, strained, seemingly hurt by the secrecy.

I hadn't considered it, but now that Caspian's pointed it out, something clicks. That day at Oakly's family's lake house, Gaster mentioned secrets not even the boys knew.

This was his secret.

"I'm sorry, Caspian. Everyone. I didn't want to keep this a secret, but I didn't have a choice. Until now," Gaster says softly, then clears his throat. "Orien's gift emerged at fifteen. He was the youngest of our time until you, Corentin."

"No, he emerged at seventeen," Corentin argues immediately.

"That's when he openly shared his gift with everyone, but he truly emerged two years prior. His first vision came the night after his fifteenth birthday. He swore off his birthday after that. Ordered everyone to never mention his day of life from that point on." He sighs, shaking his head and squeezing his eyes for a moment before carrying on. "He couldn't share everything he saw with me, but he was inconsolable and told me we had a *Guardria* bond, but no one could know until the time was right. He made me vow to keep that secret with him, and I did because truthfully, at the time, I thought he'd just had a vivid night terror or something. He was frantic about it, so I made the vow to calm him.

"Lo and behold, he was telling the truth. The moment the vow was sealed with our magic, our awakening happened, then the bond snapped in place. I was over the moon. The draw to the Vito family that I'd felt for many, many years prior didn't exactly make sense to me, but I'd chalked it up to having finally met what felt like family. Then it all clicked into place with Orien's bond. Generations of the Vito line needed me, but he needed me and my guidance the most. He wasn't thrilled at first about the bond, but that had more to do with everything else he saw that night. He learned a lot in his emerging, including the fact he would be Nexus-less. Also, I'm afraid, he learned of the time and way of his passing.

"As for your mother believing me, Orien had told her many times that if I were to say something about him, then to believe me. She, of course, denied my claim that he'd passed at first, but after a few minutes of pacing, she knew the truth. On a soul level she knew it. You could feel his absence in the palace like his life force to it was tangible. Then it was just...gone."

Caspian sinks back into his seat, staring at Gaster in a whole other light, and slowly but surely, the sense of betrayal evaporates in all of them, but it leaves behind a deep, deep feeling of loss. One that coats my tongue so thick in ash, I could choke on it.

"So you just broke the vow?" Tillman asks.

"Not me. The vow broke when Willow entered the south wing. That's why I was able to get close to her and you all weren't. Orien's power wasn't holding me back. Then what happened between us when we entered unlocked a few of the memories, reminding me that I'm the one who gave him his middle name and nickname. I can't believe that boy took that memory from everyone who knew him...The rest surfaced as we watched his last day unfold," Gaster says softly, smiling as he looks around the space.

"What happened between the two of you before we came in?" Caspian asks, catching on to that little tidbit.

With a shaky voice and watery eyes, I explain how Elementra severed our bond so she could weave CC's back in with ours, reconnecting the three of us. My heart and soul become lighter with my words, but the knowledge that Gaster spent eight years dealing with that level of suffering while I could hardly bear minutes of it splits me open.

My suffering was nulled. How the Memoria stone took that level of pain away from me, I'm not sure, but I'm grateful. I never would've survived the nonmagical realm if I was that crippled in my grief.

Tears flow down my face in streams as that thought puts yet another piece together for me. Elementra, CC, and the Memoria stone somehow worked together to keep that away from me so I could survive. They knew I was going to be alone again, so they tried to protect me as best as they could emotionally.

Draken's quick to kneel in front of me, purring as he wipes the water off my cheeks, then lays his forehead to mine. "How about we explore? I know your mind is all over the place right now, but that curiosity still burns bright. Maybe that'll help the memories and thoughts settle down a little."

That's exactly what I want.

As if his words have given my mind permission to slow down, focus on something else, I grace him with a huge smile. My dragon always knows what I want and need, even before I do.

"I'd like that. If everyone else is up to it," I mumble.

Everyone's interest piques and washes over me. They want to know just as badly as I do—hell, maybe more—what's hiding behind these walls.

"Here, take this before you go on your adventure, Willow," Gaster says, passing me another healing vial.

"Are you okay with exploring?" I ask him, then tilt my head back.

A brilliant smile breaks out across his face. It's so contagious that I can't help but mimic him. Why he's so happy, I don't know, but his aura is breathtaking and mine soaks it up like a sponge.

"This is a moment only meant for the five of you. CC meant what he said by this is your space. He and I are the only two who've been in here in hundreds of years and still only you all can enter the ward. Plus, you and I are not the only ones who've had our memories returned. I will go run interference while you all take your time."

The pride in his voice sparks a bit of excitement in each of us, and our gazes naturally look at the hall that leaves this room. There's so much mystery to that corridor and what lies behind it. My heart flutters with anticipation, stronger than the throbbing in my mind.

"Who else—"

"Oh shit..." I murmur as my hand flies to my mouth, cutting Corentin's question off.

The memories slowly start coming to the forefront of my mind before settling into their new homes. Conversation after conversation replays through the years. My eyes trace the wording on the letters repeatedly.

"Your mom. She knows all about me. Well, we know all about each other. CC took her memories as well. Often at that. Your dads as well, just not as much," I whisper, staring at Gaster's mischievous eyes. He knew all about this, the whole time. Well, when his memories were his own to know.

"You're going to have to give us more detail than that, little wanderer," Draken says.

"CC spent years telling me about Aurora. Passing communications between the two of us. He never told me who she was to me, but as I got older, started asking more questions about my mom, girl things, and so on, he sought out help from the only person he knew to ask," I mumble.

"Did Mom know who Willow was in all of this, Gaster?" Corentin asks, narrowing his eyes.

"Technically, yes, but she never got to keep her memories. Every conversation, every letter, was kept from her. I'm only privy to this because he warned me this would happen. She knew that Willow was your Primary and was in the nonmagical realm, and Orien told her that was how it had to be. So Aurora took what little and every opportunity he gave her to be there for Willow."

A smile breaks out across my face as the memories continue to unravel for me. He started telling me stories about Aurora when I was eight years old, and he allowed us to communicate with one another through letters when I turned fourteen. I received a letter a month from then until I was almost eighteen years old.

"Where are our letters, Gaster?" I ask.

"That, child, I do not know, but we will find out. I'll go and speak with her and her boys while you all get settled in. Come out when you're ready," he says cheerily, gives my head a kiss, then makes his way out of the ward with hurried steps.

"I'm so fucking confused," Draken says, running his hands through his hair, huffing so forcefully, smoke blows from his nose.

"What's there to be confused about, dragon? Our uncle was tasked with laying the pieces set forth by Elementra. That's why he was granted the gift of sight. His dutiful meddling started with Willow's mom, then his duty became Willow. Elementra blessed them with a *Guardria* bond because she needed the guidance and love of someone from this realm to prepare her for the shit show she was setting her up for. He also had to lay all the pieces for not only us but every single person in our lives so we'd be ready for her arrival. Mom got to have a closer relationship with her because Willow wasn't allowed to know about her mom, probably for protection from saying anything to her father, and she needed a female role model. What don't you get?" Caspian's words are straightforward, cold.

A lump forms in my throat at hearing it. The matter-of-fact tone doesn't hide the hurt and sense of abandonment laced within. His emotions speak louder than his words, though, and they're confusing. His understanding of the entire situation is clear. Out of everyone, he seems to be the most understanding, but nonetheless, he's very upset with his uncle.

"Well, when you put it like that, I get it..." Draken trails off solemnly.

"Come on, little warrior, let's explore," Tillman says, laying his hand on my back and steering me out of the growing tension.

Corentin and Draken promptly take up both my sides, while Tillman takes the lead. Caspian, despite his dark mood, presses himself to my back and I exhale heavily as I feel some of his anger leak out at the touch of his body to mine.

I tell myself not to obsess or bombard him with questions because when he's ready, he's going to talk about exactly how he feels with me or the guys. Someone will hear about it. The others, though...I'm going to have to prompt them first.

"Are you all upset with me?"

Tillman stops walking so fast, if Corentin and Draken didn't tighten their grips on my fingers, I would've smacked into his massive back.

"Why would we be upset with you?" he asks when he turns on his heels to face me.

"Everything we just learned...It's a lot. Elementra basically took your uncle, made him my pseudo father, and everyone was kept in the dark, with their memories taken, willingly and unwillingly, because of me."

"And what active role did you play in that, princess?" Corentin asks.

"Well, I don't know...all of it, it feels like."

"Wrong. None of it. You had no more control over any of this than we did. He wasn't taken from us. He was still there for us plenty. Not as much as he was when we were younger, but he was still a very active adult in our lives. Are we grieving, saddened? Yes, of course, but we're not upset, mad, or weirded out. We aren't feeling any of the negative things toward you that you have running through your mind right now, princess."

A whoosh of air rushes out of me. Leave it to Corentin to just give it to me straight like that.

"Thank you," I murmur, squeezing his hand.

"There's nothing to thank me for. It's the truth. Sure, we still need more answers, but so do you. We're in this together. All the same," he says softly, leaning over and laying a sweet kiss on my forehead.

I nod to Tillman, silently giving him the go-ahead, though he lingers for a moment, his gaze piercing through me, searching for any hint of doubt. Whatever he sees must satisfy him because, without a word, he turns and continues his stride.

The hall itself is normal—nothing grand or remarkable—but the fork at the end pulls at my curiosity, making my pulse quicken. As if on cue, four chuckles echo around me, and I roll my eyes. They still find amusement in this and I doubt I'll ever change. Everything new stirs excitement in me, no matter how small.

"Hopefully, it always will," Tillman says, smirking slyly back at me over his shoulder.

Blushing like a schoolgirl from that devious little wink he shoots me, I focus my eyes back forward and set my mind solely on seeing everything I can. Which, at the moment, is nothing.

After walking the realm's longest stretch of light gray walls, we come to the fork. To the left, it leads down a much smaller hallway, then double doors, whereas the right leads to a set of stairs. My gaze bounces back and forth in indecision. I want—no, need to see it all, but which way first?

"We'll clear this floor first, princess, then make our way up," Corentin declares, leading us to the left, making the decision for me.

I practically bounce on my toes as Tillman places his palm on the doors and pushes them wide, his eyes devouring everything before allowing me to pass him.

"No one's in here. You don't have to clear it like we're infiltrating a Mastery structure." I chuckle, patting his chest as I walk past him.

"Never know." He shrugs off my suggestion, but I'm already too focused on the room we just entered.

The kitchen.

The walls are lined with copper pots and pans that hang from intricate iron hooks, while shiny marble countertops stretch far, providing plenty of space for someone's—not mine—cooking creativity. The floor is laid with large, smooth stones that seem to release a gentle heat that I can feel through the soles of my shoes.

In the center, a massive wooden table dominates the space. Spread across it are different herbs, jars of what look like flours, seasonings, dried pastas. Everything preserved and ready to be used.

Taking a deep breath, I swear the air is filled with the scent of fresh bread and a hint of something sweet, like the promise of a dessert yet to come even though I know for a fact this space hasn't been used in centuries, possibly ever.

"Damn. Chef and Mrs. Grace are going to have a field day in here." Draken whistles.

"You think they're going to want to come here?" I whirl around on my heel excitedly.

"Oh yeah. Where we go, they go. They aren't going to let you or sweet baby Corentin starve. Also, unless we're planning on eating sandwiches for breakfast, lunch, and dinner, we'll need them. This kitchen is the shit compared to ours at the mansion or the east wing." Draken earns himself a little love tap on the shoulder from Corentin, but we all laugh because it's true.

They're at Corentin's beck and call willingly, lovingly. He's a sweet prince in their eyes. Plus, they spoil me with treats nonstop.

My eyes continue to trace the space, and I notice four exit points. One leads outside, where I can see a patio area much like ours at the mansion off to the right, and my heart thunders with excitement about eating out there, looking over the gardens.

Another exit leads up to a set of stairs that I can't wait to take two at a time to see what's up there. The third and the last one, I'm not totally sure because wooden doors block it.

As I approach the mysterious door that's at the back of the kitchen first rather than the other by the stairs, a gold plaque stops my nosiness, and my hand pauses on the knob.

Molva Quarters.

Of course.

Admittedly, it took me an embarrassingly long time to put two and two together that Mrs. Grace and Chef, which is his real name, and the rest of the house staff, Oscar, Lou, and Flint, are in a Nexus together. I caught Mrs. Grace with two of them teasing and touching in the kitchen once, and I backed out quietly like I caught them being naughty.

Corentin makes his way over to me with a small smile on his face as he traces the plaque tenderly. "Their Nexus has been taking care of the Vito family since my uncle was a child. When we moved out of the central quarters and into the east wing on our own, he asked them to move there with us. Look after us. They've been with us since we were children, bouncing from wing to wing, then the mansion. Now they'll come here."

"Well, thank goodness for that. I can't cook for shit," I say teasingly, hiding the emotion clogging my throat.

I don't get very much interaction with them since they're always so busy, but they go out of their way to take care of us and our mansion. So I'm incredibly thankful that they're able and willing to bounce between locations for us.

Deciding I have no business snooping through it since this is going to be their personal space, I turn on my heel and make my way toward the door by the stairs. Beating Tillman there, much to his disapproval, I poke my head in and find a formal dining room. It's nice, grand, just as the one at the mansion is, and I already know, even though it's beautiful, it won't get much use from us unless we have guests.

Allowing the guys a second to poke their heads in as well, I impatiently head to the stairs alone, which gets them moving. They all follow, just as excited as me now, with little chuckles falling from their lips that I know are directed at my elated curiosity.

Up two short flights of stairs, we come to another hallway and two large wooden doors conceal the room to our left. Tillman, not giving me the opportunity to barge in first, cuts in front of me and slings the doors open. I grow nervous and halt my steps when his feet quit moving suddenly, but before I know it, he's throwing his head back, laughing. That reaction spurs me forward so I can see.

Stopping, mesmerized, a laugh bubbles out of me as well as I see a breakfast room that matches ours at the mansion to perfection. The only difference really is the scenery behind the massive floor-to-ceiling windows. Instead of a thick forest, our view is the pristine, beautiful gardens that do eventually lead to a forest.

We all take just a moment to look around at the similarities and familiarity of the space, then we head out. The smile that takes over my face feels permanent for the time being. The more I see, the more at home I feel and the need to see the rest becomes persistent.

On this same floor, we come across a lounge that I know is crafted more for the guys than me. It's obvious the one downstairs that we were in was built to perfection for me.

Coming up a few more flights of stairs, skipping the random guest rooms and other extra spaces, I know we've hit the last floor and my feet skid to a stop as a gasp falls from my lips.

This hallway seems to defy the laid-out design we've seen so far. The width between the walls is far larger, and on each side there're two doors, totaling four new rooms.

At the very end of this gargantuan stretch, the hallway forks left and right, obscuring what lies each way.

"Hell yeah. I think we found our rooms." Draken cheers, rubbing his hands together with childlike excitement.

Taking in each door from my frozen position, I know he's right. I don't even have to enter them, and I know which room belongs to who. I feel their signatures coming off the doors like the room itself has already been infused with pieces of them.

"Draken, that's your room there. The first one on the left," I whisper.

"How do you know that, little wanderer?" he asks, cocking his brow at me with a twitch of his lip.

"I just do."

He rushes over to it and lays his hand on the knob before turning toward us. "Well, what the hell are you all waiting for? Come on."

He doesn't waste another second as he slings the door open with a chuckle on his lips that fades just as fast as it came. His features grow more serious, more revered, and I hustle into his side.

Straight ahead on the massive stretch of wall is a mural.

Two dragons, one auburn, one silver, are in a playful flight with fire flowing from their mouths. Their tails are intertwined, with the much larger auburn dragon flying beneath the smaller silver one. Tears prick my eyes as we take a step forward. Then another. And together, we raise our hands and lay our palms on our counterparts.

Letting my gaze wander, the entire room is painted in a similar design. Three of the four walls depict our dragons doing various things together. Laying our foreheads together, our heads tilted to the sky, breathing fire. It's like a live portrait of the things we've done together.

I swallow my gasp as my eyes land on the last wall. The mural here is smaller, nestled between bookshelves lined with more knickknacks than books. When he turns and spots it, his steps falter, and he stumbles back.

Perfectly centered is a painting of the moment we shared in the air on the way here, I swear. We're in flight, with who looks scarily like Corentin on my back. Tillman and Caspian ride on top of his, and a smaller golden dragon flies amongst us, with a rider on hers.

"Holy fuck. He knew," Draken whispers, running his finger over the painting of Tanith.

"It would seem so," I murmur, laying my head on his shoulder, linking our fingers.

"Damn, it had to be hard, painful, keeping all these secrets," he says, leaning down to lay his lips on my forehead.

"I only have a taste of what he had to keep to himself, but it sure isn't easy. It's what's for the best, though. It keeps everyone safe."

"You're incredible. You know that right, little wanderer?"

"So are you, dragon. So are you," I mumble, squeezing in close to him.

"I got to say, Draken, I'm a little jealous of this chair," Tillman says playfully from behind us, and we whip around to see what he's talking about.

His hulking form seems so small honestly as he sits in a chair that has sprawling wings coming off the back. Its rich auburn color pops in the sunlight that filters in not only from the window but above us. The ceiling is vaulted, with skylights that allow the sun to pour in.

"Shit, scoot over. Let me see," Draken says, not giving Tillman time to do as he said. Instead, he plops down in his lap, causing us to laugh and Tillman to yell for him to get his heavy ass off.

I turn from their playful banter as my eyes drift back toward the bookshelves. The few spines I see are so beautiful and colorful compared to the typical black and brown leather we usually see. These aren't your everyday Elementra books.

"Draken, come look at these," I say, sliding one off the shelf.

The Keeper Line.

Shit.

"Is that..."

"Yeah. History of the dragons, Essemist Keep, Keeper's line," I answer before he can finish his question and pass it to him.

He eyes them warily for a moment, running his hand down the cover. With a small sigh, he nods once but then slides the book back in place.

"Later," he says, giving me a tight smile, and I don't push for more.

"How in the realm did you get those?" I ask, not exactly expecting an answer but hopeful for one.

"You will know with time."

Huffing, I roll my eyes as we start making our way out Draken's door. The space fits his energy and his excitement perfectly. It'll be a comforting place for him, that's for sure.

"Did you notice that you had a bathroom and a closet but no bed?" Corentin asks.

"Yeah, I noticed. Why would I need a bed? I'm not sleeping anywhere without Willow," Draken deadpans.

I noticed it as well and thought the same thing. He hasn't slept in a room without me practically since my first month here. Nothing's going to change that, nor would I want it to. With any of them. They all have to sleep with me.

I won't have it any other way.

"That's yours," I say, hip bumping my gentle giant as he snorts at my thoughts, and we face the first door on the opposite side of the hall.

With a small smile and a nod, he strides toward the door, covering the distance in just a few steps. The calmness that seeps from his room is potent, and my shoulders relax and a soft sigh flows through my lips. He can sense it too and his muscles uncoil right in front of me.

I spot the greenery around the room the second the door is opened, and Tillman's small laugh pulls me forward.

Stepping in behind him, my shoes disintegrate into nothing, and my feet travel the small distance to the center of the room to stand beside him where my toes sink into the floor that's made of living moss. It's soft and cool underfoot, with patches of wildflowers that add bursts of color.

The walls are a mix of smooth stone and thick, twisting vines that climb toward the ceiling, creating a canopy of leaves. There's a desk that resembles the one in our treehouse, and a few of the smaller workout items he uses when he practices his breathing and meditation before a mission are tucked underneath it.

A hammock made of woven vines hangs between two tree trunks that rise from the floor, providing the perfect place to laze around, and I can picture some afternoon naps taking place there.

"Tillman," I murmur, in absolute awe of how this room fits him so precisely.

"I couldn't have designed this any better myself. Fuck, he knew us so well," he says before making his way over to the desk and picking up a frame.

It's been molded to hold three separate pictures, and the center image is the one that catches my eye. It's his fourteenth birthday. My heart flips at the scene of him and his mom. Engraved in the frame below them are their names.

Tilly and Tillme.

Tillme?

"Another time, little warrior," he says softly, running his finger down the frame before setting it back in its spot.

I get the sense my gentle giant has been holding out on some things with me. Like this sweet little nickname. I cock my brow in invitation for him to talk, but he pointedly ignores me, and his skin grows red with embarrassment.

Later then.

We take a few minutes checking everything out, and the guys tease Tillman on his need for a place so peaceful so he doesn't explode and make the realm crumble. It's half-truth, half teasing, I know, but Tillman's ability to calm himself, find his center, his willpower, is astonishing to witness. He's calmer than any other being I've ever met, and that takes strength, resilience, patience. And I look up to him so much for that.

Exiting his space, we walk the few feet down toward the other door on this side. I take a shaky breath because I have no clue what to expect on the inside.

"This is you, your highness," I say, looking over my shoulder at Corentin. He's tense, with his hands shoved in his pockets, and I know he's nervous about what he's going to see as well.

But like the control master he is, he relaxes his features, pulls his shoulders back, and with no hesitation, opens the door.

The sight startles him as his steps falter, and I chuckle at his surprise.

Yep, this is definitely all Corentin.

The air itself exudes quiet authority and comfort. Dark, polished wood lines the walls, with tall bookshelves filled with leather-bound books and meticulously organized scrolls.

A huge mahogany desk sits in the center. Its surface neat, shiny, and precisely arranged with parchments, pens, and a journal. Can't lie, when I look at it, I just picture him using his air to sling everything off it before he bends me over it.

My face flames at the thought, and I elbow Tillman when he chuckles, but really, it's this collected, controlled environment that brings on the safety of me having such a dirty fantasy. The headmaster loses control sometimes. Over me. Only me.

Clearing my throat when Corentin turns his darkened eyes my way, I take in the rest of the room as though I'm not thinking about him fucking me senseless in his new room. My fidgeting and squeezing my thighs together definitely don't go unnoticed. It just goes unaddressed.

Forcing myself to focus, I eye the high-backed chair, upholstered in rich, navy leather. It's large enough I could snuggle up on his lap and not disturb his work. As I cross the room to get a look at the little bar in the corner, an intricately woven rug muffles my footsteps, further justifying I wouldn't bother his concentration if I want to be in here with him.

"Do you have a sudden fear that he won't be spending time with you or something, little warrior?" Tillman asks, rudely butting into my thoughts.

"Not exactly...maybe. You know how he gets after big reveals. He hides himself away in his work," I admit.

"I don't think you have to worry about that anymore, Will." He shoots me a small smile and I release a deep breath.

Since seeing the magnitude of the decision CC laid in front of Corentin, yeah, I've been worried. Worried about each of them honestly, but Tillman and Draken are handling this far better than the Vito brothers. So of course I've thought the worst.

My eyes track Corentin as he makes his way to the large windows. They let in soft, natural light that casts a warm glow on the room and the breeze that blows in when he cracks the window truly breathes life into this space. I feel a little bit of my worries fade away when he smiles out into the distance, then turns that tender look on me.

"I like it," he says casually, but he can't hide his excitement from me. I don't call him out, but the way my bond flutters, he more than approves of his space.

Finally, we walk out of the room and Corentin shuts the door behind him as we stare at what we know is Caspian's room.

My dark protector has been unusually quiet and I hate it. He's not one for pointless conversations with other people, but with us, we typically get input, crass jokes, and mischief every now and then. None of that has been present. Just his comment to Draken before we started our tour, followed by this emotionally charged silence.

None of us move, allowing him the decision.

He finally makes it when he grabs my hand and drags me forward alongside him. Emotionless, face as hard as stone, he throws the door open and looks around.

His body flinches, but that's the most he moves as his eyes take in his room. My gaze does the same, and my heart rate spikes as I stare at the beauty in front of me.

It's a sanctuary.

For his mind, his body, and his soul.

The room is cloaked in quiet and low amber lighting, and a much cooler breeze blows through here than any other room we've seen.

The walls are completely lined with bookshelves. If I listened closely enough, I swear I could hear each shelf groaning under the weight of all this knowledge. In the center of the room, an overstuffed armchair with an attached ottoman sits, angled toward a small, low-burning fireplace. The chair is upholstered in black velvet, with a purple blanket over its back, and a small side table stands beside it. It's just big enough for two cups of coffee and a book.

There's a free-standing brass lamp that casts a warm, focused beam of light that's positioned perfectly for you to see the pages of your book. My attention lingers there. It's so easy for my mind to paint a picture of the two of us cuddled up in that chair under our blanket.

The fantasy is broken as the door shuts, cutting me off from the view.

"You don't want to go in?" I ask quietly, looking up into those haunted whiskey eyes.

"Not right now, Primary," he says gruffly before leaning down and capturing my lips in a sweet, gentle kiss.

His shadows wrap around him in a layer of armor when he pulls back and my heart cracks a little, but I'm thankful he didn't fade through the walls. He's staying here by my side as we finish our tour, despite wanting to disappear for a while.

Silently following Tillman's lead, we continue our path to the end of the hallway. When we reach the fork, he turns to me. "Which way, Will, right or left?"

Aww, shit. I don't want to decide.

"Left," CC says.

"Left," I quickly repeat out loud when I see Corentin about to decide for me.

I do glance to the right when we round the corner and all there is, is a single door, and my eyes widen when I feel my own magic pulsing through it.

My bedroom will be last.

The left hallway matches the right. There's only a single door, but unlike every other room in this hall, I can't feel anyone's magic coming through the wood. Instead, it feels ancient, powerful, but not distinct enough for me to say it's Elementra's or CC's, or, well, anyone's I know.

When I reach for the knob, anticipation on the verge of killing me, I hear CC's laughter ring through my mind, and I roll my eyes.

"Don't travel all the way in the room just yet, Willow. Your mind needs a break and to be at full strength before you venture around in here," he says.

I pause, relaying the message to the guys, and they each clam up slightly with the uncertainty of what's behind the door, but I just vibrate with excitement. I heed his warning despite wanting to ignore him, though.

"Holy shit. What is this?" I ask quietly as I slowly open the door.

"I call it an amplifier room," CC answers cryptically, and I tell the guys.

"We saw a bit of this in his memories. I've never heard of such a thing," Caspian says as he eyes the space and the guys all grunt in agreement.

"Can you tell us about this?" I ask out loud, but I don't open my mind for the guys to hear his reply. They finally seem to be relaxing fully now, and I don't want CC's voice to surprise them.

"You should ask Gaster for his notes on the Valorian Veil."

"The Valorian Veil? The home of the gods? Why?"

"You'll find your answers there."

Humming, I once again inform the guys, then turn all my attention back to the space in front of me. I can feel the pull of the magic in here attempting to draw me closer, so I take CC's warning more seriously and step back out the doorway. I can't see the entirety of the room from here, but I see enough to sate my curiosity for now, until I can explore to my heart's desire.

The walls are covered in a smooth, reflective material that seems to shift and change, showing glimpses of places I've never seen, and I shake my head out from the dizziness I feel from staring so hard. How this is possible, I haven't a clue. I'd think the material would reflect what's in the room like mirrors, but that's not the case at all.

Looking down, the floor is a mixture of tiny, polished stones that form intricate patterns, drawing my eyes and mind into a state of focus. I find myself again having to shake my head, and I take another step back.

Fuck, what is this?

Exhaling sharply, I blink rapidly, then focus on the center of the room. There's what looks like a pallet of pillows and blankets on a circular platform. The largest crystals I've ever seen surround it. They rise from the floor, and I have no doubt they'd come up to at least my hips.

I can't see the ceiling from out here, but I know there're no windows or skylights in there. The room is shrouded in darkness, with only the faint glows of the crystals and stones in the floor.

Not willing to risk any damage to my mind since it's finally starting to settle, I back up even more, nodding to the guys to let them know I'm done.

We're all a concoction of confusion and wonder about that room and its different magic. I know I'll have to ask Gaster for that information sooner rather than later to give myself some peace, but right now, I have a single-minded focus on my room as the door grows closer. A ball of nerves creeps up and gets stuck in my throat, but I swallow it down.

"This is where I leave you for now, filia mea," CC says, and I jerk my hand away from the handle.

"What is that supposed to mean?"

"It just means my presence is not needed in this room. I, nor Gaster, have stepped foot in here since it was designed. You will never need to worry about me coming to you while you are in the comfort of your room. This is your space. Your peace. And no one shall interrupt that without your say so."

"I mean, you won't be gone long, right? I don't have to go in there right this minute." My panic rises like a tide and the guys close in around me as it pulses to them. I just got him back. I don't want him to go yet. Ever.

"This is not forever, Willow. Go. See your space and enjoy your Nexus. This is for all of you. I'll always be here. Just not in there."

I suck in a harsh sob that wants to escape me because unlike any other time he's gone silent, this time, I actually feel his presence leave me. I didn't notice before that I was physically feeling him, but now that he's dismissed himself, the slight heat I was unaware of in my Memoria stone cools, and a thin veil lifts from my mind.

"What's wrong?" Corentin asks, tilting my chin up, forcing my eyes to collide with his.

"He's gone. Again."

"What does that mean, princess?"

I tell him exactly what just happened as a few stray tears slide down my cheeks. He's quick to wipe them away and dry their streaks before smiling at me softly.

"He's respecting your privacy and space, princess. If he says he's not gone for long or that he'll be back, he means it. I, for one, am thankful he won't be invading this space and bringing forth any unwanted secrets here. This is supposed to be your hideaway, your peace. Not somewhere where worry follows you."

I release a tense breath as his words settle my pounding heart. He's right. Of course he is. When he puts it like that, it makes more sense. No, I don't want my room tainted with anything negative. I want this to be a place of carefree nature and comfort with my men.

They all exhale when they feel me release the emotions that were just plaguing me. It's something I've seen occur a couple times now, and I'm pretty sure our bonding last night has caused an increase in everything between us, not just our elements and gifts. We obviously either can't block each other out now as we once could or none of us are putting enough strength behind it to truly enforce it.

Keeping that in mind, I send out a burst of love to each of them, and my body feels warm giddiness when they each send it back.

Gathering my courage, I put my hand on the doorknob and turn before I chicken out. My first few steps draw a blinding smile to my face and a mixture of laughter and a sob pours out of me.

In front of me is the exact replica of my bedroom at the mansion. There're only a few different details that I can spot and my heart swells with its flawlessness.

A crunch under my foot startles me, and I freeze, peering down. The folded cream parchment causes my eyes to widen, and I lurch for it, flipping over the envelope to find my name scribbled across. The guys close in as I tear it open, my breath unsteady as I begin to read aloud.

Willow, boys,

If you're reading this, then that means I've already told Willow I wouldn't be joining you all in this room's exploration.

I made a few tweaks that fit the wing, but for the most part, boys, this design was the four of you. You all crafted it to perfection just for her and I didn't want to disturb that.

I hope you all enjoy your new home, whether it becomes your permanent residence, temporary, or just somewhere you stay when you pass through in your years before ruling. I just wanted you all to have a space that was completely your own.

Untouched and untainted by the realm we live in.

I know the days seem long and dark, but I have more faith in the five of you than any other beings to ever cross this realm.

I love you, all five of you, so very much and I am so proud.

I will always be with you.

CC...Uncle Orien...Uncle Oreo...whatever...xoxo

I laugh at the signature. I can almost picture his puzzled face, not knowing which name to sign it as. The troubles of wearing many masks, I guess, but no matter the name, we know who he is. The multiple parts of him.

Blinking away the water soaking my lashes, I clutch the letter close to my chest, then look around at the perfection in front of me.

They really did get it right the first time. They knew exactly what to make of my space within the first week of me being here, and there isn't a thing about it I want changed.

Speaking of which...

My head whips to the other side of the room as I hustle to the bathroom and throw the door open. You barely hear my relieved sigh over the laughter coming from behind me. Men just don't understand the importance of a bathroom, and my oasis is by far the best. Nothing about it should ever change.

Walking back into the room with them, Draken grips my hand and leads me to the only real change we see. At the mansion, between my bookshelves, sits my comfy reading nook that I like to laze on. Here, there're French doors that open to the outside.

Draken laughs as he pushes them wide, exposing the beautiful balcony, and my eyes eat up the little space.

An awning spreads out above us, shading most of the area with cool shadows. A cozy couch rests against the wall, a table in front of it, and I can already imagine myself there—sleepy mornings with a cup of coffee, snuggled up beside someone.

To one side, a patio table with five chairs faces an expanse of green that fades seamlessly into the forest. On the other, if you lean over the railing, you can catch a glimpse of our garden and the gravel path, but from our height, we're concealed from sight. The space feels wonderfully private.

"This is fucking nice," Draken says as he plops down on the couch, and I follow right along with him.

"I'd have to agree with you, Draken," Tillman says, taking up my other side. "We should've thought about this."

"No. I love my reading nook," I say, shaking my head and squeezing his hand.

"We're going to stay in the wing today, princess. Chef, Mrs. Grace, and the others are prepping the kitchen now. We'll see my parents tomorrow," Corentin declares, sitting down beside Tillman and lacing his fingers behind his head.

"How? No one can get through the ward but us?" I ask, sitting up so I can look at him.

"When I touched the plaque, I felt their signatures already on the quarters. The ward knew to allow them entry through their doorway. They can come and go now through their rooms," he says as he closes his eyes, letting his know-it-all smirk linger on his lips.

"And your parents?"

"Already let them know the plan. They're fine with it and they're taking their own time today coming to terms with the memories that unlocked for them. That's the plan for everyone today."

I can't help but smirk and settle in between Draken and Tillman. If Corentin's already taken care of it all, fine by me. Once Caspian finally decides to take a seat on Draken's other side. I really do relax.

My mind silences. My heart beats normally for the first time today. And my soul sings out in completeness.

For now, everything's okay.

Five

Caspian

This is infuriating.

It's no secret at all, emotions haven't been my strong suit for the larger part of my life. Since my kidnapping, I found it much easier to separate the feelings from the logic.

Well, at least I could if I didn't allow my anger to swallow me whole. That's about the only feeling I allowed myself to have.

If it made logical sense, so be it. It didn't need to be explained or labeled. A feeling didn't need to be attached to it. It was what it was.

The little temptress, who's currently sound asleep on my chest, came into my life, brought all my emotions to the surface, and now, I can't separate them from logic.

It's fucking maddening.

Before her, I could've found out everything we did today, and it would've gone one of two ways.

One, I would've lost my shit, killed some people, then drunk myself into a stupor, cussing my uncle the entire time.

Or two, it would've been the opposite. I would've heard this information, accepted it, and shoved anything that tried to rise in me down until I felt nothing at all. Then I would've moved on.

But no, of fucking course not. I can't do either of those things. My mind, heart, and soul simply won't allow it.

The three parts that make me who I am are working against me. Forcing me to feel it all. Embrace it despite my dark attempts to ignore it.

I hate the fact that I'm mad, confused, heartbroken, understanding, guilty. Fuck, there are others in there too. I just can't put a word to them.

Looking down at the curvy body pressed so close to mine that we're almost one, I smirk. She did nothing wrong crashing into my life or making me feel things. It's a blessing to feel every part of her. It's everything else that's confusing.

I command my shadows to caress every surface of her. She caught me multiple times today staring at her or staring off into space. She never called me out, not once. She'll allow me to sit with these traitorous feelings until I figure it out on my own, then she'll listen to everything I need to say.

Which could take forever for all I know.

I tried today, tried hard to pull myself out of the funk this news put me in. We spent the day together, hiding away and growing more familiar with this wing. This whole part of the palace that is now apparently ours. Made and designed specifically for us because every fucking adult in our lives was told one way or another how our lives would go.

It was just us who fucking didn't know.

Closing my eyes shut, I breathe through the darkness that rises in me quickly, then like a caged animal, it sprints through my body furiously because it has nowhere to go, doesn't know where to go.

It's trapped. Confused.

I have enough humility in me to admit that I still have a way to go with managing my darker side, but at the same time, I'm now a man I wouldn't have recognized a year ago—hell, months—and I'm proud of that fact. I've learned through my little Primary and on my own how to pull myself back from the ledge, but today has me feeling like my feet are glued in place. I can't jump off the edge, nor can I step down from it. I'm just stuck.

Allowing my shadows to travel her body once more, I command them to wrap around her, and I place her on my brother's chest. His hands instinctively hold her, pulling her close as she whimpers through the sudden jolting. I give it a second to make sure she settles down completely before I shadow out of the room.

It's this damn wing.

I both hate it and fucking love it.

I need a break from it to clear my mind.

Shadowing through the wings, I end up standing in a room I loathe even more. The bare walls, made bed, and empty bookshelves do nothing to soothe the racing thoughts and new fears that've been rising in me since our encounter with the Summum-Master. It's just all been building up and I feel like today was my cherry on top. This fucking nightmare of a bedroom that lies lifeless in the east wing doesn't help a bit.

After I was rescued and brought back here, I grew to hate this room. With a passion. I had no choice but to lie in this bed that I park my ass on, for over a week while I healed physically. It only took a day for my anger to grow to unspeakable heights as I stared at these four walls with nothing to distract my mind.

It was its own brand of torture that I've yet to let go of.

Letting my mind drift back to those memories is a surefire way to summon the darkness, and I feel it rising fast, trampling over any other emotion as my vision starts to blur.

A sharp knock snaps me back, and I whip my head toward the sound. Only two people could have followed me this quickly—it takes a split second to know exactly who's on the other side.

"It's open, Core," I grunt, then blow out a harsh breath and run my hands down my face.

He slowly pushes the door open and leans against the frame, staring at me. We hold each other's gazes for what feels like an eternity.

His shoulders sag as he takes a few steps into the room, then kicks the door shut behind him. So uncharacteristically of him, he plops down haphazardly on the bed beside me and flings himself back, covering his face with his arms.

"You okay?" I ask.

Not gonna lie, I'm a little taken aback by his actions. He's been so put together, smiling, teasing all day with the Primary, and this whole exasperated demeanor is throwing me.

"Me? I'm not the one who shadowed out of the bedroom in the middle of the night," he says without bothering to remove his hand from his face.

"Speaking of which, you're supposed to be holding my Primary right now. I left her in your care," I say, attempting to take the focus off me.

"You may believe you travel like smoke on the wind, brother, but I can assure you, you didn't get out of the hallway before she was up, attempting to follow you." A small smirk pulls at the corner of his lips.

"And you stopped her?" I ask.

"Stopped isn't the right word. I suggested it would be best if I came to find you since she doesn't know her way around. Tillman and Draken told her they'd stay up with her, distract her, while I came to hunt you down." The smile that spreads across his smug face is tempting enough to make me forget all that's plaguing me tonight. I know good and fucking well what the dragon's and Mr. Patience's definition of distracting her is.

Yeah, her tight little pussy and the sound of my name screaming from her throat would make this all better.

"She thinks you're mad at her," he says seriously, distracting me from those delicious thoughts, and I snap my gaze to him,

"I'm not mad at her. I'm mad at the situation she's in and at everything else. She's gonna go mental at any point in time with all this shit going on."

A small snort escapes him, and he covers his mouth with his hand before clearing his throat. "I think you might be underestimating the resilience of our Primary."

"I'm not underestimating anything about her. She's a force of nature, but even hurricanes run out of hot water eventually, Core."

He doesn't respond with more than a grunt as he nods and limply lets his arm fall beside him.

We drift into comforting silence, neither of us knowing what to say, like we've done so many times in the past. I can't count on my fingers the number of times he sat in this room or allowed me in his and neither of us spoke a word. Just sat.

Slowly, I decide to lean myself back until I'm pressed to the mattress beside him. I can remember the last time we were in this position. It was after one of my darkest days. I'd beaten a couple of the fuck boys at the academy to the brink of death for talking shit about Draken, then acted like they were his best friends.

He had it hard enough. Mom had him join the academy with us so we wouldn't be separated, and having never been to a school, it was an adjustment jumping right into a level three academy. He was so upset with me for hurting his friends and I refused to tell anyone why.

Mom called us all home after the incident and I got a tongue-lashing for nearly killing them boys, and my dads were furious I wouldn't talk about it. But I told Corentin. We laid on this exact bed, in this exact position, and I told him what they said and why I did what I did.

"No, I'm not okay, Cas," he finally says, rubbing his hands across his cheeks before sighing. "I've tried all day to put on a brave and understanding face for her, but on the inside, I'm freaking the fuck out. Not because of everything Uncle Orien's done. It all makes sense to me. It was strategic. Between him and Elementra, they laid out the best possible plan for her success. Although they didn't protect her physically, they tried to emotionally. They helped build up the will that she'd need here. Elementra couldn't have picked a better man to take care of her through her childhood and adolescence.

"But I can't help but feel bitter that everyone but us was prepared for it. Fuck, even our mom got to be a part of her life before we did. We were the only ones not prepared to be given a Primary that's responsible for saving an entire fucking realm. We're having to learn along with her, and there's no doubt in my mind now that her memories have unlocked so fast, so forcefully at once, changes are heading our way. I have to prepare for it. I have to be ready. I can't fail us again."

His words are a sucker punch to the stomach. He's always worried so much about us, always putting himself below us. Fuck, he has absolutely no idea how much he's done for us and how he's never once in his life failed us.

Me. He's never failed me.

A shuddering breath leaves me as my own memories come barreling to the surface and his petrified eyes sear themselves on my brain.

"I let Willow watch the day of my kidnapping all the way through until Aunt Tilly got there for me. Together, we saw it all," I mumble and his head whips toward me, his gaze burning a hole in my cheek.

"Watch. You let her see the memories?" he asks quietly.

"Yeah, every bit of it. Many things surfaced for me that I'd blocked out, things I'm not sure I'm ready to talk about yet, if ever, with anyone other than her, but the thing that stuck out to me the most was you. How close you were to reaching me."

His eyes instantly shut down as his body flinches. The guilt surfaces like a tidal wave, crashing through him relentlessly, but this will hopefully be the last time it ever does. Fuck, I hope I can make him see.

"I've never thanked you for that. I've never thanked you for trying to save me."

"You don't have to. It was my—"

"It wasn't your responsibility, Core. I wasn't your responsibility. I was a fifteen-year-old boy, and you were only sixteen. Yeah, far more mature and responsible than I was, but you were a boy nonetheless," I say firmly, locking my eyes onto his as his chest heaves heavily.

"I may have not seen every step you took to get to me, but I know you pushed yourself harder, faster than you ever had before in your life. I know without a shadow of a doubt you would've traded places with me that day and I know you're still carrying around an eighteen-year-old guilt that's not yours to carry. You didn't fail me that day, Corentin. And you've never failed me a day after.

"I need you to let go of that, brother. I wouldn't be sitting here right now if not for you. You've carried me our entire lives and I'm beyond grateful for it. I'd tell you, you don't have to do that anymore, that I'm okay now, but I don't think you'll ever change at this point, so just know that you can carry me, us, but you can't carry this guilt anymore. Let it go for me, please."

Despite having my hands locked together in a death grip, my fingers tremble as I watch the relief wash over my brother. I don't think he even notices the weight leaving his body as if it's been waiting for my permission to do so.

Another piece of me seems to click in place the lighter he gets and the softer his face becomes. I never knew my words affected him until now, and I vow from this moment going forward, I'll let him know what he means to me. Our Nexus. I'll tell him he's the glue that holds it all together, but we'll be strong for him too.

"Thank you, Caspian," he whispers with a bashful smirk because his ass doesn't know what to say. Other than giving a lesson or explaining something I've learned, that's probably the most open with my words I've been with anyone other than Willow in years and I've got him completely flustered.

But deep down inside, I know it's not only my words that've freed my brother from his guilt today.

"His memories...How are you handling that?"

"If I spill, you spill," he says, narrowing his eyes on me. The look screams I'm not getting out of talking about my own shit if he's going to talk about his.

Fuck it.

"I'm mad. So fucking mad. But I'm also happy. I'm confused, yet I understand it all," I groan, pulling at my roots, searching for the words. "I had you, the guys, Gaster, and Uncle Orien. I was so far gone mentally, if it hadn't been for you all, I would've given in to the call of darkness a long time ago. I would've laid waste to every rebel I could find, then I would've taken myself to the beyond. The four of you kept me tethered. Especially Uncle Orien. He didn't badger me to talk or tell him anything. I have a feeling it's because the fucker knew, but he didn't push. He fed my need to be more, to be stronger by giving me knowledge.

"He was a safe place for me. He was the person I knew I didn't have to speak to, but he'd know what I needed. The timelines to when it was obvious he was splitting his time between us and Willow, to gradually becoming more time spent with her add up in my mind to when she turned fourteen and she emerged. Now that we saw his memories, I have no doubt that's why he talked to Mom and taught me how to use my shadows to evade her.

"He knew I'd need some space, a distraction to keep me from tailing him constantly like he'd caught me doing time and time again. Yeah, I'm pissed just like you that we were kept in the dark. I've felt for years that he abandoned me. I told myself I was getting too old to need him so much anyways and I let that fester into hatred. Not that I truly hated him. I just hated that I felt like he was leaving me. Now..." I trail off, gulping because I don't know if I can continue.

Corentin doesn't push. He waits me out, but I need another minute to collect myself, so I nod to him, silently telling him to say something.

"I feel free," he says softly. "I've blamed myself for his death for so many years. I've blamed myself for your kidnapping. I've blamed myself for a lot, and part of me still takes some of the blame, but I think that's simply because I don't know any different yet. Regrettably, I'll admit, I didn't notice his absence the way you did, but it also didn't feel like an absence to me.

"Every time I saw him, he knew exactly what I'd been up to, so I guess it made the time feel less extended. Now that we know what we know, I'm pretty sure that was purposeful. If I had caught wind that he kept disappearing more and more, I'd have obsessed over it until I found him. So he paved the way for that not to happen. Watching what we did this morning freed me from my guilt of not having breakfast with him. It freed me from beating myself up over not spending more time with him. He was taking care of Willow, while we learned to take care of ourselves."

His words settle the one thing in my mind that's made this entire revelation bearable for me.

Her.

Without him, where would she be? What all wouldn't she have been protected from? Before he died, he loved her, cared for her, nurtured the already resilient, strong, and formidable personality she had. I thought she was crazy as shit when she first arrived and was taking everything in stride, but now I just know, that's my Primary. That's how she survived. Nothing can beat her down. Not even a realm full of magical beings and monsters in the dark.

"I guess the only thing I struggle with now is how I spent years being resentful toward him, when really, he was doing everything in his power to protect us, prepare our future for us. Knowing the truth, I know, she needed him more than I did.

"My Primary didn't get the luxury of only suffering for thirty-three days. She endured twenty years. Bottling it up and moving along to survive, keep herself as safe as she could. Now I know it's very possible she's only here with us because of him. I think I'm madder at myself for acting like a child. Being mad at him when he was busy saving my soul." I scoff, disgusted with myself.

I don't just mean the soul that tethers me to this realm, to our creator. I mean the soul that resides in her. It's mine as well. She is my soul. I am hers. I belong to her. She's the very reason for my beating heart that's slowly but surely pumping red instead of black.

"In his memory, he hoped and prayed one day I'd forgive him. There's nothing for me to forgive Core. If anything, it's his forgiveness I seek. I hope he knows how much I love him, look up to him, and how grateful I am for him."

My lungs deflate with my omission, and another blackened piece of my soul seems to flourish. There's too much truth in front of me now to continue holding onto unwanted, undeserved bitterness. My uncle didn't nor does he now deserve my misplaced hatred.

The air that I continue to exhale sends a crackling of magic pulsing through the room. Magic that doesn't belong to either of us, and in milliseconds, Corentin and I are on our feet, gifts at the ready faster than the speed of sound.

Following the low, shimmering light, my eyes land on a ball of magic circling in my empty bookshelf. With confident strides, we clear the room just as the magic dissolves and I halt my steps, frozen in time as I stare down at the envelope with my name scripted across it.

My hands tremble as my fingers run over the cream-colored parchment. It's been waiting for me to see my truth, find my way, my soul, and now…it's here.

"Sneaky bastard. He knew I wouldn't seek solace in the room he made for me just yet," I whisper as my eyes trace his handwriting. Taking a steady breath, then blowing it out softly, I command my shadows to take it to my pocket dimension. "Later."

"I'm so proud of you, Caspian," Corentin says seriously.

Casting my gaze to him, I swallow the lump forming in my throat. Honestly, I nearly choke on it, but nonetheless, he doesn't call me out. He just stares at me with those whiskey eyes that match mine and even in the darkened room, they shine bright.

"Thanks, Core," I say before chuckling when he grunts at the pulse of pleasure that pumps through our bonds. "Seems the naughty little Primary is getting the distraction she needed."

"She deserves all the distractions we can give her. A whole other side of her life just opened back up and I have no idea if it's a good or a bad thing."

"Let's be honest, probably both. If the past few months are anything to go by, something good is always accompanied by something bad and vice versa. I'm happy she's finally getting her answers, but it'll come at an emotional cost. One I wish she didn't have to face right now. We just bonded, for fuck's sake."

"I'll make time for us, I swear. I won't let this war consume every second. Even if we have to steal moments of time, I'll make it so." He swears seriously.

"I know you will." I grip his shoulder tightly and turn us toward the door.

I have a Primary to punish for scaring me today.

At least that's what I'm going to tell her.

She enjoys it.

There's a weightlessness to our steps as we leave my bedroom and start walking back down the hall. The sound of my door shutting follows us, and I vow to leave my worries behind in that room that I no longer need. I don't need to hate it, love it, or even think about it anymore. It's served its purpose for me. It's just a room now.

My fears of what's about to come for my Primary feel less...demanding, if that makes sense. My anger at my uncle is null. I came into that room feeling like a worked-up, over-emotional mess, but now it's no longer overruling every other thought that's running through my mind.

I'm thinking clearly for the first time today. Thank fuck.

Once again, it seems all I needed was my brother to show me the way, but at least this time, I've done something for him in return.

"What are you doing?" he asks when I latch onto his shoulder.

"Stealing a moment in time."

Shadowing us across the palace, I chuckle darkly as we hover in the shadows, watching Draken and Tillman lavish the Primary with kisses and caresses. My dick is painfully hard the second her sweet melody of moans reaches my ears. They have her spread out across the bed, completely naked and exposed. Like a fragile little offering for the monster who's about to consume her.

"You make my brothers so weak, Primary," I say darkly, revealing us from the shadows.

"Excuse me?" She pants as her maddening eyes narrow on me.

"I told you earlier you were in trouble. And look what I return to. Them bowing to your every whim without even the thought of punishment."

Draken's giddiness at the prospect of what's going on hits me first and I shoot him a little wink, encouraging the beast to play my game. Tillman doesn't hide the fact that he's in on it when he moves away from her, laughing lightly as she whimpers at the loss of his touch.

They both join Corentin and me at the foot of the bed, where we stare my feisty little Primary down. Her chest heaves, making those glorious fucking tits rise and fall with each breath. If I didn't have the control I do, one would already be between my teeth.

"I didn't do anything to deserve a punishment," she argues, but she can't hide the flare of desire in her eyes.

I see it. I see it all.

"You did and you know it. You nearly caused us to lose our minds today," I say with a sly smirk on my lips.

"I can't help when that happens. If this is the case for every time some shit goes down, I should be able to punish you all when you worry me."

"Never said you couldn't, Primary."

A devious little smirk crosses those plump lips I'm ready to sink my tongue between. Her teasing is enough to make me feral, but still, I don't budge. I'll let her believe she can dish out some punishment if it pleases her. We all know there's never true punishment. The only punishment is the wait. The anticipation.

Between Corentin and me, we've rewired what the word punishment means in her mind. Never again will she hear that word and associate it with something vile or harmful. She'll think of us and the pleasure we plan to wring from her body.

"Fine then. What's my punishment?"

"On your knees, Primary. Crawl to your men," I command.

Her bravado breaks for a split second. It was so quick, I would've missed it if I wasn't staring her down.

"Don't make me repeat myself."

Her eyes flare with flames at the order in my tone and slowly, fucking drop dead sexily, the little tease spreads her thighs enough to have us all groaning before she gets her legs under her and leans down to all fours.

I bite my lip to keep myself from snatching her up and fucking her stupid right here and now. This woman, I swear.

"Now what?" She casts those eyes up to me.

Fuck, how beautiful she is on her knees for us.

"Pleasure us, Primary. All of us."

Her throat bobs as she looks between us, then her head whips back to me at the sound of my sweatpants hitting the ground.

That tongue that I know will make me fall apart darts out and licks her bottom lip as my cock springs free inches from her mouth. I practically smell her want to suck me down.

I have every intention of letting her.

"Open up, Primary."

I hold in my groan as her body shivers, but she does as I tell her to and I give her no warning.

As soon as that hot tongue touches my cock, my hips buck forward until I hit the back of her throat. My head tilts back as she gags, but that just spurs her on. Her need to make me fall apart for her pushes her on.

"Don't forget my brothers. They need just as much attention as me."

She hums around me, and I feel it in my bones. Fuck, I could explode right now. Paint that pretty throat with my cum, but not yet.

The guys all lose their pants and like the fucking goddess she is, she gets to work. One hand wraps around Corentin's length, dragging a hiss from his lips, and the other locks on to Tillman, who hums approvingly.

"Oh fuck," the dragon groans.

Looking over, the clever little Primary's wrapped her shadows around his dick and is working him over just the same as the rest of us.

"So fucking good at pleasuring your men. You look perfect bowed before us, Primary. We're the only ones you'll ever bow to. The only ones who will ever have the privilege of seeing you on your knees," I praise and the words send her into a frenzy.

I wrap my hand around those wild curls so I can see that beautiful face while I fuck it, and the tears streaming down her cheeks are nearly my undoing. She's the most gorgeous creature I've ever had the pleasure of laying my dark gaze on and having her swallow down almost every inch of me is the sexiest thing I've ever seen.

She thinks she's sly, but I see her shadows creeping between her legs, needing to take care of the throbbing in her pussy. I don't allow it, though.

I command mine out, blocking her path, and at the same time, I pull her off my cock.

"Naughty Primary. Your pleasure belongs to us."

"Please, Caspian," she begs through her teary, desire-drenched eyes.

"Get behind her, dragon," I command.

He swats her shadows off his dick and is behind her, lining himself up in a millisecond. She attempts to lean back into me, but I hold her head firmly.

"You'll come when he says you can," I tell her before moving to the side, and Tillman immediately takes up my spot.

They've fucked her together enough times now that they don't need to communicate. So as Draken grips her hips, tugging her ass up and making her back arch, Tillman laces his fingers through her hair, lining her mouth up to him, and in one swift move, she's full of half her men.

It's a fucking sight to be seen.

Corentin and I make our way onto the bed, surrounding her, and just as I feel the itch in my chest that she's getting close, Corentin slaps his hand down on that peachy ass, and I pinch her clit.

"Come on my dick, sweetness. Now," Draken commands, all beast.

My eyes close of their own accord as her muffled scream rings out around the room.

So sweet.

The guys continue to pound into her through her release relentlessly and I continue to play with whatever part of her body I please as she can't do anything but moan beneath us in ecstasy.

According to the messages being relayed from Tillman, she can barely form a coherent thought, but it's clear enough to know she's in fucking paradise.

It doesn't take long for her tight little body to start shaking and shivering all over once again, and by the erratic thrusts of my brothers, she's taking them down with her this time.

I squeeze the base of my dick to hold back my own release as her pleasure sweeps through me like a tornado.

Her cloudy eyes look up to meet mine, and I let a devilish smile cross my lips. "We're not done yet, Primary. You've got two to go."

"Yes," she moans as her eyes roll back.

Nodding to Corentin, he grabs Willow and in one smooth move, lays himself down and sits her on top of him. She doesn't hesitate to line him up and slam herself down the second his tip touches her.

Her head tips back, and her hair sprawls down her spine as a drawn-out moan escapes her throat and I pounce.

I can't help it. That fucking curvy body calls to mine and I need to be plastered to it. I need the heat of her skin to melt away my ice.

Gripping her jaw, I tilt her head back even further and capture her mouth. Her tongue tangles with mine as I drink down the taste of her. Her muffled moans vibrate through me as my brother fucks her into oblivion and I could stay like this for hours, swallowing down her sweet sounds, but I need to hear my name tear from that tight throat of hers.

Breaking our kiss, I keep my hand gripped on the back of her neck as I lead her upper body down till her chest is pressed to Corentin's. His wide eyes meet mine, uncertainty skirting across his features, but I just grin.

Calling forth my element, I coat my fingers in water, then manipulate its compounds until it creates a slicker lube. As soon as the cold gel teases her tight little ass, she tenses beneath me.

"Cas..."

"Yes, Primary," I say, stilling my finger.

"Will it hurt?" she asks in my mind.

Both fear and desperation color her tone. She wants this so fucking bad, but the unknown of what a cock in her ass will feel like has her hesitating.

"I've prepared you enough that it won't be painfully foreign, but until your body relaxes and lets me past your muscles, it's going to hurt. After that, you'll know nothing but pleasure," I tell her honestly.

"You'll make sure it doesn't hurt long?"

Fuck, that pitiful little question shouldn't make my cock even harder, but it does. How my deadly Primary can become so fragile, so soft and sweet when she's in our hands is my fucking drug.

Elementra, I'm addicted to her.

"No. I won't let it hurt long, sweet Willow."

Her body shudders, but that seems to do the trick as her muscles relax against my brother and he runs his hands over every inch of her, slowly pumping in and out, keeping her on the edge of euphoria.

Draken and Tillman gather closer, making sure she's thoroughly distracted but also, let's be honest, they're not going to miss out on seeing her take two of us together for the first time.

My finger passes her tight muscle and her back instantly arches, with a sultry little sound falling from her lips. I take that as my go-ahead to add another and slowly start stretching her out. With every pump, her moves grow more erratic. I know my poor brother is having to hold back from exploding inside of her. The way that tight little pussy is trying its hardest to slam into him and my hand is driving him mad.

I chuckle when I pull my fingers out and she cries in protest, but her sounds are silenced as soon as she feels my hot tip press against her.

"Breathe for us, princess. He's going to take care of you," Corentin coaches right before he captures her mouth in a brutal kiss.

After lubing my cock up, I slowly start working my way in.

Her body locks up tighter than a fortress, so I give her a moment, shallowly pushing the head of my cock against the layer of muscle keeping me out.

"Relax, little wanderer. Let him in," the dragon purrs as he runs circles around her clit, and her body melts like butter.

Corentin continues his slow pace and at his nod, I push my way through her barrier.

Her cries are music to my ears.

We hold still as she comes completely undone between us, exploding like a fucking volcano. She's clenched around us so tightly, I grunt and bite my tongue to keep from following her over the edge.

"Good girl, princess."

"You did so fucking good, Primary."

"Fuck me. I'm so full," she pants, her limbs trembling uncontrollably. "Move, please move."

Gripping her hips, I pull out about halfway, then thrust back in. It steals the breath from her lungs, my lungs, and I groan at how fucking good it feels, how fucking tight she is.

My control finally snaps when she pushes herself back into me, trying to take more than I'm offering.

With no warning, my hand comes down on her ass, and that guttural moan she lets out sends us into a frenzy. There's nothing the little Primary can do but hold on to my brother's shoulders so tightly she's leaving nail imprints as we fuck her together.

I no longer hold back as I plunge into her ass just as hard, just as fast as I would if it were her sweet little pussy wrapped around my cock. And she doesn't protest. She takes all of us, everything we give because we were made for her.

As if to prove my point, the ambitious creature commands her shadows back out and wraps them around Tillman's and Draken's dicks, pulling groans from their chests.

Greedy Primary.

The weight of my body presses her more firmly into Corentin until she's completely sandwiched between us. Completely at our mercy. The thin little layer of skin separating us feels so fragile and I swear if we're not careful, we'll rip this perfect fucking goddess right in two.

"Core, Cas, please, please," she begs so fucking beautifully.

Her body locks up like a vise and she throws her head back on a silent scream. All the air gets sucked out of the room as she combusts between us.

Corentin caves first, coming inside her with a deep grunt of her name. He attempts to hold her hips still while he spills himself in her, but I flick his hands out of my way and continue my brutal pace until my spine burns with the need to let go.

And fucking let go I do.

Slamming her down once more on our cocks, dark spots color my vision as I come in her ass. It drags her own orgasm out and she screams around us so loud the fucking bookshelves rattle.

I sink forward, laying my forehead on her spine, and leave a trail of kisses. I smile against her bones when she trembles at the cool touch of my lips and a small chuckle falls from my throat as I hear Draken curse as he cleans himself up and all I can do is shake my head.

All it takes is one little Primary to make four men crumble.

Multiple times.

"You're incredible, my little Primary. Un-fucking-describable."

I hear her happy little hum, but it swiftly turns into a whimper as I pull out of her and my brother slips free from her pussy. That one small noise is enough to get the dragon in frantic mode, and before I know it, he's got her scooped up in his arms, headed to the bathroom.

I have every intention of joining, but first, I crash onto the bed, catching my breath.

"Fuck, she's gonna be the death of me." I laugh as I tuck my arm behind my head.

"Agreed," Corentin grunts. Looking over at him, he's got his eyes closed and a stupid grin plastered to his face. And he's glowing. I don't think he's realized that yet.

"Damn, that's the way to go," Tillman says as he strides toward the bathroom with a chuckle.

Peering through the door he leaves open, I watch him and Draken give her kisses and a sweet, sleepy smile crosses her face as she snuggles deeper into the dragon's chest as he lowers them in the bath.

It's crazy. Perfection.

We fuck her like a bunch of savages and she's just as happy as she can be with it. I continue to stare as her small smile stays on her lips as her eyes flutter shut.

Elementra, she's everything.

Six

Willow

The sounds of low laughter, the wind blowing through the cracked door, and the gentle stream of the waterfall in the bathroom pull me from my slumber.

Really, it should've kept me asleep with how peaceful the noise is. How peaceful the whole atmosphere is.

Stretching my limbs, groaning happily as I starfish across our bed, a small laugh tumbles out of me when I think about how long it's been since I've had a bed to myself. Even with my arms and legs sprawled out as far as I can reach, I'm nowhere near touching any end and there's still enough room for my men to join me.

I wouldn't want it any other way.

Crawling out of bed quietly, I tiptoe across the floor to the bathroom, smiling as the sound of the four of them laughing and their talking grows louder. I don't want them to hear or realize I'm awake and come piling in here. I'd rather join them out there.

Quickly taking care of what I need to and plopping my hair on top of my head in a bun, I rush out the French doors to our new balcony and hum happily when the aroma of coffee and the fresh morning air fills my senses.

"Well, look who decided to join us," Draken teases as he lifts me off my feet and spins me around. He attacks my throat in playful kisses, causing me to laugh and fight my way out of his grip.

He doesn't let me get far, though, as he grips the back of my neck and pulls me in for a blistering kiss.

Fuck, this dragon knows how to properly greet a girl when she wakes up.

"How did you sleep, princess?" Corentin asks as he passes me a cup of coffee when Draken sits me comfortably on Tillman's lap.

"Amazing actually," I say, sighing happily at my first taste of sugary goodness.

"I bet so after that mind-blowing—"

"Draken," Corentin and Tillman bark, while Caspian chuckles darkly. My face flames red as his gaze traces all over me. I don't know what he's looking for, but the longer he looks, the hotter I grow.

"Orgy," Draken whispers in my mind, breaking me out of the inferno Caspian's eyes put me in.

Shaking my head, laughing over the rim of my mug, I lean my head back onto my gentle giant's chest as he twirls my hair around his fingers. "I should be exhausted honestly. Even after the mind-blowing orgy," I say slyly, grinning and shooting Draken a wink as they all groan around me, "I slept like the dead even though my mind never shut off."

"What do you mean it didn't shut off? I didn't hear any thoughts all night," Tillman says, halting his soothing caresses.

"Not thoughts, dreams. Well, actually memories. My mind spent the night uncovering new ones, replaying those that had alternate endings. None of the negative shit. They each were peaceful, fond, and loving. It's a relief, honestly. I don't feel like my brain is soup anymore."

"Good then, little warrior," he says softly, kissing me on the top of my head.

"We're due to meet everyone for breakfast in a few, princess," Corentin says, setting his drink down and lacing his fingers.

My serious man.

He's waiting for me to say something, gauge how I'm feeling about that. He'll be shocked to find out I'm incredibly excited. There's not an ounce of nervousness in me.

"I can't wait to be officially introduced." I chuckle when all four of them seemingly freeze and look at me like I spoke in another language. "Why did you all expect me to be nervous or worried about this?"

"Well, because yesterday was a lot. Plus, we don't exactly know the relationship you formed with Momma Vito. We just figured you'd be as nervous as you were when we first got here," Draken says.

Ah, I see.

Turning my attention back to Corentin, he'll be the one to take charge and explain everything to his mom and dads about me when the time comes, so I give him a small, reassuring smile.

"I don't know exactly what CC informed your dads. All my communication was with your mom, and I didn't keep too much a secret from her, aside from everything Franklin did to me. She was...let's just say in my eyes, she was my idol growing up. I can't begin to explain how happy I am that she's also my mother-in-law. That was a sweet little secret kept from me. Just based on what Gaster said, she knew I was your Primary, so I imagine there's not much from my life back in the nonmagical realm she doesn't know. I've waited what feels like my entire life to meet her."

I blush a little, thinking about all the letters we wrote to one another. She was the one who explained to me what a period was. She taught me about basic feminine hygiene. How to do my hair, makeup, all kinds of girly shit I never would've known about had it not been for her. Not only that, but she also just talked to me. Told me about her day, gave me tips on my earth element. She was just there for me.

The sound of one of their timekeepers ringing pulls me out of my mind and I smile around at all of them. I see the hints of concern in their eyes, but I'm fine. I'll probably drift into my memories a lot here at first, but they'll calm down with time. For now, they're just fresh and new to me, so I allow myself to wander into them when they come forth.

"Is that the alarm to get ready?" I ask, setting my coffee down.

"The alarm to head down there," Caspian says with a smirk, to which I nearly choke on my drink.

"What? You all were just gonna let me sleep till the last second? I need to look halfway decent," I shout as I sprint back through the French doors. Their laughs follow me in, and I'm tempted to lock them all out.

No, I'm not nervous and I know Aurora wouldn't expect me to come down in a ballgown, looking flawless, but damn, I'm in Tillman's shirt, no underwear, with my hair on top of my head.

I look freshly fucked.

"Vulgar mind, little warrior. Keep those thoughts to yourself during breakfast, yeah?" Tillman says with a smirk when he emerges in the bathroom behind me.

I narrow my eyes because he has the nastiest mouth I've ever heard. Granted, yes, he mostly whispers it to me in my mind, but still, the man has a dirty mouth.

"You love my dirty mouth."

"You don't know that."

"I do. Your pussy doesn't lie," he says with a wink as my body comes alive. The caress of his element sweeping over me, dressing me in a flowy sundress, does nothing but add to the fire.

"Come on, you two, we're gonna be the last ones to join," Corentin says from the doorway with a sly smile on his lips that tells me Tillman didn't just speak that in my mind but everyone's.

After he dresses me and I do what I can with my hair, I purposely shimmy my ass right across his dick as I scoot by him, laughing mischievously as I run through the door when he tries to grab me. I only make it three steps before being swooped up in shadows.

"Naughty Primary," Caspian murmurs against my lips.

"He started it," I say breathlessly.

"Behave or I'll finish it."

With that, he hits me with a brutal kiss before passing me off to Draken and Corentin, who latch on to each hand, basically dragging me from the room since my head is spinning.

Fuck, these men drive me wild.

How's a girl supposed to focus on anything when they just ooze sex appeal?

Lucky for me, as we approach the ward, and no more sexual comments or innuendos are being thrown my way, I can focus on something other than them. For example, I hope and pray Aurora is as excited to officially meet me as I am her. Now that both of our memories of one another are returned, I hope there's no awkwardness, no hesitation, and we skip right to the part of her loving me.

Damn, that's a little desperate, Willow.

"Not desperate at all, Will. There's no doubt she already loves you. Aunt Rory has always been one to step up and love someone who needs it," Tillman says gently in my mind.

I smile gratefully at him, although I hear the underlying sadness that he tries to hide. I won't bring it up yet, but the burning need to ask him if he's okay and about the cute nickname has been heavy on my mind. It would seem my calm, collected, seemingly unaffected gentle giant isn't as healed from his past as he's led me to believe.

"We're now officially late. We'll transport to the central quarters once we're through the ward," Corentin says exasperatedly as he shoves his communicator in his pocket. I snicker at his flustered state although I shouldn't, but he acts like this is a business meeting. Not breakfast with his parents.

"Yes, your highness," I tease, earning myself a small twitch of his lips.

Pushing out of the ward is painless, thankfully, and in seconds, we're on the other side. It's a relief to see that nothing is destroyed or at least it's still not destroyed from my loss of control and the ward coming down. I already feel bad enough for what I did to the central foyer.

The guys give me no time to get a full look around. Before I know it, we're stepping out of a transport in front of a set of double doors and I can hear the murmuring voices behind it clearly.

"They will be here momentarily, Aurora, calm yourself," a male voice commands, but there's a lightness in his tone. I can't tell which of my fathers-in-law it is, but the authority mixed with softness in his voice reminds me of Corentin.

"Calm down? Did you seriously just tell me to calm down?" Aurora fires back, causing me to laugh.

The room silences as the sound travels through the doors and I prepare myself when I hear chairs skid backward and the pattering of feet basically running my way.

"For fuck's sake. Brace yourself, Primary. They're all apparently going to greet you at the door," Caspian says sarcastically.

He's right, though, because when the doors fly open, Aurora is center stage, nestled between her men. A few feet behind them are Gaster and Keeper, smiling at us.

"Hi," I say shyly, suddenly choked with emotions.

"Oh, my girl. It really has been a lifetime," Aurora says as her arms come around me, pulling me into her chest, and I melt.

After a long, loving moment, she pulls back, cupping my cheeks and smiling so brightly at me it's nearly blinding. This is everything I always wanted it to be.

"I'm so glad you're finally home," she whispers as tears gather in her eyes.

"I'm happy to have finally found my home."

"I was preparing to go stand outside your ward until you came out. The wait was killing me. What in the realm took you all so long?" she asks, standing back and crossing her arms.

I chuckle as my face turns red, but Corentin's quick to my rescue as he pulls me in close, squeezing my hip. "We were sleeping in, Mom. We had a long day yesterday. How about some quick introductions and let's eat? I'm starving."

"Of course, of course," she says nonchalantly with an eye roll and then waves him off. Again, I can't help but laugh.

She's exactly how I pictured her. CC described her to a T. Loving and funny but with so much sass to spare. Those were his exact words, and I see it now. Although I know for a fact, she could turn this sweet and kind persona around in a heartbeat if need be. She told me once how she liked to keep her Matriarchal side away from her family as much as possible. She wanted them to experience the less stressed side of her, but that doesn't mean she wouldn't let it come out if the situation called for it.

Her voice is light and playful, which makes the memories of her letters to me so much more animated because when I let my mind's eye read over her words, I hear her voice now instead of my own.

"Willow, I'd like to properly introduce you to your Patera-Nexus. This is Roye, Theo, Neil, and you've met Dyce already," Aurora says, pointing to each of her men.

"Yeah, her favorite father-in-law as she called me," Dyce says as he damn near tackles me in a hug.

"I have five fathers-in-law. I won't be picking favorites," I say, chuckling as he sets me back on the ground and the guys pull me back in the middle of them. The rest of my Patera-Nexus all roll their eyes at Dyce then smile warmly at me.

It catches me off guard at first when they each step up and take a turn hugging me tightly, but I let the surprise go and just embrace it. I'll have to play catch-up on learning about them.

Suddenly, appreciation and excitement hit me square in my chest, and my eyes dart behind Aurora, where I find Keeper beaming at me. I give him a small smile when I realize it was my claim of five fathers-in-law that he's so excited about. It felt natural to say it and I don't feel anything negative coming from Draken about it right now, so I just move on without drawing too much attention to it.

"I'm ready for another cup of coffee and some food. Whatever's on the table smells delicious," I say, attempting to peer over the wall Aurora and her men have created.

My eyes nearly fall out of my head at the spread in front of me. From one end of the table that'll seat at least twenty people to the other, there's an array of food. It's as if every breakfast dish I've had since arriving in Elementra is on this table, waiting to be devoured.

"Are we feeding an army?" Corentin says, looking over the mound of food.

"Chef came early this morning and started ordering my kitchen around. Apparently, nothing but the best for you lot," Dyce teases.

My happy hum at the first bite of a steamy breakfast casserole spurs everyone else on and we easily, seamlessly fall into conversation. It's so normal, natural, I get choked up when I think about how this is truly the first time I've been in the room with all of them. It doesn't feel that way. It feels as though it's only been a while since we were all together.

"I wanted to wait until you all had at least a plate of food before I brought this up," Aurora says as she clears her throat and sets her silverware down.

"Here we go," Caspian murmurs. Even in my mind, sarcasm drips from his words.

"We figured you'd want to talk, Mom," Corentin says, his tone the opposite of his brother's.

"I want to explain a few things as simply as possible because Orien sure knew how to weave a confusing web," she says, rolling her eyes lovingly before looking at me seriously. "The first time he told me about you, he told me to call you *filia mea* on the day I meet you in person. He told me what it meant, where it came from, then took the memory. The night before he passed, once he'd taken my memories back already, he told me a different version as if he wanted a backup plan. He told me one day I'd meet my sons' Primary, and I'm to call her *filia mea*. He told me again what it meant, where it came from, and said I had two opinions. One, tell you its meaning, or two, allow you to find out on your own. I had all intentions of telling you, but I had no idea calling you that would cause what it did and I'm so sorry about that." She pauses, clearing her throat again and closing her eyes while she catches her breath. "I think it's best for you to find out on your own now."

"It's okay and I agree," I whisper, reassuring her I'm not upset she won't tell me.

She nods, blowing out a breath, then continues, "Other than the communication you and I had, he didn't give us any warning or a heads-up about what to expect once you got here. We knew you were the boys' Primary, and we knew Elementra was tasking you all with something beyond our understanding at the time, but that's pretty much it. And with the way Corentin, no offense, son, has been slacking on his communications with me, I know it was because of things going on with you. I'm not upset now that I understand that, but I need to know the truth. I need to know you all are safe."

The concern and sincerity in her voice cuts me. I didn't really think about it until now how the aftermath of everything would make her feel. It was one thing to be left in the dark when she had no clue who I was other than a random seer, but now that she's put two and two together, it's written all over her face that she's worried sick.

"We didn't mean to hurt you by keeping Willow a secret. It was just for the best. Once you know everything, it'll be easier to understand," Corentin says softly and I squeeze his hand to help try to wash away the guilt I feel pouring from him.

"I believe that. I do. I just want some answers. You all don't have to include every little personal detail, but at least the big stuff," she pleads.

I turn my head to Corentin, giving him permission with my eyes to let everything out. There's nothing I need to hide from her anymore, any of them, so if he wants, he can tell it all.

"Do you want me to just tell them, or would you rather show them?" he asks, and my eyes widen at the choice. I would've thought for sure he would've jumped all over the opportunity to finally spill all the beans.

"Really?"

"This is your life we're discussing, princess. You should have the choice of how everyone finds out everything."

My heart thuds wildly in my chest and I give him a grateful smile. I didn't think of this being an option. Why, I don't know. I guess I'm just used to him being the one delivering all the news, but the more I think about it, the more I do want to be the one to be honest about it all.

"I'd like to show you all what we've been leaving out, if that's okay?" I ask, turning to Aurora and my Patera-Nexus.

"Show us? How would you do that?" Roye asks skeptically, arching his brow.

Caspian and Draken snort and shake their heads while Corentin, Tillman, Gaster, and even Keeper smile at me. Aurora and the guys just look around as if we've lost our minds.

"My magic will need to lock onto your magical signatures, then I can broadcast the events to you. You'll see it through my mind as if you were watching my memories."

Quietness falls over them that makes me fidget in my seat. They're shocked still with their mouths gaping open and the collective tension grows in the room.

"How...is that possible?" Aurora asks quietly after a long stretch of silence.

"It'll make sense soon. As soon as I show you."

She pulls herself out of her stupor faster than her men and gives me a confident, ready, and willing nod before hissing her men's names to get them back on track. I chuckle as they shake themselves out and stare at me in amazement.

Most of the people I spend my days with, you know, my men, Gaster, Oakly, her Nexus, and lately Lyker, Aria, and their Nexus, have grown used to me being able to do shit normal people can't, so it's funny to me to see the royal family frozen in astonishment.

"Full disclosure, there're going to be some things that are hard to see, and I apologize for that. There will also be parts I skip over. Trust that there's a reason you don't need to see it," I murmur awkwardly, completely ignoring Draken's knowing chuckle.

"Center yourself, little warrior. Think back to the moment you'd like to start, then breathe. These are your memories to control, not someone else's, so show as little or as much as you want. Imagine yourself speeding through time on the parts you want to skip. It may even be best to black it out," Tillman coaches gently in my mind and I instinctively start regulating my breathing.

"Everyone ready?" I ask and at the echoing consents, I push my magic out.

There's a little resistance from my fathers-in-law, and by accident, I swear, I force my way right through it. I do shoot them a guilty smile when they startle, but that's all the time for reactions we have before my mind sucks them in and I close my eyes.

I start at the beginning.

And by beginning, I mean the moment I walked up on my tree and found my gift on my birthday.

From there, I let them see it all.

Donald's initiation, Gaster rescuing me, our original bond snapping in place, Oakly, her bond snapping in place. The moment in the breakfast room when Corentin and I had our awakening.

My first day of classes including that ass beating I took. Plus the ass beating Tillman gave Claven.

I don't let them witness it all, but I show them the moments of Draken's and my awakening. Followed by mine and Tillman's.

I relive the panic I felt during Tillman and Caspian's kidnappings. Caspian telling me the truth and my earth element breaking free. I skip over me running off to Oakly's then returning. That feels too personal to share.

I smugly show off the altercation between Gima and me. Knowing what we know now, I wish I had done worse. Nonetheless, we carry on through the memories at the speed of light.

The at the time Terravile pack Alpha, Jarod, showing up at the academy. Me seeing his mark and putting together who the rebels plaguing Elementra are. Gaster teaching me the concealment and dimension spell. Followed by my first gift emerging. The sight.

For the obvious, I skip over Draken's and my bonding, but I show them the morning after. My fire. My dragon. My first flight. The two-day coma.

Elementra.

The visions of Lyker that haunted my dreams. The deadly cures and why Gaster brought a batch of them here. The Alpha trials at Terravile. Me taking the deadly dagger. What would've happened if I hadn't taken the dagger to the stomach. Saving Aria.

The morning following Tillman's and my bonding. My gift of Mind Transference. How the sound of everyone's voices brought me to my knees in pain.

The debrief we had where we discussed my first assumption of what the Mastery was doing to the individuals they were kidnapping. Meeting Layton, followed by his medically induced coma he's still in. All the Terravile Mastery members dying in the castle that triggered my first trip to the past.

The Summum-Master. Keeper.

The beginning of our planning for getting in the Forsaken Forest.

The vision I had of what was going to happen to the academy. Even as deep in my mind as I am, a lump still forms in my throat. Fuck, I was so angry, scared. But it had to be done.

My kidnapping.

I don't conceal the torture Franklin put me through.

Donald. Max. Bryce...Trex.

The cuts, bites, burning, bruises, blood draining.

Or all the information I learned. CC's guidance.

Sitting on that bathroom floor, giving up on myself for the first time in my life. Our mental link snapping in place.

I don't hide the vile things said to me that day. I don't shy away from Donald's crude words and vulgar intentions. I let it all be seen so my hatred is understood even more than it already is.

The battle. Max's death. My inability to heal all at once.

Capturing Trex. Capturing Franklin.

The Bane of Essence.

The damage done to my body.

I show the sweet glances Corentin shared with me the morning after our bonding.

What Tillman showed me with his mind about Gima's part in the academy's ward coming down.

Finding out that Trex is a pawn in all this and his brother's need for our help. Franklin's story about my mother. The past, where Elementra allowed me to see my mom escape the chains in Franklin's torture room. I show that snippet with pride. She was such a badass.

My gift of Light Bending emerging. How no one could hear or see me in the clearing by our tree.

Nikoli identifying all the ingredients in the Bane of Essence. Jamie rerunning my blood and discovering Lyker is my brother. Going to Terravile to tell him the truth. CC's memory of my mom coming through the portal. The day she had to leave Lyker behind and return to Franklin.

Our mom's house. Finding the Willowrrie flower.

The meaning of my name.

The grueling training Oakly and I were put through in preparation for us to leave for the forest. Then me falling into the past as we vialed up the Bane of Essence.

I skip over Keeper's past as that's not my moment to share. That will be a story first for him and Draken to talk about. Hopefully.

Franklin... The Summum-Master's my grandfather.

I slow down the moment and let his words ring clear in my mind for everyone to hear, but I also don't hide my loathing, my zero intentions of acknowledging that blood relation. Then with pride swelling in my chest, I show the moment when, with my men, my brother, and Ry, my brother from a bond by my side, we end my torturer's life. How I sealed his fate using the same powerful words Aurora did when she had to make that same difficult decision.

My dream walking with Tanith and how she instructed me on how to save Keeper.

I can't show the moment my shadows emerged with Caspian, but I show the morning my water tried to drown me, and my shadows came out to play that day.

The Forsaken Forest.

The moment I moved Oakly out of the way would make me laugh at any other time. She was pissed, to say the least. That humor flees me as Keeper pins me to the tree, baring his fangs, ready to rip my throat out. I allow the words I whispered that the guys didn't hear the first time around play out loud and clear. They've never pushed me for all the information. The revelation of him being Draken's father was enough of answers for all of them.

The battle saving Tanith.

The rage-filled beating I gave Donald. I wish more than anything I had killed him right then and there. Been done with it. But his time will come. He won't escape this realm alive.

The Summum-Master's and my exchange. His dark promises, as well as mine. The explosion of power.

I will be his ruin.

The bomb Keeper dropped about my bloodline being the guardians of the portals. I'm still ignoring that, but my time of ignorance is ending.

Concealing my naked body, I show the moment my gifts and elements exploded out of me after our bonding. I'm not even sure what it means fully aside from the fact that our souls are now truly tied together, but that level of power I released seems relevant.

Meeting Aurora. Her triggering my memories.

The South Wing.

Slowly, I start cutting away the strings of magic that're tied to my mind, starting with Aurora and the rest of my Patera-Nexus, then making my way around my men. The moment I cut the last string, I sway in my chair and my vision doubles.

Fuck.

Without missing a beat, Corentin shoves a healing vial between my lips and tilts my chin back for me. I still can't muster the strength to open my eyes. I had no clue it was going to take this much out of me, but this is also the first time I've shown months' worth of memories.

My mind scrambles, attempting to put all the newly constructed pieces back together again and in the meantime, I sit here statue-still, regulating my breathing so I don't throw up.

"That was..." one of the guys' dads says, but I haven't heard them talk enough, aside from Dyce, to know their voices.

"Give it a minute, Dad. She needs a moment," Caspian says harshly. I grin despite the pain the muscles in my face cause in my head.

"Take another one, princess. That one is taking too long to kick in, or it just isn't enough, but your pain's killing me," Corentin whispers as he presses another vial to my mouth.

"What do you mean?" I slur.

He laughs quietly, running his fingers down my temple gently.

"I've felt every part of you I've wanted to since we bonded as a Nexus, princess. There's not a part of you I can't feel."

"You feel me all the time or when you focus?" I ask, far more aware than I was two seconds ago.

"When I focus."

Blinking my eyes open, I look at him, stunned, then slowly, not to spin my brain around again, I seek out the others. They're all wearing matching smirks.

They all can feel me. Not just through my bond.

Holy shit.

"I should've pushed harder. I should've made him bring you home the day you emerged. I should've ordered it," Aurora says. Before I even turn to look at her, I hear the tears in her tone.

My heart splits open when I see the steady streams pouring out of her eyes. Her emotional pain cuts me deep and the darkening of her aura makes me wish I didn't show her all of that, but they needed to see it. They needed to be caught up because our time is coming. I feel it in my soul.

Things are changing. Rapidly.

"It all worked out the way it was supposed to," I say gently and she shakes her head, balling her fist on the table.

"What was your life like after he died and we lost communication? Did you...what did he leave you to live through there?" she asks angrily, and I understand that anger, but it's not his fault.

Shaking my head, I give her a small, sad smile. "There's no need to dredge that up. I don't know exactly why I had to stay there, after my emerging or my eighteenth birthday came. You saw his memories and where he left it off. I still must figure that out, but you have to believe it was the right thing to do. I believe that."

The argument is sitting on her tongue. It's written all over her face. All over her men's face. The tremble in each of their arms, the quiet, serious demeanors show the restraint they're using to hold their emotions back right now.

"Listen, I know what you all just saw and found out is hard. It's been very hard for us from the second I stepped foot in this realm, but regardless if we like it or not, it's out of our hands. For the most part. We have decisions to make at every turn and those decisions have consequences that lay our paths for us. We have to accept the path that was laid for us prior to now. With our loss of memories, gaining them back, and everything we have in front of us, we just have to move forward. We have a society to crumble and a realm to save."

My words are firm, and I leave no room for argument.

If we start falling down the pits of could've, would've, should've, we'll never get anything done. And if I continue to bury my head in the sand about the truth of who I am, we're going to lose this war.

We can't afford that.

I refuse it.

"Our daughter-in-law is right, my angel," Dyce says quietly and his sweet nickname for Aurora makes my lip tremble.

How freaking cute. And fitting. She looks like an angel.

"I know. It's still difficult to accept. We could've taken care of her," she says quietly, looking into his eyes while he nods.

"We could've, but it wasn't our job yet. It was Orien's, then it was Willow's own responsibility. Not that that means she should've experienced whatever she did, but obviously, being here would've been worse. We believe that. And we take care of her now," he states.

I don't even mind that they're speaking as if I'm not sitting right here because their sweet words and his sound reasoning calm me down as much as they do her.

"Well, then it's decided. We start training tomorrow," she says with a confident nod, forcefully wiping her tears away.

Yes, exact—wait, what?

"I'm sorry. Did you say training? Training for what?" I ask.

Full-fledged panic mode.

If she says to rule the realm, I'll die right now.

"Calm down, my girl. I have no intentions of throwing the throne at you all," she says with a little laugh at my horror-stricken face. "There's so much none of you know about what it truly means to be a completed *true* Nexus. Things you won't find in your books and lessons. We'll be teaching you. Starting tomorrow."

Turning my gaze to the two most knowledgeable people I know, Gaster has a smirk on his face, while Caspian looks utterly confused. Neither reaction gives me any reassurance.

What the hell is Nexus training going to look like?

Seven

Draken

I get it, asshole. I get it.

My dragon chuffs, not happy with being called an asshole, but he sure as shit is being one right now.

I'm just trying to sit here and enjoy my brothers' embarrassment as Momma Vito goes on and on telling Willow all about them as children. She's pulling out the good stuff.

Like how the big, bad Vito boys used to hate storms and would kick their dads out of bed because they needed to sleep with her.

I think that shit is cute, but judging by both of their red, stoic faces, they don't appreciate it.

Tillman's no better.

She's doing a good job of reminding him of all the embarrassing, personal shit he called people out for when his gift emerged. He thought he was so cool blabbing people's thoughts out, having no clue as a careless teenager how mortifying it was to the adults around. He knows that shit now. Willow's gasps and quiet, playful scoldings make him look thoroughly uncomfortable.

It's hilarious.

There's nothing Momma Vito could say that would embarrass me. My little wanderer knows I did some stupid shit in my teens, but let's be honest, I was the baby, so I did no wrong.

"I'll be back. Give the guys hell while I'm gone," I say, bending down in front of Willow before stealing a quick kiss.

"You okay?" she asks.

"Yeah, the beast needs to stretch his wings. Don't fuss over me, little wanderer."

"Do you want company or is this a solo thing?" she asks, completely understanding.

"Solo if that's okay."

"Of course it is. Be careful."

She gives me a sweet little smile and a wink when we break our kiss and her musical laughter follows me out into the hall. That little noise is enough to settle my dragon's ass down so I can make it outside.

He's been on the frits since she burst through the ward in the south wing without us. He calmed down once we got through, but rewatching everything this morning through her eyes was a lot.

It's a whole different perspective when we watch things like that. For example, her first day of fucking classes. Yeah, I saw it all go down, but I was trying to fight my way to her, so I missed bits and pieces. Seeing it all today, from start to finish, has my dragon ready to fly to the fucker's house and eat him.

We should've killed him rather than almost drown him.

Jogging out of the central foyer and through the doors, I take a deep breath of fresh air. It's been too long since I flew over the Central. Granted, people used to run inside when they saw me in the air, or they'd drop down and cower. I couldn't give a fuck now, though. These clear skies are calling my name today.

Rounding the corner of the gardens where the clearing breaks out, my steps slow and I subtly sigh. Not loud enough to be heard but enough to get the aggravation out of my system before they notice I'm here.

Well, before he notices.

I'm trying, sort of, to get on board with this whole vampire king being my dad thing.

Okay, it's not really a 'thing.' It's real.

It's not just one thing holding me back. It's multiple things. All the questions I have, self-consciousness, fear. There's a hefty dose of all of it mixed in there.

My initial reaction was to try to blame it on the fact that accepting him would diminish the Vito dads' stance in my life, but I quickly shut that down. No one can replace them. They're my dads, through and through. If Keeper can't get on board with acknowledging that, accepting that he's an addition and not the only one who holds that title in my heart, then that's my answer on where he stands.

I guess I got a couple more fears to go along with that excuse. Like I need to know what happened between him and my mom, but I'm not ready to hear it or explain what I've been through. And I'm just scared to build a relationship with him.

There's no doubt that if what he says is true about Willow's bloodline, then she'll get the portal to Essemist Keep open. Then he'll be gone. How do we have a relationship realms away?

We don't. That's the answer.

I want to be happy about this, accept it as fully as my little wanderer has. I haven't told her not to claim him or anything like that, so subconsciously, I fucking guess I'm already getting on board.

Hell if I know.

See what I mean?

This shit is too confusing and complicated.

Mustering up a smile, I approach Keeper where he and Tanith are having a stare off. It's easy to tell they're communicating and whatever he's saying is annoying her based on her chuffing and the small balls of smoke blowing from her nose.

"Hello, Draken," Tanith says, bowing her head to me as I walk up.

"What's up Tanith? Gone for a flight yet today?" I ask as I lay my forehead to her.

"No. My lord is nervous about scaring the townsfolk. I am a dragon that feeds on knowledge, for Essemist's sake, not a Baccum. I'm not going to eat the little people," she scoffs and the sarcastic tone has me laughing.

"She's complaining about flying, isn't she?" Keeper asks, throwing his hands up and shaking his head.

Clearing my throat and cutting my laughter off, I say, "Yeah. Something about she's a dragon not a Baccum. Whatever the hell that is."

"Nasty creatures. They don't take small sips but rather suck their victims dry until there's not a drop of blood left," he says with a grimace that matches my own. "And, Tanith, you know good and well I was not comparing you to them. I simply pointed out the people of Elementra are not used to seeing any other dragon aside from Draken fly the skies and it may be intimidating for them."

"Understood, but I am no threat to them. If the Matriarch is comfortable with me frolicking around her gardens, her people will be just fine."

I smirk at the feisty dragon in front of me. I don't quite understand Keeper's and her bonded relationship yet, but I'm pretty sure she's not asking permission if she can fly or not. I got a feeling it's more of a respect thing. She'd have already taken to the skies if she felt like it. She's just considering his unease in the situation, but she's making her unhappiness about it known.

"It's really not a problem. I'm going up now. My dragon needs to stretch his wings," I say, not exactly inviting them but offering the opportunity if they want to take it.

"See. Draken is going up and we will join him," Tanith declares, earning a laugh from me and a grunt from Keeper.

"You're sure that's fine? I don't want to cause trouble for the Matriarch or her men," he says, turning to me.

"If it were a problem, Momma Vito would've told you not to fly," I say, turning from him to get ready to shift.

Deciding to shift into the size Tanith is, I tilt my head back and let the magic wash over me. It's such a freeing feeling. When he gets in moods like this, I walk around with tight, itching skin until I set him loose.

Stretching out my wings and neck, I shake the rest of my body out as I get in a balanced stance and then look to see if Tanith is ready.

Keeper's gaze instantly lands on mine, and I pause my movements. Just as he looked at me the first time I shifted in front of him, I catch him staring mesmerized again, and I don't know what the hell to think about it. I mean, he has his own bonded dragon. It's not like this is some spectacular new thing for him.

"Oh, but it is, young one," Tanith says, and I cut my eyes to her.

"You ready?"

"After you." She laughs.

Smart-ass dragon.

Since Keeper's in a tizzy about flying over the people in the Central, I lead us in the direction of the mansion instead. There's nothing but forest from here to there and it's all our land, so there's no one else to worry about. When he gets more comfortable with letting Tanith fly more places, I'll take Willow and her to where the Central meets Terrian. The mountains and cliffs there are killer to fly between.

Letting my dragon take the helm since he's the one who needed this little excursion, I fade into my mind, trying to put together the pieces of all the shit that's been going on here lately. It's all a clusterfuck to me, and I want to figure out the fastest and best way to end this shit so we can have a long, relaxing life.

Sooner rather than later.

"You and your young flight have had many changes in the small amount of time you've been together," Tanith says, breaking me out of my thoughts.

"How do you do that?" I ask.

"Do what?"

"I know you can't read my mind, or at least I never read anything that said dragons could read minds, but you always seem to know what I'm—even Willow—is thinking."

"It is my ability to gather impressions. Your thoughts pulsate. Let's call it a signal, and I can interpret its meaning."

I startle at her words for a second.

Shit, we can do that too. Except we don't gather impressions from other people. We get them from our dragons.

"What about that confused you, Draken?"

"Not confused me, per se, but Willow's and my dragon pass impressions to us. It's how we communicate with them. If communicating is what you want to call it."

"Fascinating. I've been curious as to how you and her speak with your counterparts since you are one and the same."

"Curious? You seem to already know it all."

"No, not all. But I have generations' worth of knowledge stored in my mind that does allow me a greater sense of understanding. But you and your beloved are the first of your kind. Just like your father and me. That is why he looks at you like something magnificent. It is because you are."

Father...Not going there.

"In the books I've bothered to read on dragons, nowhere said that you feed on knowledge and that's how you grow to be so intelligent," I say rather than acknowledging anything else she said.

"It is common knowledge in Essemist Keep, but many from other realms dared not come near us. Fear of being eaten, which is such an offensive notion. Dragons do not eat people for the fun of it. So the tales told of our kind leave out very viable information. There's also our communal knowledge that we do not broadcast with others outside of our kind."

"Communal knowledge?"

"Yes. Yours and your beloved's are already beginning to come forth. I just don't know what all will be available to the two of you or where all it will come from."

"I don't know what that is."

I rack my brain, trying to remember if I've ever heard of that in dragons, but nothing's coming to me. When she says a flight, I know what she means by that. That's what a group of dragons that stay together is called, but I'm sure I read that somewhere.

"Just as any animal is born with their instincts, dragons hatch with that as well, but due to our nature, we're born with a little more. Communal knowledge is information that is passed down to us through our parents and

members of our flight. The ceremony of a hatchling is a spectacular sight to see.

"The entire flight will gather around the nest and softly purr, encouraging the little one to break through the fortified shell. It's the first test for the young dragon. Their eggs are as strong as stone, and it is quite the tiring process to break yourself free, but once you do, the cracking of the shell will sound for miles around before it shatters around you. It will shake the realm itself, letting everyone know a dragon was just born.

"After that, the first of your kind to greet you are your parents. Your father, followed by your mother, will lay their heads to yours. It cultivates the bond between parent and child. During that bonding, all the knowledge the parents have gathered over the years will pass to the young dragon, and it will store itself in their mind. Once the parents have partaken in their bond, the entire flight will share their knowledge with the little one as well.

"There is still much development and growing the young dragon must learn and go through, but as they age, there will be things that they just know, things they are just aware of, and that is the communal knowledge that's been shared with them."

My heart thunders in my chest as I picture a huge flight of dragons waiting for a hatchling to be born, then celebrate it by giving it the knowledge it's going to need to survive. I'd bet everything I do know that it's a powerful, emotional moment.

Damn, I wish I had experienced that.

"So Willow and I have communal knowledge?" I ask.

Not that I doubt Tanith's words. It's just the honest truth that I've never been the smartest person in the room. I feel like school, life, well, everything would've been a lot easier on me in my earlier years if I had this knowledge she's speaking about.

"Yes. I have no doubt about that. I've already sensed it in both of you. I'm just not sure how your communal knowledge was shared with you and from who it all comes from. I know you have pieces of me. Your dragons and their interactions prove that, but for the rest, I am unsure. You both were born from bodies, where I was born from an egg and had a ceremony."

"Other than you sensing it, how would we know we have this knowledge? Gotta be honest with you, Tanith, I've never been one to just know shit, nor have I ever liked learning."

She laughs like I'm kidding, but I really have always hated school, reading, anything that forced me to sit still for a long period of time. I got to move around, burn off the energy that's always running through me.

"Do you remember your earlier years of life? Earlier than the normal being would?" she asks.

"No, I don't think—"

I stop when my senses are assaulted with the past. The dark burgundy walls of the brothel, the way my mom always smelled sweet, her singing voice that could put me right to sleep. I remember it all clearly. I remember the exact spot she's buried in and what she was wearing when she was laid in the ground.

"Yeah, I can."

"That is a sign of communal knowledge. The ability for your memories to begin imprinting strongly enough to stick at a young age."

I drift into silence at that. For many, I can see where that ability would be badass to have, but I don't really feel the same. I'm thankful to be able to remember my mom, don't get me wrong, but I could do without all the other trauma that came along with it.

Willow too, no doubt. I've always wondered how it was that she could remember things from when she was so young, but I chalked it up to the Memoria stone. Guess that wasn't the case.

Soaring through the clouds, a speck in the distance comes into view and my chest rumbles with happiness. I love that fucking mansion. There're so many fond memories there and it's created an escape my brothers and I needed over the years. Now it's also where we bonded our Primary. The greatest gift of all time.

I already know our time is going to be split between here and the palace now, but this house and everything about it will always be ours.

Staring out over the crystal-clear skies, I'm starting to feel like Corentin. My mind just won't shut up and it's driving me crazy. Up here is where I'm supposed to be able to leave my worries behind, but since one of my worries came up here with me, I can't unfocus.

Unfocus? Is that even a word?

"Tanith, when Keeper touched me the first time I shifted in front of him, something happened," I say rather than flat out asking what I want to know.

"That's correct."

Seriously? That's all she's going to give me.

"What happened?"

"I don't believe you're ready for that answer," she says matter-of-factly.

"What? Why?" I ask. Butthurt.

"Because you're not ready to accept him for who he is to you. That's quite all right. You deserve time to wrap your mind around this."

"Well, why didn't he take some time? He was told I was his son and that was that. End of discussion. I don't get it. He didn't even need to think about it," I say, getting a little defensive even though she just told me it was okay.

"No, he didn't need time. That's just the way my Lord is. Once his mind is made up, that is that. There's no need for a fuss or questions. It's both reassuring and incredibly frustrating. He's a very stubborn man when he wants to be."

Her teasing settles my nerves, but at the same time, it makes me feel like shit. For the most part, my entire life, I've always been the same way as she's describing him. Quick to make up my mind, make a decision, then I stuck to it no matter what. Unless my brothers had a good argument as to why it was a bad decision. Even then, though, I didn't always listen. Like with Willow. The second I saw her and she called Tillman 'mine,' I was fully committed. That was that.

I'm struggling with this, though, and it's making me feel childish.

"Willow said you chose to bond him. Can I ask how or why you did that?"

"Much like this realm, in Essemist Keep, many of us with a higher consciousness, vampires, creatures, dragons alike are given fated beloveds. For dragons, you know instantly when you come across yours and you are to decide right then and there if you will accept the bond or not."

"Um, but...you...he," I stutter because she said fated beloveds. There's no way they have that sort of relationship.

Her deep, ethereal chuckle vibrates through my mind, and I don't know whether to let it calm me down or freak me the fuck out.

"Our bond is different, yes. There's no romance or intimacy. I am the first of my kind to ever form a cross-species bond. Although I recognized him instantly, just as I would've had he been a dragon, the deep primal claim, like you feel over your beloved, was absent. Just an awareness that I needed him and he needed me."

Thank fuck for that. I was about to freak the hell out.

"So you felt the bond and accepted it?"

"Yes."

"How does that work? If that's not a too personal question."

Fuck, I should just stop asking questions while I'm ahead here.

"Not too personal at all, but maybe you should ask him," she says before letting out a small, rumbling roar, then descends toward the back lawn of the mansion.

Shit. Seriously. Come on.

Following her rather than leaving her behind and turning back like I'm tempted to, I touch down a few seconds behind her and watch as Keeper slides off her back and stretches his body out. Smiling as always. I guess I get it, though. Hundreds of years trapped in a forest would make me appreciate my freedom as well.

"Go on, Draken, shift back," she orders lightly with a laugh.

Meddling dragon.

Letting the magic wash over me, in milliseconds, I'm left standing on two feet. My annoyance with Tanith swiftly leaves me as I gaze at our pool, the patio table, the spot in the lawn a few feet over where my little wanderer and I completed our bonding ceremony. We haven't been gone long enough to miss it all, but after seeing and knowing the significance of the south wing, it just makes me cherish the mansion even more.

"This place and the palace are truly spectacular, Draken. The architecture here is very different from in the Keep but no less fascinating," Keeper says enthusiastically, smiling around at everything with total interest although he's seen it before.

I hum in agreement, not knowing what to say before closing my eyes for a second, and mentally yell at myself to stop being an asshole for no good reason. Sighing, I turn a little more toward him and ask, "What's it like? In the Keep, I mean."

A tight smile crosses his lips and his eyes cloud over. I instantly kick myself for asking because of course that would dredge up his longing. I can't imagine what I would feel like being locked out of Elementra for hundreds of years. It would've killed me, honestly.

"Sorry, you don't have to talk about it," I say quietly.

"No, it's fine. It's just been a long time since I've allowed myself to think about it," he says, then looks back at Tanith, his smile morphing into a real one. "The Keep is like nothing else. The realm itself is ancient and timeless, a place where centuries have passed without significant changes. Popular to the lore I'm sure that's spread about, we do tend to live in massive castles that are made with obsidian or slate. They have tall towers and spires that are darker in color, but the insides are typically grand, bright. My mother loved to redecorate. Goodness, it would be like entering a new home every full moon..." He trails off, falling deep in his thoughts.

Guilt squeezes my chest. I was just trying to take Tanith's advice and speak with him. I didn't mean to upset him.

"Is there any sort of magic there like here or...?" I ask, trying to pull him from wherever he's getting lost at.

"Oh yes. The air is filled with the hum of magic, both of our own abilities and from those who've ventured there. It's elegant and refined. Tradition and grace are very much valued and contrary to what you've seen, the vampires who live there are sophisticated and cultured. The bloodlust is a nasty side effect to our kind, stripping away their love for art, music, learning, intelligence..." He trails off once again, shaking his head, but he's quick to get himself back on track this time. "The realm has a peaceful atmosphere, but there's always an underlying sense of power and strength. It's a beautiful but also a humbling reminder that the land is full of beings and creatures who possess great abilities."

"Speaking of creatures…" I turn my head to Tanith and cock a brow, judging if now's the time to ask my burning question. Her little huff is confirmation enough, so I ask, "How did the two of you bond?"

To my utter shock, he throws his head back, laughing. And I mean fucking laughing. Holding his belly and all as he bends forward and continues to snicker like I just told the realm's funniest joke. I can't help but cock my head to the side and stare at him.

"Oh my, I thought surely Tanith would've already bragged about that," he says as he wipes his tears dry before clearing his throat. "She tried to kill me, of course."

I don't think I've ever gasped so hard in my life. My hand flies up to my chest in some form of offended shock 'cause I didn't expect that nor do I know what to do. Is it okay to laugh like he did? Should I be concerned? Hell, I don't know, so I stare at Tanith in disbelief as her chuckle trickles through my mind.

Crazy-ass dragon.

"Why did she try to kill you?"

"To accept the bond, you must prove to each other you're equal in all things. For dragons, that's both intelligence and strength. So when I strolled up to her flight like I was some hot shit vampire heir about to request knowledge—granted, keep in mind I was very young—she sensed the bond and attacked. I didn't have the slightest clue what was happening until I struck out at her, attempting to defend myself. I felt the pull of the bond. In that moment, we both had a choice to make, whether to continue the fight, let the bond solidify, or go our separate ways and let it sever. Well, you see what we chose. She chose, really. She took about a five-second break, staring at me before snatching me off the ground with her claws. It was a brutal battle," he says, smiling at Tanith like he won in the end.

"He was a fierce competitor. Obviously, no match for me, but nonetheless he gave it his all and was worthy." She snorts, and they both laugh. Him out loud, her in our minds.

Well, shit.

I stay in a sort of state of shock for a moment before a loud laugh bursts out of me. I picture in my mind him just strolling up cocky as shit in front of a flight of dragons, then all of a sudden this golden beast tries to eat him. That shit is hilarious.

It's pretty badass if I'm being honest. There he was, a small vampire man, well, he's pretty big, almost as big as me, but still, compared to a dragon, he's puny, and he stood his ground. Held his own against a magnificent creature, and apparently, formed a first of their kind bond.

Shit.

"That shit is so funny. I can see Tanith trying to eat you. It wouldn't surprise me if she tried it now." I continue laughing even as he joins me, and I feel a little of my apprehension melt away. Maybe he isn't too bad. "I didn't realize you could've chosen not to accept the bond."

"It would've been rather painful to do, but it's our decision in the end. The two of us were too curious in nature to ever reject something like this, but for example, a vampire-vampire pairing could've been very different. Bonds in the Keep aren't like bonds here. Not everyone is given a beloved who, in fact, loves them unconditionally. Their souls made perfect for each other. Very few get the pleasure of a bond like that. Beloveds who find that do not fare well apart," he says solemnly. I obviously once again dredged up something bad for him.

"Well, I think what the two of you have is pretty cool. Plus, if not for this first of your kind bond, me and Willow wouldn't have our dragons," I say cheerily, trying to lighten the mood once again.

"You and your beloved are magnificent, Draken."

His smile is true. Even the beast in my chest can sniff out the sincerity behind his words. Nothing about him or what he says is a charade or a way to pander to me.

"I'll speak freely, young one. Continue talking to him, ask him questions. He's eager to know you but will not push the boundaries you've laid before him. I won't tell you the things we've spoken about in private, but I will tell you he wants to get to know you and be a part of your life. He will follow along at your pace," Tanith says so softly, I know she feels as though she's crossed a line but thought I needed to hear it.

Maybe I did.

She's closer to him and knows him better than anyone. Her giving me permission to take my time takes the pressure off me to just jump right in. My family already seems to be on team keep Keeper, but I know they'll support me and my decisions no matter what. Nor will they push me to move quicker with him. So maybe getting to know him, at my own pace, is okay.

"Thank you, Tanith."

"Of course, Draken."

I blow a hefty breath out and that exhale seems to finally drain away the tension that's been weighing me and my dragon down. We have enough to worry about in the realm right now that adding my newfound daddy issues on top of it was exhausting me.

I'll get to know him. Slowly.

Just as I go to open my mouth and say something to Keeper, I feel the sweet invasion across my chest and a smirk crosses my lips. My little wanderer is about to check on me. Can't hide anything from her even miles away from her.

"Draken, where are you?" she asks. She tries to hide the concern in her tone, but I instantly hear it. It's not concern for me, though.

Something's wrong.

"Are you okay?" I ask, stomping away from Keeper and Tanith, preparing to shift back.

"I'm fine. I need you to come back now. Tanith and Keeper as well."

"I'm on the way."

"Something's up. Willow needs us," I shout just before the shift takes over.

Roaring, I beat my wings furiously, picking up unimaginable speeds in a matter of seconds. Physically, I know she's fine, but her tone and the worry pumping through my chest from her has my beast pushing himself to the max.

"What has happened?" Tanith asks.

I didn't even notice because I was so focused on feeling Willow, but she's keeping pace with me easily. Her face is fierce as though we're flying into battle and her body is cutting through the rays of the sun like a golden sword. Why the hell we've been lollygagging around if she could fly like this beats me.

"I don't know. She didn't say, but she's upset and said she needed the three of us back."

"Then let us fly, young dragon."

With that, Tanith's body takes off, attaining speeds I'm not even sure I can reach. It's as though she's got a touch of the vampire's speed mixed in with her own.

As if the thought that he can't keep up offends my dragon, he pushes harder. Shooting us through the air so fast, the trees beneath us are nothing but a sea of blurring green. The typical fifteen-minute flight is over in less than five.

My worry peaks as we approach the Central clearing and standing there waiting is my little wanderer, with tears in her eyes, my brothers, Gaster, and the Vito parents.

What the fuck happened?

My claws don't even touch the grass before I'm shifting back into my human form and sprinting to Willow. The second she's wrapped in my arms, I feel the tremble in her limbs.

"Are you okay? What's going on?" I ask frantically.

"We need to go to the healing wing now. Layton's having seizures and he's bleeding from his nose and ears. The Summum-Master is about to break through Aria's rune. She's already there, trying to fight him off, and Jamie is attempting to heal him, but he doesn't have long, Draken."

No. No. No.

Fuck no.

We can't lose this kid.

"I will need an enchanted dagger with a Reservoir gem to reverse the rune. We must hurry. If the Summum-Master can cut through the rune blocking him, it will not take anything to kill the boy," Keeper says immediately, stepping up beside me, no questions asked.

"Done," Willow declares, and without missing a beat, she steps back from us, planting her feet in the ground as she opens her pocket dimension.

The familiar swirling pool of silver opens and she stretches her arm in for only a brief second before she pulls it back out with a dagger clenched in her hand. I forgot all about her taking that dagger off the dead pussycat. My mind hasn't even thought about it since she was rescued, and I've seen it through her twice now.

She's truly the smartest fucking person I've ever met in my life.

"This is one of the daggers, right?" she asks, handing it over to Keeper.

He nods as soon as she places it in his hands, and the blood, whoever's blood that is sitting inside the gem, begins to bubble as he whispers in his language.

"Yes. A powerful one at that. Very good, Adored," he says proudly, but my fierce goddess just nods sternly, then turns to Tillman.

"On me, we need to move," he commands and we all latch on to him.

In milliseconds, we're stepping out of the transport in the private sector of the Central healing wing, and the screams of Layton's mom pierce my ears, making my feet freeze and my heart thud uncontrollably.

No, fuck no. We aren't too late. I won't accept that.

"Go, please," I bark at Keeper, grabbing his sleeve and running toward the screams. I truly thought the Summum-Master had forgotten about the kid. He hasn't fucked with him like Trex since the day he killed all the shifters.

Surprisingly, Keeper latches onto my arm, and with a stupid fucking amount of strength, drags me, literally drags my thousand-pound ass through the halls in the blink of an eye.

The scene in front of me is horrific. There's blood pooling underneath Layton's head as he shakes and convulses in his bed, and his mother is sunk to the floor, screaming and shaking in the arms of her men, begging for someone to save her baby.

It's fucking gut-wrenching, heartbreaking, and it chills my blood.

Jamie and Aria are sweating, with pale faces as they each work as hard as they can to save him.

Aria's ghostly, clouded eyes shoot up at us and although I can't even see her irises, I see the plea in them.

"I can't hold on much longer."

"Come, son. You must do as I say. Hold his head and with your blessed gifts of this realm, push your magic beneath his skin. Bless it with good intentions. The rune tied to him is far different than the others that are tied to the heart. His is wrapped intricately through his mind. Now is not the time to explain it all to you, but you must think about weaving a positive reality for him. Do it now. Soul Seer, do not release your rune until my signal. Healer, make sure his mind does not explode and take away the pain I will cause."

Explode. Are you fucking kidding me?

It's as though I'm having an out-of-body experience as I jump to the front of the bed and grip Layton's head between my hands. His warm, sticky blood dribbles between my fingers, and although blood has never bothered me, I get queasy at the sight of his.

"Hold his head still," Keeper commands, and with no complaint or question, I do as I'm told. "Focus, son. A positive reality. What will his life look like after this curse is removed?"

Focus. Focus.

What will it look like?

Freedom. It'll look like freedom.

He'll have the opportunity to go to a real academy and learn about his amazing and rare gift. He'll learn it's a blessing not a curse to be one of a kind. Or at least one of an extremely low few in his case. It'll be scary at first, being the youngest at an academy full of young adults who've been training for years, but he'll catch up. He's smart. I know it. Eventually, he'll meet his Nexus brothers. Hell, maybe I can talk Corentin into letting him visit the other academies, see if his bond snaps in place with anyone.

He'll have all his parents, who obviously love him tremendously and will do anything for him. He'll never have to worry again about them being killed for loving and looking for him. He'll never have to be separated from them by force again.

He's going to have a great life.

Come on, Keeper. Fix this kid. Fuck, he deserves a great life.

He deserves so much better than what he's had to deal with over the last year and I swear here and now to help however I can. I push the best intentions my mind can come up with and lace it with the bubbly, cheery side of myself. I want this kid to be happy-go-lucky all the time. Not because he has to put on an act for everyone else but because his life is going to be great and that, in turn, just makes him that way.

Keeper's soft, accented whispers echo around the room. I don't understand the language, but the power behind it is immense. It's stirring up my own magic in my chest and I pull on that feeling, bolstering it and pushing it out.

A small growl slips out of me when Keeper presses the tip of the dagger to Layton's forehead and it takes everything in me not to knock it away. This is something that has to be done.

Rather than tracing out the M that's now visible on Layton's forehead, he drags the dagger slowly backward. Instead of it slicing his skin, each traced line seems to erase the scarred tissue, leaving behind clear pale skin.

Layton bellows out in agony, although his mind isn't even aware of what's going on, and the sound is horrifying. Every time he screams, his mother's wails get even louder, and together, they make a traumatic melody that I know I'll never be able to forget.

"Almost done," Keeper grunts just as he traces over the last line on the M. When he pulls the dagger away from Layton's head, he presses the tip of it to his finger until a pool of blue blood sits on the tip.

While still pushing the best possible intentions and path for Layton through to him, Keeper's blood travels through the dagger, through the hilt, and when it drops into the Reservoir gem, the blood begins to sizzle.

The noise silences everyone in the room, or maybe all I can hear is the sizzle 'cause I'm so focused on it, but rapidly, it boils the blood down until it's nothing. It completely dissolves.

A painful, loud gasp falls from Layton's throat as his eyes open wide in panic for a brief moment before they clear. His chest heaves heavily as his eyes cut back and forth, trying to see the room, but I'm still holding him in place.

"It's okay, calm down. You're okay," I purr softly.

"Dr-Draken."

"Yeah, buddy, I'm here."

"He's gone. He's out of my head."

"Yeah, he's gone. You're going to be okay," I whisper.

A small smile graces his lips and his eyes begin to flutter shut. My heart pounds against my rib cage, attempting to fall out of my chest as panic grips me.

"No, no, no, Layton, wake up. Wake up," I shout as my fingers twitch on his cheeks.

"It's okay, Draken, he's fine. He just passed out. He's exhausted, but he's okay and he's alive," Jamie says as he lays his hand on my arm.

Gently, he pats my shoulder, silently instructing me to let go of Layton, so I do and backpedal until I hit the wall behind me.

Sliding down until my ass hits the ground, I drape my bloody hands over my knees and watch as he heals and cleans Layton up.

Soft, warm hands grip my cheeks and turn my face from the sight of this kid I've grown to be quite protective of until I'm staring into a pool of shiny diamonds.

"I'm so proud of you, my dragon. You did so good. Even asleep, his aura is so bright, it's blinding," my little wanderer whispers.

"I didn't do much."

"Don't discredit yourself, Draken. Those were some of the most powerful intentions I've ever felt. I have a feeling he's going to wake up a completely different person. For the better."

"You mean that?" I ask.

"I know that."

When her lips meet mine, I melt into her. That was one of the most emotionally draining experiences of my life, outside of everything she's been through, and for a second there, I thought we lost him. I thought all the promises and words of assurance I'd given to his parents were going to be for nothing.

Her promising eyes are all I can focus on now when she pulls back and smiles at me. Her pride for me in this moment floods my bond, and I swear it rejuvenates me.

"Let's give them some time to check on Layton, and we'll visit later, okay?"

"Yeah. Good idea," I say as I make eye contact with Sira. There are tears still streaming down her face, but the gratitude reflected at me makes my throat close up.

"You were remarkable, Draken. I've never experienced anything like that in my life," Keeper says, smiling when Willow and I walk out of Layton's room.

"What do you mean?"

"That amount of power you put off. I've never been fed magic before. That was exhilarating." He beams as he squeezes my shoulder.

I'm sorry, did I just hear him right?

"Fed magic? What in the realm are you talking about?" I ask, utterly fucking confused.

"You mean you didn't do it on purpose?" he asks, cocking his head to the side. My frustration grows swiftly, but before I can say anything, Willow cuts in, no doubt sensing my rising irritation.

"If something strange or different happened, Keeper, it's best to just explain it all," she orders gently.

"Well, you all recall me explaining how the Summum-Master would make me drink blood before a binding ritual to maximize my power?" he asks, leaving out the tidbit that it was my little wanderer's blood or her mom's or grandma's, but anyhow, at our nods, he continues. "I don't have to consume anything prior to the ritual or as you just saw, undoing it, but if I don't feed, it would leave me quite drained and hungry. Just now, though, you were putting off enough magic to feed me and keep me sustained. It traveled through my bloodstream like electricity. It was highly potent. I feel as though I was just a glutton with my food."

He's still fucking beaming from ear to ear with excitement and I'm still as confused. I don't know how that's possible, nor did I do that on purpose.

"What were you thinking about, dragon, when you were pushing your magic into Layton?" Caspian asks.

"All kinds of shit. A better life for him mostly."

"At any point did you think of Keeper?" Gaster asks, stepping up beside Caspian, looking at me just as curious.

"Well, yeah, I guess. I thought about him being able to fix Layton. Can you just give it to me straight? One of you?" I ask with a frustrated sigh.

"I can only assume, my boy, we may need to talk to Tanith, but just as she can push knowledge on to others and she can absorb it, I believe you did feed him your magic. You pushed it onto him while you were thinking about what was best for Layton."

How...

"Tanith, can you hear me?" I ask. I've never tried to talk to her while she's not been in front of me, but this can't wait, so I might as well try.

"Of course I can."

"I just fed Keeper my magic."

"Congratulations, young one. That is exciting news."

Her nonchalance at this makes me growl, and her laugh in my mind doesn't help. Damn know-it-all dragon.

"Will you please explain this to us? This is confusing."

"I suppose so, although you all should learn some patience."

Keeper snorts, letting me know he heard it, but I don't find the humor right now. Maybe after she explains.

"As a dragon, you've always had an ability to push out what you absorb. For typical dragons, it's knowledge. But you are the first of your kind and you feed off magic, therefore you push out magic."

"I've never done this before. How does this even work? Layman's terms, please," I ask and Willow squeezes my hand in solidarity.

"Well, my lord is a being that survives off lifeforces. Yes, the main consumption is blood because it is the most potent, but there are many forms of lifeforces. Your magic is one of your lifeforces. So you pushed it out, and he consumed it because it was a source of food. It is something his body would've naturally done, just as it was natural for your body to push it out."

"Tanith, will he be able to push his magic onto anyone else or just Keeper?" Willow asks.

"Anyone."

"Thank you," Willow says before turning her attention to me.

"You've been doing this. The only reason it wasn't so obvious was because you were doing it on me and I also have and rely on my magic.

Keeper noticed it so starkly because he doesn't have Elementra-blessed gifts."

"What do you mean, little wanderer?"

"Think about all the times I needed to be healed and how quickly that happened. How quickly my magic refilled itself. Every time, you were right there with me. Probably touching me. Of course having all of you guys touch me helps, but it's been expedited because you've been feeding it directly to me."

"I'll be damned, dragon. You've been doing it to all of us," Caspian says with a smirk and a shake of his head. "It's different than what healers like Jamie do. They fix the damage done to the body, and our magic does the rest. You've been filling our magic reserves, which, in turn, speeds everything else up."

Well, fuck me.

"So I can push my magic into each of you? I can keep you all from ever being drained?"

"Yes," they all echo.

I stand there statue-still for a second as that shocks me down to my core. This is amazing. An ability that's going to protect them, keep them from ever getting dangerously low and not being able to take care of themselves.

Holy shit, I can power them.

"This is so fucking cool," I holler, picking Willow up and crashing her into the center of my brothers. "I've been inside all of you."

"Draken." my brothers shout and my little wanderer throws her head back, laughing.

I'm gonna feed them magic until it's coming out of their asses.

Eight

Willow

My love for training hasn't grown a bit.

Although I'm thankful for it and it's definitely given me more confidence in myself, I still hate working up the sweat.

I have no clue what Aurora has in store for us this morning and she gave us no hints at breakfast what to expect, but after yesterday's revelation about Draken's ability, she grew even more excited and couldn't wait to get us together.

After that startling, amazing discovery, Tanith mentally walked Draken through on how to purposefully feed us his magic. Up until now, his emotions in the moments were leading the way, which makes sense. Every time I was hurt, he and his dragon were worked up. The same with the guys. He goes into his natural protective mode, and it just leaks out.

Once she gave him instructions on what to do, he mastered it quickly. He had us so full of magic, my eyes were glowing for hours, Corentin looked as though he had a spotlight on him everywhere he went, Tillman had a headache from basically hearing every thought in the healing wing, and Caspian was a walking cloud of smoke.

We had to stand barefoot in the garden and force it out.

I told Aurora then would've been a better time to train, but she said absolutely not. We could possibly destroy her palace.

Which was a fair concern at that moment.

Before we left the healing wing, leaving Layton there still asleep but healing well, according to Jamie, we paid Trex a visit and it killed me to see the sight of him.

The restraint it's taking him to hold the Summum-Master back from breaking down Aria's rune is slowly killing him. I can see it written all over his sunken eyes, thin cheeks, and pale skin. He refuses to see Keeper, and he refuses to remove the rune himself out of fear the Summum-Master will kill his brothers. So finding them and bringing them home is moving up higher on the to-do list.

"This isn't going to be like our training, right?" I ask Tillman as we make our way to the gym in the central wing.

"I doubt it, but I couldn't tell you, little warrior. She wouldn't go over the plan with me."

"You should've just read her mind. Knowing Momma Vito, she's about to make us practice our hugging and talking about our feelings," Draken says sarcastically, and Caspian immediately stops walking.

"You're joking. We can do that on our own. We don't need her help with that."

I laugh at his disgusted face. Seems that he'd be willing to do that with us just not in the presence of his parents, so I'll count that as a win.

"Just because I can read her mind doesn't mean I'm going to. I'm not going to invade her privacy like that," Tillman says as we start walking again.

"You have no problem invading all our privacy no matter how much we've told you to knock it off," Corentin says snidely, tapping away at his communicator.

Fuck. I want to eat him up right now. He's dressed in E.F.-issued black workout sweats and an all-black shirt, same as the others, but I've never actually seen Corentin work out or train, nor dress down like this besides pajamas. Those two days he took over my training for Tillman when they got kidnapped, he was in his slacks and a button-up with the sleeves rolled quarter length. Still drop dead sexy, but he was dressed, ready for work. Right now, though...it takes everything in me not to jump all over him.

"Don't slip on your drool, little wanderer."

"I'm not drooling, thank you very much."

"Yeah, you are. You're looking at the boss man like he's your last meal."

"Well, if I were in a situation to need a last meal, you four would be exactly what I'd consume. I'd—"

"Enough, you two. Don't start that shit before we walk in here," Tillman butts in, eyeing Draken and me like we're torturing him before casting his glare back to Corentin. "You all don't need privacy from me. What runs through Aunt Rory's mind is none of my business. Whatever she has in store for us this morning isn't going to be any harder or worse than what I've already put any of you through."

Ugh. Says the giant who lives for working out.

He makes sure to send me a saucy little wink before shoving the double doors to the gym wide open for us. My feet halt as I gaze around because this sure as shit isn't what I expected when they said gym.

It's just a big-ass open room.

I mean, there is gym equipment around, but they're practically pushed into the corner, out of the way. There're windows allowing for natural light to come in, and then the bare hardwood floor.

That's it.

No mats, no obstacle course. Nothing of the sort.

Aurora and my Patera-Nexus stand in the middle of the room, talking amongst themselves as we take a couple more steps in and then wait a few feet in front of them.

"So this gym is...different," I say.

"This isn't the traditional workout gym you're used to, daughter-in-law, no, but this gym has been fortified to withstand our gifts. So it'll hold your Nexus's as well. Hopefully," Dyce says with a devious wink.

I see he's hoping for some mischief today.

"Why does it need to withstand any of our gifts?" I ask, cocking my brow.

"You'll see, my girl. I'm so excited. We'll show you first, then we'll start working with you all. There's going to be so much that you all can do that even we can't, but you still need to learn structure and how to work as a unit. Go stand against that wall, all of you. Go on, chop, chop. You've kept me waiting long enough," Aurora orders, waving us off with a happy little chuckle that her men melt at.

Damn, I hope my guys look at me like that after two hundred years together.

I cock my head curiously as Neil walks over to the far side of the gym and lays his hand on the wall. My eyes nearly bug out when a door pops open, and he just walks into the secret, mysterious room. With a chuckle and a grip on my arm, I'm brought back to reality as Tillman laughs and shakes his head at me. My curious little heart took control there for a second and my feet were moving faster than my mind.

"Did you all know about the cool secret room?" I ask.

"How do you know it's cool, Primary?" Caspian asks instead of answering me, with a little twitch to his lips.

"Because it's a secret. That automatically makes it cool. Will one of you answer me?"

"No, princess. We were unaware of the cool secret room. This is my parents' private gym. This is probably the first time any of us have stepped in here since we were kids. We did most of our working out with our dads down at the palace E.F. compound," Corentin fully explains. Thankfully. But that just makes me bounce on my toes in more excitement.

I love a good surprise. Good being the operative word.

"Okay, kids, no one panic. Nor do we need your help," Neil says cryptically as he comes back out of the room holding a glowing box.

"What's that?" I ask.

"You'll see," Roye says as he cracks his neck and shakes his limbs.

What the hell is about to happen?

Neil sets the box down about six or so feet in front of Aurora and the others, then moves to stand in the single file line they've created. I watch intently, with my heart thudding wildly with excitement, waiting for whatever they're about to do with that box.

Together, Aurora, Roye, Dyce, Neil, and Theo all raise their palms and command the box to open.

There's a quiet beat before literal chaos explodes around the room.

I jump, startled at the sudden noise and bodies piling out of the box.

Not just any bodies. Mastery members.

I attempt to step forward, but Tillman grabs hold of me. Whipping my head up to him, I see a mixture of confusion and astonishment written across his features.

"They're not real, little warrior. Watch."

Focusing on what's going on in front of me like he commanded, my breathing quickens when I rapidly count out the fifty or so Mastery members circling Aurora and her men. They've moved now into a defensive position, with Aurora tucked in the middle of their protective ring.

Suddenly, the first Mastery member strikes out, and Theo throws out...well, I don't know what that is that just came out of his hand, but it threw the Mastery member across the room. When he or she, whoever's behind the robe hits the wall, they vaporize and fade to nothing. The glowing vapor gets sucked back into the box and then all hell breaks loose.

I swiftly realize I only know Aurora's and Dyce's gifts and elements. The others I'm completely clueless about and I'll be learning on the go.

We stare, enthralled at the sight before us. Like a choreographed dance that they've done a million times, Aurora and her Nexus work seamlessly together, fighting off the massive gathering of fake Mastery members.

With graceful steps and precise moves, Aurora twirls between the men, shooting out her earth element, laying her hands on them for support, and her blue eyes are glowing as she mutters so low I can't hear her.

Each of her men cast out elements, moving around in the circle with exact steps and synchronized strikes. It's as if every one of them knows when to attack, when to move out of the way, and which one is to be the closest to Aurora. I've never seen such a display of a group of people being so in tune. I thought my guys worked flawlessly together, but this...this is something else.

"What the fuck?" Caspian mutters.

"This is amazing," I respond breathlessly.

"Yeah, sure, but did you all just see earth come out of Theo or am I seeing shit?" he asks frantically.

"You're not seeing shit," Corentin says sternly, with his eyes narrowed, following every move his parents make.

"And that's not normal because..." I trail off because obviously I don't know what they're talking about.

"Uncle Theo's element is air, Will," Tillman says, watching the show just as keenly, if not more now.

What?

None of us say or ask anything else as we focus back on the show being put on before us. The guys' confusion and awe grow as the numbers begin to dwindle down. The smaller the attacking group gets, the faster they move in, and the faster Aurora and her men retaliate. Before the last of the Mastery members fall to nothing but particles and get sucked into the box, they're all basically a blur of motion I struggle to keep up with.

Silence reigns as the box pulls in the last of the fallen, and with a loud almost zipping sound, it vibrates violently, then settles back to its glowing, still state.

My mouth gapes open, with my jaw nearly on the ground as I stare at Aurora and her men, who are smiling at one another, breathing heavily, and high-fiving like they didn't just put on the most badass battle I've ever seen.

Sure, we've gone against numbers like this and come out on top, but that was just extraordinary. They barely moved from their first positions in that circle, and they took down fifty Mastery members as if it was a walk in the park. Within minutes. Yeah, they were fake, but still, that was impressive.

"What in the realm was that?" Caspian barks as the silence stretches on too long.

"That, son, was the unity of a true and completed Nexus," Roye says.

"How were you all using elements you don't possess?" Corentin asks immediately.

Aurora puts her hands up, halting all questions and answers as she catches her breath with a dazzling, energetic smile on her face. She's practically glowing right now in the aftermath of that display.

"There is a lot to explain, so just allow me to do that first, then ask your questions afterward. Okay?" she asks and when we all nod, she lowers her hands.

"That is an illusion box. Tilly and Ian were the main creators, but her whole Nexus took part in it as well," she says softly, smiling at Tillman.

Ian...

Looking over at Tillman, he's tense, still, but he's trying to shake it off. Ian was one of his dads. He had the gift of Illusion, apparently a strong one. He's only told me their names and talked about them twice with me. The first time was the night I woke him from his nightmare, and the second, the conversation struck up after we found out Trex's brother was an illusionist.

It was just a small moment, a quick conversation where he talked about them freely then changed the subject. I'm starting to see now that my big, gentle giant has been doing a wonderful job of hiding his hurt from me.

It's just in this moment that I'm realizing all the times he's distracted me and changed the subject anytime his parents have been brought up. I've fallen for it and moved on without complaint each time because every now and then he'll make comments about how they'd have loved me, and that's given me a sense of knowing more about them than I truly do.

Oh my gosh, he did it with that cute nickname too.

It sends a pang through me that I try to shove down because he obviously hasn't wanted to talk about this or just hasn't felt comfortable enough to bring it up. When or if he wants to talk about it, he will, but until now, I always thought he's been completely open with me about how losing all his parents affected him. That's not the case, I see.

I swallow down any hurt or negative feelings I may have because it's not my place to push him or any of them to talk to me about things like this if they don't want to. So it's unfair of me to be upset that he hasn't brought it up. I obviously don't do the best job, though, because he squeezes my hand.

"Tilly used her knowledge of fighting and instructed Ian on what an ideal fighting scenario would look like had any of us got stuck in a situation like this where we'd be outnumbered and surrounded. Since the illusions aren't real, we still needed a way to measure the damage we'd take if one were to strike us, so Hudsen embedded the rebels with his electricity. They give small zaps every time they hit you.

"Those first few training sessions were rough and needless to say, we got shocked enough times to decide we had to start working better together. Drudy, as you know, wasn't one to be forthcoming with everything it meant to be a true Primary, so Tilly and I were on our own in learning. Until my sneaky brother gifted us a book," Aurora says, nodding at Neil, who carries the glowing box back into the secret room and emerges with hopefully the book she's referring to.

My eyes zero in on the bound leather and my heart knows it's full of CC's handwriting without me even needing to see it. His signature is all over it and the tie between him and me pulses in my chest.

"He'd been compiling research on true Primaries and their true abilities once their Nexus was complete. I have a feeling he got a lot of this information from his visions, and..." She trails off, looking at me sadly before clearing her throat. "From your mom, Willow."

My heart flutters at the mention of her. I may be biased, obviously, but I'm positive my mom was the best true Primary to walk this realm. I haven't been given the luxury of seeing everything she was capable of, nor do I know much of her Nexus outside of what Lyker's told me. But there's no doubt they were incredible.

"I believe the guardian bloodline, which is what Keeper has referred to you as, Willow, were, are, a more evolved line. You can manipulate multiple elements, gifts, and so did your mom. Tilly and I were only able to learn how to push our elements through our Nexus members, even if they don't possess our element. Even that helped tremendously, but I have a feeling for all of you, it'll be so much more because you have all four elements at your disposal. Plus, you possess each of their gifts. I think you'll be able to strengthen that as well."

I gaze at my men, who are staring at their mom like she's grown a second head, but something about her words settles itself inside my chest. Our bonding already strengthened their power, they've got new abilities as well, but if I were to combine my power with theirs...Shit.

"May I?" I ask, pointing to the book in Aurora's hand.

"Of course." She hands it to me gently.

As I run my fingers down the cover, a tingle passes through them and I smile, sensing his familiar magic. Opening it up to the first page, tears immediately well in my eyes at his handwriting. The ink is still plenty legible even after all this time. Aurora has taken great care of this book.

The Primary is the sole Source of the Nexus. They're the center being who can fully activate a Nexus as one and balance the power of air, earth, water, and fire.

I smile down at the words I've read before. They're in my journal, and it's the first thing I read on Primaries after the truth was revealed to me about being the guys' true Primary. What surprises me, though, are the paragraphs after the introduction. It's an insert I've never read before.

Touch is a vital component of a Nexus and a natural want for a Primary. Their need to have physical contact with the members of their Nexus is ingrained in their DNA because they naturally seek to strengthen them. It is the gateway for the growth and development of the forming or formed bond and without it, the power will not flow properly from one member to the next. A Nexus cannot be strong if they are not close.

The Primary is the conduct that has the ability to pass on the manipulation of all of Elementra's blessings through touch. It is only through the Primary's guidance that the Nexus can tap into the full strength of the completed bond.

"That's why you were touching one of them constantly just then," I murmur out loud.

"Yes. As I said, Tilly and I only got as far as our elements flowing through them, but I believe you'll be able to pass on all of Elementra's blessings," Aurora says. She had to have memorized this book to know exactly what I was referring to because she doesn't look down at the book but instead holds my gaze.

"May I borrow this?" I ask as I close the book.

"It's yours now, my girl. I'm pretty sure I was only supposed to watch after it until you got here," she says sweetly, smiling proudly at me.

"Thank you," I say, then walk the book over to the windowsill. When I join them again, I clap my hands and rub them together. "So where do we begin?"

Everyone chuckles at me, but I'm pumped now. From Aurora's and her men's badass display of their power to my new reading material, I'm ready to conquer it all. If what Aurora believes is true and I can pass my power through me into my men, which strengthens their abilities, I'm ready for it.

It also makes more sense now as to why she was so excited about Draken's newest ability. With him being able to feed me his magic, I won't grow tired of pushing power into them. We'll basically have our own give-and-take system that doesn't tire us out.

And in a war against a psychopath that has possibly hundreds of stolen gifts, we can't get caught at anything less than full strength.

"Let's start small. I'll push my earth element through Roye and walk you through what I do. He has an earth element, and it was easiest for me to learn with him first," Aurora says, but I hold my hand up because I'm utterly confused about what my Patera-Nexus, aside from Dyce, is capable of since they bounced around so much, and I saw each of them use an earth element because of her.

"Can I have a quick breakdown of your gifts and elements?"

Each of my fathers-in-law puffs up at my question. Their eagerness is heady, and I laugh at the smug smirks on their faces. It's clear where my men, all four of them, get their cockiness from.

"You've opened a wormhole now, my girl," Aurora says, snorting.

"Come on then, daughter-in-law. See if you can guess them. You already know my beast, but put that magical signature gift to good use on the rest." Dyce cheers, pulling me forward before I can answer, and my guys grumble behind me.

Roye steps up first with his arms crossed and a sly smirk on his face. He's not using his gift yet judging by the absence of the subtle vibration

I feel when people are actively using their gifts, so I don't know what he's waiting for.

"Come on, Draken. You'll be the prop."

Prop? What in the realm does he need a prop for?

Draken snickers and jogs up happily for whatever's about to happen and I arch a brow at him, earning myself a wink. "You think you can handle my dragon?" he asks excitedly.

"There's no room in here for you to shift," Roye says, shaking his head.

"Oh, but on the contrary," Draken says, giving no one any warning before he sprints farther from us, and in the middle of this damn gym, shifts into his fifteen-foot form.

"When did he learn to change his size?" Theo asks, whipping his head to us.

"After we bonded. We both can shift to whatever size we please," I say proudly as I look at my fearsome dragon. Luckily, the gym is big enough with the incredibly high ceilings and huge space, but he probably should've warned them.

"Well, this is going to be an awkward hold. Don't flap around or swipe me with your tail, Draken," Roye says as he marches up to Draken, then...crawls underneath him.

What the fuck is he doing?

Suddenly, Draken's off the ground.

And not because he's flapping his wings.

Roye stands tall underneath his belly, literally holding him up as if he were nothing more than a workout bar. I quickly shake myself out of my stupor so I can cast my gift out and pick up on Roye's, although it's fucking obvious.

"Holy shit. He has super strength," I mumble.

"That I do, Willow," Roye says proudly before tossing Draken to the ground. The entire gym shakes, and we all wobble on our feet before righting ourselves.

I never would've believed this if I hadn't just seen it with my own eyes, but that is fucking astonishing.

"You barely even shook. Someone's been working out, huh?" Draken teases, squeezing Roye's biceps as soon as he shifts back.

"That was amazing," I exclaim excitedly, then turn to the other two of my Patera-Nexus. "Who's next? Oh, Theo, what was that thing you did to the fake Mastery member?"

"That was my gift," he says, smiling, then cutting his eye to Roye, he hits him with that same blast of whatever his gift is.

This must be something they do a lot because Roye, although caught off guard, steels himself and doesn't fly into the wall but does slide feet from us.

"Forcefields, Willow. Unlike a shield that would surround us in a protective barrier, I send mine out. Whoever is the poor sap to collide with it gets forced away. My element is air," he says as he then wraps Roye in a vortex of it.

"Enough. Neil, your turn," Roye barks, over being the guinea pig.

"Willow, if you would," Neil says, holding his hand out for me to take.

Before I can even place mine in his, though, I'm snatched back, and all my men are yelling no at the same time.

"You boys are being ridiculous. I'd never hurt her. I'll just make sure everything is in place as it should be."

In place?

"He's an Osteokinesis, little warrior," Tillman informs me.

"Which is?"

"He can manipulate bones. Any way he wants to," Caspian says, still holding on to me protectively.

Well, that's terrifyingly cool.

"Can you crack my back?" I ask excitedly as the thought comes to me. I am a little stiff this morning and that would work wonders.

"Crack your back?" Neil asks, confused.

"Yeah, you know, when your bones or body feel stiff, you crack them to loosen up."

He still looks at me as though I've lost it, but he nods nonetheless and I pull myself out of my guys' grasps. They're being crazy if they seriously think he's going to do anything that hurts.

"Ah, I believe I see what you mean. You're holding a lot of tension in your vertebrae," Neil says when I finally lay my hand in his. His gift washes over me, and there's this strange, itchy feeling flowing through my body.

I don't have time to clarify or confirm with him when every bone in my spine cracks. I can't help but arch into the sensation and I groan as the stiff feeling fades to complete relaxation. There's never been a time in my life where my entire back has been cracked and shit, it feels spectacular.

"Better?" he asks.

"So much. Thank you."

"Anytime. My element is water. It comes in quite handy when manipulating the fluid in the bones," he says, then everyone chuckles at the shocked expression on my face.

Here I am thinking about how he'd make a damn good chiropractor and everyone else has murder on their minds. Granted, that's a pretty perfect gift for either scenario.

Okay, so we've got Dyce our Tasmonium shifter with a fire element. Roye with super strength and earth. Theo is a Forcefield with an air element. Neil is an Osteokinesis aka bone breaker with a water element. Aurora, of course, an empath with an earth element.

Got it.

"Enough show and tell. We've got work to do. Come on, Roye," Aurora orders playfully, laughing as Roye strings her up and pulls her to him in vines. The guys all groan and grunt, faking gagging noises while I laugh at the adorable affection. "Okay, okay, Willow, watch closely, then I'll explain what I'm doing."

I focus my attention on where Roye's holding out his hand and Aurora is hovering hers right above it. The shift of energy in the air is their earth elements on the surface already. The power grows in the atmosphere as she slowly lowers her palm until they're pressed together, and once they touch, the entire foundation shakes until a small flower bursts through the floor at their feet.

I could see the flow of the element the entire time as I called my gift to the surface. It traveled from both of their chests, down their arms, where it waited in their hands until it was united. I just don't know how they commanded it together.

When I say that out loud, Aurora nods. "Yes, we command our elements out individually as we would any other time, but the trick to combining them is I must command the two to mingle, at the same time he commands his to obey. That took us quite some time to perfect because anytime we spoke to each other, it would break the connection. We just had to learn to work together, become more in sync. This is where you all will have an advantage. Maybe speaking telepathically won't break your connections. How about you give it a go with your air? That's the element that broke free first."

Corentin and I look at each other at the same time, and his cocky smirk makes my knees weak.

Holding his hand out for me to take, our fingers lace together as he strolls us to the middle of the room with a certainty that boosts my own confidence. His control is in full swing, and part of me is lapping it up and soaking it in with every stride. While the other part of me is screaming to simmer the hell down before we embarrass ourselves.

"Ready, princess?"

"Ready, your highness," I say, then blow out a nervous breath.

"Okay, you two, see if you can move this ball. Just try to focus on lifting it or moving it at first. Nothing crazy," Aurora says from behind us.

Just as they had done, Corentin lays his hand out, palm facing up, and he calls his element to the surface. When I feel his air caress me, I call mine out and it pushes against my skin, practically begging to mingle with his.

That reaction makes a lot more sense now.

"On my count," Corentin orders and I nod. *"Three...two...one."*

"Obey," he says, but my *"Mingle,"* comes a second afterward.

Instead of mingling, his air shoves my hand from hovering above his, causing the air I sent out to blast from my palm straight in front of us. The earth ball Aurora created goes flying into the wall, shattering to pieces on impact.

"Whoops," I say, letting my hand fall to my side.

"That's okay, try again." Aurora molds the broken earth back together and places it back in its spot.

"Okay, on one or after?" I ask.

"After. As soon as I say one, we'll send our commands out," he clarifies and I nod. *"Three...two...one."*

"Obey."

"Mingle."

I want to dance with joy when the feeling of his element weaving itself with mine flows through my body. I feel both powerful and light as a feather. It's the most amazing, crazy sensation with the elements I've ever felt.

That elation is a little premature, though, as the power continues to build and I realize I don't have a damn clue how to pass it back to him or what to do with it. I'm supposed to be powering him, not myself.

Mentally, I imagine the element flowing back through our hands and through him, but that doesn't work. The force of the air just continues to grow within my chest.

"Shit, what do I do with it now? It won't go back to you."

"Release it, princess. This was a step my mother obviously forgot to mention or didn't think we'd get so quickly," he says and there's a subtle strain to his voice. My element is pulling more and more from him and he's trying to hold it back.

Fuck.

Commanding the air out, my mind works overtime, and I can't think properly about the best way of dispelling some of this power. All that crosses my thoughts is how I may accidentally sweep everyone up in a damn tornado if I just release it, so I follow the original instructions given to us and hit Aurora's earth ball.

The structure shakes violently and I gasp, covering my mouth with my hands as the earth ball turns into a cannonball. It soars so fast toward the wall, I don't have time to stop it before it crashes through the solid stone, leaving a gaping hole right through to the outside.

"Shit," I say, whipping around to face my Patera-Nexus, "I broke your unbreakable gym. I'm sorry."

They each stare at me with shocked eyes and slack jaws.

Draken's snickering starts out soft, small, and when I cut my narrowed eyes to him, he loses it completely, dragging everyone with him into a fit of hysterical laughter.

"You should've seen your face, little wanderer. You look so surprised." He continues to laugh as he holds his belly, and I cross my arms, staring him down.

"It's not funny, dragon," I complain.

"Oh, but it is." He wipes his eyes and chuckles under his breath.

"Well, that was a pleasant surprise. Looks like we'll need to reinforce the gym," Roye says and when I turn to him, apology ready on the tongue, his wide, prideful smile halts me.

He's not looking at me, though. He's beaming at Corentin and the aura around my man is blinding. This is not the reaction I expected to destroying a whole wall, but if it makes Corentin this happy seeing his dad proud of him, I sure as shit am not about to ruin the moment.

"Don't fret about the wall, Willow. Roye, you and Tillme go patch that up and reinforce it for now while I walk them through what happened," Aurora says.

Tillme...

Tillman's face colors pink and he refuses to make eye contact with me, but he does give my forehead a kiss as he walks past me. I have to bite my mental tongue from asking about it and I force my gift not to reach out to his mind.

"You knew that would happen, Mom?" Corentin asks.

"I didn't know she'd send the ball all the way through the wall, but yes, I knew that first time her element would take over."

"Why didn't you tell us that?" I ask.

"I didn't want to put any pressure on either of you to get it. It's incredibly frustrating to try over and over and never see the results. I wanted you to just focus on getting your elements to mingle first. Next, you can work on sending that extra kick back to him. That starts before you even command your element out. You have to zero in on him, his element, and with strict intentions to go to him. It gets even more complicated when you start mixing elements they don't possess," she explains gently.

I blow out a subtle breath because when she puts it like that, it feels complicated. Just now, my element was solely focused on me and pulling from him. That was harder than I honestly thought it was going to be, and now it seems even more difficult.

"It's okay, princess. We're not meant to master this in a day. Let's try one more time, then you can practice with one of the others," Corentin says, tilting my chin up and laying a sweet kiss to my lips.

That's rich coming from Mr. Controlling himself. He knows as well as I do, I want to master this now. Anything new, I want to figure it out immediately. He's the same way about absolutely everything and the only reason he isn't currently is because he doesn't want to upset me.

We're getting this shit right. Right now.

"If he's Mr. Controlling, you're Mrs. Impatience," Tillman chuckles, and I glare at him as he winks at me.

Exhaling and shaking my body out, I clear my mind of all things but Corentin.

Chocolate and allspice fill my senses as I lean more into him. The sweet but dominant scent fits him so perfectly. His dirty-blond hair, styled without a strand out of place, would look wrong on anyone else dressed in workout clothes but not him. It's a delightful mix between his normal controlled routine and this new attempt at wearing something other than suits all the time.

His sharp whiskey eyes see everything. They remember everything, plan for everything. I'm sure even now, he's taken in the liberty of thinking through every scenario that can go right or wrong for us on this next attempt, and he's ready for however it'll go.

There's a warm breeze, like lying in a hammock on a beach, that always surrounds him. It's the perfect blend of cool air and the heat his light puts off. I fixate on the small glow to his skin now, knowing, feeling his beautiful gift just waiting under the surface for my touch.

"One more go, princess. Ready?"

"Ready, your highness."

"Three...two...one."

"Obey."

"Mingle."

My element flows out of me, wrapping itself around his, and I push, commanding it to follow my orders and move through him. There's only the slightest bit of resistance before it does just that. I hear the gasps and quiet murmurs behind us, but my attention is solely on Corentin.

He grunts as the combination of my air and his flows through his limbs and he latches onto its strength like the commander he is. His light is shining bright in a halo around him, and it's breathtaking, exhilarating.

I'm so in love with this man.

As he raises his hand to command the air out, the reality of what has everyone behind me whispering about slaps me in the face.

There're six Corentins.

"Core..."

"Yeah, princess?" he asks excitedly. There's almost an otherworldly note to his deep voice. Like power is lacing even his mental tone.

"How are you feeling? Do you have good control over the elements?" I ask, trying to keep the shock, the worry, the confusion of what the hell is happening out of my voice.

"It feels completely natural yet unbelievably powerful. I have them under control. I think I could hold it for a while before having to push it out. Your power is exhilarating, princess."

Fuck, I want to swoon at his words, but now's probably not the time.

"So you feel powerful, pretty amped up, huh?"

"Exactly. Why?" he finally asks as he looks down at me with a panty-melting smirk.

"Because there're multiple of you. I think I pushed too hard."

"What are you—" he starts, but his sight follows where I'm pointing my finger. *"Shit. I'm reflecting myself."*

His eyes swing back to mine and I expected to see a little shock, maybe some panic because that's what I'm feeling, but he's even more collected, confident.

With a flirty wink, he flicks his finger at Aurora's ball, sending it flying straight up into the air, then he turns to me.

All six of him surround me.

"You forced my ability to power up, princess. I haven't done that since my emerging," he whispers as he grips my chin.

"Making multiples of yourself...that's your boost in power?" I ask breathlessly as the heat in his eyes traps me.

"Holding reflections is more technical, but yeah, I can make multiples of myself." He smirks at my flustered state, but I can't help it.

Between the power I feel him radiating, that look he's giving me, and the fact I'm surrounded by more than one of him, even though they are only reflections, I'm about to be a puddle at his feet.

With a sweet, soft kiss, he breaks our connection as his duplicates return into him and he stretches his body out. Everyone swarms us, praising and congratulating us on what just happened.

Meanwhile, all I can think about is what I would do if I could get my hands on more than one Corentin at a time.

Nine

Willow

Staring out over the view this morning is a beautiful, peaceful picture.

The guys all had things they needed to take care of this morning, and while they each invited me to join them, I decided on a little alone time. Which I'm pretty sure they all knew I needed because they didn't push back. Plus, Gaster is meeting me here in a few. There're things we need to discuss and things I can't keep ignoring.

So in the rare blissful few moments of silence, I take in and cherish the scene in front of me.

The sun hasn't crested the trees just yet, but it's poking out, getting ready to warm the ground. The cool morning breeze has just enough chill to it that I need a thin blanket out here on the balcony, and the perfectly made cup of coffee Corentin handed me before he left warms my hands.

Just as I bring the mug to my lips, my communicator buzzes on my thigh and as soon as I see the name across the screen, I smile.

Damn, I've missed her.

"Fuck, I've missed your voice," Oakly says as soon as I accept the call.

"I haven't even said anything yet." I chuckle, but as her own laugh joins mine, the sound fills the gaping hole of longing that was in my chest. "I've missed you too."

"I'm sorry I didn't come to the healing wing with Jamie. I've just been..."

"Wrapped up in your men's arms because you completed your bonds?" I snicker at her outraged gasp, and I wish she were here to see my smug face.

Thank fuck I don't actually feel the way Oakly feels during her spicy time with her men because damn, that would be so awkward, but yeah, I felt the moment she seemed to...well, I don't know how to explain it. Her bond felt stronger, and I knew what that meant.

"Please, for the love of Elementra, tell me you did not see that in some creepy-ass vision."

"No, absolutely not." I laugh at the mortification in her tone, then clear my throat. "Our bond strengthened again, just like after you bonded the first time, but more...if that makes sense."

"Holy shit, it does. You...you're fully bonded too. I felt it," she whispers before squealing so loud I have to pull the communicator from my ear. "This is the coolest and weirdest thing ever."

We fall into fits of laughter. This, by my definition, isn't the weirdest thing that's happened, but it's something, that's for sure. It makes sense now, though, why I haven't felt a desperate need to see her like I normally would. Both of our bonds are a little distracted with the bigger bonds taking over our emotions currently.

Once our teasing and laughing tapers off, we easily jump right into catching up on everything that's been happening for both of us. I tell her about the memories, the south wing, CC, and like the amazing sister she is, she laughs, cries, and cusses him out on my behalf. Her excitement for me having almost all my memories returned matches my own, though, and her support means the world to me.

"What is that noise coming out of you?" I ask as she lets out a long, exaggerated groan.

"My parents are blowing me up. They've been blowing me up since Corentin sent out the announcement of the academy shutting down. They laid off a little bit when I told them I was selected to join the mission we were going on, you know, excluding the part about kidnapping an ancient vampire, but since we've gotten back, they've been relentless. They want to know where I'm staying, who I'm staying with, blah, blah, blah. Well, last night they took it too far. I kinda snapped..."

"Snapped how? Don't leave me hanging like that."

She lets out a sigh and I swear I can see her eyes rolling. "They had invited me to dinner last night, which I know I should've just said no to, but then I would've had to come up with an explanation as to why I didn't want to come, so I just ignored them. Right before bed, they started blowing me up again. So then I got scared that something had happened to one of them and I answered. Wrong freaking shit to do. My dad went ballistic on me about how much I made a fool of him and embarrassed him."

"I don't understand. How did you make a fool of him and embarrass him by ignoring their calls and not going to dinner?" I ask.

"They..." Her voice wells with emotions and her sudden sniffling has me sitting straight up.

What have those assholes done?

"Oakly, what did they do?" I accidentally, not really, growl.

"They'd arranged me a Nexus and I was supposed to meet them at dinner. The Razy Nexus. Fucking elite brats who are higher up in the Central and Aeradora society."

My ears ring as the rage, sadness, and abandonment vibrate through her broken tone. I have to breathe through my dragon's immediate need to defend her and my own fierce emotions make my skin hot at hearing her so upset.

This is the shit I just can't understand about some families in this society. She's a true Primary to a wonderful group of men. Hell, if we want to get technical, Ry's standing elevates the entire Nexus to the point you'd think her social ladder parents would be thrilled. What should matter is her happiness, the fact she's cherished, cared for, and not just that, those men build her up and encourage her to be more than a pretty face.

She's a badass.

"So you snapped and told them you had a Nexus, a true Nexus," I conclude.

"Yeah, and they didn't take it well. Demanded I come home and introduce them," she mumbles.

"Are you going to? I mean, fuck them. I'll fly over there right now and tell them to fuck off. We'll show them how high up in society you are when you roll up on a dragon's back." She thinks I'm kidding by the way a small laugh breaks through her tear-drenched voice, but I'm not.

"Yeah, we're going to go the day after tomorrow. The last damn thing I want is to spend the remainder of break with my parents. It's not going to go how they believe it's going to, though. Ry's already declared they're taking full Nexus responsibility over me, and I won't be leaving that house as a Folder but a Mercie. He's supposed to be talking to Corentin and Tillman today about it. You know since we technically broke quite a few rules."

"You lost me completely. What the hell does that mean? And why would he need Corentin's and Tillman's permission for that?" I ask, completely confused in the conversation now. The only thing I understood was the part of changing her last name to theirs.

"I forget sometimes you didn't grow up here," she snorts before saying, "I'm not sure how to put this without it being a long explanation or pissing you off."

Oh, welp I already know it's going to piss me off now.

"Might as well just spit it out."

"There're rules written within the academy handbook. Rules specifically for unbonded females, Primaries," she says vaguely, not explaining shit.

"Get on with it, Oakly. I don't have time to go hunt down this so-called handbook I've never heard of until this second."

Shitty on my part, yeah, but Corentin never brought it up, so it's not that important for me to know, I guess.

She sighs deeply, and I already know from that alone, whatever it is, is some shit that's going to irk my nerves.

"You wouldn't have heard of this because it doesn't too much apply to you. Because you're a...charge, so to speak, and you're already your Nexus's responsibility. For those of us females who aren't, who have parents, they have to sign off on our Nexuses while we're still at the academy. True or chosen. They decide when to give up their responsibility over us until we finish the academy. I wasn't supposed to fully bond the guys without my parents' knowledge of them."

She delivers the news softly as if me being called a charge would hurt my feelings, but I couldn't give a fuck about that part. That's not the part that has my blood boiling.

"Oakly, what the hell do you mean they're supposed to sign over responsibility of you and they needed knowledge of them before your bonding?"

"See, I knew you were going to get pissed." She tsks as if I shouldn't be mad.

"Hell yeah, I am. That all just sounded as though Primaries need our parents' permission on who we decide to spend our lives with. And why the hell does anyone have to take responsibility for us? We aren't children."

"Technically, we're supposed to get their permission for, well, everything. It all started when true Primary bonds became more and more rare. People were bonding however they saw fit, and society decided that there needed to be more power balance involved. So their solution to that was parents would be responsible for their daughters' well-being until they completed the highest level of the academies. That includes everything, even who they bond with. If the parents didn't feel like it was a good fit, they wouldn't allow it. It's barbaric, old-fashioned, and a way outdated practice, but neither the five, nor the elite society will agree to change it.

"Corentin's bent the rules plenty for many people. Me included. He was technically supposed to inform my parents the moment Ry's and my awakening happened, but he didn't."

I pinch the bridge of my nose and breathe while I process this bullshit. This is a level of control I'd expect from the Mastery, but everyone else in Elementra? No. This is ridiculous.

"This is bullshit, Oak, but that's beside the current point. This is something that'll get fixed. If Corentin's already bending the rules and not informing parents, that means he's already working on a way to get rid of it completely. And I'll make sure to see it through, but for now, explain to me what this means for you. What happens when you get to your parents'?"

"Well, I'm hoping it's going to be a civil discussion. The deed's already done. But the plan is we're all going to go have breakfast with them and be as sweet and fake as possible. The guys will hopefully charm my parents, they sign over responsibility of me, and we leave. And I never speak to them again."

I snort at the sarcasm and nonchalance of her plan. From the shit I've heard her talk about her parents, I don't see it going according to that plan. At all. I see screaming, yelling, Ry losing his shit. Jamie may charm and calm everyone down until her parents say something sideways about her, then he's going to flip as well.

"Okay, well, what's the backup plan? What if they refuse to sign over responsibility of you?" Those words taste like ash on my tongue.

That's something that's going to change, one way or another. Hopefully, as soon as we get rid of the two of the five betraying us. Aurora can fill the seats with people who aren't corrupted by the Mastery and their disgusting beliefs.

"The next step is more complicated. The proper channel would be to go to the ruling council of our territory, but each of my dads are from a territory, Mom's from the Central. None of the five of them would agree to claim one of the other territories as home, so they've been pandering all five territories their whole lives."

Of course.

"Couldn't I just get Aurora involved? Get her to sign this shit and be done?" I ask, growing frustrated with this whole stupid-ass situation she is in.

"Fuck, the way you speak of the Matriarch as though she's just a friend is crazy to me." She squeals, causing me to laugh.

"Sorry, I kinda forget she's the Queen. But she's also my mother-in-law and yeah, a really good friend. I'll call in a favor."

She blows out a breath so harsh I hear her lips flapping together and I laugh at her dramatics. "I mean, yeah, she could sign off and it would be done and over with, but I'd prefer to talk with my parents first. The last thing I want is for them to realize how close I truly am to the ruling family now because of you. That's another reason why I haven't told them about our bond. They'll smell an opportunity and be completely fake. I'm just ready to cut ties with them, Willy."

The sadness in her tone eats at my heart and I wish like hell she had a better relationship with her parents. It's so unfair. All she's ever wanted was their love, but all they wanted was a top spot in society and they've treated her like shit her whole life because she doesn't feel the same.

"I know. Go with your plan and hopefully they'll agree. But we have this plan as backup. One way or another, we'll get you from under them, so you'll be free to do and love your men however you see fit. Okay?" I ask softly.

"Yeah, sounds good. We'll let Jamie do all the talking." She sniffles.

"That sounds perfect. It's all going to be fine and afterward, you all will come stay here at the palace with us for the few remaining days of the academy closure."

"At the palace? You aren't going back to the mansion during the break?" she asks, surprised. It surprises me too.

"Probably not for break. We'll have to work out the logistics after the academy opens back up, but I...I love the south wing and there's much I need to learn here. I know CC well, so I know there're more secrets hidden within these walls that I have to figure out. I love the mansion too, though. I don't want to only live in one, but for right now, I'm meant to be here," I admit.

The south wing is where my heart's calling me to be, for now.

I haven't said it out loud to the guys yet, but they know, they feel it too. They've also put off exploring their rooms to the full extent, just like I've put off exploring the rooms I know were made for my benefit.

"Shit. Never in my life did I think I'd ever visit the palace. Now I'm about to be hanging out there like I'm somebody special." Oakly snorts.

"First off, you are special. Secondly, get used to it. I don't think you've thought it all the way through, Oaks. You'll be living here one day with me. Tillman will be commander of the entire E.F. army when he takes over from Roye, which will pull Ry, Nikoli, and San in higher positions. Jamie will become the palace's healer and Master Inventor. You're my sister. You'll automatically become my most trusted advisor. You'll be working alongside Gaster as Master Archivist. Hell, knowing him, in two hundred years when I pop out a kid, he's going to want to step down and you'll be taking over completely."

My laugh fades out as everything I just said in a teasing manner slaps me back into reality. The silence coming from the other side of the communicator screams the deafening truth of it all. I've been listening, learning the structure of the ruling family, and I guess subconsciously, I've already started accepting it and working it out in my mind.

"Holy shit, Oakly," I whisper.

"Yeah, talk about a fucking wake-up call."

"That's going to be our lives one day. Two hundred years sounds so far away, but it's not, is it?" I ask as my own emotions race to the surface.

"No, it's not. We've got other things to worry about first, though, right? You know, like finishing at the academy, traveling, sightseeing, our bonding ceremonies. No need to fret over the other stuff right now. Right?" she asks as her own panic bleeds through her words.

"And saving the realm," I mumble.

"Fuck, yeah. That too. See, plenty for us to do before we become sensible, responsible adults who rule the realm. We've got plenty of time."

"Yeah...yeah. Plenty of time."

We manage to end our conversation on a much happier, funnier note, making plans for the tour I'll give her when she gets here, how she, Aurora, and I will enjoy some coffee and girl time. All in all, we're our happy, normal selves by the end of it.

Deep inside, though, I can't shake the feeling...

The clock for the realm is ticking.

"Eager to learn about the Valorian Veil?" Gaster asks as he plops down beside me on the couch in the lounge with a single journal. Far less than I thought there'd be when CC told me to ask for his notes.

"I don't know if I'd say eager to learn about it, but I am eager to go inside the amplifier room."

"Ah, yes, of course. The Eye of the Veil," he says dreamily.

"I'm sorry?"

"It'll explain more in here. That's a story I haven't told in some time," he says as he passes over a journal that's seen better days.

I'm careful as I untwine the thin leather string that's holding the cover closed and I'm surprised when I find that the parchment inside looks fresh, new even.

"When the portals closed, I enchanted my journals from the other realms to preserve them better. Quite a few of my journals on Elementra are preserved as such as well. Some are not. Depends on my mood and the information inside," he says with a smirk when I give him a questioning look.

"I'll admit, Gaster, I expected books and books on this realm when CC told me to ask about your notes. I didn't expect only a single journal," I say as I flip through the pages.

I come across a particular spot where it's actually missing a page, and my finger runs down the jagged, ripped edges. Of course my curiosity burns to know what's missing, but as I read the page before it, it's mostly information on Elementra.

"I spent a good number of years in the Valorian Veil, but times were getting rough there before I left. It happened quickly, fiercely, so I only grabbed this one journal. It had the most valuable information in there and then I fled. The portal to the Veil closed first, and that's no surprise to me. Whether it was your ancestors or Elementra who closed that portal, I don't know, but they knew that realm was on its own verge of war, and we needed no part of it."

War. It seems to be a trend.

There was always a war in the nonmagical realm. There's a war in Elementra and apparently, the gods can't get along either. I wonder if the vampires, the giants, and the casters have figured out better ways to exist.

"May I borrow this?" I ask.

"I've already sent it to your journal. I just wanted to show you the original as well." He pats my hand and takes the journal from me.

"I've been meaning to ask you about that, Gaster..." I trail off at his knowing smile. He's been waiting for me to bring it up on my own.

"Your infinity journal. Yes, apparently, I've presented it to you twice now."

"You made it for my birthday and CC gave it to me as a present. I remember the day he asked for it back. I'd run to my tree crying because Franklin had destroyed my room. I'd stolen a book from his study with the intention of reading it then returning it. I'd done it many times and not gotten caught, but that time, I guess I stole a book I had no business reading. When I told CC, he said it was too dangerous for my journal to stay in my room anymore and that he'd bring it with him every day for me to write in. He'd never explain to me why, though. I even made the argument that Franklin couldn't read the words because he didn't have magic, but we know the truth now. How did you get possession of it again?"

"I'm not entirely sure, child. I found it in my cottage, and I could sense my magic intertwined with it. I couldn't bring myself to throw it away. Once you arrived, I thought to myself, how perfect. It's even her favorite color. Then I added my notes and research to it. When I first made it, it was under CC's directions," he says softly, with apologetic eyes.

"I hid it in his office while he was molding your necklace. I knew it'd be safe there."

My body shivers as CC's voice filters through my mind. This is the first time he's spoken since before I walked into my bedroom, despite my multiple attempts at asking questions and getting nothing in return.

"So this is how our communication will go? You randomly popping into my head." I try to keep my tone light, although I'm already getting emotional. I'm torn between being thrilled I hear him and upset that it's not consistent. I wish he could talk to me always.

"Yes and no. There needs to be a purpose, remember?"

"And there's a purpose now?"

"Yes. It's time for you to go into the amplifier room. No more dillydallying, missy."

My sudden chuckle causes a lone tear to fall down my cheek and I wipe it away quickly before looking up at Gaster. He can already tell there's something going on in my mind and he's patiently waiting for an answer. He smiles warmly at me as I tell him where CC hid the journal and he full-on laughs when I grumble about the dillydallying.

"There's obviously something you need to see. The Eye of the Veil is the actual name. CC renamed it to his own needs. Made it plain and simple," he scoffs and rolls his eyes before carrying on. "It's a tool used to amplify the gift of the sight."

"There are people in the Valorian Veil with the sight as well?"

"From my understanding, there's a person. They're spoken of as if they're a myth or a legend. Some refer to them as the Oracle, the Fates chosen, a god. Some even believe they are a Fate themselves. Their title varies depending on who you ask, but regardless, they're revered, and it's said they use the Eye of the Veil to magnify the messages they receive from the Fates."

"The Fates? I thought the realm was made mostly of gods?"

"That is true, but gods had to come from somewhere, child. The Fates is what I refer to their creator as because it's simpler. The history of the Valorian Veil is a long and detailed one."

"A long and detailed story we don't have time for," I grumble when he gives me a small smile.

"Another time. As for the Eye of the Veil, the individual who developed it used a glass dome that magnified the stars, brought them closer to the sight, if you will. They believe the stars conceal the gateway to those above even the gods. Those that blessed this individual with knowledge of the future. Much like I've seen in both CC and you, their ability was a struggle at first and did not come as easily to them as they would've hoped. So they created a tool to help them. When CC emerged with the sight, I created the amplifier room in hopes it would help him.

"Instead of the glass dome, obviously, I used gems from the realm known for their amplifying properties as well as ones that help you balance yourself, stay calm, and bring forth your intuitive nature. You noticed the reflective walls, yes?"

"Yes, but they have images on them or paintings, I guess. I'm not sure what's on their surfaces," I say, thinking back to when I looked in there. My mind was all over the place, but I know whatever I saw surely wasn't any place I've seen before.

"Ah, so something was trying to come through then." He nods, running his hand down his beard.

"What? No, a vision wasn't coming through. I just saw whatever the paintings on the walls were."

"There are no paintings, child. The room is enchanted to broadcast what's in your mind."

No way.

"Way, Willow. I got to the point in my life where my visions came daily and sometimes it was difficult to replay the paths. So Gaster and I came up with the broadcasting enchantment. It's a permanent fixture. When you're sitting in the center dais, the vision you have in your mind will play around you and you'll be able to watch it. Like a movie."

"Like a movie. Haven't heard that in a while," I whisper because I don't know what to say. That's advanced level innovation mixed in with some magic.

"So I go in there and what, a vision is just going to hit me?"

"Possibly. If there's something you need to see. It has great strength, so there's no telling the pull it will have. It's very possible the reason something happened when you looked in there on your tour was because your mind and mental shield was weak from the memories unlocking. Who knows what may happen now," Gaster says, but he has that same excited gleam in his eye that he always has when something is about to happen.

"I guess there's only one way to find out," I say with a huff as I push myself off the couch.

"That's the spirit, Willow." He cheers, giving himself away.

Making our way out of the lounge and down the hall to the stairs, there's an excited bounce to Gaster's steps as there's a nervous falter in mine. My visions are already intense when they come on their own. Purposefully amplifying them is frightening. I'm hopeful that I'll see something that helps us, but realistically, I'm mentally preparing for the worst.

"So will I have no choice once I'm in here? A vision's going to come no matter what, like they do already but more...?"

"It may, but that is not the only purpose of the amplifier room. Yes, what Gaster said is true, it does enhance the visions, but more so, it was most beneficial to me in learning to control the sight. By coming here more frequently, I eventually mastered calling on the gift on my own."

My feet trip over air as my lungs take a huge gulp. His words made my brain short-circuit and it takes effort to fully process what he just said. Thank goodness for Gaster's closeness because if not for his arm, I would've face-planted the floor.

"My goodness, child."

"I can stop the random-ass visions that just pop up on me and control when they come?" I ask CC rather than answer Gaster, but I do pat his hand to say I'm okay.

"Visions that have great importance, whether they're past, present, or future, will always come with no say so from you. But by learning to control the gift itself, you can learn to see more than what is being shown to you. You can learn to call upon the gift in times of indecision and guidance. Having more knowledge and the possible paths will always be better than being in a situation blind."

Of course I'd like to have full control over when I'm suddenly sucked into a vision, but I understand that in times like this, things are forever changing, and I'm being shown what needs to be shown at just the right time. So I take not being able to control that with a grain of salt and I fuel my motivation with the fact that I can learn to control the gift enough to give me the advantage of seeing more, on my time, and how I see fit.

"I can work with that. Being able to control it even a smidge is better than what it's doing for me now by only showing up randomly," I say.

He doesn't respond to me, but his agreement grips my mind like a hug. As we hit my hall, I hope the silence is him just biding his time until we got in here and I'm not about to receive the silent treatment again.

"Listen closely, child, because as you know, I can't go in there with you," Gaster says and I immediately halt our walking.

"I most certainly did not know that."

"Then you simply didn't think about it. Of course I can't join you to possibly see the future," he says with a smart-ass smirk and an arched brow that cause me to huff in frustration.

"That very reasonable thought didn't even occur to me," I say, running my hands down my face.

"I know, child, you have much on your mind, but it's going to be all right. I will be right out here if you need me, so listen to my instructions," he says, patting my arm encouragingly, and when I give him a clipped nod, he continues. "When you first get in there, I want you to make sure your mental shield is locked up tight. Don't allow the magic in the room to pull on your own until you've had time to familiarize yourself with the space. It's going to be dark once the door shuts but call forth your dragon to help with that.

"Only once you're comfortable with the space do I want you to sit or lie on the platform and completely clear your mind. Empty all your thoughts. Only then should you lower your block. It may be difficult this first time around, so don't feel obligated to watch the walls if a vision does come through. Just focus on the vision."

I blow out my breath, repeating his instructions out loud to make sure I understand them clearly. My way of stalling. They're straightforward and easy to follow, but now that we're standing outside the door to the amplifier room, I already feel its call. My magic is fidgeting in my chest, begging to be released, but my mind is at war with what I may see.

"Wish me luck," I mumble as I place my shaking hand on the knob.

"You don't need luck, Willow. Everything you're meant to see will come one way or another. Use this as an opportunity to take some control and see it first on your terms. You've got it," Gaster says encouragingly.

With the light shining through the door, the room looks just as it did the first time I saw it, with the exception of the images playing across the walls. The center platform has a light glow to it where it's surrounded by the large crystals and the floor is shimmering with the crystals that are embedded in its foundations.

I shut the door slowly, sending myself straight into darkness that only lasts a second, then it's as though I've stepped into a whole new world.

The light coming from the crystals intensifies and their glow reflects off every other one in the room. It's as if I'm standing in the middle of the night sky, walking amongst the stars. I'm careful with my steps even though I know the small shimmering dots are embedded in the floor. My mind tries its hardest to convince me I'll feel their sharp but smooth textures across my toes.

Now that there's no light shining in, the massive hip high crystals show off their distinct colors and I find myself mesmerized by their appearance. As much as I want to head straight for them, I force myself to follow Gaster's instructions and become familiarized with the rest of the room.

My hand glides gently across the reflective walls and I'm not surprised to find their surface as smooth as glass. I can only hope it's as strong as it seems.

The enchantment that fills the space between the platform and the walls pulses beneath my palms, and I grit my teeth to ignore the call because I'm finding that I badly want it to flow through me.

The room isn't that big, so after a quick exploration, I finally sate my need to observe the crystals that surround the platform. All five of them are incredibly impressive and of all the caves I've visited in my time on Elementra, I've never come across crystals like this.

My hand finds the crystal closest to me and its cool surface seeps into my bones, relaxing me as I allow its power to touch me slightly. Its blueish color is gorgeous and just the sight of it calms all my nerves. Makes my senses sharper.

"That's the Blue Calgate. Its purpose is to calm and alleviate stress and anxiety. It encourages unwavering focus," CC says softly as if speaking too loud will disrupt the atmosphere.

"That's exactly what it's doing now."

I move to the next and repeat my process. The difference between this one and the Blue Calgate is obviously its coloring but also the emotions I feel coming from it. I feel balanced and strong.

"The Mountain Malachite. It enhances one's natural strength. The outside of this crystal is practically indestructible, but if you were to break through the surface, you'd find the inside to be soft."

Hard on the outside, soft on the inside.

I hum softly, running my hands over the beautiful shades of green. The colors are stacked and layered as if it's built up its own defenses over time.

"This one?" I ask quietly as my hands cup the fiery red crystal. Its jagged edges are sharp, but there's something about it that calls to me regardless of its fearful appearance.

"The Revitalian. It revitalizes your energy, your creativity as well as promotes bold action and clearer thinking."

Yeah, I sense that. I'm fighting off the massive smile and the want to perch my ass on the platform and start seeing our future.

"The Shadow Light stone," he says as my hand grazes the next.

Something about this stone brings forth a multitude of emotions and I find myself fighting back tears and a laugh. It's a confusing concoction that eventually tapers off until I'm smiling at it softly with water welled in my eyes.

"The purpose of this stone is to bring forth both negative and positive reactions before showing clarity to the situation."

"Last but not least," I mumble.

The stunning purple crystal is larger than the rest and it sits at the head of the platform. Four spires breech from its connected foundation and its striking, formidable appearance makes my breathing quicken and my heart races. My trembling fingers reach out slowly, and the second my skin touches it, nothing else seems to matter. I'm wrapped in a cocoon.

"This looks like a cluster of amethyst from the nonmagical realm," I murmur.

"An amethyst, yes, but not from the nonmagical. This is an Angel Aura Amethyst. It's from the Valorian Veil and is the ultimate form of divine connection and protection. Elementra herself blessed it when it was brought to this realm."

I allow his words to seep into my very being as I take in all the crystals surrounding me. They each have incredible properties and purposes, yes, but I notice something far more distinct.

"CC, they each represent my Nexus. Each of these crystals matches the color of the bonds between me and the guys as well as their personalities. Why?"

"Because you all were made with the strongest of intentions. Each of you represents the strongest of the strong. Of mind, heart, body, and soul. I know it's a lot, the responsibility put on all of you, but you are worthy, and you are capable. It may not seem that way and I recognize the unfairness of it all, believe me. I felt it, your mother felt it, any before us who were chosen for this felt it. It took me centuries, until my eyes laid upon you the first time, to understand it, but you are a blessing. This is a blessing despite how it may seem. Elementra has given you, your Nexus, the power to make the realm what it should be. If you can achieve it, there will finally be harmony."

Tears flow down my face in silent streams as I continue to look around the crystals surrounding me. As hard as it is to admit, this journey has been a blessing to me. Yes, there have been some incredibly difficult obstacles and far too many near-death encounters, but without what I've been through, if I hadn't been chosen for this, I'd be living a miserable existence in the nonmagical realm. Or hell, I may have never been born.

I'd be nothing.

Here, I'm something.

That realization brings forth another that hits me like a ton of bricks.

Elementra may have orchestrated my entire existence, and CC dictated much of how the trajectory of my adolescence would go, but now, they've both left the decisions up to me. That's why everything's happened the way it has lately.

"You both are no longer going to be making the decisions for me. It's all on me from here on out. You're both leaving me. That's why it was time for my memories to unlock. Time for me to come here." Panic grips the tone of my voice even mentally.

Oh my God, that's why my visions were the way they were before we saved Keeper, why my gut instinct seemed to intensify, why the need to bond the guys became so strong. They're leaving me to finish this on my own.

"We will never leave you, filia mea. Do not think that way. But we can no longer help influence your decisions. There are still plenty of clues and information I've laid for you, but we've guided you in the preferred way as much as we can. We will still be here for you, don't believe otherwise. But we can no longer tell you the paths to take."

It's on my tongue to argue that they haven't told me anything straight out. That I've already had to figure it out on my own, but clarity sweeps through me. I peer down at where my hand is resting on the Shadow Light stone and blow out a harsh breath, then close my eyes.

They have been telling me, just not as clear as I would've liked, but I see it now. The phantom pushes, the pulls, the calm that overcomes me in times of indecision. They have been telling me.

"This is where your new journey begins, filia mea. It's time."

His words fade through my mind like smoke on the wind, and the loneliness that overwhelms me tells me he's gone for now. That was the guidance and purpose for his presence for the time being.

Now it's on me.

Wiping the tears from my eyes, I turn in place on the center of the platform, letting my hands glide across the crystals as I go. Their powers soak beneath my skin and I breathe deeply, absorbing everything they're willing to give me.

Slowly, I lower myself down and roll the material of the soft plush purple blanket between my fingers. A genuine smile crosses my face because even this small gesture shows the care and attention he put into making me as comfortable as possible when he dropped this news on me.

Let's see what's in store for us.

Focusing on the wall in front of me, I clear my mind. I empty out everything I just learned, all my thoughts on what's to come, and I just focus completely on the reflection of myself on the surface of the wall. I'd like to attempt to see the vision, if one comes, play out across the room. If I can't manage it this first time, I'll work on it.

As my body relaxes to the point I feel weightless and my mind quiets, I call forth my magic, commanding it free.

For a brief, blissful second, there's nothing.

Then...

There's everything.

Time is meaningless as passages of moments speed across my mind faster than my eyes can follow. There's no beginning. No end. Just blurs of things that've already seen the light of day, things that are happening as I sit here, and things to come.

The movement slows, stopping on a point in time that just recently occurred. A moment in time that means more to me than anything.

Our bonding.

I'm suspended in the air with gifts and elements shooting out of my very being, slamming into the chest of my men, connecting us as one. From this angle, seeing myself, I look like a beacon of pure power. When it happened, I felt its intensity, but this is something else.

It's the dawn of a new era we didn't even know we were entering.

Time moves again faster than I can grip onto the vision.

Then again. Then again.

Over and over, different paths shoot across my mind, and I can't make sense of any of it. I'm not seeing anything, yet I'm seeing everything. These are visions that will come through when I most need them.

For now, they're just a blip, a blur in time.

The blur finally forms a being like a pixelated picture coming into focus and I suck in a startled breath.

The Summum-Master dances around, shooting power out of his body with the ferocity of a volcanic eruption. Blood. Bodies. Destruction.

It's everywhere. Everything.

Just before the moment begins to move again, I swear he's staring into my soul, and I catch the briefest glimpse of eyes black as night. Before the image fades once more, I hear the quietest whisper.

Choice.

Wait, what choice?

I don't get that answer, and no more whispers are to be heard as an agonizing scream tears from my throat.

It feels as though my whole body is on fire. It's not my flame that flows through my veins, but I swear lava. My skin feels like it's melting from its unforgiving heat, and I continue to bellow as I throw myself on all fours.

Stop. Please fucking stop.

There's no stopping the burn. Everything around me is a blazing inferno.

With all the strength I possess, I throw myself off the platform, hitting the floor with a bone-jarring thud, but still, I'm on fire. Not just my body but my soul. It's submerged, burning to ash.

Forcing my limbs to obey me, I start to crawl to the door.

Break the connection. I have to break it.

Tears and snot fall down my face as I sob my way to where I remember the knob being. Every move I make is painful and the reflective walls are a river of orange coated in soot.

"Gaster..." I try to call out, but my broken whimper is barely audible even to my ears.

"Gaster, please..." I cry out mentally.

Just a few feet in front of me, the door slams open and light pours in, snapping my mind out of the chokehold it was in. I collapse on the ground, curling in on myself as my sobs tear through me.

"Willow."

No sooner my name leaves his lips than I'm lifted off the ground with strength I didn't even know he still possessed and moved into the brightly lit hallway.

"Calm down, child, everything's okay. You're okay," he murmurs and shushes over and over, but I can't stop the tremors and tears. "What happened?"

"I...I don't know. I've never physically felt anything from my visions. Until now," I stutter, trying to make sense of what just happened to me.

"Felt? You felt what you saw?" His body startles as he asks the question and it solidifies it even more for me that that wasn't normal.

"Yeah. Burning," I pant out.

"Burning, as in you were burning?"

"I don't know, Gaster...I don't know."

Although in my heart I feel the possibilities. Either that was my soul burning or the realm. The two would go hand in hand.

If a piece of my soul were to burn, I'd burn this realm to the ground.

Ten

Corentin

So many things to do. So little time.

The two weeks break I—if that's what I can call it for us—put the academy on for our mission is rapidly coming to an end and at this point, it seems like my days are blurring together.

Classes will resume in a few days' time, and the mound of things to work through on my desk is astronomical. The Summum-Master never retaliated on either the academy or Rebel Castle, so I feel confident allowing classes to start again. With extra security and protection in place, of course, but for now, Rebel Castle will remain vacant.

Running my hands down my face, I shake my head and dissect the heap of tasks that need to be taken care of by priority. It's honestly hard to focus on anything related to the academy when my true desire and focus is everything that revolves around Willow and hunting down the Mastery.

The academy will always be one of my biggest responsibilities, but it seems so minuscule in the grand scheme of everything else. Alas, the students have no part in this war, and they rely on a safe environment to learn and grow in. So that's what I'll provide for them.

"Why so stressed, brother?"

The years of practice of not being fazed by Caspian's sudden appearance instinctively kicks in and the flinch that surely would've come out of anyone else merely sends a twitch across my eye. He catches the movement, though, and smugly smiles as he rounds my new desk.

"Aren't you supposed to be doing research on Willow's bloodline, the portals, or anything else that could help with the thousands of things we have going on?" I ask as I lace my fingers in front of me and stare him down.

Arrogant little shit.

"That's what I've been doing for two days now. I wanted a break to go check on my little Primary, then come see you," he says as he plops down in the chair across from me, knowing good and well he's got my attention.

I asked my princess to join me both yesterday morning and today. Yesterday, she declined for some alone time, which turned into a rough day after she entered the amplifier room, and today she said she didn't want to distract any of us from what we have going on. Opting to spend time with my mom and practice more of mingling our power. I said that was fine, when really, it took everything in me not to drag her into this office, where she'd be by my side all day.

"And what was she up to?" I ask nonchalantly.

"Discussing dresses for the Spring Ball and our bonding ceremony." This time my flinch escapes.

"You're kidding?"

"Afraid not, brother. Looks like we'll be attending both."

"You don't seem nearly as upset about that as I figured you would be," I say, arching my brow.

"The ball will give me an opportunity to spy on all the families and figure out who the second family betraying us is. Whichever they are, they're doing a fucking remarkable job staying under the radar. None of Mom's little spies are picking shit up."

"You don't think we'll have it figured out sooner? There's still plenty of time before then."

"No, I don't think we will. We've uncovered too much to their liking as it is. They'll be more careful, more cautious of everything they do from here on out. Without the vampire to lay more runes and Franklin gone, we've hit them where it hurts. They won't make anything easy from this point on," he says confidently and I believe every word of it.

Caspian has an amazing ability to think much like the good and the bad guy. Placing himself in the villain's shoes is an easy feat for him. Pulling him out has been the struggle in the past, but I'm pretty sure those days are behind us now.

"And our bonding ceremony. How do you feel about that?"

"If it makes the little temptress happy, so be it. Plus, I enjoy stringing her up and ripping her nice clothes off her. You three lovesick fools will enjoy it as well," he says with a feral grin, and I snort at his bullshit.

"Three? You're forgetting one, Caspian," Tillman says as he suddenly walks through my door.

"Ah, Mr. I'm going to avoid my Primary until she forgets I've got trauma, what's brought you here?" Caspian asks sarcastically and I don't hide my snicker at Tillman's deadly glare.

Yeah, we've all noticed it.

His head whips to me and his eyes narrow, causing me to laugh harder. It's only a matter of time before my princess gets the truth out of him. Granted, Tillman really has handled his problems the best out of all of us, but regardless, Willow deserves the truth.

We've seen pretty much all of her, especially Caspian, and I'm sure there were things she would've rather preferred to never come to light, but they did. So the least all of us could do is share pieces of ourselves with her.

Even the dark parts.

His shoulders deflate and it's obvious he heard those thoughts. I wipe the smile from my face while preening in victory on the inside.

"Thought you were down at the palace compound?" I ask.

"I was. I'm getting ready to escort Draken and Keeper to the prison and let Keeper remove some runes. Those prisoners don't have shit we need, but according to Keeper, the more runes removed, the weaker the Summum-Master will get. Wanted to see if either of you cared to join?" he asks, crossing his arms all stoic and serious.

"I'm in," Caspian says, immediately hopping out of his chair.

"I've got to stay and take care of things. Let me know if anything of value does come up. Did you invite Willow to join?"

"I did. She's staying back. Coming to see you in a few, actually," he says with a twitch of his lip, no doubt sensing the instant spike in my pulse and the excited thoughts running through my mind.

Caspian was teasing earlier, calling us lovesick fools without referring to himself, but I don't have a leg to stand on if I attempted to deny that claim. Willow's got me wrapped around her finger. The guys know it, she knows, and I for damn sure know it.

"I'll see you all for dinner," I say, dismissing them condescendingly, mostly teasing, with a wave of my hand.

My office falls back into silence as their laughs follow them out my door and I lean myself back in my chair as I gaze around the space. It's perfect. Really, it is, and it provides me a kind of comfort I no longer feel in the office in my room back at the mansion. And a comfort I've never felt at the academy.

In here, I feel peaceful, more focused, and more motivated while working. Like every turn of a page or stroke of my pen is meaningful, calculated, and precise in a way that sets my anxiety at ease. My uncle did a phenomenal job setting up a space that is so entirely me but also encompasses a side of me that I didn't even realize I'd locked away.

My point's proven as I mindlessly fall into work and the time passes me by.

Quicker than I realize, I'm signing off on the last form that needed my attention from the academy. I gaze at the literal stack of things I needed to get done over the next few days and gawk in shock as if it's all completed.

Grabbing a handful of files, I start flipping back through them, glaring in astonishment as they all are complete in my usual perfection. Checking my timekeeper, I rapidly stand from my desk as I notice only two hours have passed by.

What the fuck?

Impossible.

"What's impossible, your highness?"

Whipping my head up, Willow's leaning against the doorframe with her arms and ankles crossed, smirking at me in my panic. Just the sight of her has my heart rate slowing and the tightness in my skin loosens from the pressure of my gift.

"Something weird just happened, princess," I tell her honestly. However I just got through that amount of work in that amount of time is impossible. Even with my keen focus, I never should've been able to finish it that fast.

Her face grows serious as she pushes from the entryway, shutting the door behind her with a blast of her air. In just a few strides, she's in front of me and I'm pulling her into my chest. I breathe deeply, inhaling her sugary scent until my lungs fill like they're on the verge of popping.

"What happened?" she asks, reaching up and cupping my cheek, looking at me with worry crossing every one of her features.

I run my thumb across her forehead, smoothing out the lines there that are forming because of me. I don't want her to worry, nor do I think this is necessarily a bad thing, just a strange one.

"I just finished all my paperwork and caught up for the academy."

"Oh...well, that's a good thing, right?" she asks, confused.

"It is, but the weird thing is, that was easily two days' worth of work, and I just finished it in two hours. I don't even recall going through all of it, but I did. I checked. It's all complete," I tell her, pointing to the now finished stack of papers.

"May I?" she asks, laying her hand to the pile, and I nod.

She rummages through them and the lines in her brow become deeper the farther down the stack she goes. It's quite a collection of work.

Request for class transfers, Geo's correspondences, approvals for increases in lesson plans for certain advanced classes, current performance metrics for the final year students. Plus, all things Headmaster upkeep.

It all needed to be addressed prior to the students returning, and I had planned it out where I'd bust out as much as I could over the next two days while spending time with my Nexus.

"So you recall sitting here working but not actually flying through all of this?" she asks as she places the last page of my stack back in its place.

"Exactly. I don't know where my mind went."

She hums to herself, staring at my desk as if it's the realm's greatest mystery, and I run my thumb across my bottom lip to hide my smirk. I track her fingers as they run mindlessly in circles on my desk and the concentration etched into her features is the cutest fucking sight. This woman makes me melt at the simplest things.

Lovesick.

Something catches her attention, though, as her fingers stop their movement and she gently peels up the corner of my desk mat. A sudden, almost crazed laugh bursts out of her and my eyes widen with worry that she's cracked like Caspian warned she might.

"Sneaky little shit," she mutters as she begins clearing off my desk.

"Princess, everything okay?" I ask as she shoves my papers into my arms.

"I've found the cause of your hyper focus."

"I don't think the new desk mat made me work harder, Willow," I say, placing the papers down, and grip her shoulders.

"Not the mat, what's under the mat. CC left you a little surprise," she says, flicking my hands off her and getting back to quickly clearing everything off my desk.

I don't question her frantic insistence anymore and allow her to continue stripping my desk bare until there's nothing left but the dark smooth wood and the navy rectangular leather mat that stretches across its surface.

"Would you like the honors? I'm fidgeting I'm so excited, so make your decision quickly." She cheers, tapping her nails on the desk.

"The honors of what?" I ask. Still confused and a tad bit more concerned with her behavior.

She huffs and rolls her eyes before pointing to the mat as if I should already know what she's so worked up about. "Remove the mat. You'll see. Come on, just trust me, please."

She shoves my chair out of the way, then grips onto my arm and pulls me until I'm standing center of my desk. The excitement that's thrumming through her bleeds into my chest and I look down at her with a million questions running through my mind, but I settle on believing if she's this excited and wonderstruck, there's something to be seen.

Probably faster and more anticlimactic than she would've made it, I snatch the mat off the desk.

The leather slips from my fingers and hits the ground with an audible slap as I stare with my mouth gaping open at the surface of my desk. It's not wood as I would've sworn, but glass. Underneath the thick clear layer are green, red, marbled, and purple stone shards laid out in the shape of the sun on a large slab of blue crystal.

Placing my palm in the center, a wave of calm focus spirals its way through me, and my mental to-do list begins to organize itself clearer than I've ever seen it before. It's as though all distractions have fled and left behind an unwavering mindset.

"I just learned about these," Willow whispers, trailing her fingers down my hand.

"What is this, princess?" I ask as I remove my hand from the glass and suck in a sharp breath as the power releases me.

She begins explaining her amplifier room in quiet detail as her fingernail traces the outline of the sun. Yesterday, she was shaken up by whatever she saw and didn't want to talk much about the room other than it's a room full of crystals. Now, I listen with keen fascination as she describes the rare, powerful stones that represent the many strengths we as individuals and a Nexus, have.

It's intriguing, to say the least.

My uncle thought things down to damn stones.

Crazy.

"They'll enhance your gifts more and more with time, from what I understand. You'll start being able to control this boost rather than it controlling you. Or at least I hope that's the case."

The slight waver in her voice that she tries to hide has my hand reaching out to pull her closer to me without any thought. Her sight has given us more advantages than we'd have any other way, but I hate it. I'm grateful for all the things my uncle gave her but not that.

"Gift, princess. I only have one." I chuckle as she rolls her eyes, then as I run my fingers down her spine, I say softly, "Plus, it didn't enhance my gift just now. It...I don't know. Enhanced me."

"Your hard work, dedication, focus, drive. They're all key parts of your personality. I believe they're gifts. In their own right. The crystals enhanced all your natural strengths."

The pride shining in her piercing silver eyes makes a hum vibrate in the back of my throat. Even if I couldn't feel the truth of her words in my chest, where our bond seems to sing, the devotion and surety skirting across her features would tell me everything I need to know.

My lip tilts up when her face darkens in a blush, and she turns from my hungry gaze. I don't bother to hide it from her. There's nothing quite as sexy as your woman looking at you like she has unwavering confidence in all you do.

"Corentin," she whispers as her body flinches.

The surprise in her tone instantly doses that rising desire. It's as if she's seen a ghost and I immediately tighten my arms around her.

"What's wrong?"

"Look," she says, pointing her finger down to the ground.

My gaze follows her direction, as does my body's reaction when I flinch as well.

Corentin.

The wind gets knocked out of me as I glare at my name written across a letter that's taped to the back of my leather mat. The two of us know exactly who it's from by the handwriting alone.

All I can do is stare at it for what feels like an eternity. I don't have the control not to read it like my brother, though. It's already a festering need to know what's inked across that parchment.

"I can give you a minute," Willow says softly as I bend down and pull the letter free.

"No. Stay," I command, lacing my fingers through hers and pulling her down into my lap as I sink into my chair.

I position her until she's laid back on my chest, where she can read the letter with me. There's nothing he could say that I wouldn't want her to know. She's aware of all my failures, plus the many embarrassing stories my mom has decided to share since we've been here.

Releasing a breath harsh enough to ruffle Willow's hair, I allow the laugh that leaves her to soak into my heart and calm its frantic rhythm. The weight of this thin parchment feels as though it's a thousand pounds, yet so fragile as I easily tear through its seal.

Now or never.

Nephew,

I'll admit completing your room was the most difficult. I asked myself countless times, "What do you do for someone who does it all for himself? Someone who dedicates so much of their life to the needs of others that they've neglected to allow themselves their own enjoyment." Then it dawned on me. This is just you, my boy. You find enjoyment and happiness in the prosperity of others. Despite the cost to yourself.

You've been the first of many things, Corentin. First born, first to wake in the morning, first to emerge, first to get their work done, first to have a plan, first to make a decision, youngest to become Headmaster.

You've also been last so many times.

Last to call it a day, last to relax, last to the dinner table, last to eat his food, last to finally lay his head down at night.

So many firsts. So many lasts. So many responsibilities.

I wanted nothing more than to alleviate some of those obligations for you, but in reality, I gave you more. It was a brutal pill for me to swallow because although I knew you could handle it, I didn't want you to have to. I didn't want any of you to face what I have, but unfortunately, you all will face more.

So my only solution to this was to give you the tools you needed to continue to be yourself but also find and embrace the side of you that will seem so foreign, it will feel wrong at times.

The purpose of each crystal you've now found embedded in your desk has been explained to you and I can confirm that you will gain control over their abilities with continued practice. Soon enough, you'll recall everything you fly through. There is no magic or enchantment making the work complete itself. It's all you and your know-how, just at an accelerated rate due to the untiring concentration.

This is my gift to you, nephew.

Time.

There's far too much for you to miss out on now. Grasp the moments given to you and never let them go.

I'm so proud of you, Corentin. What all you've done. Who you've become and who you will continue to grow to be.

Take care, my boy.

Uncle Orien xoxo.

My hands tremble as I read the letter repeatedly. He's given me something that here lately has felt so fleeting in my life. The race against an imaginary clock that never seems to stop ticking.

Willow feels it too, as have my brothers. We've all felt the pressure that we're now on a time crunch. We've made moves in the realm against our enemy that has upped the ante in this war. It's a silent companion every day as we slowly unravel the remaining mysteries. Despite the lack of retaliation, we know we set something in motion.

Leaning forward, I place the letter in my top drawer where I can easily pull it out and read it anytime I find myself lost to my work. It'll stay there as a reminder that I have people who care about me. The work can wait.

This is my gift to you, nephew.

Time.

"Tell me, princess, what would you like to do with the rest of your afternoon?" I ask quietly and lay a kiss on the side of her neck.

"You don't have other things to do?" she asks, craning around to look at me.

"I can take care of that later. For now, a large chunk of my day's opened up."

The breathtaking smile that takes over her face has my heart once again pounding wildly in my chest. Just like when I told her I'd ride with her in her dragon form, she's looking at me now as though I've handed her the realm's greatest gift.

Little does she know, being able to spend my day with her means more to me than anything.

"Have you worked on your newest ability boost any more?" she asks.

"I have," I say confidently, grinning at the gasp that leaves her when two more of me surround her.

I've managed to teach myself how to command my replicates to do more than mimic me. With enough concentration, I can make them pose differently, move independently, and hold a more solid form like she and Caspian have learned to do with their shadows.

I can't hold on to that long, but I have every intention of mastering it. Especially when I command one of them to tilt her chin up and a heady little whimper falls from her lips.

"That's quite the nifty gift," she says breathlessly, and my dick immediately responds to her husky tone.

"Why is that, princess? Is four men not enough for you?" I ask as I lay kisses across the erratic pulse in her neck.

"Four is plenty enough, but..."

Her shaky breath brings a sly smile to my lips, and I gently bite her shoulder before ordering, "Finish your sentence."

"There're multiples of you. It's intimidatingly sexy."

I hum approvingly as her legs part automatically for my hand as I trail my fingers on the inside of her thighs. I can feel the heat coming off her pussy and I know she's already soaking wet for me.

"What's so intimidating, princess?"

"They have a commanding presence just like you. I'm torn between being freaked out and so fucking turned on," she admits honestly.

"Let's see which it is," I say before growling low when my fingers caress her slick pussy. "Why are you wearing a dress with no underwear?"

"Wishful thinking." She moans as I start circling her clit.

"So you came in here with the intention of getting fucked, huh?"

"Yes."

Music to my ears.

Commanding my reflections to merge into one, I mentally picture myself undressing, and like my gift is actually mine to control, it follows the directions.

"Eyes open and spread your legs as far as you can baby. Let me see your pussy."

"But—"

My hand swats the inside of her thigh, silencing her argument, and she arches into me as her gasp echoes around the room.

"Good girl. Now watch me while I watch you," I whisper in her ear as her legs loop around mine and open completely.

Undoing my pants, letting my cock spring free, I command my reflection to slowly start undoing his belt. Realistically, I could just make all the clothes vanish, but by her squirming and the soft moans falling from her mouth, my princess is enjoying the show.

"Corentin," she groans when I fist myself.

Real me and reflection.

"Watch me. Watch how you make me, my gift, everything come undone for you." I groan when I line my dick up and her hot core tries its damnedest to suck me in.

She's so wet, she's dripping down my cock, making it easy for my fist to glide up and down. I circle her clit, in sync with my own movements, and when my reflection steps closer, she clenches around my tip so tightly I nearly sink myself inside of her.

"Can...can you hold this form?" she asks through her pants.

"We'll find out, princess." I release my dick and wrap my hand around her hair.

I know what she wants by the thrumming desire pulsing in my bond. If she wants to suck my dick and be fucked by me at the same time, who am I to stop her?

"Fuck." I hiss through my teeth. "Didn't expect that."

"What?"

"I feel it. I feel what you're doing to my reflection."

"Do...do you like it?"

Her nervous question makes my head fall back against my chair and a groan falls from my chest. Do I like it? What a question.

"I get to take your pussy and mouth at the same time, princess. It's the greatest fucking feeling in the realm."

When she hums in the back of her throat, I slam into her in one hard thrust. The double sensation is almost unbearable and my muscles tense. Everything she does to my reflection, I feel tenfold.

It's nearly impossible for me to hold my control over my reflection and myself, so eventually, my moves merge as one. Every brutal pump into her pussy is mimicked in her mouth. She moans and hums greedily, taking every inch of what I'm giving her.

"Come, princess. Choke my cock," I command.

Circling her clit faster, her movements grow desperate. Her pleasure rips through her so forcefully it pierces my spine, and I lose my hold on my reflection. As it fades to nothing, the sounds of her screams echo through my office and I grip her hips, slamming her down on me until I'm coming apart inside her.

She collapses back into my chest, and I run my hands up and down her sides as we both catch our breaths. I don't think I could even get up and walk right now if I wanted to. Never in my fucking life have I ever felt anything like that.

Two slow claps start from the corner of my office, and I meet my brothers' stares, chuckling at Willow's startled, "Shit."

Draken has a hungry grin across his face, while Caspian has his head cocked to the side, trying to figure out what he just watched. I'm not sure he even notices he's clapping with Draken. Tillman's arms are crossed, staring in fascination.

"I don't know if I'm fucking jealous or really impressed, boss man. And, little wanderer, you were phenomenal as always. I damn near came in my pants."

"Seriously, Draken," I grunt.

"Impressed, dragon, that's the answer. Don't be jealous that you can't duplicate yourself and fuck me," Willow says with a sassy tone that has us all groaning.

"Filthy mouth, little warrior," Tillman says as he comes over and gives her forehead a kiss.

"Some privacy maybe? I'm still inside of her, for fuck's sake," I mentally bark.

All it gets me is a round of laughs from my brothers and Caspian takes it upon himself to come over and lift Willow off my lap. She doesn't hesitate to cuddle into his chest, and he looks down at her, conflicted. I shake my head as I put myself away and internally laugh because I know what his ass is about to say.

"Naughty little Primary."

"I'm naughty for craving a member of my Nexus and I just happened to get two for the price of one?" She cocks her brow and I smirk smugly at their glares.

"Logically no, but because I'm apparently a jealous asshole, yes," he says seriously.

"Get over it, brother. There're things you can do with your shadows that we can't," I tell him as I join them in my sitting area.

"I don't need any extras to give my little wanderer everything she wants, plus some," Draken says with full conviction as he scoots closer to Willow and Caspian. "So while we were working hard, the two of you were getting freaky. Not cool. Not cool at all," he says as he attacks her neck with kisses.

"Corentin got plenty of work done today. He's actually ahead of schedule," Willow brags, preening with pride for me, and my chest swells.

As she jumps right into explaining what happened, I lean back in the lounge chair, lacing my hands behind my head and smirking at their gaping mouths.

Today was a win for me all the way around.

I'll take every win I can get.

Eleven

Willow

Ugh, the beauty of this field is breathtaking.

With Draken's warm chest against my back and the sun setting, the trees in the distance cast just the right amount of light to make the flowers look like they're dancing in waves of colors. It's a picture-perfect moment.

It's magical. Peaceful.

I wish I could just sit here forever in his embrace, but for the life of me, there's something I should be doing or there's something I'm supposed to remember right now, but I can't. My mind is nagging me to pay attention, but attention to what, I have no clue.

"Stop that. We have to focus." I giggle, shoving Draken away.

Why did my laugh sound so funny?

"What do we have to focus on? We're in a field of flowers, doing fuck all nothing." He lays me back and continues to attack my neck in kisses.

"Draken," I squeal. "We should be doing something, though."

He doesn't listen as his kisses start trailing their way down my chest and my body alights, pushing away the doubt in my mind. His hands glide softly up my thighs and I arch into him, begging him to go higher.

Wait, where's his warmth? His hands are cold.

His touch is always warm, fiery, and it always calls mine to the surface to join.

"Draken, wait. Something's not right."

He looks down at me and cocks his head to the side as if that sounds absolutely foreign to him. I mimic his stare, and we hold that position for a long moment until he starts talking, but I don't hear his words anymore. My eyes narrow as I force myself to concentrate and the dazed look in his eyes slowly pushes clarity to enter my senses.

This is a dream. I'm dreaming.

Damn. It seems so real.

"What are we doing here, Draken?" I ask quietly.

"We're relaxing, of course, little wanderer. We can do other stuff if you want," he says with a wiggle of his brows.

I snort a laugh because dream him seems so much like real him, and for the life of me, it takes all my mental strength to keep clarity of the situation. I'm aware now this isn't real, but shit, it doesn't feel that way, and part of me really wants to just give in and let the dream overtake me. One little slip into the fantasy and I'd drift right back into my blissful ignorance.

But I can't. I don't have lucid dreams for no reason.

"Focus on me for a moment, dragon," I purr softly.

"All I ever focus on is you." He smiles down at me, leaning in for another kiss that I allow.

Cupping both of his cheeks, I pull his face back to look at me. "Is there a reason we're here, dragon? You can tell me," I whisper softly against his lips.

Leaning in, his breath brushes across my ear, and I repress the shiver that wants to escape me.

Fuck, it's so real.

"We're not alone."

I attempt to pull him closer, ask what that means, but he slips through my fingers, literally. My dream Draken fades to nothing and I sit up straight, searching my surroundings.

What the hell is happening right now?

Standing, I turn in circles slowly. There's no sign of dream Draken anywhere. There's nothing actually but flowers and a tree line. I'm not alone, though. Now that it's been brought to my attention, I feel the eyes watching me.

"Show yourself. What do you want?" I yell out, continuing my turning.

The cracking of a branch has me whipping my body around to the noise and although heavy silence falls over the field, it's deafening as I face off with a man I've never met a day in my life.

His jet-black hair frames his face in tight curls and it seems darker than night laid against his pale skin. His eyes, although bright with touches of both blue and green, barely hold any life. I see a flickering of it in there somewhere, but it's far, far down in there. He stands statue-still, staring at me as I glare at him.

There's something oddly familiar about him despite me knowing I have no clue who this is. His clothes give me no clue as he's not dressed in an E.F. uniform, or robe, or anything that even resembles what we wear.

"Wait!" I shout as he turns around and takes off through the trees.

My feet move faster than my mind as I charge after him. Whatever his reasoning is for being here, I'm supposed to know. I need to talk to him. This is the strangest dream walking I've ever done, but every time it happens, we get one step closer to ending the Mastery. I can't let him get away without knowing what he needs me for.

"Please stop. I won't hurt you," I call out as loud as I can as the distance between us continues to get farther apart.

Fuck, he's fast for this to be a dream.

Suddenly, he slams to a stop and pivots on his heels until he's glaring at me with so much malice, I halt my pounding feet about twenty feet away from him. I sense the hatred rolling off him in waves and my body tenses under the pressure of it.

I don't know what I could've done to this man, but whatever he believes it is, it's strong. He truly loathes me.

"Won't hurt me." He laughs humorlessly, taking a step closer to me. "You've already done plenty of that."

"How? I don't even know you," I say softly, holding my hands out in front of me.

"No, not directly. But I know all about you, Willow. And I'll kill you for what you've done to my brother."

His brother?

"No, wait, please stop."

I charge forward, but I'm too late.

"Wait," I scream, sitting straight up in bed.

My limbs flail about around me as if I'm still trying to run, waking all my men up in the process. Tillman and Draken are up and out of bed in a millisecond with their elements and gifts at the ready. Corentin's body slams into mine until I'm pressed into the mattress and shadows that are thick enough to steal my sight drape over us.

"Where's the threat?" Tillman shouts at the same time Corentin asks, "Willow, what's going on?"

"Everything's okay. Everyone can stand down. It was a dream." I pant mentally.

The rush of the dream plus waking up and scaring the shit out of everyone has stolen all the air in my lungs. I can barely breathe under the weight of Corentin and the adrenaline, but my words seem to simmer everyone down. The dark cloud slowly recedes, returning my sight, and Corentin gracefully gets off me, pulling me into his lap.

"Some fucking dream, Primary," Caspian says, heaving from the side of the bed.

"I know. I'm sorry for scaring everyone. It was so weird. Weirdest dream walking I've ever done."

I don't feel any need to keep anything about the dream from them since I didn't learn anything of value and the more I talk, the more their confusion festers. Not that I expected them to figure anything out for me when I have no clue what was going on, but their uncertainty makes me feel worse.

"You haven't done anything to anyone's brother that we're aware of. I mean, maybe you offed a Mastery member who was in a Nexus during one of our many battles, but even then, why would you be sent to them to help them?" Draken asks.

"The people I can think of weren't real Nexuses, so I doubt they'd feel that strongly about harming her. It would just be their ridiculous loyalty to the Mastery, and they wouldn't want her help," Caspian bites out bitterly.

"Yeah, I don't know. I don't recall harming anyone's brother directly either, though. The last few fights, we've killed off most larger groups of Mastery members. It sounds pretty bad when I say it out loud, but we don't take many prisoners..."

"Oh my God."

"What?" Corentin, Caspian, and Draken ask at once.

"Oh, shit," Tillman mumbles and my eyes meet his. He just heard my thoughts, so he knows.

"Trex," I whisper.

"What about him?" Draken asks.

"That was his brother. That was Dec. The Dream Walker," I say with wide eyes as I look at each of them. "Holy shit, that wasn't my dream walking at all. That was my real dream, and he entered it."

They each begin talking and asking questions at once. The noise grows louder around the room to the point I slam my eyes shut and raise my hand, asking them to stop. All the while, their pissed off emotions trample across my chest. Needless to say, my men aren't too happy about another man entering my dreams, then threatening me on top of that.

"I'll kill him," Caspian says darkly.

"We'll kill him," Draken agrees, nodding along easily.

"No one is killing anyone. We need to talk to Trex. This makes so much more sense," I say, throwing the covers off me and attempting to get out of bed.

"Hold on a second, princess. We're not going anywhere right now. Everyone, calm down and get back in bed. We'll decide what we're doing in the morning," Corentin says, although I know that's bullshit. They're each bright-eyed and bushy-tailed.

No one's going back to sleep.

Nor do we have to. As if this was planned perfectly, Tillman's time-keeper begins blaring through the room and we each turn our heads to look at it.

"It's morning time, your highness. Time to get ready," I order as I hop out of the bed and sprint to the shower.

Their murmuring voices follow me under the spray of water, but no one tries to stop me or slow me down as I take the realm's quickest shower. They obviously got the memo because by the time I've stepped out of the bathroom, fully clothed, ready to go, my room is deserted.

Leaving my bedroom to go rush them along, it's like clockwork as they each step back out of their rooms when I turn the corner on their hall, and I let a saucy little smirk cross my face.

"You all should've just joined me. Sure, you have bathrooms, but what's the point of using them when mine is big enough for all of us?" My smirk blooms into a full smile as they each groan and wait for me to walk into their protective circle before carrying on down the hall.

"There's a reason we don't shower with you every morning, little warrior," Tillman says, peering over his shoulder.

"Oh yeah? What's the reason?"

"'Cause we'd run the water out, little wanderer," Draken says with his own sexy little smile.

"The water doesn't run out."

"Don't underestimate the time we could spend in there fucking you senseless, Primary. You wanted to get shit done this morning. You made that clear. That wouldn't be happening if we joined you," Caspian says behind me, sending a chill down my spine.

Elementra.

"You're probably right. Next time," I say, breathless.

They each chuckle at my flustered state and all it does is send more heat blazing through my core.

This damn bonding honeymoon period is making me a horny glutton for these men.

"We're having breakfast first, then we'll leave. Codi just messaged back and said Trex isn't doing well this morning, so he's slow moving. We'll give him some time to get up and going," Corentin says as he scowls down at his communicator.

Well, that's one way to dry up all dirty thoughts.

"We have to figure out a solution for him. He's going to die," I say quietly.

I really thought when we got to Keeper, we'd easily fix Trex's and Layton's problems. Start them fresh in their new lives.

I never even considered what Trex had said about the Summum-Master knowing if his rune came down, he'd kill his brothers. The sad reality is Trex isn't willing to risk that, but in turn, it's going to kill him slowly.

"After we eat, I'll go ask my—Keeper to join us. Maybe he has an idea or some advice on what we can do in the meantime." Draken offers, coughing to cover his slip-up.

I smile gratefully and don't say a thing about what he almost called Keeper. They've been spending more time together and time with Tanith. It's beginning to sway him even if he isn't ready to admit that. I try not to push, but I can see the bond building right in front of my eyes.

I scarf my breakfast down like a woman starved despite Corentin ordering me to slow down and declaring we aren't leaving right yet. He said that Lyker and Aria are meeting us at the healing wing as well, so now I'm really ready to go. Trex can take all the time he needs this morning and I won't rush him as I play catch-up with my brother and one of my best friends.

"Come on, little wanderer. The more you bounce your leg, the more anxious my dragon gets. Let's go find Keeper and let him know the plan. The guys will be ready to go by then." Draken grips my hand and pulls me out of my chair.

"Thank goodness. All that bouncing was giving me motion sickness," Caspian sasses behind a smart-ass smirk.

He's full of shit. He knows good and well, between his water element and shadows, both of which are fluid and forever moving, he doesn't get motion sickness.

Giving Tillman and Corentin a kiss before I walk out, I blow Caspian one with a little of my air behind it and laugh my way out of the breakfast room as he loses his spot in his book. His dark chuckle follows me out into the hall and my chest grows giddy with anticipation for his payback.

"You're hiding your nervousness and stress behind horniness." Draken tucks me under his arm and I startle.

Damn it, how has he been doing that lately?

He's like Caspian, calling me out on my shit.

"I am not." *I am.*

He snorts, shaking his head and looking at me like I'm the realm's worst liar. "Don't take me for a fool. You can't hide from me. I know our bonding has sparked this increased sex drive, but you're instigating it now."

"I'm not trying to." I sigh, glancing up at him with a tight smile. "I just feel all over the place. My heightened horniness is easier to focus on than anything else. Even if we don't act on it, it's the more pleasant of emotions I've been feeling lately," I tell him honestly.

"Well, be honest with me, little wanderer. I'll help you with whatever I can. What's got your mind the most out of sorts? Other than the obvious never-ending shit list."

"That's the answer, dragon. Our never-ending shit list that continues to grow. I don't know what the biggest problem to face first is, so I think about all of it, all the time. Plus, it doesn't help that whatever happened to me in the amplifier room has me on edge about everything. I'm waiting for the palace to be burnt down or something."

"Firstly, we both know we don't need to worry about anything being burnt down. Between the two of us, we could put out any fire. Second, decide what you think the biggest issue is and let's put our focus there. If there's anything we learned so far, little wanderer, it's one issue leads to another, then another and then we fix it all at once," he says confidently.

I want to argue that it's not that simple. Things don't just fall into place for us, but I bite my tongue when I think about that.

That's exactly what happens.

Not as simply or as smoothly. We always have to face some shit. Get put into dangerous situations. But one way or another, the answers to multiple problems surface at once.

"You're right," I say, squeezing his arm and smiling up at him before releasing a deep breath. *The biggest issue.* The problem that's been plaguing me for days. "My blood. The Summum-Master having a stash of it and the fact my blood opens the portal to the nonmagical realm. We need to do two things there. One, find out more about the capabilities my blood possesses and two, we need to locate where he has the stash. He can't continue to use it. There's no telling the issues he's causing elsewhere."

If this were the nonmagical realm, I'd be worried about him pinning murders and other heinous crimes on me with the way he carries a vial of my blood around his neck. It makes me sick to my stomach thinking about what past generations had to go through for him to collect a stockpile. Now he's using it however he sees fit like it's his right to.

"Okay then. We start there, little wanderer. The other stuff will fall into place and be taken care of as it needs to be taken care of."

A weight seems to lift off my shoulders with his nonchalance. Just that easy, he's put my racing mind at ease. Of course I won't just stop thinking about all the other issues we're facing. Like now, we're still going to check on Trex and tell him what's happened, but I don't feel like I'm suffocating anymore.

"I love how you do that," I say with a playful smile.

"Do what?" he asks.

"You always know when something's wrong and you do exactly what I need you to, to make it better, even without me saying anything. I'm incredibly grateful for that."

"That is the tie between beloveds, dear Adored. You probably do it to him as well and don't even realize it. Plus add in all your other connections the two of you share, I'm surprised either of you can get anything past the other," Keeper says, scaring the shit out of me as we round the corner in the gardens that connect the south wing and central.

"Where in the realm did you come from?" I ask, placing my hand over my racing heart.

Damn vampire stealth and hearing. I'm lucky to be alive.

"That is dramatic, Adored."

Tanith snorts in my mind.

"Is it, though?" I ask sarcastically.

"I was coming to see if the two of you wanted to join Tanith and me for her morning flight actually. She must've called to the two of you," Keeper says as he wraps me in a hug.

"We were coming to look for you. She didn't call for us. We're going to the healing wing and wanted to know if you'd join us. We could possibly use your help," Draken tells him, clapping him on the shoulder as he releases me.

"Of course. Help with what?"

As Draken starts explaining to Keeper my dream and Trex's condition this morning, I walk over to where Tanith is basking in the sun like a spoiled dragon princess.

"Good morning," I say, laying my forehead to her snout.

"Morning, Adored. You look tired."

"Thanks, Tanith. You're supposed to say I'm glowing, radiant, beautiful, you know?"

"Of course you're all those things, but you always are. Today, you look tired, so I informed you of such."

I smile, shaking my head at her. The more time I'm around her, it's obvious why she and Gaster get along so well. Take out their plethora of knowledge, I'm sure they'd still enjoy each other's sassy-ass company.

"Appreciate it. Your impressions are getting stronger. I'm almost confident you really can read minds but aren't telling us."

"Unlike you, that isn't an ability I'll ever have, but you're correct about the impressions. They are growing increasingly easier and more detailed. As yours should be. I believe my growth is because of the two of you, having my bonded back, and spending so much time in this land. The magic is so strong, I can see it."

I nod along with her. I've seen the magic before as well and it is pure, powerful, and I wouldn't be surprised in the slightest that she can see it. The impression thing, she hit the nail on the head.

After Draken filled me in on everything they discussed the day he learned he could feed us his magic, my dragon has been a lot more vocal, if you will. It feels even easier than before to determine her wants and needs. She seems to completely settle now, knowing I understand her better.

"The guys are ready. Do you want us to transport with them or fly?" Draken asks, slinging his arm over my shoulder before greeting Tanith.

"Let's fly. It isn't a long trip, and it'll give the guys time to get everyone together."

"Sounds good," he says with a huge smile and I know that's what he wanted but was giving me the choice. So I chose what would make him happy.

It's maybe seconds after that, the guys join us, giving me kisses bye before they transport out and we hit the skies.

Draken's playful maneuvering and twining of our tails always get me going. The guys all want to pick about how I'm wild up here in my flights, but it's most certainly Draken's fault. He instigates the playfulness.

As we level out after a few moments of crazy twists and turns, my heart warms as I catch a glimpse of Keeper looking at us with the softest smile. It's impossible for me to see him in the light I do the other vampires. All the horrors I know to be true, and the ones exaggerated by others, he just doesn't fit that description. But there's a nagging question that's been in the back of my mind.

"May I ask you a question, Tanith?"

"Oh my, this is going to be good," she says back, cutting me a look with her eyes.

"Very funny. The term beloved. Is it one used freely, like a sweet nickname in Essemist Keep?"

"You mean as your men all address you as things that are not your name?" she asks.

"Yeah. Like princess, little warrior, little wanderer. Caspian calls me Primary, which is technically what I am and his sweet name for me. I guess I'm a princess too, but they call that the Awaiting Matriarch here."

"I see. No, beloved is not tossed around like that. It is more as your Shadow Walker uses his words. Beloved is a sacred title. One only given to ones truly beloved."

I was afraid of that.

"How many beloveds can a person have? You know like I have four true Nexus members."

"One."

"At a time or?" I ask slowly.

"No, young one, in a lifetime. It's an undeniable connection that's not even broken with death. Why the sudden interest?"

"Just...curiosity."

"Oh, don't begin to lie to me now, Willow. We share freely," she says seriously.

"I know, but I don't think it's my place to share," I say sadly despite trying to hide the heartbreak in my tone.

It doesn't get past her.

"Ah, I see. You don't feel like it's not your place to tell your beloved the truth."

"So you know?"

"Of course. My lord has not spoken about it, nor has he grieved properly, but I know. Just as I felt Draken come into this realm, I felt her leave it."

"I think if Keeper told him, it would bridge the small gap remaining between them. Draken wants answers about his mom, but he's afraid to ask."

"And my lord is afraid to speak."

"So what? They're just going to ignore it indefinitely?" I ask incredulously.

"Probably. These are immortal men we're discussing, dear. They believe they have all the time in the realms to do as they please. Sometimes they need a push or a swift claw to the ass. Whichever you prefer."

"What I prefer? So you think I should tell him?"

"I do."

"Well, then why don't you tell Keeper to talk about it then?"

"Oh, absolutely not. It'll cause a fight and I'm liable to eat him. You can't eat your beloved."

"You can't eat your bonded," I argue.

"I most certainly can. I've tried a couple of times over the last few hundred years. He's rather fast."

Oh, what the hell?

"Listen, Adored, there are many responsibilities to being a beloved. Being bonded in any romantic capacity. One of those is being the bearer of news.

Whether bad or good, you are always honest no matter what. No matter how difficult. And in turn, you must also be the one to comfort and care for their feelings. I believe it will do more harm than good for Draken to hear this directly from my lord.

"He will blame him rather than understand the predicament he was in. Coming from you, he will receive both honesty and comfort. My lord will take my advice on pretty much anything, but broaching the subject of his passed beloved will not go over well for the two of us. He is still firmly in his angry stages of grieving. Despite not showing any of you that side. He had no outlet other than the forest that held him prisoner and essentially took the love of his life and child from him."

My heart splinters as I recall the look on his face as he told her she had to leave. He was determined he'd have her, hold her once again, and I can't imagine what he felt to know she was gone. That still leaves me with so many questions, though. I need those answers if I'm going to tell Draken this.

"The vampires told the Summum-Master—"

"Coming in for a landing, ladies. Don't squash the tiny humans," Draken says cheerily and I wrap a tight leash around my bond, squeezing in any hurt I may feel.

"By tiny humans, you mean our Nexus?" I ask, trying to push out a teasing tone.

"Exactly. They're so small from up here." He laughs and I let the sound fill my heart.

"We will continue our discussion, young one. Or you may leave it up to the boys to figure out the rest of the answers," she says, vaguely telling me she'll tell me all I want to know, but it's probably best to let them sort it out.

Shaking out my massive head when my claws touch dirt, I let my magic wash over me and take with it the worry of our conversation. As the bright light obscures my form, I tell myself repeatedly, one problem at a time. I'll tell him when the time's right.

For now, let's focus on the Dream Walker who has some serious misguided hatred for me.

"Did you have a good flight?" Tillman asks as he wraps me in his arms.

"I did. It was the perfect amount of time to let my dragon spread her wings and not throw a hissy fit."

"Too bad little flights don't soothe my dragon. She's still just as sassy," Keeper says and Tanith bumps him with her snout, causing all of us to laugh. My dragon chuffs in my chest as if she's offended, but it's the truth. She doesn't overrule or push as hard as Draken's or Tanith, for the matter, but she sure as shit will annoy the hell out of me until I give in.

"Is he ready for us or does he need another minute?" I ask and my question silences everyone, causing the hairs on my arms to stand.

"Prepare yourself, Will. He doesn't look good. He's worse than he was the other day. It's getting hard for him to keep food down and he's incredibly weak," Tillman says softly.

Turning to Keeper with pleading eyes, I ask, "Is there anything you can do for him?"

"He was adamant last time he wanted me nowhere near him. Understandably. But if he'll allow it, there's a way for me to help. The Soul Seer and I may be able to help him enough that he'll be almost...normal. It's completely up to him, though."

"Again, the name's Aria. I think he'll give in this time. It's not looking good, Willow," Aria says sadly as she joins the group, and I immediately pull her in for a hug.

"Fortune teller," Lyker says as I approach him next.

"Alphahole. Thank you both for coming," I say, muffled as he squashes my face into his chest.

"Of course. Aria was insistent that she needed to come save the mind reader. Plus, I brought you something," he says teasingly.

"You brought me something?" I ask excitedly as the guys begin herding us in the doors of the healing wing.

"Don't sound too happy about it. I don't even know what it is, but it looks important. I found it while I was rummaging through the house, trying to clean some stuff up." He chuckles, but my hands freeze as I reach for the book he so nonchalantly tries to pass me.

I can't even bring myself to grab it. My mom's magical signature pulses off of it and a lump forms in my throat as I look at the bright silver engraving on the black front cover.

"You're kinda freaking me out here, sis. Is it cursed? Should I not have touched it?" Lyker asks in a panic and my hand shoots out to clutch the book when he goes to drop it.

"Don't be ridiculous. It's not cursed. It...it was Mom's," I stutter.

Opening the first page, I startle at the first cream-colored page, and the next, then the next. I flip through the pages as my heart thunders wilder with every turn. I'm not sure what I was expecting, but it wasn't for the pages to be blank.

Confusion contorts my face until I run my finger down the seam in the middle of the book and the enchantment attached to the binding gives me a small shock.

"She's concealed the words inside," I mumble.

"Figured as much, but I couldn't get anything to reveal. I tried the reveal spell, untangling the enchantment, and my blood, but nothing worked." I glance up at him and realize everyone, including myself, has stopped walking and is staring at us.

Giving them a tight smile, I close the book back and trace the Nexus mark that's engraved on the cover counterclockwise just as she did to open the portal. A shaky breath falls from my lips as her magic calls to mine in my chest and the mark begins to glow. It's over just as fast as it started, and I don't have to open the book again to know the pages are still blank.

Clearing my throat, I give my brother a grateful smile as I open my pocket dimension. "Thank you for bringing this to me. I'll let you know as soon as I get it unconcealed."

"No worries, fortune teller. I have no doubt you'll figure it out," he says confidently, smiling and clapping me on the shoulder as we continue to walk down the hall once more.

"One thing after another, little wanderer."

My eyes cut to Draken, and I return the little smirk crossing his lips.

"One thing after another."

Finally reaching the room that Trex and Codi are waiting for us in, my feet try to trip me up on my first glance at him, but I force the smile to stay on my face. He looks like he's lost another ten pounds since I've seen him. His eyes are even more sunken in, now accompanied by large dark bags underneath them. His skin that was once just very pale is starting to turn gray.

"Don't start planning my remembrance of life yet. I'm still here," He snarks playfully, and it makes me want to sob. He looks seconds from dying.

"Stupid question, I know, but how are you feeling?" I ask as I lower myself in the seat in front of him.

Corentin's quick with serving me a cup of coffee and then surprises me by putting one in front of Trex. He squeezes his shoulder and gives him a firm nod, which Trex returns. Something about the exchange makes the water well faster in my eyes and I rapidly blink it away before they all notice.

I feel like I'm looking at a ghost already.

What the fuck are we going to do?

"As well as I can feel right now, I suppose. You didn't come to talk about me, though. What's going on, Willow?" he asks knowingly, getting straight to the point.

"I had a dream last night."

"Okay. About me? Was it a vision?" He cocks his brow.

"Yes, about you, but not exactly. Dec visited me," I tell him and watch the hope, surprise, and confusion cross his sickly face in a matter of seconds.

"Is he okay? What did he say? Do you know where he is?"

"He wouldn't really talk to me and what he did say wasn't pleasant. He hates me, Trex. I'm not sure what the Summum-Master has told him, but he believes I've done something to you, and he swore to kill me for it."

His mouth gapes open and he slumps back in his chair defeatedly. I feel like the realm's biggest asshole for bothering him with this while he's struggling, but if I'm going to get answers from anyone, it'll be him.

"There's no telling. During our annual meets, we aren't allowed to speak about what we've been doing. We're monitored the whole time, but

I wouldn't be surprised if the Summum-Master has made it seem like you kidnapped me against my will or something along those lines. So Dec and X probably do look at you like you've signed my death warrant." He gives me a teasing smirk that I know means you kinda did do that, and I can't help but snort.

"Where were your annual meets?" Caspian asks from the corner of the room.

"I have no clue. We were blindfolded and bounced through transports until we finally ended up together. It was never the same spots."

Disappointing but not surprising. Those locations would be a good starting point for us, even if they weren't promising.

"With his lingering threat, do you think he'll visit me again? Is there something I can tell him to convince him that you're okay and we're looking for them? I need something to make him believe me, then maybe he can tell me where they are."

He stares off into space, drifting into his memory as he thinks about his brothers. The room is silent as we patiently wait for him and I really want to pry into his mind to see what's going on. Obviously, I won't. I don't think his brain can take much more.

A slow smile continues to grow across his face until finally a bolstering laugh bellows out of him, startling me out of my staring.

"Tell him he knows good and damn well that last blackened berry pie was mine."

"Come again?" I ask, dumbfounded.

"It's been a running joke since we were thirteen. Xander's mom always cooked us mini pies on our birthdays. A mountain of them. I mean, the things were no bigger than a child's palm, so we would devour them. For my birthday, I asked for blackened berry pies, and I saved the last one for a midnight snack. His ass ate it but has sworn for years he didn't. I know he did. I reminded him of that every single year until, well...you know."

Despite the sad ending that I know came, I smile at such a fond memory. This is exactly something I'd need to know to prove to Dec that Trex told me. It's sweet, personal, and a joke the two, technically, three of them have shared. I'm glad they have moments like this to hold onto.

"Any other advice you can give me? I'll try to work with my gift on finding him, but is there a way I can try to, I don't know, summon him to my dreams?"

"Yes and no, I believe. Dec used to always say he knew when we were trying to contact him, but I don't know if that's true because I never recalled purposely doing that as a kid. Since we've been separated, I haven't dared try, nor do I think the rune would allow us to. There's possibly a way for you to think of him intently while you're dreaming, but I'd imagine it would take you being willing to let your mental guard down. It had to be down pretty good anyway for him to get through your defenses this time."

My face flushes and I ignore its growing heat. Yeah, I can confidently say they were down because dream Draken had me thoroughly distracted.

"I'll give that a try. Now I need a favor from you."

"And that is?" he asks suspiciously.

"Let Keeper and Aria help you. If they have a way to help you with the rune without removing it, allow them to. You can't die, Trex. Not when we're so close to...ending this."

My voice breaks and I don't bother attempting to hide it. We're close, even if it doesn't feel that way. Everyone I've come across so far in this crazy, hard journey has a purpose, a role to play, even if I don't know what it is yet. I can't allow him to die before he serves his.

"I'm not willing to do anything that puts them at risk," he says firmly.

"This will put your brothers at no risk. The rune will remain but be weaker." Keeper's accent flutters through the room and Trex instantly tenses.

"I didn't agree to seeing him," Trex says, narrowing his eyes on me.

"I know and I'm sorry. I didn't push it last time we were here, and I wouldn't push it this time, but this is serious, Trex. You're almost unrecognizable. I don't mean to be rude or blunt, but you don't have much time. I know it, you know it. If you hope for any chance of seeing your brothers again, we have to do something." I see the argument forming on his tongue and my anger rises quickly. I don't mean for it to, but he can't be so damn hypocritical of Keeper. "He was put in an unwinnable circumstance just as you and you both have done what you had to survive. Let go of your disdain for him. At least long enough to let him help you," I bark harshly before blowing out a deep breath and softening my final word, "Please."

His eyes bounce between Keeper and me repeatedly, then they turn to Codi, who's been quietly supportive throughout this whole conversation. His face now, though, is one full of pissed off determination and as bad as it sounds, hope rises within me.

"Willow's right. I'm sure both of you have regret for what you've been forced to do, but you have no reason to punish him or be a dick when you were in the same situation. If you need someone to blame, fine, blame someone, but the right someone. The vampire isn't the one. If you decide to not let him help when he can without jeopardizing our brothers, then you're just being a selfish prick. Don't do that to me, to us."

My eyes nearly bug out of my head at Codi's tone. I've never heard him angry and he sure as shit isn't softening his words for his brother right now. Trex doesn't seem to take any offense whatsoever. He just sighs and rolls his eyes.

"Fine. What do you have to do?"

Well, shit, should've just had Codi talk to him to begin with.

"I will need to mark your rune. It will weaken its power over your mind but only from your perspective. The Summum-Master won't be able to tell the difference. Then the Soul—I mean Aria—can place her rune back on your mind and it will further separate the connection," Keeper tells him, also not sounding the least bit offended over being the main topic of conversation.

"That sounds simple enough," Codi says, nodding like he's the one who gets the final say.

"Too simple. What's the catch?" Trex asks.

"No catch. You just probably won't like the method of marking the rune," Keeper says, shrugging.

"Elaborate." Trex hisses.

"I am the middle between the rune and the Summum-Master. I must mark your rune with my blood. As in, I'll be smearing my vile, vampire, bright blue, royal blood all throughout your mark," Keeper says with a mocking, unhinged smile as Trex cringes.

Indecision wars within his eyes, and just before Codi gets ready to go in on his ass again, Trex holds his hand up to him and mutters, "Fine."

"Excellent." Keeper claps.

In a blink of an eye, with no warning to any of us, he's around the table, holding Trex's head between his hands. Draken quickly steps around as well, I'm assuming to lend some magic if needed.

"No squirming, boy. This will only tingle. Maybe burn a little." Keeper laughs as Trex's eyes grow wide and I pinch the bridge of my nose and sigh.

Should've known that Keeper's calm indifference was just his way of mentally torturing Trex while he helped him. Draken most certainly inherited that sly psycho shit from him.

The rest of us fall silent as Keeper's eyes begin to bleed red and glow brighter as he speaks in his native language. The sound is smooth like velvet and tranquil. As Trex's body fully relaxes, basically slumps in his seat, Keeper presses his index finger to his fang, slicing it open.

I stare in unwavering fascination as he traces Trex's M on his forehead backward, just as he did to Layton but with the dagger. The red outline of the scar turns blue as Keeper's blood sits on the surface, boiling. Slight hisses fall from Trex's lips, but other than that, he doesn't budge or flinch. I don't know if it's the words Keeper spoke softly or his stubborn pride that keeps him from showing any signs of discomfort, but he stays statue-still.

Like water running down a drain, Keeper's blood sinks beneath the M and glows brightly before fading to nothing.

"Aria now, if you will please," Keeper says quietly.

She presses her fingers to Trex's temples and her eyes shift into their white cloudy voids. Unlike Keeper, she doesn't have to speak and her gift caresses my skin as it flows from her to him.

There's a palpable release of tension in the room when they both step away from him. His chest expands, and the sharp inhale echoes around the room. Codi's quick to pass him a healing vial, and without ever opening his eyes, Trex tilts it back in one shot.

I swear I want to yell at him, tell him to open his eyes, say something, but instead, I knot my sweaty, twitching fingers together. I wait patiently with quickened breaths as his gray skin begins to pinken and the sunken dunes beneath his eyes fill out. My gaze traces the aura starting to create a silhouette around him and I slowly smile as the yellow surrounds him like the sun.

"Trex, you all right?" Codi asks.

Finally, his lids flash open, revealing brown eyes that are brighter, livelier than they've ever been. At least compared to how I've ever seen them.

"Never been better, brother," Trex says, then turns his gaze back to me.

My heart pounds in my chest as his eyes flare, his mind taking back at least a little bit of control over itself. I know what he's about to do, and as I open my mouth to tell him no, don't risk it, but he shakes his head at me.

"The nonmagical realm's portal is the weakest of the six due to its lack of magic. It's grown weaker with the vampires taking over the forest and Elementra's power bleeding in there minimally. That's why the Summum-Master's able to pass through it with only a drop of your blood. From the nonmagical realm, he can pass through the other portals with your blood. It takes time, though. And yes, there are portals in all the other realms that reach each other. Your family only blocked out Elementra. A fatal flaw in their plan was not closing *all* access points until he was dealt with.

"Your blood, your family's blood can open portals anywhere. You aren't restricted to physical barriers like we are. The Summum-Master can do so as well but with a great loss of the stockpile he has of your blood, so he only does that sparingly. Only once in his lifetime if I can recall.

"You need to destroy that stockpile. It's going to be hard. Not because it's heavily guarded by members of the Mastery but because he has it protected by many powerful relics, runes, artifacts, things our eyes have never seen, from all the realms. Those will be your obstacles."

"I...we don't know where to even look," I whisper, completely enthralled by his almost otherworldly voice as he just spewed all that information out rapidly.

His own gift is flaring to life, blocking out any resistance or pain he may be feelings telling me this. He doesn't have long to take advantage of this momentary block, it's evident in the trembling of his limbs.

"You're not going to be able to look. You must track. Don't take that lightly, naively believing it'll be easy because you're bonded to the realm's strongest tracker. When I say it's guarded by things we aren't even aware of, I mean it."

"How do you know this?"

"I've listened, spied, been completely compliant for years around him and Franklin. People tend to become loose-lipped when they think of you as nothing more than a slave. Donald likes to brag about all the secrets he's privy to as well. They never thought in a million years I'd say anything that would jeopardize the well-being of my brothers and I'm notorious for acting like I don't give a shit."

By the time he finishes his sentence, his voice is back to normal and the bright, melted chocolate shine in his eyes fades back to normal. He sways just a smidge and gratefully accepts the second healing vial Codi hands him.

"Thank you, Trex," I mumble.

"Don't thank me, Willow. It's the least I can do."

Turning my head to the side, my men stand strong as if none of this is a surprise to them, but I feel the shock, excitement, and unwavering devotion to me filter into my heart from each of them. My gaze lingers on my dragon as he gives me a small smile and runs his thumb across his lips.

"One issue leads to another, then another and then we fix it all at once, little wanderer."

Seems that way, dragon. It seems that way.

Twelve

Tillman

"You were perfect this morning, little warrior," I whisper low to Will as I wrap her in my arms when we leave Aunt Rory and our uncles' gym.

The feeling of her earth element still flowing through my blood makes me feel invincible. The power packed into her tiny little body is fucking insane and I swear everything within me swells with pride.

I chuckle at the blush crawling across her cheeks as she peers up at me through her lashes. She's a bashful thing when she wants to be, and I'll forever eat this shit up. Between my praises and dirty words, I could have her colored pink all day every day.

"You weren't too bad yourself," she purrs as her eyes travel the length of my body.

"Don't go there, little warrior. I have work to do," I groan low in my mind.

"Fine, but remember you started it."

Her laugh fills my heart, and I lean down to cut the sound off with my mouth. I'd much rather just carry her back to our wing and spend the day with her in one of our rooms, but Uncle Roye's already waiting for me at the end of the hall.

"You think the two of you fortified the gym enough we won't break it anymore?" Draken asks when I back her into his waiting arms.

"No doubt. We used pretty much the full force of our elements together just then. I don't think anyone, except maybe our Nexus, will be able to break it. Even then it'll have to be intentional," I tell him as I smirk down at her warmly.

"Don't put any ideas in the little Primary's head. She's already gung-ho on mastering this in a week," Caspian says sarcastically as he and Corentin move in to surround her.

"I'm right here, you know," she says, rolling her eyes.

"I can clearly see when there's a goddess in front of me," he says low, causing those sassy-ass eyes to dilate.

"Enough, all of you. We've all got things to do. I'll see you soon, princess," Corentin says before getting himself a quick kiss, followed by Cas.

"You all are mine later," she purrs, pulling groans from each of our chests.

Corentin transports to his office and Cas takes to the shadows as Draken slings his arm over her shoulder and strolls her down the hall away from me. The two of their laughs carry back my way and I can't help but watch her as she goes. The way that woman enthralls me is crazy.

"Fix yourself before you go out there showing everyone what's mine," she says slyly, shooting me a wink before turning the corner to leave.

Fuck. Me.

I let my head fall back, groaning, but I do what she says. She'd kick my fucking ass if I walked out there sporting a hard-on. Even if she is the reason it's there.

It's ridiculous how she makes us all act like teenage boys.

Although it takes considerable effort to push the thought of my foul-minded little warrior out of my head, I have everything under control by the time I make it down the hall and out the door that leads to the training fields.

There's a small army of E.F. members mulling around, waiting for orders, and I make my face stern before they can see anything other than their steadfast leader.

"Formation," Uncle Roye and I bellow at the same time.

The double command has the young E.F. members scattering like mice to get in their assigned positions and the more well-seasoned ones do exactly as they should. Uncle Roye chuckles and I see his smirk out the side of my eye, but I keep my gaze focused straight. If these recruits see my more relaxed side this early on, they'll think they can joke and fuck around with me as well.

Not happening.

"Three laps. Go," I command, sending them on their way.

"You're so much like her, it's scary sometimes." Uncle Roye again laughs. At least this time he waits until they're all out of earshot.

"Well, she was the best of the best, so I got it honest," I say before turning and walking toward the next group of soldiers.

"That she was," he agrees quietly with a small sigh.

I don't bother saying anything else. Not willing to open that can of worms out in the open for any of our men or the few women out here to hear.

It's no secret that I'm a legend amongst the E.F. members. Besides the fact that I'm the youngest to ever hold the role of E.F. Leader, my mom made quite the name for herself, and I've followed those footsteps closely.

This is the longest stretch of time we've stayed at the palace since we started at the academy all those years ago, and apparently, it has everyone feeling nostalgic. I've heard my mom's name plus the nickname she gave me more times in the few days we've been here than I have in the last decade. It has not only me on the edge, but Will's picked up on it quickly and she wants answers. Answers I don't know how to give her.

Every morning during our Nexus training with my aunt and uncles, something is said that has Will's eyes cutting to my pinkening cheeks. Every comparison, every compliment, is coated in a small comment about how they'd be so proud or something along those lines.

It's not that I'm trying to hide anything from her. It's just simply a subject I don't talk about. I've accepted what I've had to accept and that was that. I grieved and overcame it.

Or at least that's what I thought.

Every morning after training, when I come out here with Uncle Roye, I see the envious looks the recruits shoot my way. I hear their thoughts about the stories they heard of my mom and her Nexus. They make remarks about how cool it must have been to have a mom and dads who were badass, revered, and to be feared when their teams arrived at missions. How everyone knew shit was about to get real when they arrived.

It's the truth. That's exactly how it was for them, how it's becoming for my Nexus now, and I can't help the sadness that rises in me, wishing they were here to witness it.

What would they have taught us?

Would they have been proud of me for winning the E.F. Leader trials so early or would they have told me to wait?

Would Mom want to take over this crazy-ass war we're in or would she let me lead like Uncle Roye's been doing?

Their whispers make me ask myself questions I haven't considered in a long time, and I just fucking wish my mind would block it all out. Ignore it. I want to just continue to accept what I can't change, believe that they would've been proud of me and my Nexus without any of the other feelings surfacing with those thoughts.

"Got your eye on any of the recruits to take back with you?" Uncle Roye asks, snapping me out of my mind.

"Not sure yet. Are they all as needy as that other little shit you recommended?" I ask, cocking my brow.

Based on his recommendation, I placed a fairly new but hungry E.F. member at the south wing gates to see how he does. He went to a third-year academy in Aeradora, graduated early, then transferred here to the palace, but he's Nexus-less still.

He wants to transfer to the academy, hoping to find his brothers, and I've already approved for him to accompany us to see for himself, but damn, he's got to learn some independence before I agree to let him transfer there full time. He calls me damn near every few hours. For absolutely nothing. I don't need to give him permission to piss.

Uncle Roye swears the kid's worth the headache, but I've yet to see it.

He's not really a kid. Damn, he's freshly twenty-nine, older than Draken, but fuck if he doesn't act as immature as a teenager.

"Rich is only needy because he wants your attention. His water element damn near competes with Cas's. Well, would have prior to him bonding, but still. He just needs some guidance and his brothers." Uncle Roye defends, although he's smirking. He knows the kid is needy.

"We'll see. As for the others, regardless of whether I truly think they're capable or not, they'll have to get their shit together at the academy. The missions aren't for the weak. Especially if we're getting ready to face shit from other realms."

"Uh. Thought about how you're going to approach that? You know I'll help however I can, but even we haven't had to face relics not of Elementra," he says, finally gaining a sense of seriousness.

"Gaster and Cas are working overtime to comb through information on any relics they can come across. That's step one. We have to get a sense of the threat and how to destroy them. Not knowing what all Willow's blood is capable of is a huge unknown, but we do know that we have to get rid of that supply. Cutting off the Summum-Master's ability to continue moving through realms is the main priority."

"So you all believe the mind reader?" he asks.

There's no accusation in his tone, but I'm not surprised with us being betrayed at every turn that he's hesitant to believe someone who's still technically under the Mastery's control.

"Yeah, we do. There's no reason not to. His intentions may still lean on the selfish side, but all of ours would be if our brothers' lives were at stake. More than that, though, he, just like Keeper, wants the revenge owed to him. He wouldn't lie to Willow. He needs her to find his brothers. That's his sole motivation."

"Then we'll start implementing harder trainings just in case you need the recruits. I'll get Theo out here and start working with the groups on deflections. I'm sure his forcefields will be different than whatever the relics do, but they'll have a sense of defending themselves against a power that can shove your ass across hundreds of yards."

"Yeah, there's no fucking telling. I can tell you, though, I won't be taking any of the completed Nexuses to the academy or Mastery missions," I say as I watch one of the few Primaries out here in the training field flip a man twice her size over her back.

I hide my smirk behind my hand so none of them see me laughing at him, but I make sure to watch this moment keenly so I can show Willow later. She'll eat this shit up.

"Why not? The one you're staring at right now is one of the fiercest members we've got. She kicks ass and takes names."

"I don't doubt that one bit, but you now know what the Mastery is doing. Primaries, females in general, are targeted so they can decide who they want paired and which men get power boosts. They don't give a fuck they're fully bonded. They can mark them and force them into a life of misery. We can't risk having completed Nexuses ripped apart. It's senseless and would kill her. What would her skills mean then?" I ask.

It's sickening and it makes my stomach revolt. The thought that Willow came so close to experiencing that herself makes me see red.

No. Fuck no. We won't be risking anyone like that.

If I could, I'd wrap Will up in soft moss and lock her away. Obviously, I know that's a reality that'll never happen, but I can dream.

"We're gonna end them, Tillme. I swear."

"I know, Uncle Roye. I know." I sigh, clapping him back on the shoulder as we focus back on the sparing and drills being run.

He's done phenomenal with every member here truly. I just don't say it out loud for the recruits to hear. They'll get that, minimally, from me if they return to the academy with us.

That's everyone's goal, well, for any who want to see the fight up close. Most members who are stationed here at the palace are responsible for territory patrols and smaller scale missions. Those who come to the academy know what's in store for them.

While walking through the large compound observing the E.F. members, I keep both my eyes and my ears open, but my mind wanders to everything else.

I've been running through the possibilities of what Trex said to Willow nonstop. I fucking hate the idea of her attempting to coax Dec into her dreams, but at the same time, it seems that's going to be the fastest way to find them. Once we find them, I have a feeling we'll find out a shit ton more. Simply because we can remove all their runes.

The three of them have been Mastery pawns for over ten years now. The information they may hold could be invaluable. The fact that Trex was able to give us what he could on her blood while still having the rune in place just tells me they know shit we need to know. Even if it's something as simple as the Summum-Master's fucking eating habits, it'll be more on him than we currently have.

Not only that but also their gifts will be useful to us in this battle. Fucking top notch mind manipulating gifts. I won't force them to fight, but Codi certainly will, so there's that.

Draken and I made a quick stop by Layton's when we left Trex, and the kid looked brand-new. He's completely different than the scared little chameleon we first found. I didn't want to pry too far into his mind, fearful that I could harm something that was just fixed, but I did peek.

There isn't much left in there that we don't already know now, but the one thing that stuck out is that the Summum-Master does have monthly meetings with the two families that are on the council. It seems they plan their meetings after they've met with the royal family and it's never the same time, place, or location. That would be far too easy, and the Summum-Master is far too smart to do some stupid shit like that.

Despite all of us already assuming some sort of correspondence was taking place between them, it's helpful to know it's a definite occurrence. We immediately informed Aunt Rory and our uncles since they have people watching all the families, but still, none of them are acting any sort of way. Even the Everglows who we know for sure are traitors haven't done anything to draw attention to themselves or the Mastery.

So as of now, we're at a dead end on family two.

The buzzing of my communicator pulls me out of my thoughts, and I forget myself for a second as I let a long, drawn-out groan escape me that has the group in front of me straightening their shoulders.

This kid, man.

Again.

"Yeah, Rich," I grunt.

"Sir. There's an individual outside the gates attempting to get in. He claims he's your second-in-command's brother, but your second isn't with him."

"I am his brother, you fucking newb. Tillman, get out here now before I kill this fucking kid."

The sound of Nikoli screaming has me moving through a transport without even ending the call. Never have I heard him bellow in rage like that and my stomach bottoms out. I've heard that tone before, though. Plenty of other times in my line of work.

Something's happened to his brothers.

My best friend.

My steps stagger as I appear in just enough time to watch Rich wrap Nikoli up in a globe full of water. My eyes do widen at the punch of power behind it, but his biggest mistake wasn't unleashing that power and holding onto it.

Within a second, Nikoli's bursting through the encasing with his own water element and lays the kid out with a single punch. His body thuds to the ground beside another motionless form.

Jamie.

"Get me a fucking healer here, now," I bellow out to the E.F. members charging this way, causing them to halt their run before nodding at me. "Nikoli, what the hell is going on?" I yell as I latch onto his heaving shoulders just as he goes to continue beating into the unconscious guard.

"Tillman, they're gone. They're fucking gone," he shouts, shoving away from me, snatching at his roots as his anger completely takes over.

Drawing my gift to the surface, I shove it out full force.

"Calm down and talk to me," I command.

Slowly, impressively so, Nikoli's fight gives out and he drops down to his knees beside Jamie. He lays his hand to his neck, checking for a pulse before his rage-filled eyes snap up to meet mine.

"They were drugged and taken. I didn't detect it in my drink before it was too late. By the time my gift burned through, they'd already taken Oakly, San, and Ry, plus Oakly's parents. I was barely able to grab Jamie and transport here. They're alive. For now..." he says before another hair-raising scream of rage passes through his throat.

All the blood in my body rushes to my ears and I barely hear the pounding footsteps of my men running toward us. My vision blurs to the point I can't make out the healer kneeling beside Jamie, and I have to force stone around my boots to stop my swaying.

When an E.F. member attempts to pull Nikoli off the ground away from Jamie, another fight breaks out, spurring my mind back into reality.

"Get the fuck off him. The next one of you to attempt to keep my second from his Nexus member will be answering to me directly," I say deadly low, but they all hear it, and their fearful gazes snap up to mine as they slowly back away from Nikoli.

Deep breath. Deep fucking breath.

Leader Tillman is needed.

Focus, Tillman.

"Tillme, focus. Your emotions are everywhere."

"Where else should they be, Mom? They've got him. They got Cas," I scream, pulling at the roots of my hair as the ground trembles beneath me.

"And we are going to find him, son, I swear. But first you must calm down. Center yourself. Focus on the earth beneath your feet. Pull on its strength. Clear your mind. Deep breath for me now."

Deep breath. Deep breath. Center yourself.

"There you go. You got it. Now focus on the minds around you. Hear what you can. Make sure none of the guards were aware of this."

"I can do that."

"I know you can, Tillme. We're going to find him."

Deep breath.

Snapping my eyes back open, I let the calm and center strength I've always had to find in moments like this wash over me. I clear away the fucking panic coursing through my veins and focus on the order of operations that now have to take place.

"Where's Willow?" I ask my brothers through our connection, attempting to keep my voice level.

"Sitting with Tanith reading. What's up, T-Man?" Draken asks in his natural chipper tone and my heart clenches painfully.

"Leave her right there for now. Don't say anything. The rest of you get to the gates at the south wing now."

"What's happened, Tillman?" Corentin asks, instantly picking up a problem.

He doesn't give me enough time to respond before he and Caspian pop up just a few feet from me. Their stoic and angry glares crumble for a split second as they see the healer working hard on Jamie. Their calculating eyes watch as Nikoli hits the ground on his knees again and rocks back and forth.

When they both look at me at the same time, all I can do is nod.

They already know something's happened to the others.

"You're lucky she's all transfixed in her book right now or I wouldn't—" Draken starts as soon as he steps up behind Corentin and Caspian until he sees what's happening. "What the fuck is going on?"

I relay the small amount of information Nikoli has given me to them and they each morph into different men. Their anger, worry, and need for revenge are instantaneous and then the profound realization of why I didn't want Willow here just yet sets in.

"She's going to burn this fucking realm down," Caspian says without a hint of his normal giddiness at the prospect of trouble. Even he in this moment understands how bad this could go.

Our Primary's sister, her Perfecta Anima, has been kidnapped.

"Exactly. As soon as Jamie's healed up and stable, we'll get as much information as possible from them both. I'll look into their minds to see what transpired leading up to the kidnapping. You," I bark, pointing at a random E.F. member, "go to the palace compound. Tell Commander

Roye to begin rounding up teams for an emergency mission on my orders. Tell him my second has been taken hostage."

"We can't keep this from her long, Tillman. I understand and agree until we know more, we don't tell her, but we have to tell her as soon as possible," Corentin says.

"Tell me what?"

That sassy, "ha-ha I got you" tone has the four of us freezing in our spots. Our bodies instinctively try to press closer together and block the sight of Jamie and Nikoli from her.

One look and she'll know.

To my complete and utter fear, one look and she's going to make this entire palace crumble.

Caspian commands his shadows out to block the scene in front of us and we slowly turn to face her. It's obvious that we're attempting to hide something from her, and it becomes even more pronounced as we all slam our blocks into place. She instantly feels it, even if we aren't capable of truly blocking her out because of our bond, but she doesn't push us.

The feisty smirk slides off her face, leaving behind a mixture of confusion and hurt skirting across her features. It slices my fucking heart open and I want more than anything to make it better because what we're about to tell her is going to cause her even more pain.

When she stumbles back a step, naturally, we all reach out toward her.

"Why...What's going on?" she asks in a voice so small my throat closes.

"Listen to me, Primary," Caspian says so softly, her eyes well with tears when she whips her head to him. "I need you to stay calm. Push your emotions to the side and bring just logical thoughts forward. Can you do that for me?"

"Cas...what is going on?"

"We'll tell you as soon as you promise me that. We aren't trying to hide anything from you. We just wanted to be more prepared before telling you what's happening, but since that's not going to be the case now, you have to listen to me. Put your emotions away, Willow," he commands gently.

She takes multiple breaths, trying to calm the erratic rise and fall of her chest. She slams her eyes shut, just as I had done, as she clenches her fist at her side. We give her all the time she needs and fuck me, I wish it took longer for her to collect herself than it does.

In just a few seconds, she's opening those deadly silver eyes that are crystal clear and focused, ready for whatever news we're about to share.

At her nod, Caspian pinches his lips together. Pulling his shadows back, the four of us part for her to come stand in the center of us.

The second she's between us, I feel her flinch as her eyes land on Jamie and Nikoli.

"Oakly..." she murmurs.

The sound of her voice has Nikoli's head whipping up toward her, and fast as lightning, he's on his feet, coming to stand in front of her.

"Willow, I need you to track her. Please find her. I can barely feel her now," he begs, gripping onto her hands. We attempt to move him away from her because in his own worry and panic right now, he doesn't see her storm rising to the surface.

"Nikoli, what happened to my sister?" she asks.

Eerily calm.

"We were drugged at breakfast. They took her, Ry, and San, her parents. I don't know where they are."

She staggers back from him as though he's burned her, and she tries to catch her breath. The battle that just began raging in her is obvious. Just as fast as that calm demeanor came, it vanishes with that news. We all try to reach out and grab her, but she crashes down faster than we can.

The moment her knees hit the ground, the grass splits open and the fissure travels its way through the forest in front of us. Although we can't see it, we hear the limbs breaking apart like bones snapping and we feel the vibrations in the earth as the trees are uprooted. They hit the forest floor with deafening thuds that make my chest pound in sync.

Falling to my knees in front of her, I lock my gaze on her now purple irises. They aren't slits, so I know it's still her in there, but barely. Just fucking barely. There're no sobs falling from her chest or tears streaming from her eyes, but the flames burning in their depths are brutal.

Deadly.

"Come back to me, little warrior. We're right here. We've got to get down to the bottom of this and begin searching for them. You have to be in your right frame of mind to find her. She needs you right now. I need you," I whisper as I grip her cheeks.

I need her. My best friend needs her.

Her body startles underneath my hands and a small silver ring forms around her pupils, but that's as far as the color travels. The deep, drawn-out exhale that fans my face is strong enough to nearly blow me over, but after it's finished, I know I have her back.

"I'll find them. I'll find them for us. I swear."

"I know you will, little warrior. I know you will."

Her features close off from me. From everyone. She drifts deep inside of her mind, and the fear pumping through her chest is strong enough to take my breath away.

I don't dive in her mind, but I know she's reliving what she's already been through.

"Draken, get her to the compound command room," I say softly while kissing her head and pulling her to her feet. She doesn't so much as blink as I pass her into his arms, and we all share a look. "Go. I'll be there in a moment."

"You, healer," I bark as soon as Draken transports out. "What's going on?"

"Immobilizer drug. A hefty dose," he grunts.

"Get him moved to the command room now. Call in another healer and someone get Rich a healing vial. I want word if anyone shows up at any of the palace gates. Understood?"

"Yes, sir," the entire group echoes.

"Core, go get the rest of your parents. Cas, go find Keeper and Gaster. Meet at the command room," I order, pulling my communicator out.

In the blink of an eye, they're gone, followed by the small group of E.F. members, along with Nikoli and Jamie.

"Tillman, I didn't—"

"Get to the palace command room. You, Aria, and your Nexus will have entry."

"What's happened now?"

"Ry, Oakly, and San have been taken."

"Fuck," he shouts, barking commands at whoever's around him. "Fortune teller?"

"Okay for now. Shutting down."

"Elementra help any who get in her way. We'll be there in five."

I end the call without anything else and press the device to my forehead while I breathe through the fucking turmoil rolling through me.

It's a battle to collect myself once again, but I finally do, and I push my gift out.

"Oakly, come on, you little shit. You know you hate it when I'm in your head."

Nothing.

I'm met with unforgiving silence. There's not even static on the other end. Just empty fucking quietness and I clench my teeth so hard I'm surprised one of them doesn't break, but I don't let it deter me. I try again.

"San, come on, man. You've read everything you could get your hands on about this shit. Just talk back to me."

Nothing.

The pebbles that decorate the walkway up the south wing drive vibrate around my boots with every step I take. It's just a little leak of my element, but it needs an outlet. It needs somewhere to bleed.

Come on, man. You got this.

"Ry...Please, brother, answer me," I murmur.

Nothing.

Whipping around, I bellow as I unleash my earth element on the forest in front of me. The trees that survived my little warrior's slip of control stand no chance as I let my anger out. I let it pour out of me until the red tint that's obscuring my vision clears and I can see the sea of green laid before me.

Heaving, I shake my head and place my hands on my hips. Then pace. I search, beg, plead for the balance that's been my constant for nearly my whole life. The settle my parents taught me to find.

It seems elusive until I tilt my head up and stare at the side of our balcony that now will have a view of a destroyed forest.

My better half. My true balance.

She needs me. She needs my strength. And I need hers.

Blowing out a deep breath, I walk back out the gate and cross the small distance to the tree line. Or well, what was a tree line. The small trek gives me enough time to catch my breath and get the rage I feel under control fully.

Taking a knee, I close my eyes and focus my mind.

We'll find them.

My earth element flows into the cool dirt as I dig my fingers into the forgiving ground. My breathing levels, my mind silences, and my heart rate slows as one of the blessings I've been given fixes the senseless destruction I caused. It fixes the bleeding rage pouring through me and I find the side of myself that everyone else is waiting on.

Hang on, guys. Your family's coming.

Thirteen

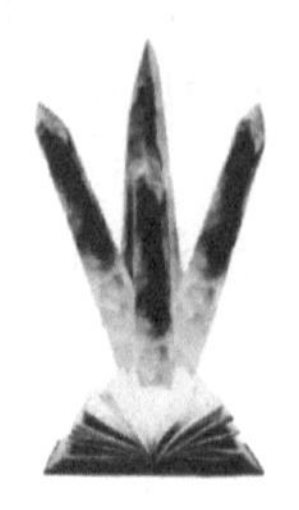

Willow

It's by the grace of Elementra that I'm holding myself together.

I don't remember standing from the ground or being moved to the palace command room. Nor do I have any idea when Gaster, Keeper, all the Vito parents, Lyker, Aria, Lennox, Kyan, and Zane arrived, but here they all are, surrounding me and attempting to lend me their strength while I stare off into nothingness.

Aurora's trying her hardest to push some positive emotions onto me. Her gentle gift caresses my skin like a warm breeze, but I can't absorb it or accept it. The anger, hurt, and fear that're pulsing through me basically burn it away the second it touches me.

My eyes tracked Gaster's pacing until they nearly went crossed and after that, I sank into my mind and haven't been able to pull myself out since.

The guys aren't trying to reach me anymore. Tillman ordered when it was time to finalize a plan, he'd tell me. They all know, if I allow my mind to grip reality too much, I'm going to snap.

My thread is so thin as it is.

If I listen to Nikoli's or Jamie's voices too much, I lose the control I have on my elements. They've each stared at me with both apologies and a heady dose of hope in their eyes and I can't bear it.

It'll be my undoing.

I've come so far with believing in myself. Up until now.

Until this very moment where it means more than it ever has.

The doubt plaguing me is going to make me physically ill. How could I have been so stupid, so naïve to believe it would be okay for Oakly and me to put off training me to track long distances? Of course she's walked me through it. Discussed it in sure-fire detail, but we've never actually practiced because of my aversion to transporting.

That pathetic fucking fear is eating away at my soul now.

It's going to cost me my sister's life.

Trembles shake the command room's walls, and fine powder falls from the ceiling as everyone falls silent and stares at me. I hate the pity I see in their eyes. The understanding is just as bad. I should be above this. A dark thought shouldn't have me on the cusp of crumbling, but here I am.

Falling the fuck apart on the inside.

"I need a minute. I'll be outside," I say stoically, stepping away from Aurora's warmth.

"Draken go with her," Corentin says gently, but I hold up my hand to my dragon man.

"Solo trip for now, dragon," I mumble.

"If you need me, any of us..."

"I know."

I practically power walk until I burst through to the outside.

The palace command area is different than the academy's.

Where I could've left the academy's command room and walked through the gym to get outside, here at the palace, the command room is its own separate building. Once I burst through the doors, I'm met with a training yard that is teeming with E.F. members.

Those who don't know me give me a wide berth and even wider glances. Those who do give me determined nods. Ready to go whenever my men or I, I guess, command it.

I round the building like my ass is on fire to get away from all the eyes. I can't hold my heartbreak in any longer.

As nothing but trees come into sight, I slow my steps and tilt my head to the sky as I pace around. It's a failing effort to get my breathing under control and as the rays continue to warm my face, my tears burn as they slide down my cheeks.

It's not long before my legs give out and I sink down into the grass and grip handfuls of it. I want to bellow, rage, fucking burn everything to ash until I find her. The sobs that come up and out from the depths of my soul are painful as I hold in my silent screams. The agony that wants to tear out of me would no doubt be heard for miles around.

"Oakly, please. Please let me in."

I plead and beg for the millionth time. Wherever they've moved her and half her Nexus is concealed. I don't feel our bond more than enough to know that she's alive and she won't answer any of my mental yelling.

"CC, Elementra, one of you. Please. Please tell me what I can do. Don't abandon me in this. Please guide me." I cry.

This moment, more than any other I've faced, is when I need them. This is a situation where their guidance would benefit me more than ever. I can't lose her.

"You must calm yourself, filia mea. All the tools you need to find your Perfecta Anima have already been provided to you, but you must search within yourself. You will never be able to do that if you do not balance your emotions."

Fuck, I want to scream at him. Ask him how dare he tell me to calm down in a time like this, but the reaction slaps me in the face.

I'm not oblivious to the fact that I've reacted quite emotionally since my men parted like the fucking Red Sea to show me half of Oakly's Nexus on the ground. One being healed, one losing his ever-loving mind. But how else am I supposed to react? I'm all too aware of what my best friend could be facing right now.

Drawing in a lungful of air, I pull my legs beneath me so I can sit crisscross in the grass and try to meditate the way Gaster has tried so many freaking times to teach me. He swears by the silent, still method, but I just can't focus on this shit. The quieter my surroundings get, the louder my mind responds. So instead of being quiet, I sing.

Air, earth, water, fire so bright,
Four elements, pure and right.
Air we breathe, wise and sweet,
Earth stands strong, soil beneath our feet.
Water flows, broken and whole,
Fire's warmth feeds the soul.
Remember these with joy and cheer,
The elements become one, the world becomes clear.

Repeatedly, I sing the lullaby that's come to my rescue more times than I can even recall. The enchantment that started it all. As the melody plays in my head, my diversions poke their way through the darkness as well. A small, watery smile crosses my face as times that seem so long ago play across my mind, but it's over far too fast for my liking.

As I continue to sing and each line brings forth a more positive emotion, I use this moment to fortify my diversion spell. Give it an upgrade, if you will. I lace all my happy new memories with my lullaby like background music as each one comes forward.

Of course the guys are front and center. I keep all their original moments that I used when I first made this spell and add on from our time together since then.

Gaster. CC. Lyker, Aria, Lennox, Zane, and Kyan. Then Aurora and my Patera-Nexus.

Ry, San, Jamie, and Nikoli. My brothers born from a bond.

Finally, Oakly. My sister. My best friend. My backbone.

I try to replay every single second of our time together. Every laugh she's drawn from my mouth. Every narrowed, sideways look she's shot me when I do something to her disliking. Fuck, her absolute brilliance. She's so smart.

I let it all out and allow it to solidify my spell.

The calm I was so desperately looking for coats my body in a blanket of protection and I exhale hard enough to blow the tears off my lips.

Okay, Willow, think.

You've been in the exact situation she's now in.

You know what happens and you know what to do.

As painful as it is, I bring forth the day of my kidnapping to the front of my mind. I picture how I was pulled through multiple transports, drugged by the immobilizing tonic, and then placed in the cell inside the concealed structure.

So based on the time that's passed and my inability to reach her, it's easy to assume she's already inside the concealed structure.

Fuck, okay.

I had to break it while I was trapped in there, but the roles are reversed now.

How do I break it from the outside?

How do I reach her?

How do I...

Shit.

"CC, can I use the spell to break through this barrier between her and me? Not to bring down the entire concealment, but enough of the block I can feel and talk to her?"

"I do not know, filia mea...Can you?"

My heart pounds against my rib cage as his no answer-answer fills it to the brim with hope. Determination floods my system and I dig my fingers into the earth to pull on the extra power.

"Fuck yes, I can."

Centering myself, I call forth all my power, building it up to exponential heights and then the spell I'll never be able to erase from my mind. It's so permanently engrained in my memories now, it's as easy as breathing to recite.

"Clarity is shown through my knowing eyes,
spread the knowledge to those who are blind.
Crumble the deception of the disguise,
reveal the truth for those to find."

I feel the crackling across my mind and hope blooms throughout my chest like a field of wildflowers. I snatch up the feeling and hold onto it for dear life, but after a few more seconds pass and the buzzing dissipates with no connection to Oakly opening, I scream out in rage.

"No!"

My fists pound into the earth in sheer fucking anger and each strike has the ground quaking beneath me.

"Why would you make me believe that would work?" I cry out in my mind, blaming CC for my failure.

"You can make it work, Willow. Do not doubt yourself. Think of the words in the spell. You must manipulate them to do exactly as you want."

Growling, I recite the infuriating spell in my mind over and over. Every time, I come up short on another answer. Those are the words to the spell. Therefore, it should work. Damn it.

"That spell will bring down an entire concealed structure."

"Yes, I know—"

An entire...

"You infuriating man. After all this is said and done, I swear, you, Elementra, and I will be having a long-ass discussion about these riddles. You hear me? I'm over the mind games. I'll make damn sure the next savior gets step by step freaking instructions on what the hell to do. I'll write the manual myself."

I heave as both my anger and frustration bleed out of me. I understand the method to the madness, I do, but this shit is too much sometimes. I'm on borrowed time to save someone who means the world to me. I don't have time to figure out on my own that I must reword the spell in order for it to work for this particular situation.

Thankfully, that lesson from him comes barreling through my mind the moment I understand that's what I'm supposed to do. Part of me wants to absolutely flip out that he taught me how to do this when I was only fifteen because if not for the Memoria stone, I surely would've forgotten this by now. The other part tells me to just be thankful.

"After all is said and done, filia mea, the realm...hopefully won't need another savior if you succeed."

"Great, thanks a lot. No pressure."

His laugh soothes me and pisses me off in equal parts, but I latch on to the soothing bits like a leach and drink it dry until it fills my body back with the calm and patience I had moments before the original spell failed.

Once again centering myself, I think about the words I need to replace for this to work. I have to focus solely on her, gaining entry into her mind, and not the location of where she is. I don't need everyone to see where we need to go. I just need to know.

With the strongest intentions, fully focused on Oakly and only her, I release my power.

"*Clarity is shown through my knowing eyes,*
Give me the knowledge, for it is I who is blind.
Crumble the deception inside the disguise,
reveal her truth for my mind to find."

Gasping, my mind opens up and the block that sat between the two of us shatters into thousands of pieces. The rush of her bond filling my chest cavity has a harsh sob burning its way up my throat.

Pushing myself through her mind, I can tell she's unconscious. I rip away the murky fog that seems to sit on her awareness like a sheer curtain and I cover my mouth with my hand as I feel her startle awake.

"Oakly, it's me. Please tell me you hear me," I beg.

"Willy..." she mumbles and the drugged-induced slur stabs me in the gut.

"It's me. I need you to wake up fully, Oakly, at least mentally. Can you do that for me, please?"

"I...my eyes won't move."

"It's okay, everything's going to be okay. Do you hear me? I'm coming for you, I promise."

I try my hardest to keep my tone level when really, I just want to bawl my eyes out. Her broken, confused speech sends panic washing over my body until it's hard to hold myself up.

The long pause she takes has my heart racing and my beast prowling in my chest. I need her to talk. I need her to breathe. I just need her to tell me she's okay, even though I know she's not.

"Don't. Don't fall back asleep, Oakly, please," I beg when I feel her mentally drifting again.

"It's...so hard. I'm so heavy...so hot," she stammers.

"I know. I'm so sorry. Nikoli and Jamie are here. They're safe. We're coming for you. I'll find you. I'll track you. I swear. Please, please hold on."

"No tracking."

"Don't say that. I swear I'm fucking coming. Do you understand me?" I yell, the defeat in her voice causing me to lose my composure.

"Don't have to track. I'm in...Pyra."

Her words fade out with her subconsciousness, and I bellow her name through our mental link to try to pull her back to me. Nothing works as I feel her slip further into the darkness and panic grips my heart. She's been given something far stronger than the immobilizing drug and I don't have much time.

I was freezing when I was drugged, not hot. I only started sweating when they tortured me. What drug could—

No. The heat. She's hot.

Pyra.

My vision.

Pure white-hot fear consumes me as I shove myself to my feet, staggering as I try to take a step. After the second failed attempt to walk, I command my shadows to engulf me. I move through the thick stone walls as if they're paper and burst through to the command room.

"She's in Pyra," I practically scream as all eyes turn to me.

Everyone stops moving and stares at me as though I've surely cracked now. Their softening gazes have my body heating with rage, and forcefully, I shove my mind into every last person in the room. Replaying everything that just happened outside.

"I said, she's in Pyra. We need to move."

I'm proud of the firm, steady command in my voice although my body sways harshly. Between the amount of magic I've used in the last few minutes to the overwhelming fear consuming me, I'm minutes from hitting the ground.

In less than the blink of an eye, my men surround me and Caspian latches onto my arm, pressing a healing vial to my lips.

"She's inside of Pyra. Not meaning she's in the lava, but that's where they have her concealed. From this moment on, assume to know nothing of the inside of the volcano. It's been manipulated now to be a Mastery structure. Uncle Roye, I need teams of your strongest earth and water elementals. Debrief them for what we're doing. We're moving out in fifteen minutes. Once there, Willow is going to identify the best way to infiltrate using her sight. We'll be blind going in. That's the best and all we've got for now. Go get ready," Tillman orders.

His full-fledged leader mode settles the warring worry and panic inside of me, and I suck up everything I can. Pairing that with my dragon's battle-ready determination, I let the emotions of the two of them blanket me in an impenetrable armor. Mix that in with Caspian's and Draken's bloodthirsty rage and Corentin's cold detachment, I basically disassociate myself...well from myself.

I go completely cold on the inside. Fortifying my internal walls as we prepare to go save members of our family.

The sound around the room grows again as everyone discusses and finalizes plans. I listen keenly, I do, but realistically, in my mind, these plans may be for nothing once we get there. Pyra may be swarmed with Mastery members and they each will meet their end today.

No one will receive mercy from me.

I keep my gaze trained on where a healer is doing a final checkup on Jamie as I cross the room, and everyone's eyes follow me. There's no doubt my murderous thoughts are bleeding out everywhere, but everyone is the same. They're just not used to mine being so potent.

"How are you feeling?" I ask with more control than I actually feel.

"Better. That was a hefty dose of immobilizer, but we've got it all out. I'll take a few more healing vials just to be on the safe side," he says confidently, nodding to the other healer as they finish up.

"Good. I don't want to upset you when I tell you this, but you need to be prepared."

His eyes snap up to mine, on the brink of a freak-out, but all I can do is give him a tight smile. I don't have anything else to offer.

"She's drugged with something stronger. I don't know what, but it's not your typical immobilizing drug like I was given, or you were. You need to have extra healing vials with you. Keep close to Draken if you can, so if you need a magical boost, he can give it to you."

"You...you think it's that bad?" he asks.

"For her, at least, yes. I have no clue the state Ry or San is in."

It seems the calmest of my best friend's men has a murderous side to him as well because in the blink of an eye, his whole aura shifts to a rage I've never seen from him. As a medical professional, he's typically pretty good at keeping his wits about him. But not now. Not with this knowledge about his Primary.

"Little warrior, Jamie, come on. It's almost time," Tillman calls out from the doorway of the command room.

Marching my way through the doors, my other three men are already waiting there for me, and as always, they surround me protectively. Their energies match that of my own. There're no silly jokes to break the tension, no sexual innuendos to cheer me up, no chin tilting, no purrs, nothing.

Just deadly men ready to exact some vengeance.

"Child, a word before you go, please," Gaster says softly, meeting us before we approach the large gathering of E.F. members.

Nodding, I break away from my men as they step to the other side to speak to Aurora, Neil, and Theo. Dyce and Roye will be joining us. From the bits and pieces I actually paid attention to, they all never leave Aurora. Half of them always stay behind.

Out of the corner of my eye, I catch a glimpse of Keeper, laying his head to Tanith's and that tells me all I need to know about him joining us. I'm sure she isn't all that thrilled about it, but she's not stopping him.

"Willow, come back to me," Gaster says softly as he turns to face me and grips my shoulders.

"Of course I will, Gaster. I always do."

"No, child, I mean in this moment. I can't allow you to leave here with the emotions rolling off you. You have every right to be angry, hurt, upset, and want vengeance. Everything you feel is valid, but the heartless detachment is not you, my girl. Come back to me now, before you go."

His words fracture the icy encasing I'd placed myself in. I try my hardest to seal it back up, but he tries even harder to tear it down. He shoves himself at our bond full force, and no matter the amount of power, magic, gifts, or elements I possess, I simply don't stand a chance against him.

"Gaster," I croak. "Why?"

"Because this is not you. Do what you must and what feels right to protect and take care of the ones you love, but you do it with heart, with compassion, with love. I don't mean that in a sense of allowing these vile creatures to get away with what they've done, but you're much stronger when the love you feel for everyone is at the forefront of your intentions. You keep your soul pure, Willow. You do not allow it to be tainted," he states firmly, pulling me into his chest.

And I fucking shatter.

I cry and cry until I can't anymore. I let the hatred I'd been feeling up until this point bleed out of me and into him. He takes it and does away with it as though it is nothing. He holds me tighter, allowing me to fall apart.

When I pull back and wipe the tears from my eyes, my entire body feels weightless, and I sigh in relief.

"Better, child?"

"Much. I didn't realize that was weighing me down."

"It is not in you to be cold, Willow. Everything you do is with burning passion. This may be a deadly mission, but you approach it with the intention of saving your sister, her men, not with the intention of killing. That will be an event nonetheless, but that will not be your main goal."

"Thank you, Gaster," I sniffle before giving him my first real smile since this whole shit show started.

"It is my pleasure. Now go bring my other granddaughter home to me. She is in deep shit when I get my hands on her."

My jaw hits the ground, and I stare in astonishment. Honestly confused about what just came out of his mouth. "Gaster, did you just cuss?"

"I did. That's how bad that girl has me riled up. You missed some not so pleasant words come from me as well when you were being rescued." He gives me a sassy wink as he leads me back over to my men and I watch as each of their shoulders drop in relief.

It isn't just them, though. As Tillman's deflate, I swear the entire small army waiting for his orders does as well.

"Sorry about that. Got a little murderous."

"More than murderous," Caspian says as he grips my jaw and turns my face so he can peer into each of my eyes. Obviously the darkness had been leaking much, much closer to the surface than I realized. "Good, now we can focus properly. How one little fierce Primary can have an army of highly trained men ready to tuck tail and run."

"I wasn't that bad." I argue when he shakes his head at me.

"Primary, your abyss is almost as black as mine. I was beginning to question if we were ever going to be able to get you out," he says sternly, letting me know how serious he feels about this.

"I'm sorry," I whisper.

"Don't be, but next time you're close to the edge, call for me. I'll come," he whispers before pressing his lips to mine.

Wordlessly, he passes me to each of my other men and they all shower me with the same love and devotion.

It's very scary to realize how in these last view moments, I was able to become nothing but mindless in my pursuit to get what I want and my readiness to do whatever necessary. Everyone else be damned.

Maybe I take after the Summum-Master a little more than I'd like to accept.

"No." Tillman turns to me and harshly barks. I can't help but straighten at the tone he used, and he doesn't break my eye contact until I give him a nod of acceptance. Once he finally looks away, I blow out the breath I was holding.

Fuck, he's intense when he wants to be.

"Listen up. We're transporting to Pyra. Everyone, meet on the decimated side to stay out of any line of sight. We'll maneuver around from there. We have no other information than that. Be ready for anything. Move out in sixty seconds," he orders.

I use those quick sixty seconds to send Aurora and the remainder of my Patera-Nexus a reassuring nod. I tell Tanith I'll watch over Keeper and at the sign of trouble, I'll reach out to her.

I look at both Nikoli and Jamie. I give them my best reassuring smile and their shoulders sag. I should've known better than to let my anger take over. They were looking to me for guidance and reassurance their Primary is going to be okay, and I let them down.

I vow with only my eyes that I won't do that again.

My brother, Aria, Lennox, Kyan, and Zane stand strong to our right. There's no hint of hesitancy in any of them and the seriousness in their expressions makes my chest swell with pride. I'm so thankful that despite the new position Lyker holds, the small amount of spare time he has, he, his brothers, and Aria are always ready to step up for our family.

My fingers lace their way through Tillman's as Corentin's mental countdown reaches twenty, and I squeeze his hand both for his grounding and my own.

Closing my eyes, I take a deep breath, preparing myself for what I'll see when they open again.

The heat that caresses my face the second I'm guided out of the transport is suffocating. It's at least fifteen degrees hotter than in the Central, add that in with the sight in front of me as my eyes open, and I can barely breathe.

Standing probably one hundred or so feet away, covered in a thin veil of shadows, my eyes travel up and up until my neck is craned back, looking for the top of Pyra. It's a beautiful, intimidating sight and why it took Nikoli and his team as long as it did to locate the crimson root now makes a hell of a lot more sense.

The obsidian black seems to stretch endlessly both in the sky and across the land. It's a wall of a rock that gives me no sight to the other side. From my studies, there's two sides to the volcano that everyone refers to.

The facial side. It's the view everyone in Pyrathia sees when they gaze at Pyra. There's a large distance between the nearest town to the volcano's edge, but supposedly, it doesn't matter where in this territory you are. You can see Pyra and all her glory.

The other, the one we came in on, is the decimated side.

Craning my neck around and peering through the scatter of E.F. members, I figure out quickly why it's referred to that. As far as my eye can see is nothing but black volcanic rock that's hardened over the countless millennia of her existence. There're no homes, trees, grass, bushes, just nothing. It's gorgeous in an intimidating sense. One that reminds you of how powerful this beast of nature truly is.

"What do you see, Will?" Tillman asks.

When my gaze turns back to Pyra, I scan the long stretch of darkness for any sign of life. It appears as an endless stretch of black until movement far in the distance, at least a couple football fields away, catches my eye. A meek amount of pale skin pokes out from underneath the black robes hiding them and if not for their careless movements, I never would've spotted them.

"Way down that stretch, there's a group of people. I can barely see them," I say, pointing my finger to the right.

"We'll start heading that way," Tillman says, but I grasp onto his hand before he can give the signal.

"They'll see us coming in no time. They haven't spotted us yet because of how far away we are and Caspian's coverage, but they'll no doubt see a black cloud heading toward them and sound the alarm."

"Bring down the concealment, Primary, and we'll charge," Caspian says darkly, but I shake my head at him.

"There's still too much of a stretch between us. I don't know how to explain the distance in tactical terms for you, but it's at least four training fields between us and them right now."

"Fuck," all four of them mutter.

It would take us far too long to run that distance and have the element of surprise on our side. The other opinion would be to transport closer and shock them, but even then, that leaves our army transporting blindly and potentially still scattered out.

"Conceal us, little wanderer," Draken says.

"I—"

"Yes, you can. If you can tear down a concealment the size that structure was, you can conceal all of us," he says confidently, cutting off my rebuttal.

"Feed her your magic, dragon. Primary, ground yourself and concentrate. No more doubt. Just do it," Caspian commands sternly.

Cocking my eyes up to him, there isn't a shred of uncertainty in his features or his bond. None of that is to be found in any of my men. When I glance over at Nikoli and Jamie, both shaking where they stand, any remaining hesitancy flees me.

They feel them. I feel her now that I concentrate on her and that's all the motivation I need.

Reciting the concealment spell in my mind, practice before pushing my power out, I pause as the words repeat.

Conceal my possession from curious eyes. Only to me, you reveal its disguise.

That's not going to work. They aren't my possessions.

Calling my magic forth in my chest, I lace it with the intention to conceal those around me who are here to find my family, but only from those who intend to hurt us.

"Conceal my people from harmful eyes. Only to us, you reveal their disguise."

My power flows across our army like a gentle breeze and only a few surprised noises flutter through the group.

Gazing around, I still see everyone clearly, and by the glances they're all sharing, they still see each other.

"Time to test it out. I'll tell Uncle Roye to stay back and man everyone while our Nexus goes and checks. We'll have them transport to us once we have the clear," Tillman says.

A smug-ass grin crosses his face when Roye startles and whips his wide eyes to Tillman, but he recovers quickly enough. With a nod to us, I turn the five of us toward the Mastery members.

"Caspian, move us about a training field away in this direction."

Wrapping his shadows around us, he doesn't question me at all and in a split second, his blanket of coverage falls away from us. I blow out a subtle breath as none of the Mastery members acknowledge us, and two more times, Caspian moves us closer.

Standing less than a hundred feet from the guards, their voices are finally audible, and they're none the wiser that we're now standing right on top of them.

"Clear," Tillman relays in our minds.

Transports open and the entirety of our army steps up behind us and I continue to bounce my gaze from them to the Mastery members until they're all gathered back with us.

Facing the volcano head-on, I scan the wall of darkness while simultaneously getting a headcount now that we're close enough to tell. A wash of Corentin's magic covers us in a silencing bubble and I shiver at the feel of it before turning toward him.

"Twenty out here. We'll send a small team forward to take them out while you find the entrance, princess. How do you want to proceed from there, Tillman?" he asks.

"Keep one alive. We can question them about the layout inside before moving in blind. That'll give us a better advantage over getting to the three of them quicker."

"Allow me the honor. Twenty is light work," Keeper practically purrs when he steps up, eyes already crimson.

"Why do you get to do it?" Dyce immediately asks, crossing his arms.

"You may join...if you can keep up." Keeper winks and I shake my head at the two of them.

Guess I'm getting that battle I pictured.

"Enough, you two. Keep it clean and quiet. Move out," Tillman orders.

That's all Tillman had to say and suddenly, what appears to be a race between two teenage boys ensues. That is until Keeper reaches the Mastery members. By the time Dyce reaches him in his Tasmonium form, four bodies have already hit the ground and the remaining rebels look around frantically for what the hell is happening.

Just as I imagined. The two of them work seamlessly together. Keeper dances around with unmatched speeds as Dyce's large, extended jaws wrap around unsuspecting victims. It's brutal, bloody, and they take down the nineteen members without ever breaking a sweat.

Kicking and screaming, unable to even see the beast that has him by the collar, Dyce drags the twentieth member by his robes and tosses him into our silencing bubble. He tries to pry himself free of the invisible restraints he finds himself in, but Caspian has him coiled tight.

"His heart's going to fall out if I pry," Tillman says.

"Then just ask him. This information probably isn't even blocked."

The look they all give me has me rolling my eyes, and without waiting for them, I reveal only myself. I'm instantly offended when the asshole stops his thrashing and sighs a breath of relief.

Idiot.

"I don't have time for small talk. Tell me exactly what the inside of the volcano looks like. Now," I command, forcing my eyes to turn violet.

I get great pleasure when the prick's gaze widens comically and his trembling starts back up, but regardless, he keeps his mouth shut, so I shift a claw and press it to his neck.

"I won't ask nicely again." I growl.

"Ch-ch-chambers, rooms. There're small hallways grooved out until the...the center magma pool," he stutters.

"Are there hostages inside?"

"Y-yes."

"How many?" I press my claw into his neck firmer when he takes too long to respond and he yelps loudly before spilling.

"I don't know. A couple rooms worth. They're spread out. Please, I just got sent here recently. I didn't move them in. Just door duty."

I remove my claw from his neck and conceal myself once again as I turn to Tillman to take over. We stare at one another for a long moment, indecision warring between us. He knows I can't kill him. Taking a life in the heat of battle is one thing, but this kid, well, man child, gave me everything I needed once I scared him shitless.

"Move him to the palace prison, then report back. He'll have his rune removed and tried fairly for his cooperation," Tillman finally orders a palace E.F. member. "Observe the wall, Will. Let's find our way in before he returns."

I hold in my small, appreciative smile because I have no doubt they all would've preferred to just kill him now and make it easier, but I am grateful and proud of his decision. It takes a lot more strength to be compassionate than not.

Taking a few steps forward, there's still nothing to be seen from here other than the haze I know to be the concealment covering this side of Pyra. I continue my trek, ignoring the bodies lying about until I can run my hands over the hot, smooth surface. Wherever the door is, it's blending in effortlessly or they have it extra shrouded.

Rubbing down every inch I can reach, all that presents itself is the faintest buzzing in my palms from the concealment, and just as I grow frustrated, I fall forward.

I hold in my sudden shriek, slapping my hand to my mouth when I stumble into an empty stone chamber that has only a single hallway leading out of it.

Intrusive magic crawls across my skin, attempting to reveal my presence as I glance around and it's a battle to shove it off me. My men's panic hits me in seconds, causing me to shiver, and I jump right back out before they flip their shit.

Slamming into a solid chest, my shoulders are gripped tightly as Corentin holds me steady. "What was that, princess?"

The calm, collected tone doesn't fool me. The tight grip and the glow on his fingertips tell me that was about to be my ass if I didn't come back out.

"I found the entrance, but we have a small issue."

"What?" they all ask at once.

"I can hold the concealment, but it's going to take a lot. There's some sort of, I don't know how to explain it, but like stripping or blocking magic when I passed through. I don't think it'll mess with our own magic, gifts, or elements but definitely spells and enchantments. I felt it trying to pull my concealment away."

"That's exactly what it's doing, Adored. Nor will you be able to transport. The Summum-Master has the enchantment placed around the forest as well. It's one of his preventative measures from spies or unfaithful followers," Keeper informs us.

Damn it. That makes sense.

"What do you want me to do?" I ask my men.

"Don't waste your energy holding the concealment. We already have the element of surprise now. What did you see?" Tillman asks.

"This opens to an empty chamber with only one way to go."

"Then that's where we're going. Palace team three, stand guard. Everyone else ready?" he asks.

At everyone's definitive nods, I release our concealment, and he leads the way. He and Corentin step through first, followed by me, then Draken and Caspian. I hold my breath until my eyes find them and I move out of the way for as many of our men to follow in.

There's no way everyone we brought with us will fit in here, but I leave that up to Tillman to handle. I can't ignore the pounding in my chest any longer. I feel her. We're so close now that I could follow the threads connecting the two of us.

My men sense it in me, and they position themselves around me wordlessly. As soon as the remainder of our family piles in behind us, we push forward.

Moving down the hall on silent steps, I bring my dragon forth, allowing my eyes to glow violet, and the dark hallway comes to life before me. There's no one in my sight, but in the short distance, I see the first break away in the wall.

The small corridor is dark and only a few feet deep, leading to a solid steel door. Without a window, crack, or crevasse, there's no way to tell who or what is behind it, but with one small nod at Caspian from Tillman, he moves through the shadows.

I try to reach out and grab him before he goes in alone, but I'm too slow. Not that it matters, though, because before I can get pissed or panic, he's popping right back out.

"Twelve alive hostages," he whispers, but I hear the strain in his tone and his emphasis on alive.

"No guards?" Tillman asks.

"No."

"Leave them for now then. They'll be safer there. Any guard we pass won't make it to them again."

That murderous promise draws a smirk to Caspian's lips, and I see the rage morph into something far more fearful. Well, not fearful to me but surely anyone we come across.

We pass three more cells laid out the exact same way as we make our way through the winding hallway and each time, we handle it the same. So far, it seems as though the design is crafted that this one hallway covers the entire stretch of this side of the volcano. I'm almost positive it'll lead directly to the magma pool, and from there, there will be other routes to take.

I only assume that because of lack of other directions to go other than straight and we've only encountered one Mastery member. I'm pretty sure he was going to the restroom that we passed.

He didn't make it.

No instructions need to be given to Caspian as we approach the fourth steel door, and I keep my eyes peeled down the empty stretch of stone so we aren't caught off guard by any wandering Mastery members.

"Everyone, get ready. Prepare yourselves," Caspian says coldly not two seconds later.

That's the only warning he gives us before wrapping me, the rest of our Nexus, Nikoli, and Jamie in his shadows and snatching us through the walls.

My dragon immediately rushes to the surface and bile collects in my mouth at the sight in front of me and the sounds flood my ears.

In the middle of the room, Ry and San are tied to a post with their backs to one another. Ry's being restrained with massive ice blocks around his hands and feet, while San's are contained in the stone blocks and shoes. Just like I was.

There're four Mastery members on each side, taking turns laying into them whether it be with a gift, a fist, or an element. They aren't even interrogating them. They're just ruthlessly beating them to the brink of death.

Ear-piercing screams leave the chests of both Nikoli and Jamie. Concealed in this cloak of darkness, that's all I hear. Their wails are so loud, they block out the grunts and groans falling from their brothers. The noise is haunting, and I know I'll never be able to wipe any of these tortured sounds from my memory.

Rage and sorrow in equal parts hit me in my heart so hard it takes my breath away. Tillman's shaking so furiously, I'm positive at any moment he's going to make Pyra erupt and no matter the amount of calm I try to push at him, it's useless.

With a petrifying bellow falling from his chest, Caspian's shadows fall away, and they pounce. Before I gather my wits about me, six of the eight men are lying dead on the ground with the other two trying their hardest to escape. It's a useless feat that I don't bother interfering with and instead I rush over to Ry and San.

"Hold on," I say softly as I reach them.

Calling on my water and earth elements, I free them from their restraints and surround them in my air before they collapse in a heap on the ground. Not only is Ry beat to hell and back, his teeth chatter so loudly, I'm surprised they're not cracking.

Gently as I possibly can, I lay my hand on his arm and command my flame to slowly warm him back up. I hold in my growls and fix my crumbling face when he sluggishly rolls his neck to the side to look at me.

"O-Oakly?"

"Let's get the two of you fixed up. Then we're going to get her. We need you two," I say as calmly as I can.

"Fuck," Jamie mutters as he slams to his knees and puts a hand each on the guys' shoulders, then he sighs in relief. "Thank fuck. It's just surface."

"What does that mean?" I ask.

"They don't have any drugs left in their systems. It's all external wounds. Give them two healing vials each, will you, please?" he asks, nodding behind him at the small sack on his back.

Doing as he asked, the tightness in my chest lessens slightly as they are both able to hold the vials themselves. His magic is already coursing through them, and when Draken lays his hand to Jamie's shoulder, his eyes begin to glow.

I watch in amazement as every extra drop of magic Draken gives Jamie, he pumps into his brothers, and the rate at which they heal right before my eyes is astonishing. Of course their bruises will linger, but the cuts, busted cheeks, lips, and swollen eyes fade away in seconds.

"You okay?" Tillman asks Ry, pulling him in for a hug as soon as he's on his feet.

"Physically? Sure," Ry grunts and my heart clenches painfully.

"We'll get her. I swear it," Tillman says seriously.

For a brief second, the Mercie brothers all embrace one another. The relief on each of their faces is minimal and when they turn to us, there's nothing left but deadly promises and readiness to find their woman.

Oakly, we're almost there, babe.

Wordlessly, Caspian covers us in darkness once again and moves us back into the hallway where all our people are waiting.

One nod from Roye and Dyce, and we're off down the endless stretch once again. I went from being surrounded by just my Nexus, to my best friends as well. They have me cocooned in a bubble made of the eight of them while we make our way down the hall. Caspian flows through the walls in a matter of seconds. I can't tell if he's killing people in the rooms as he goes or just mentally getting a head count of hostages, but regardless, we continue our steps and every time I turn around, he's right back there with us.

Nikoli quickly and quietly fills Ry and San in on everything and I feel their appreciation in my chest, but I can barely focus on it.

Without saying a word, our steps become faster. Either they're all feeding off me or Oakly's guys feel it too because we're practically sprinting as we finally see the opening at the end of the hall.

That's where she is.

Tillman tries to tell me to slow down. I both hear his words and feel his hands reach for me as I continue to run past him, all of them. But I can't stop. I won't. She's so close.

Bursting through the opening, I finally do slam to a halt as unbearable heat licks my face, but the sight in front of me is what freezes me in place.

Glaring around, there's a huge circular stone platform that stretches around a ginormous pit of magma. I can't see the fiery pool of death as it's at least a couple stories down, but the suffocating heat tells me it's close enough.

This center area is absolutely massive in size and judging by the continuous pounding of boots behind me, there's enough room for the majority, if not all the E.F. members we brought with us. A flimsy-ass railing has been placed around the edges as if that'll stop anyone from falling in, and around the entire perimeter, except for this exact hallway we just exited, are Mastery members at the ready.

But they aren't the fuckers I'm staring deadly daggers at.

"Well, well, well. About time the Nexus thieving whore showed up."

Fourteen

Willow

I'm going to kill her.

This stupid, crazy-ass stalker bitch dies today.

"Germ. Still a delusional fucking psycho, I see."

Her eyes narrow menacingly and I glare right back. Despite the sound of the boiling magma beneath me and the hushed orders behind me, our voices seem amplified in this large space. She hears the malice and intentions in my tone.

Her time is coming to an end.

"The only delusional one between the two of us, Willow, is you. How the fuck you believe you'll get out of this is beyond me. The Summum-Master has made his demands, he's given his orders, and that is that."

"So you've known about him this whole time?"

"Admittedly, no." She sighs with an eye roll. "Daddy didn't feel it was necessary I knew it all. Until I came home and told him all about the whore at the academy who was trying to steal my men. Then he informed me of my role, and I took on my position proudly. Unlike you. No worries, though. Soon enough you'll be out of the way, and me and *my* best friend will have the Nexuses promised to us."

My blood both boils and turns to ice in my veins at her words. Multiple things about how she just said that cause the hair on my neck to stand on end.

"Who the fuck are you talking about?" I ask coldly.

"Ask Caspian. He knows all about *my* best friend." Her loud-ass laugh rings so loudly in my ears, it nearly makes my eyes crossed. I can't stop the smoke that blows through my nostrils or the flames that cover my partially shifted claws.

I'll kill her. I'll kill them both.

"It's all been decided. Silvia's being a little stingy with not giving Caspian up, though, so I caved with a trade. She could take Caspian, and I'd take Ry. He's not too bad to look at."

The ground beneath my feet shakes and I'm not one hundred percent sure whose earth element was just set free. Mine, Tillman's, or Ry's. But when Ry takes off sprinting to the right, attempting to charge around this big-ass platform to reach Gima, the sides surrounding us begin to crumble into the magma below.

All of us wobble from the sudden shift and I fall forward, catching myself on the railing, holding on for dear life as my men hang on to me. The unforgiving heat that licks across my face has me peering over the side to get my first glance at the bright orange magma. It's bubbling angrily and shooting large glubs in the air as the stone continues to crumble into it. The temperature rising around me has beads of sweat instantly forming on my forehead, and I know, if any of us fall in there, there's no surviving that.

I whip my head around rapidly when Tillman bellows Ry's name and with a quick command, he has a vine wrapped around his waist, snatching his ass back off the edge before he could literally fall to his death.

Peering around me, Lyker, Aria, Lennox, Kyan, Keeper, and Roye, plus the E.F. members, have had to huddle closer together. Some are even pushed back into the hallway, and we're completely cut off from getting around any other way. My eyes scan the other side, pinpointing the earth elementals who have their palms faced out, commanding the platform around us to fall.

"On each side of us, they're using earth elements to tear apart the platform and hold it down. We need to get them back up," I frantically shout.

Tillman's orders to our earth elementals come not two seconds later and multiple people break from our hoarded circle to stand closer to the edge to bridge to gaps between us.

I hold in my protest when Roye joins one side and Lyker steps up on the other. A silent whimper pleads through my mind, begging my brother to get the fuck back. It's a useless request, though. He's got one of the strongest earth elements here and he's not just going to stand around watching.

My breaths come in harsh pants as I push myself to stand back up once the shaking finally ceases and I sneer at the manic smile on Gima's face. That stunt and her words have me on the verge of blowing this entire volcano up, but I shove the desire down. It's going to take a shit ton more than that to have us back down, and in reality, the bitch is undeniably crazy if she thinks anything she just said will come to fruition.

And Silvia can count her fucking days.

I'll hunt her down if it's the last thing I ever do.

"Where the hell is Oakly?" I growl.

"You know, I thought you were a hell of a lot smarter. The men in the Mastery speak of you as some legend, but you didn't even bother to look above you when you came through the entrance. The scouts up top watched everything go down and alerted us in here. You'd think for an animal that could fly, it'd be natural for you to look up," she says, giggling as her head tilts back and she gazes through the top of Pyra.

Slowly, not trusting this bitch whatsoever, I cast my gaze above me just as she's doing, and I choke back a sob as I stumble into my men's bodies behind me.

From the neck down, Oakly's covered in a stone encasing, and the entire contraption around her is being held in the air by a net knotted by vines. Her head is slumped to the side and she's out cold. She doesn't flinch, twitch, or move as I scream for her in my mind repeatedly.

Her name bellowing from her Nexus's throats barely registers in my ears and whatever the guys are saying to me doesn't penetrate the darkness closing in. I can't hear. I can't breathe. I can't feel my Nexus's hands on my body. I can't see through the red tinting my vision.

Every nerve ending in my body prickles painfully, causing my limbs to tremble and the rage-filled tears that slide down my cheeks are nearly scalding.

"She's their true Primary and they're fully bonded. If she dies, the four of them do as well," I say far more calmly than I feel when I snap my gaze back to Gima's and step forward to grip the railing.

"Not my Nexus, not my problem."

"But Ry—"

"Is replaceable. Corentin's who I care about the most. The others are added bonuses but again, replaceable." She flicks her hair off her shoulder as if she couldn't give a single fuck about anything or anyone but herself right now. "Anyhow...this was fun. I'll see you in a few once they capture you and bring me my men."

The delusional bitch saunters up to the railing on her side of the magma pit and when she leans over the side, looking down laughing, I hope and pray she falls in.

Of course that prayer isn't answered and when she rights herself, there's a deranged smile playing across her lips.

Then, in true psycho Gima fashion, she blows me a kiss.

Except, it isn't a kiss...it's a fireball.

And it's not heading toward me.

The entire realm tilts on its axis as the sound of snapping vines draws my gaze back up above me. I watch in delayed horror as the last bit of the netting holding Oakly in the air burns to ash.

Just as her stone casing begins to fall from the sky, time seems to freeze as our entire life together flashes right before my eyes.

No. Impossible. We have a lifetime to go.

One hundred years, two hundred years, three, four...fuck, a millennium.

Elementra, you said...

You vowed none of my bonds would ever break. You...you...

Realization hits me like a ton of bricks right to the heart and I nearly crumble under the weight of it.

My bonds don't have to be physically in this realm for them to stay intact.

No.

"Gima made her decision today, Ultima unum. Make yours."

Her soft, otherworldly voice comes and goes just as quickly.

As does my decision.

I will always choose her.

Shouting, wailing, full-fledged fucking panic collides with my chest once reality seems to catch back up. The fear of the entire army behind me, my family and all, crashes into me so hard it becomes hard to think about anything other than that, but I forcefully shove it away and take a deep breath.

"Everything's going to be okay."

I push it to my men, Ry, San, Jamie, Nikoli, my brother, his brothers, Aria, Keeper, Roye, despite not knowing if they will even hear me, but the least I can do is try.

The silence that surrounds me is of my own creation. I block everything out. Everything. The shouting, the orders, the guttural screams, the hisses coming from the magma with each new stone that disturbs its peace.

And I take a deep breath.

Just as Oakly plummets past the railing...

I dive off the side.

Commanding my earth element out, I tear away the stone prison surrounding my sister as she free-falls at breakneck speed and tears well in my eyes as her purple hair blows around her and her sundress dances wildly in the wind.

She looks like a falling angel.

A scream that's laced with my anger and fear rips painfully from my throat as I shove my air behind me to propel me down faster.

The unforgiving heat that has my skin feeling like it's melting off calls to the flames that burn in my blood, and I call the beautiful beast who blessed me with it forth.

Share control.

My power explodes out of me with my shift and a furious roar bursts free from my lungs. Pure animalistic instincts pulse through me and I allow plenty of room for it in the forefront of my mind.

Tucking my wings to my sides, I continue my nosedive and as soon as I'm confident I'm close enough, I extend my powerful legs out as far as I can and wrap my claws around her waist. The sudden swoop and unfurling of my wings cause the magma to jump up out of its pool and surround us in waves, but I shove my air out at it with full force, then command it to propel us upward.

Riding on nothing but the current of my element, I tuck my legs in as close to my chest as I can and wrap Oakly's body to mine by vines, then cocoon her protectively with my wings.

The flaming temperature of her skin sears into my scales and has a hiss whistling through my teeth. My water element instantly responds, flowing freely into her, both trying to hydrate and cool her down.

Like a missile, my large silver body crashes over the side of the stone platform and I slide until my back collides with the volcanic wall. I don't even have time to take a breath before suddenly I'm being pummeled with brutal strikes from elements and gifts.

It dawns on me instantly that I've landed us on the wrong side of the platform, and my dragon shoves more of herself forward. And I embrace it.

With a harrowing roar, I release my flames on anyone who dares to stand in my line of fire.

The deadly purple pours from my throat along with an ear-piercing screech that has the huge crowd scattering like mice away from me, but I don't allow that. Fuck no.

I command the flames to climb the walls, hunt those down who dared to try to kill my sister, kill me.

"Willow," a gentle voice calls and I whip my head around, growling viciously.

"Willy, it's me. Jamie. I need you to pull your flames back. Caspian moved me through his shadows to get me here, but now they're fighting off waves of Mastery who are trying to get to you. They need you and I need you to uncoil your wings so I can get to Oakly. Please," he says softly, holding his hands up, palms out.

"They need us. Calm down. Focus on who that is." I coax my dragon.

His sudden appearance startled her and she's on high alert, not wanting to give me back full control. With a low, rumbling warning, she sticks her snout directly to Jamie's face and inhales.

As soon as she scents the bond of our sister on him, she relaxes.

Calling my inferno back to me, I see familiar E.F. uniforms now clashing with the sorry-ass Mastery members. My men are somewhere in that chaos, killing their way toward me.

After uncoiling my wings, Jamie immediately springs into action and lifts Oakly into his arms. Once they're a few feet from me, I shift back.

"Fuck...FUCK. Willow, this isn't good," Jamie shouts as soon as I kneel beside him. "This is...this is something far different than what any of us were given. What anyone I've ever treated has been given."

My heartbeat thunders in my ears and a lump forms in my throat. Laying my hand on Oakly's forehead, I sense that she's truly burning up. This is a next level fever.

"Is it the Wymfire poison?" I ask, almost hopefully, because we have a cure for that.

"No. She'd be...dead already. I don't know what this is," he yells.

"Tell me what you need, Jamie," I croak.

"My brothers and a healing wing. This is going to take more than me, Willow."

When his watery eyes collide with mine, my heart shatters into a thousand pieces and my shadows engulf me.

I move through the darkest faster than I've ever moved before.

The first of Oakly's men I find is Nikoli and a breath of relief leaves me. He's a Detector. He'll know what this is.

I don't even announce myself as I step out of the shadows, hit the person he's fighting with my flames, then snatch him by the collar of his uniform and whisk him into the darkness with me.

I've never moved anyone through the shadows before, but my gift is running on purely heightened emotions and desperation.

When we step out, he whips around with a snarl on his lips until he realizes it's me, then his face crumbles. Just as I try to step back into the darkness, he wraps me up in his arms.

"You saved her," he whispers.

"Not yet, I haven't. Help Jamie," I say quietly, then push myself away from him.

I shove the emotions clogging my throat as far down as I possibly can. If I think too much about how she's lying on that stone, almost too hot to touch, unresponsive, and fading fast, I'll break into a million pieces. Even my men won't be able to fix me completely again.

Finding Ry and San together on the farthest side from where Oakly is, I nearly throw myself at my gentle giant when I see him with them, tearing down men left and right. He stands so strong, and I call on this part of him to build me back up in this moment.

Walking up behind him, I lay my hand on top of his outstretched one. He doesn't even flinch, doesn't even have to look down to know it's me. I feel him open himself up, welcoming my element into him, and I command them to merge.

Wrapping vines around the waist of the E.F. members in the thick of this mosh pit, he snatches them back to us, and quicker than the Mastery members can figure out what's happening, he opens the stone platform. As the thirty or so men fall to their deaths, he closes it back up.

"Jamie needs Ry and San. I'll be back," I tell him when he turns to me, but he shakes his head.

"Stay with Oakly. We'll have this cleared in a few minutes and we'll meet you over there. Roye, Dyce, and Keeper have teams with them searching the other halls. Palace teams are moving hostages out."

"If you need me—"

"I will, little warrior."

With a quick kiss to my forehead and a nod to Ry and San, I whisk us back through the shadows to join Jamie, Nikoli, and Oakly.

The sight is not what I wanted to see.

She's still completely unconscious, skin red, and Jamie's beginning to sway.

"I need Draken," he commands.

"Jamie needs you. Where are you?" I ask, panicked.

"Be there in one minute, little wanderer."

I know the one-minute time will prove to be true because the ground beneath my feet shakes with his roar and I know he'll be soaring through this volcano to get to me.

"He's coming. We should go ahead and move her to the healing wing when he gets here," I say frantically as Jamie begs Oakly to take what he's giving her.

"If we could, I already would have. Until they have these halls cleared, we can't get out with her like this. We can't transport out of here. This fucking volcano, this fucking weird magic, these fucking people," he bellows.

His brothers move in closer to him, while never taking their hands off Oakly as well and the rising tide of my anger swells once again. Not at him or his yelling. I take no offense whatsoever to it because I'm not feeling much better. The biggest difference is where Jamie might yell because he's angry, I may kill someone.

I stop my pacing as the beating of wings draws my attention and Draken, in the smallest dragon form I've seen him in, comes racing toward us.

"Little wanderer," he says, swooping me up the second he shifts back feet from us.

"It's bad, dragon," I croak.

"Don't say that. He'll heal her up and she'll be okay. I'll power him up until he's about to combust from all the magic," he purrs softly, cupping both of my cheeks.

All I can do is nod, and he accepts that for now.

I resume my fretful pacing as I watch the number of Mastery members continue to dwindle down. I don't have to hunt for Tillman when I want to find him. Other than towering over everyone, the E.F. members naturally gravitate toward him. Corentin, on the other hand, I've had to keep my eyes peeled for. One second there're five of him fighting, the next, I can't find him anywhere.

Caspian's the only one I haven't been able to see, and I grow more and more panicked as I watch Corentin approach Tillman and pull him into his light. I feel it in my chest that they're heading toward me, but my ghost is nowhere in sight.

"Cas, where are you?"

"Be there in just a moment, Primary."

"You're okay?"

"Yep."

I don't like the short answer, but he's responding and nothing in his tone or bond would suggest otherwise.

Every second—okay, constantly—I tap into Oakly's bond. I rotate from banging to hugging the mental link in our minds, begging her to please wake up, do something. Show Jamie that you're responding to his efforts.

"Princess," Corentin breathes, snatching me up and out of my mind. I hadn't realized they were right on me as I just stare at Oakly.

"Corentin, what do we do? She's not healing. She's not responding."

"They blocked off the exit we came in from. The E.F. members are protecting the hostages, but we're waiting for the others to get another hall cleared, then we're going. I promise. He may not be healing her, but he's keeping her alive, princess. I swear."

"Can't me or Caspian just shadow everyone out? I can move through the walls in here, so surely, I can move outside," I plead. I need her out of here. I need her to open her eyes.

"If it takes much longer for the halls to be cleared, that's what we'll do, baby, okay? Roye is keeping Tillman updated by the second," he says, gently pinching my chin.

I swing my head to Tillman, and although he has his arms crossed, standing strong behind Ry, I can tell by the distance in his eyes, he has his mind elsewhere. Probably in multiple other people's heads.

Nodding, just as I release an unsteady breath, a cloud of shadows forms a few feet from us and my shoulders sag in relief.

But it isn't my dark and damaged protector who steps out first.

No...

Gima is slung to the ground with her body coiled tight in shadows and a furious scowl across her face. The heavy rise and fall of her chest match mine the longer I stare at her, and the heat in this room mingles with my flames roaring back to the surface. My anger burns away my worry and my body trembles with adrenaline.

"Brought you a present, Primary."

My glare swings to Caspian and the twisted smirk on his face is all the permission my darker side seems to need.

In milliseconds, I'm out of the safety of Corentin's arms, commanding Caspian's shadows as if they were my own to put Gima on her feet and release her. The moment she steadies herself, I rear back and punch her as hard as I can with a stone-covered fist.

Her howl of pain is music to my ears. The sight of her bright red blood cascading from her nose and into her mouth feeds my fire, and with a battle cry pouring from my lips, I fucking pounce.

My legs straddle her waist and she attempts to hit me with a fire-coated palm, but a quick snatch of her wrist with my flamed fingers has her screaming in agony and I blow her element out as if it's nothing more than a candle.

Repeatedly, I rotate pounding into her face with one stone hand, and the other I leave bare so I can feel her skin split beneath my fist. I need her to feel the pain she's put me through. The torture I endured because of her assistance. Whatever is coursing through Oakly's blood. It's her fault. And she will pay me back with more than a pound of flesh.

Her eyes roll back into her head and her arms lose the feeble strength she was using to try to push me off.

I let my arms drop to my thighs as I catch my breath for a moment, then shove my magic out to open my pocket dimension in front of me.

Reaching in, I quickly snatch out two healing vials. I despise the fact I'm about to feed this bitch something my *Guardria* made with such care and love, but nonetheless, I need her alive for now.

Gripping her jaw in my hand, I pry the clenched muscles open and shove them both in her mouth. It takes a minute for her throat to start working, but after a second, she's choking and sputtering. I slam her mouth shut, making sure she drinks every drop, and patiently—not so much—wait until her blackened eyes begin to flutter back open.

"Get the fu—"

My palm flies across her cheek, cutting off her sentence, and when she slowly cranes her face back toward me, fear finally flickers in her eyes for a brief second before they narrow on me.

Delusional, yes.

But not completely stupid.

"What the fuck did you give Oakly?" I growl.

"I didn't give her shit."

"Maybe not directly, but you had a hand in it. You can tell me with your mouth, or I carve it from your mind. Make your choice."

"You can't—"

"I can and I will," I sneer.

The extremely low-cut shirt she's wearing is only tied together by a string above her belly button, so her chest is on clear display. She has no rune and the only individual who would mark her is here with us. There's no chance of her heart falling out, so if she thinks I won't melt her mind to find my answers, she's crazy.

"Have it your way, Germ."

The resistance from the block that is placed on her mind is nothing for me and I tear it down mercilessly. Her screams just barely echo in my ears, but I'm already plundering through any and everything I want to see.

This is where she's been hiding since the academy was attacked and her father has been at the helm of all the decisions being made for her. His voice isn't the one of the man we heard in Layton's mind from the meeting with the Summum-Master. Which leads me to believe that stupidly, the Everglow family was recruited by the other family who betrayed us.

Gima may act like hot shit, but the majority of the men here ignore her existence. The Summum-Master hasn't bothered to even meet her and I sift my way through, looking for Silvia, but even she hasn't been allowed to see her. All communications between the two of them are being passed through Gima's father.

They had a long discussion, I swear like a fucking business meeting on the terms and conditions of how my Nexus and Oakly's will be split between the two of them. It's sickening to hear, and the more I listen, the angrier and more aggressive I grow with my exploration of her mind.

Finally, we approach this morning and my blood boils.

Oakly was brought into a room and judging by the quick movements of her eyes, at this point, she was only drugged with the immobilizer. She's still fully aware of what's happening as a group of men get her strapped onto a table. Gima's stupid fucking ass is bouncing around laughing, waiting for them to finish. Once they do, one of them turns to her.

"They'd like a word with her, then you can come back in to watch her."

"Ugh, fine. I'll tell them to make it quick," Gima groans, rolling her eyes as she stomps to the door. When she opens it, my heart drops to my stomach.

No.

"Don't take too long, Folders. Deinde-Master Darstein will be here soon."

Tears of rage fill my eyes as Oakly's parents stroll into the room she's being held in, and I could fucking scream when Gima shuts the door behind them.

How could they?

They're perfectly fine.

Nikoli had thought they'd been taken as well, but he was wrong.

They did this.

Gima only allows a few impatient seconds to pass before she's opening the door once more and dismissing Oakly's parents from the room. None of them argue. They don't fight. Nothing.

Her mother just turns to her and says, "This is for the best, dear. This is our family's way up the hierarchy, and I knew you'd never be on board with it. Everything's going to be okay, sweetie."

Tears stream down Oakly's cheeks and no one even bothers wiping them away for her. That shit ignites even more rage in me, and I pull on Gima's mind painfully. I feel her body twitch beneath mine, but I don't give a fuck.

I listen, Oakly listens, as Gima's voice echoes around the room as she tells her everything she plans to do to my men. Every nasty fucking sexual fantasy she can concoct in her mind, she just says it out loud, then she moves on to Ry.

Her malicious intentions are clear as she strokes her fingers across Oakly's forehead softly and quietly tells her exactly what she has in store for Ry as though she's reading her a bedtime story. The disgust, hatred, and heartbreak are clear in Oakly's eyes, and I have no doubt, my sister would've killed Gima then and there if she hadn't been drugged.

A short while passes as Gima continues to taunt her before the door opens wide, and a man with a stern face and sure steps walks in with a medical tray in hand. I'm shocked to find I recognize that face but not from my own memories. Caspian's second kidnapping.

"Enough, Miss Everglow, I need to begin her preparation," he says, exasperated, dismissing Gima completely.

"I'll stay and watch," she announces, hopping off the side of Oakly's table excitedly.

"Very well." He rolls his eyes.

There's not much preparation at all other than him cleaning the area around the vein inside Oakly's wrist. He shoves a large syringe in and pushes in whatever it is that's currently keeping her from healing. Once he's done, he simply cleans the small drop of blood away and turns back to the door.

"I'll be in my lab and will be back to retrieve her when it is time. You are not to touch her whatsoever. Watch only," he commands harshly but doesn't bother to spare Gima a glance.

"Don't speak to me that way," Gima says, seething.

Doctor who the fuck ever stops in the doorway, slowly turning around to face her. "Listen here and listen well, you insolent girl. You are granted what you have because of your father's ability to brownnose his way to the top. You do not get to tell me what to do. Mind your mouth or you'll be on the table next." With that glaring threat, he leaves without another word.

Gima stands in her spot, shaking with anger before spinning around to Oakly, and begins pacing.

"How dare he speak to me that way? Wait till my father hears about this. I'll fucking show..." She stops her pacing, and a sinister smile crosses her lips. "He may believe that, but I have plans for you."

The cunt does a complete one-eighty personality switch and resumes her taunting for a few more minutes until Oakly's eyes flutter shut, and with a suck of her teeth, Gima literally fucking pouts like her favorite toy's been taken from her. She proceeds to pace around the room, huffing and sighing, I guess watching her as she was told to do, until a Mastery member bursts through the room.

"We're on lockdown. E.F.s have arrived and the heirs are amongst them. Stay in here."

Before he gets a chance to leave the room, Gima latches onto his hand. "Actually, we're bringing her to the center. Allow them through that entryway, please. Deinde-Master Darstein has had a change of plans." Her gift purrs through her lips and the unsuspecting fool falls right into it. She laces her fingers through his after he slings Oakly over his shoulder and proceeds to pump her gift into him as they travel the halls.

The entire time, she persuades him to give orders and plans to the other Mastery members, and I guess with his standing, they do nothing but obey. She orchestrates this whole thing, solely on her own, and with no permission from anyone in the Mastery who actually has a standing.

Smart, psycho bitch.

I speed through our entire encounter, but it takes me by surprise that killing Oakly was a last-minute decision. It isn't until she actually says out loud that Ry is replaceable that she considers that option and decides she doesn't give a fuck about him or Silvia getting the rest of them as her Nexus. She completely intended to hurt me for stealing what was never hers.

Snatching myself out of her mind, I practically jump off her as though she's burned me. My fists clench painfully at my sides as she moans and groans, pushing herself to her feet on wobbly legs, and slowly wipes the blood that's drippling out of her nose.

When she looks at me with a crooked smile, then dares to look over at Oakly, I snap.

My arm shoots out and I grip her hair tightly in my hand, pulling her so close to me our chests collide, but given that she's a few inches taller than me, I bring her down to her knees.

"Wait till I tell my father about this." She hisses and attempts to pry my hand from her head.

"After all of this, you're still so fucking delusional." I growl and drag her to the edge of the platform.

Finally, a sense of self-preservation kicks in and she begins begging and screaming as she thrashes around.

"No, no, you can't do this. I'll give myself over. I'll tell you everything," she bellows as she sits on the ground to try to force me to stop pulling her along.

Her resistance is nothing compared to my dragon's strength plus the unyielding anger pumping through me currently. It takes me nothing to get her just a foot shy of the drop and I crouch down in front of her.

"There's nothing you could tell me, Gima, that I don't already know. But I will tell you something, so listen close," I say low, deadly. "Elementra presents choices to all of us because it's our right to choose the path we take. Every choice has a consequence. You chose poorly. You chose to fuck with the strongest family in Elementra rather than help us destroy the plague infecting our realm. So now, I have to make my choice to rid the realm of the infection that is you."

I didn't think her eyes could narrow even more, but she proves me wrong. With a glare that could kill, she spits out, "My father will never stand for you harming me. This will mean war."

"We're already in a war and your father chose the wrong side. Any last words?" I ask coldly.

Panic, true panic, finally sets in across her face and as the tears well in her eyes, she casts them over to the side.

To my fucking men.

"Cor—"

"Never mind, I don't give a fuck."

With that, by the tangle of hair I have wrapped around my hand, I sling her headfirst over the side. I watch from the edge, holding her gaze for as long as she can hold mine, and her screams echo up to me. I don't budge until I see her body catch fire within the magma.

Hands suddenly grip me everywhere and pull me back until I'm cushioned in the middle of my Nexus. There isn't an ounce of disappointment, disgust, or anything other than pride pouring off them. Except the undercurrent of fear and worry that is still raging through all of us.

Their sweet words and praises will have to wait.

"The man who came to see you when you and Tillman were kidnapped is here. He's somewhere in the volcano and he's the one who gave Oakly whatever is coursing through her right now," I tell Caspian and immediately his eyes darken.

"I'll find him, Primary."

With that, he moves through the darkness at the speed of light.

"Keeper's got his path cleared," Tillman says not even a second later as his eyes start glowing and before I can open my mouth, he continues, "I'll tell Caspian, and he'll meet us wherever we are. He'll be fine."

We jog over to where the others are still surrounding Oakly as Jamie pumps everything he's got into her. During my fight, he's lost his E.F. uniform and his shirt is absolutely drenched in sweat. Between the heat in here, Oakly's fever, and how much power he's having to push out, he's going to have a damn stroke.

"Time to go. Guys, get her on this," Tillman commands as he maneuvers his hands around to make a gurney.

As gently as they can, Ry, San, and Nikoli lift Oakly up and place her on it while Jamie never removes his from her chest. Draken and Corentin wordlessly grab the ends so they can carry it while her men continue to hold on to her and the sight nearly fucking breaks me. She may be my *Perfecta Anima*, but they love her like a sister as well.

We're a family. If one of us hurts, we all do.

Tillman guides us to the hall Keeper was in charge of clearing and as soon as we hit it, he appears in front of us.

Falling in line with us easily, he's wearing a bloodthirsty smirk and gore that tells the story of what he's been up to. He goes to say something, I'm sure inappropriate at this moment, but he stops as he looks at Oakly's prone form.

"What's going on? Why isn't she awake?" he asks frantically.

"They've injected her with something. We've got to get her to a healing wing," Draken says seriously as our footsteps pick up pace.

"What was it?" Keeper asks.

"We don't fucking know," Nikoli growls and I see the guilt and shame crawling all over him. He has no reason to feel like that, but I don't dare say anything to him right now. They're all going to be feeling a little of that no matter what.

"With all your consent, I will identify it." Keeper immediately volunteers, and that causes us to stop in our tracks.

"What do you mean?" Jamie asks, panting.

"If you'll allow me to taste her blood, I can tell you what is plaguing her."

"You can do that?" I ask, shocked.

"I can. I can already smell that it's not lethal or harmful to me. The Summum-Master tested many of his concoctions on me to measure their potency," he says with a small growl.

I want to scream at him to fucking do it now, but ultimately, that's not my decision.

Luckily, Jamie's doctor slash scientist sides kick in quickly.

"Please. If you can identify it, it'll make treating her easier when we get out of here, but I can't pull my magic back. Without it..."

A small whimper falls from my lips, and I try to smother it down, but I had no clue it was that bad. Of course I knew it wasn't good, but I didn't know she's completely relying on him at this point.

With a firm nod, Keeper gently lifts her hand to his mouth and softly pricks her finger. As respectfully as he can, he sucks down a couple drops of blood, then lays her arm back to rest.

The air in my lungs dries up when I sense the shift in his mood. His eyes quickly bleed to crimson before flashing back to his ruby orbs. He tries to compose himself, but he's failing miserably.

"Just say it, Keeper," I whisper, mortified.

"This is the drug they administer to those they intend to steal their gifts from. There...there is no cure for this."

No.

Fifteen

Caspian

Ahhh, I do love the sounds of screaming.

Dropping the piece of shit who hid away like a coward while this hall was being cleared, I continue to fade through the darkness. The tidal wave of emotions that continues to pour into my heart from my Primary forces me to go faster, kill quickly.

In the time we've been here, I've felt her experience every emotion known to our kind and it's created quite the cacophony inside of me. One second, I'm ready to murder everyone. The next, I feel like going to my knees in front of her and holding her close.

I'll admit up until this point, I've been indifferent toward her *Perfecta Anima*. I've never wished her any harm despite her hate for me, which honestly, I deserve. I was quite the asshole to Willow when she arrived, as well as to her, and I've never bothered to apologize to her. She was always just another female, so I didn't truly care to, but that'll never be the case again after today.

Feeling the turmoil, the true heartache my Primary is experiencing right now over Oakly is like having the organ cut from my chest. I may have thought I knew what it meant to share a bond like the two of them do, but

I was clueless until today. If she dies, so will a large part of my Willow. Gone will be the woman who owns my soul and what's left of her will never be the same.

I fucking refuse to allow that to happen.

So I will do everything within my power to make sure Oakly survives today and every day going forward. I may, just maybe, apologize and work toward taking the number three spot from Corentin or Tillman.

We'll see how far hunting down this man and killing him gets me.

"Oakly's been injected with the drug that the Summum-Master uses before stealing people's gifts, according to Keeper. He claims there's no cure. We need the fucker who injected her. Roye and Dyce will stay behind while we get her to the healing wing. We're at the entrance now," Tillman reports.

"Go, brother. I'll take him to the dungeons when I find him and get those answers."

"Be careful."

"I will and...our Primary?" I ask. I already feel her enough to know, but Tillman can see and hear things I can't.

"Calm. Petrifyingly so."

My displeasure rumbles in my chest because I know what the little Primary is doing. I'm doing the same currently. But she can't live in the darkness like me, and I'm not there right now to stop her. My brothers will have to do that for me for now.

They've created such an awful habit of ignoring these signs because of me, but just because our demons match, it doesn't mean we're the same.

Where I've grown a home in the black abyss, my Primary embraces it, commands it, then sets it free. The setting it free part is where she needs the push. If not, it dims her light. And I can't have that.

The glow she's left in my soul is already flickering with the flashbacks seeing the hostages here are bringing forth. They've given up, just like I did.

"That means she's retreating and shutting down. Don't allow her to."

"There's no allowing or not allowing, Cas. She's processing—"

"She's processing nothing. She's hiding from her fear of her sister dying and everything else. She dove toward a pit of magma, incinerated over half the Mastery army that was in that center, and just beautifully killed the

bitch who caused all this. You can't let her hide in her mind, or she'll let it consume her, then shove it down until we can't reach and reassure her. Do as I tell you or I'll come do it myself," I command.

"Fine. We'll see you soon. Transporting now," he says begrudgingly.

He may not like that I'm telling him to force her to talk, but he'll do it. We don't have the time to spare for me to shadow all the way to them. I'll handle her privately when this is over and make sure everything is fine then.

I'd rather she outwardly acts batshit murderous over her being quiet. Her silence is never a good thing in moments like this.

Shadowing through more walls of this volcano, I have to admit, despite the memories this situation is bringing forth, this design was ingenious but also incredibly foolish. Pyra has given the Mastery an advantage over a monstrous compound that has so many different uses, it's unbelievable. The current floor I'm flowing through is fucking bedrooms. They had individuals living in this space.

It's probably one of the largest and most populated structures we've infiltrated, but that's where their errors lie.

Taking this down is a massive hit to their army. Regardless that the majority are grunts, with a few top soldiers mulling around, the numbers were catastrophic.

At the end of the four halls, we thought that was it, but we were wrong. Each stretch ends with an illusion wall that leads to flights of stairs. I sent E.F. members through each of them, but the current one I'm drifting down is a few floors higher than where they are, and I'm pretty positive I've cleared the pussies and stragglers who didn't join the battle earlier.

There lies the design flaw.

Since I've moved upward, I couldn't begin to tell you what's going on now in the hallways below me. They're too far apart and the volcanic rock creates a barrier thick enough to block out sound.

The higher I travel, the less I feel the pull of whatever that is that the Summum-Master used to strip away others' spells, enchantments, and the ability to escape. The tug of it against my skin continues to shrink the more I climb.

I couldn't begin to tell you where in the volcano I'm located, but judging by the temperature becoming cooler, I'm closer to the top than the bottom now. It's still warmer than I'd care for it to be, but it's no longer sweltering.

I've been rapidly moving through the walls, giving quick glances around the rooms, but the second I pass through the corner of this one, I slow. There's no outside magic surrounding it whatsoever.

Sticking close to the wall, I slowly walk around the corridor blocking my view and muffling the voice I hear. I stop to observe my surroundings once the fucker I've been looking for comes into sight.

There's no one in here with him. He's talking to himself, pacing around the huge lab.

"Found him. About to move in. He has an entire lab stationed here. No hostages. Send someone up here to retrieve this shit," I tell Tillman and feel his hope rise.

I've been a little preoccupied since I last said something to him, so it's only now that I pay attention to everyone's sense of dread. It's so strong, I could confuse it as my own.

Fuck, that can't be good.

Knocking a row of beakers off the counter with my hand, I push myself up and perch my ass on the side, smiling as he whips around, startled. I'll give him credit. He straightens himself up very quickly and doesn't cower or try to run. Yet.

"Well, well, well. I like what you've done with the place," I say smugly.

"Caspian Vito, we meet again." He attempts to nonchalantly step behind his desk. I just roll my eyes. As if that scrap of wood will protect him from me.

"That we do...Sorry, do I call you Deinde-Master or Doctor?"

His bravado slips for just a moment and then he schools his features again, but I catch it and tilt my lips up enough just to let him know I did.

"Whichever you prefer."

"To be honest, I don't give a fuck, nor do I have time for pleasantries. We need to get going, so are we doing this the hard or easy way?" I ask, clapping and rubbing my hands together.

"I won't be going anywhere with you," he shouts dramatically and attempts to transport out.

"I'm a little offended you thought of me as such a fool. You're obviously a smart man," I say sarcastically, gazing around. "Did you think I'd just make my presence known and not be prepared for you to try to leave me so soon?"

The smug bastard was too distracted to even notice both my ice and shadows crawling around his feet, locking him in place.

Hopping off the counter, with each step I take, I command my gift and element to continue their crawl up his body and by the time I reach him, they're beginning to form around his neck.

"You and I are going to have some fun, while you tell me everything about whatever the fuck you injected into my Primary's sister. If my recollection serves me—which it does—your enforcers beat me for an hour straight and not a peep passed my lips. Let's see how long you hold out." I throw my head back, laughing, then latch my hand around his neck and transport us out.

Fucker has no idea the pain I have coming for him.

I pop us right into my favorite torture room in the dungeon.

Why is it my favorite? Fuck if I know. Probably because it's the coldest room down here, but my dads and brothers know this is my room and no one can torture anyone in here without me.

It's muscle memory for me at this point to pop in right in the perfect spot, shove the asshole into his seat, and have the magical cuffs snapped in place all in the matter of seconds.

My smirk has his thrashing stilling and the panic streaking across his face smooths out as he looks around the room. The rise and fall of his chest never calms, though. Despite the collected and in control persona he's trying to show me, he's failing miserably. I've lived my life with the most in control person to walk this realm. This scum is nothing compared to him.

"Darstein, correct?" I ask as I plop my own ass on the chair in front of him.

"We both know you already know the answer to that. Get to the point," he says tensely.

"Have it your way. I was giving you an opportunity to get comfortable before we began, but I guess you're not a man for foreplay," I say huffing, slapping my hands on my knees, then pushing up from the seat.

My shadows lash out faster than he has time to flinch and slice his shirt open, exposing his unmarked chest and the one or two cuts they left behind. I tilt my head to the side curiously, while he cries out over the little paper cuts. There's no doubt he's marked somewhere, but I was honestly expecting a huge-ass branding on his heart with his standing in the Mastery.

"This is a pleasant surprise, Darstein. It's not often that I'm wrong. If your mark isn't on your heart, it must be on your head. But why?" I ask, tapping a dagger made of my gift against my lips.

"If you know about the marks, you know as well as I do that I can't talk. So if you're going to kill me, just do it already."

His tone is almost pleased, as if he's proud he'll be dying with his lips sealed. Stupid, fool.

"Ah, of course. I have a solution for that, though," I say as I let a devilish smirk cross my face.

"Bring Keeper to my torture room so he can remove this rune," I tell the dragon, and his dark chuckle morphs my smirk into a full-fledged smile.

I don't say anything else. I let my stare linger on Darstein, making him fidget uncomfortably in his chair. Only once I hear the knock at the door do I let a sinister chuckle bubble out of me.

"Gentlemen, thank you for joining us," I say mockingly as I swing the door open wide.

"N-No. How?" Darstein stutters, his bravado completely falling apart as Draken walks in, then moves to the side for Keeper.

"Darstein. You're looking...well, as you always do. The sniffling is more obvious without the Summum-Master around, though."

"You're not supposed to be here," Darstein murmurs, seemingly shell-shocked, and Keeper looks at him like he's lost his mind.

"I see you've not moved up any further into his good graces if he didn't even bother to tell you I was freed from the forest. What did you do this time to piss him off?"

Well, I must say, this entire exchange has piqued my interest. Keeper brings up a very valid point and I intend to get the answer to his question, but first things first, we have a *Perfecta Anima* to save.

"We can play catch-up in a moment. We need to figure out what we can about the injection," I say sternly.

Wordlessly, both Draken and Keeper step up to Darstein, not bothering to give him a heads-up about what's going to happen. He knows by the way he's already screaming and thrashing around like a beached fish.

As soon as Keeper removes the dagger from beneath his waistband and presses the tip of it to Darstein's head, the entire rune reveals itself and I whistle low. The marking is massive. It stretches from the arch in one of his brows to the other. This scum must have unyielding loyalty to that piece of shit despite the disregard the Summum-Master has toward him.

I watch in silent fascination as Keeper repeats the same process he did on Layton, although way less gentle, and Draken isn't attempting to flood him with happiness.

After the outline is complete and the rune begins to fade, Keeper finishes it off by adding his blood to the Reservoir gem. Darstein knows his time is now coming to an end, and when the hissing of the blood boiling stops, he chokes on a sob.

Pathetic.

"How you've had the stomach to do the things you do but can't handle this is astonishing," Keeper says, shaking his head.

"Anything I've ever done has been in the name of science."

I chuff and roll my eyes at that ridiculous excuse. "I'll explain why you're wrong in a moment. First, explain to me what it was that you injected Oakly with and how we fix it."

A smirk tips his lips upward and as I go to step toward him, quicker than I can follow, the dragon has his head snapping to the side from the force of his punch.

Gripping his most likely broken jaw, Draken forces his eyes to meet his. "Smile at the prospect of what you've done to my Primary's sister and I'll rip your lips from your fucking face."

"I...I...there is no way to fix that," Darstein bubblers.

There's a fix for everything.

"The name of the injection. The ingredients. Its purpose. Everything. Now," I bark, and command hundreds of small shadow needles to stab into his chest. He howls in pain, and I grab a handful of them, then snatch them out. "I'll pull one out for every piece of information. The longer you take, the more I add and the bigger they'll get. This is my one compromise. Pick your torture wisely."

"Okay, okay," he screams and I pull out another.

Just as he goes to open his mouth again, another knock at the door sounds, and Draken bounds over to get it. I sense Tillman's heavy-ass booted steps without even turning around. The turbulence rolling through him is enough to shake the entire foundation below.

"Anything?" he asks.

"Doctor dickhead is about to tell us all about the injection now," Draken growls, shooting Darstein a look of warning.

Tillman's eyes take on their telling glow as he begins sifting through everything he can on his own. The longer he stares, though, the more his brows crease.

That can't be good.

"Explain. Now," he orders, pulling out of Darstein's mind. On my left, Keeper pulls out his little black book that he likes to keep with him and a pencil, readying to make the list of everything. No doubt sensing we're going to need that.

"We've named it the Vessel Deterior. Its purpose is to break down the body in order for the Summum-Master to remove the gifts and elements. The ingredients..." He hesitates, and as soon as two seconds pass, I cast out five shadow forks and embed them right below his collarbone. He bellows, and everyone looks at me.

I may have skipped a couple size growths there.

Whoops.

"The ingredients are from multiple realms," he cries, heaving, trying to catch his breath, and I give him this moment rather than stab him again. "Natural born Elementrians do not die from diseases nor do we have natural causes of death, but one other realm does and another has one disease that can kill if contracted."

"The nonmagical realm and Mystara Hollow," I finish for him and he nods.

"Mystarians, much like us, could be immortal, but a couple centuries ago, a plague broke out. It was caused by an invasive plant—the Aconight plant—that blended with one of their remedy herbs. Its appearance was nearly identical, so many of the practitioners were adding that into their potions unknowingly. The herb strips their magic. Once consumed, there is no stopping it. Their magic basically...fades away. They've since identified the plant and have done away with it, aside from the supply the higher rulers keep.

"The nonmagical realm can and will die of both. Their lifespans are incredibly short, and they can die by any number of things. Fragile beings, to say the least. There are hundreds of thousands of diseases present in the realm, but one in particular called an autoimmune disease, got the Mastery's attention."

His eyes alight with wonder and I snarl before sending out a small switchblade to stab through his shoulder. Sure, I love learning about new and fascinating things, but he's getting excited over these deadly diseases that have killed across realms. I don't give a fuck if he's a scientist and this is interesting for him. I won't allow him to relish in some sort of sick satisfaction.

"Finish," I command.

"An...autoimmune disease for nonmagical beings is when the body's cells attack themselves. Rather than fighting off something as simple as a common cold, it'll kill off the healthy cells that are trying to protect it. Then lastly—"

"The Poison of Essence," Tillman grunts and we all whip our heads toward him.

"What?" I ask coldly.

"He uses a drop of the Poison of Essence," he says begrudgingly.

"I am not the creator of this. I've just been modifying and perfecting it," Darstein says defensively as if that makes him any less guilty.

"Explain the purpose of the three of them together. What is it doing to Oakly right now?" Tillman asks.

"Our bodies are created on a duality system. We have all the same components of nonmagical beings, but with the bonus of our gifts, magic, and elements. Those two function both together and separately. Our bodies could survive without our bonuses, but our bonuses must inhibit a body. Our bonuses are intricately woven in with the rest of us, so deeply, we, for the most part, cannot tell their functions apart.

"Once you mix those three ingredients together, it creates the means to separate the bonuses completely. The Aconight plant attacks the bonuses. It is not strong enough to make it fade as it does the Mystarians, but it weakens its ability to fight it off. Paired the drop of the Poison of Essence, it can tear it from the body once the body is broken down enough. That's the point of the autoimmune disease. Without the protection of our bonuses, it can attack our cells, inhibit the body's ability to heal. It's the first ever Elementra infection."

The room falls deathly silent.

I can't even breathe through the onslaught of information now coursing through my mind.

"Keeper, you got all that?" Tillman asks solemnly and Keeper's pencil stops scribbling after a moment, then he nods. "Draken, take him back to the others and give them this information. See if anyone can find a way around this."

"You're wasting your time. I've yet to come up with a reversal. Once it's in the bloodstream, there's no getting it out," Darstein says and Draken's fist flies across his face once again. This time, leaving him out cold.

"Go. We have more to discuss with him. If Willow or any of you need us, let me know," Tillman orders once again, gripping Draken on the shoulder. The dragon doesn't resist as he and Keeper leave silently, lost in their own thoughts and rage.

"What else did you see?" I ask once they shut the door.

"I didn't go far back. I heard the ingredients but didn't understand the two that weren't from here. There're some areas that are going to take a good bit of effort to uncover. He's been drugging himself to forget things. What stuck out, though, was that he has an overwhelming repeated thought about how he's better than the last scientist. I think that's the man who did what he did to you," he says cautiously, but I'm not upset he brought that up.

The opposite, actually.

I want that answer. Now.

Pulling out a healing vial from my shadows, I pop the cap and pause, glancing over at Tillman. "When he wakes up, bring up the former scientist and get an image of him from his mind. I'll be able to identify him."

At his nod, I pry Darstein's jaw open and pour the contents in, then step back and wait for him to come to. It doesn't take long. Gaster knows how to make a mean healing vial and this fucker should be grateful I allow him to absorb it.

Groaning and turning his head around, he startles when he fully comes to and sees the two of us glaring at him.

"Who did you replace in the Mastery?" Tillman immediately asks, then slaps his hand to Darstein's forehead.

The piece of shit doesn't even have to answer. He's thinking it all loud and clear for Tillman to gather all on his own. The brighter his emerald eyes glow, the more Darstein screams. He's not being gentle whatsoever in his pursuit for answers and I'm thrilled to see it.

After what feels like fucking forever, Tillman stumbles back, panting heavily and shaking his head. Laying his hand to my shoulder briefly, he sends me an image that makes my blood boil.

"That's him," I grunt and Tillman nods before tilting his own healing vial back.

"Fuck, that took a lot," he groans.

"What all did you get?"

"Everything that isn't completely wiped out from the drugs. Starting from the time he was born," he says and my eyes widen.

Well, fuck me sideways.

Looks like someone got another upgrade.

"Did he know where he is?" I ask.

"Yeah. Dead. He set him up and the Summum-Master killed him."

I'm not gonna lie and say I'm not pissed the fuck off about that. His life was mine to take, but I guess the alternative would've been he'd still be free to kill people. So I'll let it go. His replacement will have to do.

"The jealousy got the best of you, didn't it?" Tillman asks tauntingly.

Darstein's eyes narrow and his lip tilts up. "I was Master Ale's apprentice for years. I surpassed his capabilities by a mile, yet he'd do or say nothing to show the Summum-Master that I was just as skilled. They both treated me as nothing more than an insolent child."

"Then when Ale told you that you couldn't participate in a high-stakes experiment, you decided to just fuck the whole thing up and let the blame fall on him," Tillman summarizes.

"How did he do that?" I ask.

"The infection was in its early phase at this point. They weren't directly injecting it into people but instead forcing them to drink it. Its effects took longer and only those with extraordinary gifts survived long enough to have the process completed. He did something to the vial. That is the part that's practically wiped clean from his mind. You've made sure to cover your tracks so the Summum-Master didn't find out you were the cause of the failure and ultimately got his most treasured scientist killed."

"Most treasured? How many are there?" I ask.

"There were two top scientists. Master Ale and Master Drin. Drin is in the nonmagical," Darstein answers.

"Show me Drin," I command Tillman, and he immediately obliges.

My shadows shoot out of me and surround Darstein. He's my outlet for the anger seeping through my pores as the cold dead eyes flash through my mind.

Fuck these motherfuckers.

Every one of them.

"That's the man who would draw Willow's blood," I tell him.

He nods knowingly before carrying on, "He's still there. He works under Franklin, well, did. This idiot hasn't been informed of really any of the newest updates, but he probably would've found out today. The process of the infection takes about six hours to fully infect. The Summum-Master was due to arrive at Pyra to complete the transfer of Oakly's power. So we have three hours, give or take, to figure this shit out. He only knows this part of the ritual. Infecting the victim. Then the Summum-Master takes them away. Once we get Oakly figured out, maybe Keeper can fill in the rest."

Three hours...

I'll be using that time wisely.

"Head back to the others."

"If we can't—"

"Don't speak it, Tillman. Don't even fucking think it. Take what you've learned and go inform the others. Fill in any gaps they may have. I'll be there once we're done here," I order low.

He holds my darkening gaze for a long moment, making sure he still sees the man inside of the monster.

He's failed to realize—they all have other than my Primary—that the two have merged into one. There're no longer multiple sides of myself that battle for dominance. When my Primary's soul nuzzled itself inside of me all sweetly, my monster came crawling to her feet like a starved animal begging for a scrap of meat.

Now it's her soul, myself, and my monster against the demons.

I won't be telling him that currently, the three parts that make me whole are losing this internal battle.

He doesn't need to know I can't stop replaying how those hostages laid there, hopeless, begging for me to deliver them death with just their eyes. It was the same way I looked at anyone new who waltzed into my stone cage when I was taken.

No one ever granted my request. Nor did I grant theirs.

"I'll keep you updated," Tillman finally says, breaking the silence.

My eyes follow him out and when he shuts the door, I let out a deep, relieved breath.

Finally.

My demons want free.

My darkness wants to descend.

Spinning on my heel, I face a petrified Darstein. Twirling a dagger in my hand, I bend down to eye level and ask, “Any last words?”

His mouth opens and closes repeatedly as incoherent blabbering spews out.

Groaning impatiently and rolling my eyes, I slam my palm over his mouth.

“Never mind. I don’t give a fuck.”

Sixteen

Willow

"Her soul is still strong," Aria whispers beside me, pulling me out of zoning out.

I feel like I've been staring through this glass pane for days, when it's only been a couple of hours. The longest, most dreadful hours of my entire life. No amount of physical torture comes close to this level of mental and emotional suffering.

I give Aria a very unconvincing tight smile and squeeze her hand back before moving away from the glass and turning back toward the table we have set up in the hall.

Scattered across its surface is every piece of information the academy, the palace, and Gaster possess on Mystara Hollow and the nonmagical realm.

While Jamie, Draken, and a few select healers work in there on Oakly, pumping her full of magic, the rest of us are out here, reading everything we possibly can to figure out a way out of this for her.

When we first arrived, Aurora had already called in the best of the best and had this secluded room ready to go for her.

Unfortunately for one of the healers, he made the grave mistake of forgetting his bedside manners. He said that even if we could save her, she'd be brain dead from how hot her body was. Before anyone could interfere, San and Ry attacked.

I still don't know or care if he's woken up yet.

None of the other healers have dared utter a negative word.

When Keeper and Draken arrived back with the ingredients and purpose of the infection, Gaster, Neil, Theo, and Aurora jumped into action, collecting everything they could get their hands on in breathtaking time. Since then, we've been at this table.

Searching for what feels like impossible answers.

This is the first time I've ever seen San's gift in true action. It goes far beyond the realm of just reading and retaining information. He can speed through the pages in the blink of an eye. It takes him around six minutes to devour an entire book and I'm pretty sure by this point he's read everything on the table twice.

"Come see me, young one. Take a break."

I release a shuddering breath and close my eyes. Tanith's ability to soothe my dragon with gentle words is astonishing, but my fear, anxiety, and fight not to give up resist the comforting feeling.

"I can't. We're running out of time."

"And your mind is running in overdrive. If you do not give it a break, it'll never find what it's seeking."

Sighing, I bow my head and blink away the water collecting in my eyes. She's right. My mind hasn't stopped since...well, since I laid eyes on Jamie lying on the ground outside our ward and Nikoli's petrified eyes told me all I needed to know.

It's been running a mile a minute at every turn since then, but now, all I find is dead ends. I can't find a way out of this for her. And I simply can't accept that. I won't survive without her.

"Tanith wants to see me. I'll be back in a minute," I mumble to no one in particular, but my voice still draws everyone's attention.

"I'll walk you, child. Maybe some fresh air and conversation with Tanith will spark something for me," Gaster volunteers. I give him a tight smile and lace my arm through his when he offers me his elbow.

We walk in strained silence through the healing wing and out the doors to where Tanith is sitting with her head tilted toward the sun.

I almost forgot it was daylight still.

The darkened windows in the healing wing obscure the sun and heat, keeping the area cool and dimly lit. Comfortable, I guess for the patients in there.

To me, though, in this moment, it just makes it feel cold, empty.

Hopeless.

"The two of you feel drained. Be one with your realm for a moment. Take in the magic," Tanith says softly as we approach her silently.

"Thank you, Tanith," Gaster says respectfully as he bows to her, but I can't even muster up that much.

The warm rays that are heating up my chilled skin make my throat close, and another wave of tears gathers together. I don't think I should be out here enjoying the sun and the natural heat while my best friend is inside, internally burning.

Gaster doesn't give me much of an option, though, as he grips my elbow and pulls me down to the ground beside him.

"My lord has shared what all you've learned, and I believe I understand, but maybe one of you should spell it out for me. See if there's something we're missing."

"Gaster," I croak out.

As he relays the information to Tanith, I close my eyes and tilt my head to the sun, mimicking her and begging it to give me an answer.

Besides Jamie, Draken, and the healers working away at pumping their magic into Oakly nonstop, plus Elementra only knows the number of healing vials, the only other solution we've tried is giving her the Poison of Essence cure. We hoped that maybe, even though she'd only been given a drop of the poison, the cure would help do something.

It didn't.

She's still just as hot and on the cusp of death as she was without it.

"Let us assume the best as we speak," Tanith says with full conviction. *"The Poison of Essence cure stopped the flow of the poison in her blood. Draken, her Nexus member, and other healers are feeding her magic, which is keeping the Aconight plant at bay. So that leaves this disease from the nonmagical realm. What do we know of it?"*

I grit my teeth painfully. This question has already come up and all eyes turned to me for an answer. A fucking answer I didn't have because I didn't have to worry about sicknesses of that degree in the nonmagical realm.

My illnesses were physical injuries. My nose never even ran unless it was bloody, or I'd been crying. I know very minimally about what people truly suffer in the nonmagical realm.

What I do know is about the flu shot, colds, breast and ovarian cancer, and birth controls because of the posters in the doctor's office that I read a million times when I was getting my IUD implanted. Other than that, Franklin had doctors come to the estate. For obvious reasons.

I'd hear people at school talking about deadly things. Heart attacks, strokes, cancer, but it's not like anyone was giving me breakdowns of what any of it meant.

"Only what Darstein said. I didn't have to face these things during my time there, nor did I ever have to learn about it. I never even met anyone who mentioned it," I bite out.

"Do you remember Stephanie? From kindergarten?"

CC's voice causes Gaster to flinch and Tanith to growl low at the sudden invasion. My mental block was down and open to both of them so we could communicate. I didn't expect him to come through. Seeing as I've been fucking begging and crying for his directions all day.

"Are you fucking kidding me? Do you seriously expect me to remember kindergarten? Especially at a time like this?" I ask harshly.

"Calm yourself, Adored. The one who speaks is wise beyond our comprehension. If he wants you to think back to this time, you should do so. Do not give him undeserved wrath."

"He's my other Guardria, Tanith. I've been begging for his guidance all day. Years actually."

"And now he is giving it to you. I know the frustrations you feel, young one. I've lived in the shoes you are now filling for many, many years. It is much easier to take our anger out on those we love, but you must repress that desire now. This is the one you've told me of. He is doing all he can, when he can. Take his guidance," she says so softly, it douses my inferno, and I swallow down the lump in my throat.

"I'm sorry," I breathe.

"As am I, filia mea."

Gaster laces his fingers with mine and pats my hand warmly as I blow out a breath and wipe the tears soaking my face. I use his resolve and confidence to ground me. I feel like I'm seconds away from shaking so violently, I'll vibrate myself into the earth below me.

"I don't think I remember kindergarten. That was...that was the year it all started," I say quietly.

"Follow Tanith's lead," CC says.

"Tanith..."

"To go that far back, young one, you must at least recall a time you were that young. Something that sparks that time frame," she says.

A small whimper passes my lips as the first thing to come to mind is that forsaken grave Franklin put me in. I quickly wash it away and replace it with meeting CC. His presence washes over me and blankets me in the love he feels for me and I hold onto it for dear life.

"I remember a time."

"Good, now think intently about that time. What were you doing? For me, it would be learning to fly, getting my claws off the ground, controlling my wings. Dragons learn to fly between the life span of six to eight years. By ten, we are allowed to fly with our flight."

What was I doing? Other than getting my blood drained.

I started at the all-girls school.

Magnolia Prep.

Suddenly, flashes of times long ago start playing across my mind and the navy, white, and black plaid uniforms spring to my mind. The etiquette classes. The pageants. The nurse's office.

"Good, filia mea. Think of Stephanie."

Stephanie. Stephanie...

"Willow, if you won't tell us the truth about how you injured your arm, we will just have to inform your father again."

"I've already told you. His friend's needle caused the bruise," I cry.

Mrs. Smith, the school nurse, shakes her head disappointedly at me before turning on her heel and walking away. With the stupid tie hanging down my shirt, I wipe away my angry tears and cross my arms.

"Sit right here, Stephanie. Your mommy will be here in a minute," Mrs. Smith says, far nicer to the girl who sits in the chair beside me.

She doesn't look hurt to me.

"Are you okay?" she asks softly, tapping me on my shoulder.

"Fine." I sniffle, turning so she doesn't see me crying.

"I heard what you said about the needle. My doctor has to stick needles in me too. My daddy holds me sometimes when it happens."

My wide eyes turn to her in shock, and I look over her for the same bruises I have. I don't see any, but she obviously didn't make the mistake of taking her jacket off.

"Your daddy takes your blood too?" I ask.

"Oh...no. I have to get blood," she says quietly as she looks down at her hands and picks at her fingernails.

"Get blood? Like they put it in you?" I ask with a disgusted look on my face.

"Yeah. My mommy and daddy said it would make me feel better."

"You're sick?"

"I guess so." She sighs sadly before carrying on. "At least I can get sick. Then I can't get better. I thought I was better because Dr. B told my mommy I could come to school now and play with other girls, but I threw up at recess a few minutes ago and now she's coming to get me."

"So you'll have to get blood put in you again?" I ask, completely fascinated.

"Maybe. I got ice cream afterwards last time," she says with a small smile and a shrug of her shoulders.

"Maybe that's why my father takes my blood. So I can help you feel better," I say happily.

"Willow." My father's voice barks from the doorway, and I straighten in my seat as cold fear slithers across my body.

His frown smooths into an easy smile as Mrs. Smith comes to stand beside him with her arms crossed over her chest. I shrink in on myself as they both glare at me and I know I'm in trouble.

"Come. Tell your friend goodbye," my father orders.

"Bye. I hope you feel better."

I slowly rise from the chair and slink my way toward my father. Before leaving the nurse's office, I peer back over my shoulder and wave at Stephanie.

I come out of the memory gasping, desperately trying to get air into my lungs. Watching that through my adult eyes, I easily see that Stephanie was sick. Her pale skin, the whites surrounding her eyes were tinted yellow, and she was so thin, fragile. I don't remember ever seeing her at school again, but then again, I got in so much trouble that day, I didn't make many friends after that. I kept to myself and made sure to keep my jacket on.

"I'm so sorry that's what you experienced, young one," Tanith says gently, and when I cast my eyes to her and Gaster, I realize I broadcasted that to them both.

"Don't be. It's okay."

Gaster clears his throat and squeezes my hand tightly before saying, *"From what I just gathered, that child was ill, and her illness required the blood of others to help her because her body couldn't do it on its own. That's how Darstein described the disease."*

Hope, the fickle and misleading emotion, floods my system as I put a death grip on his hand. We have blood in plenty of supply.

"Okay, so we give her some blood. That'll fix it," I say excitedly, trying to push myself to my feet, but Gaster holds me down.

"Hold on, Adored. Let's work it all out again. So we know that the blood will help with the nonmagical disease. The cure will help with the poison. But what did the Mystarians do to fix the Aconight problem?" Tanith asks.

Silence.

I have no clue, and neither does Gaster. There was no information in anything we found in our archives that even alluded to the issue in their realm. This spread happened after the portals closed.

"They burned it," CC says quietly.

Despite the fire that burns through me, my body suddenly feels like I've been dunked in an ice bath. The way he said it makes the hairs along my arms and the back of my neck stand on ends. Tanith's awareness tickles its way across my skin and I know what she's going to say.

"Adored..."

"No. It could kill her," I say, shaking my head furiously.

"What could kill her?" Gaster asks, confused.

"Like I had to do for Keeper and burn the cord from inside his neck. Tanith is going to suggest I burn the Aconight plant out of her blood. But it's not that simple or straightforward. With Keeper, I had something to pinpoint and command my flame through. This is spreading throughout her entire body. It's everywhere. I'd have to boil her blood. No. Think of something else," I command frantically.

"The time has come, filia mea," CC says softly and I sob as I feel his presence leave me again.

"No, please don't leave me. Please give me another way." I cry, begging for another solution, but one never comes.

The buzzing of Gaster's communicator forces him to withdraw his hand from mine and I grab fistfuls of grass in my hands to keep myself from exploding.

"We'll be there in a second," he says after not saying anything else rather just listening to the one-sided conversation. "They need us up there. There're only a few minutes left until we hit the six-hour mark. The palace healers are trying to convince the Mercie Nexus to let go. Aurora is ready to kick them all out, but Jamie needs help."

The sadness in his tone pulls another drenched sob from my chest and I can't hold in the scream any longer. I let it pour from me as I push up on my knees and rock back and forth. All around me, it feels like the walls are closing in. I'm seconds from suffocating under the pressure of it.

I can't lose her.

"Then do what you must, young one. You have all the tools at your disposal now. Use them. The flame, the blood, the cure. Your father-in-law. Her Nexus, your own. Find a solution to the problem in front of you with

everything you have. You are a dragon, a Primary, a sister, a daughter, a granddaughter, an Awaiting Matriarch, a Guardian, and an Adored. There is nothing you cannot do," Tanith says gently but firmly.

My tear-soaked, violet eyes snap open and meet her glittering gold ones. They're so full of conviction, it nearly steals the little bit of air I'm able to suck into my lungs.

Crawling over to her, I cup her snout in my hands and lay my forehead to hers. The power beneath her scales flutters across my body, and my dragon unfurls her wings and tilts her head up. Ready.

"I can do this."

"You can do this, young one."

Nodding, I stand up, wipe my face, then basically snatch Gaster off the ground and drag him along with me. Determination spreads throughout my body as I try to put the multiple pieces of what must happen together in my mind.

"What is the plan, Willow?"

"I'm still working on that," I say, blowing out my breath. "We're going to work it out with everyone. I'm going to need their help."

The two of us race through the healing wing and the second we hit the floor Oakly's on, I hear her men yelling, and the tension rolling in waves down this hall hits me straight in the gut.

They're seconds from losing their shit and my men, my brother, his brothers, Aria, Aurora, my Patera-Nexus, and Keeper are all standing with them.

"This is unethical and inhumane. You all should allow the girl to pass. Be here with her and spend your last few moments together in peace. I will not stand to allow myself or my team to continue working on someone who is clearly gone, and you all just don't want to accept that," the head healer says sternly, staring down at the small army of my family.

"Then get the fuck out," I say calmly as I push my way into the overcrowded room.

"Excuse—"

"I didn't stutter. Get the fuck out. Your help is no longer needed," I say, dismissing the asshole who's clearly already given up on my sister.

"You have no auth—"

"My daughter has all the authority she needs, but if that isn't enough for you, then hear it from me. Get the fuck out," Aurora says dangerously low, sending the room into silence.

Except for me.

I laugh. Because obviously I've lost my mind, and I have no other choice but to laugh or I'll crumble.

"Willow, I need extra hands. It's rapidly taking over. I...I can't do it on my own," Jamie says as sweat drips into his eyes, but he doesn't dare remove his hands.

"You're not going to do it alone. We're about to heal her right now, but I need everyone's help with working this out of my mind," I say as I come to stand beside my sister.

"What have you got, trouble?" Ry asks, choked, and I can't bring myself to look at him, so instead, I squeeze Oakly's hand.

"Multiple things have to happen all at once. I have to burn the Aconight plant out of her blood. Even though we've already given her a Poison of Essence cure, I think she'll need another. She needs to receive blood as the infected bits of hers are going to be burned away. And all of you need to be touching her. She needs her connection to her Nexus. Jamie, she'll still need your magic and Draken's. She should probably be kept cool as well. I'm going to be...burning her from the inside out. I just don't know the order in which this should all happen."

The room falls eerily silent as they all stare at me. Hope and pure desperation pierce my soul, and I finally look up at my brothers born from bonds. They're each staring at me like I've just given them the winning numbers to the royal chance and their surefire belief in me has my heart swelling.

"Okay, everyone, get in positions. Jamie, stay where you are. Draken, move up by her head so you can feed her directly and Jamie. Ry, San, Nikoli, opposite side of Willow. Princess, get where you need to be. Keeper, you need to manipulate the blood transfer. Who's giving the blood?" Corentin asks, fully taking over organizing everything to perfection.

"Willow should. Her blood is the strongest and I will add some of my own as well to give her a boost in lifeforce," Keeper easily agrees, coming to stand beside me.

"Good. Next, Tillman ground Willow, keep her thoughts clear. I'll keep my air circulating around Oakly to keep her cool."

"I'll add my water. It's her element as well and she'll need to be hydrated," Caspian says, stepping out of the cover of darkness, and my eyes fill with tears once again when they lock on his.

All I can muster is a mouthed thank you and I suck down a sob ready to escape me when I feel his shadows circle my wrist.

"Willow, start out soft and slow. Build up as you go and as Jamie pushes his magic into her. The rest of you, keep skin to skin contact no matter what. Keeper, you'll be able to tell when the transfer needs to begin?" Corentin asks.

"I will. Adored, I will slice your wrist and Oakly's, if that's okay?"

"Do whatever you need to."

"Okay, princess, begin. You got this," Corentin says firmly and I nod to him before seeking out each of Oakly's men.

The look in their watery gazes speaks a thousand words.

One way or another, they're going to be with her. It's decided by more than their own love for her. Their souls have spoken. If this doesn't work and we lose her, we lose them as well. They've accepted that and they're okay with it. They've made peace with it.

I haven't.

I don't believe the five of them realize what they mean to us.

That's the weird thing about grief. It's a selfish emotion.

I know as well as anyone in this room, the space Elementra would have ready for any of us in the beyond is just as magical, just as perfect as this physical plane she's created, yet we aren't willing to let them go there. We don't want to be here without them.

I'll be selfish enough for all of us to admit that.

I'm not losing any of them.

"We're going to heal her. I'm not going to lose any of you today."

"We know, Willy," all four say as one, and a mixture of a sob and a snort escapes me.

"Go on, trouble. Bring my firecracker back," Ry commands as a lone tear finally drips from his eye and I nod.

"Come on, Oak. You heard your most bossy of men. You're in so much trouble with him."

Leaning down, I lay a kiss to her nose and rub my hands down her arm while simultaneously encouraging her to fight and apologizing for what I'm about to do to her. This is going to be so painful. I know it without a shadow of a doubt, but it's what must be done.

My flame slowly travels through my veins, and I squeeze my eyes shut tight as they pierce through her skin. Her nerve endings cause her body to twitch and the agonizing gasps I hear from her men make my heart thud wildly, but I can't risk peeling my lids open to check anything for myself.

Heavy hands lay on my shoulders, though the weight feels like feathers, and suddenly, the sounds become mere whispers in the wind. There're no thoughts. There're no fears.

There's nothing but Oakly.

Draken's magic washes over the room and forces me to take a deep breath from the abrupt fullness I feel. I use the extra boost just given to me and push a little harder. The heat that's coming through my palms is a mixture of her fever and my flame, and a bead of sweat travels its way down my neck until a cool breeze stops its path.

The multitude of emotions filtering through the room tramples my chest, but I can't shift my focus enough to block it out.

I embrace it.

I allow the heightened sense and feelings of everyone in this room and the hall bolster my resolve, then I shove it out.

I push. And push. And push harder.

The heat intensifies to unmeasurable heights and the multiple groans from around the room ring loudly in my ears, but I don't relent. I don't pull it back because even though I know my flame is blazing, it won't truly hurt anyone in here.

Other than Oakly. She will be the only one who may be burned beyond repair if I'm not careful.

The hisses that are falling from the lips of Ry, San, Jamie, and Nikoli suddenly morph into agonizing screams, and it takes me a moment to realize my throat is roaring right along with theirs.

Heart-wrenching pain engulfs me as I feel the threads that keep Oakly's soul stitched to mine begin to unravel.

"What's happening?" My brother's concerned voice filters through my mind, but I can't answer him.

"Their souls are splitting apart," Aria quietly whispers, but I hear it.

Loud and clear.

"No!" I scream as I hold Oakly's arm tighter.

"Willow, you have to stop. It's killing her. It's too much."

My eyes snap open and collide with San's. His face is set firm, although his lip trembles. He nods in retaliation to the insistent shaking of my head, but I refuse. I'm not letting her go.

My frantic gaze searches each of their eyes. There's a war raging in each of them that I understand down to the depths of my soul. Part of us is fighting tooth and nail right now, not willing to let her go. The other side, the one that doesn't want to surface just yet, believes this is the end of the line.

"I can't. I need her. She's my sister," I cry, begging them to keep pushing, keep trying.

I whip my head to Oakly and force my mind into hers. There's no consciousness on the other side, but still I plead.

"Oakly, fight. Do you hear me? Fight with all you have. Fight for the love that's out here waiting for your hazel eyes to snap open. Fight for your Nexus, who will wage literal war for you, then turn around and hand feed you pastries because they're your favorites. They're going to love you forever, Oak. Here, in this realm. Fight for the want to prove yourself as the best archivist to walk the realm. No doubt Gaster will train you to the point you surpass him, and he'll be none the prouder.

"Fight for me. Please. Fight for us. Fight for the future we're going to have together. Fight for our bonding ceremonies. Fight for our adventures. Our

girl days. Our gossip sessions. Our trainings. The children we'll have in two hundred years that are going to give us hell. Please fight."

Another excruciating bellow falls from my lips as another strand slips undone between our souls. The thread of our connection is growing thinner by the second and I know any moment now, our bond will break, then be made whole again.

But she won't physically be here with me anymore.

"I swear by all the fucking power within me, Oakly Mercie, if you leave me, I'll crawl to the fucking beyond and drag you back out here by your beautiful purple hair. Don't keep fucking tempting me," I scream as my emotions become an overwhelming concoction of grief and anger.

Power surges through the room, causing Jamie to take a desperate, harsh inhale that echoes through the space so piercingly it penetrates the heartbreak overriding all my senses.

"Don't you stop now, Willow. Her body is sucking my magic dry. Draken," Jamie grunts painfully.

My dragon man's power pulses through the room and it springs everyone into action.

Wind, water, and a mountain of certainty coats not only my body but Oakly's, and when Keeper turns my wrist outward to drag his razor-sharp nail down my wrist, I nod at him encouragingly.

When he does the same to Oakly, his smooth accent floats around the room and I gasp as I feel my blood pulling from my veins. It's the same sensation as when I'd be drained, but there's no pain, no needles, and no tubing. Just a direct transfer of my life essence to hers.

Drag after drag of my blood pours into Oakly to the point my head begins to swim, but the strong arms that wrap themselves around my waist hold me up and I hold onto my determination for dear life.

I watch through blurry eyes as Keeper lifts his wrist to his mouth and punctures the vein until his cobalt blood streams down his chin. As the two lifeforces merge, a river of purple blood flows into the cut on Oakly's wrist and Jamie takes a deep breath.

"Gaster," Corentin commands.

Gaster hurriedly makes his way through the sea of us and gently opens Oakly's jaw. The pure white liquid miracle of the Poison of Essence travels through her lips and the room falls deadly silent as we wait.

Watch.

Tillman's chest catches me as everything that makes Oakly explodes out of her and sends all of us skittering backward. Her water, her gift, her magic swarm her body protectively. Healing it back whole.

Her purple hair fans out around her and the shine that always makes it look like it's brushed with glitter shimmers from her roots until it touches her ends. Her pale skin slowly starts to gain back its sun-kissed glow, and when her finger twitches, me as well as her entire Nexus jump back to her sides.

My lungs beg for me to breathe, but I can't.

There's no air left for me when Oakly inhales what feels like a never-ending gasp.

Brown, green, and gold flares to life as her eyes snap open, glowing with the overwhelming amount of power coursing through her. For a moment in time, she just stares up at the brightly lit ceiling before blinking them in rapid succession. When her gaze turns to her Nexus, they pounce.

Wrapping her up in their hands, they hug, kiss, cover her until I can barely see her through their massive bodies. Their words of praise and love to her have me covering my mouth to hold in my sobs of relief, but that doesn't stop my body.

My knees finally give out on me and I crumble to the floor in a heap as I hold on to the side of her bed for support. My men instantly surround me, holding me close.

I cry even harder when I feel a fingernail tickle the top of my hand and I immediately turn my palm, lacing our fingers together.

"Willy."

Seventeen

Willow

The guys' murmuring travels into Oakly's room where we're lying on her bed, pretending not to eavesdrop.

Well, I'm pretending. She's lost to her own thoughts.

I waited patiently on the floor while her men lavished her in love, Jamie gave her a thorough check, and then they just held her while I held her hand. As soon as her fingers gripped me tighter, attempting to pull me closer, I crawled in bed beside her.

That's where I've been since.

Aria joined us for a little while as well, reassuring us our souls were as strong as ever before my brother told her it was time for them to go. The only other visitor was Gaster. I thought his rapid shifts between scolding then crying while giving us hugs were going to be her undoing, but she held strong and soaked up the love he showered her in. Plus, the calming tea and pastries helped.

Now the two of us sit together in silence. It's not our normal comforting kind, though. The tension surrounding her is deafening.

My fingers trail through her hair mindlessly as she sighs to herself and I'm waiting for her to speak. The reality of what happened today has just settled in her mind and she wants to ask me about the in between then and now, but she doesn't. She's not ready.

Yet.

Based on the plans I hear from the guys outside and the pieces of information I'm picking up by eavesdropping in their minds, they're preparing to separate us so we can both get some rest. My body tenses at the notion, even though I feel Oakly's desire to be surrounded by her guys keenly in my chest.

For her wants and desires, I'll leave her side, but it's only because I feel that's what her soul's practically begging for.

"They're getting ready to kick me out."

"Selfish men."

I snort as she rolls over, facing me, and we lie here, staring at one another. I fight back the tears that want to fill my eyes because I see the waterworks welling in hers. I don't want to be the cause of them falling.

Physically, she looks as she always has, but now there's a piece inside of her that will feel foreign, at least to herself, for some time to come.

I'm all too familiar with it. I never wanted her to know it.

It's the weight of the demons that sit in the back of your mind.

Emotional and mental traumas aren't things everyone will experience in their lifetimes, and I'm so happy for those who will never know that type of turmoil. As for my best friend, though, she'd already known a touch of it through her parents' lack of acceptance of her.

Now it's layered. Darker. More pronounced.

She doesn't know how to cope with this level, but I'll be here for her. I'll guide her.

"They're going to hog your attention for a little while, and I'll allow that. But then I need some time with you."

"There's no doubt I'm going to need a break from them." She smiles and I know it's forced.

We're both bullshitting just to fill the silence.

"Get some sleep or snuggles or whatever it is you need, and I'll see you tomorrow."

I lay a quick peck to her nose and genuine laughs fall from both of us as she tries to swat me away. The noise seems to call out to our men as they stampede in here like their asses are on fire and we smirk in their direction.

The relief that drapes across the Mercie men is tangible as they surround us on the bed. I take that as my cue to get up and as soon as I hold my hand out, four others latch onto it and pull me up.

"I told the guys to give me just a little while and I'll have the wing cleaned out for all of you. Tillman will come get and escort you when it's ready," Corentin says as he comes to my side and smiles down at Oakly.

"Wing?" she asks.

"We're clearing out the east wing. That's where you all will be staying from here on out. At least until we all return to the academy."

Her wide eyes swing to her men, then to me, and I hide my snicker behind my hand. That was a piece of information I overheard, but I figured I'd let him tell her.

"I already told you, you'd be visiting me here. You didn't seriously think we were going to let the five of you out of our sight, did you?" I ask teasingly.

"Holy shit," she breathes. "I didn't really think about where we'd be staying at all, to be honest, but the palace? We're staying at the palace?"

"Staying isn't really the word, *Perfecta Anima.* I give it a day and you and your entire Nexus will be moved in," Caspian says sarcastically, although he's not lying.

If I have it my way anyways.

She snorts, rolling her eyes at his tone, and I bite my lip to hide my smirk from them both. That's until Caspian's face grows more serious, and he steps closer to her side. I sense the shift in him, and I don't have the slightest clue what it is he's about to say or do.

"Oakly, I..." He pauses as her eyes grow to the size of saucers. Everyone's in the room do, actually, and I hold my breath because that's the first time he's ever addressed her by her name. "I killed the man who injected you. He'll never hurt you or anyone else again," he says sincerely.

Her gaze softens as she looks at my dark and damaged protector, and my love for him bursts out of me before I can contain it. He's not a man of many words to people outside of our Nexus, but she knows, in his own way, he just publicly apologized to her.

"That puts you in spot number two," she chokes out with a smile.

"Hey," Corentin and Tillman shout, but Cas is all dark smirks when he looks over at Draken.

"I believe I can beat the dragon out."

"We'll see about that," Oakly teases and the tears I'd been fighting to hold back flood freely.

It's always been poking fun about her having favorites, although it most certainly started out that way. We agreed when we first started speaking through our mental link that she'd carry on her little joke of having my men compete for the top spot in her eyes even though she'd already deemed them all worthy by that point.

I could never pick a favorite of her men because they each balance her so perfectly and they've grown to be more than random guys in my life. Just as my men have become for her.

"We'll be back soon," Tillman says as he gives Ry and the others hugs, then ushers us out of the room. My eyes linger on Oakly for another moment until her men perch their asses on her bed, blocking her from my sight.

My feet feel like they're being weighed down by stone as we make our way out into the hall, but I sigh happily when I see our research table's already been cleared and cleaned up. Plus, there's no one else out here. Leaving me alone with my men.

"What's the plan, your highness?" I ask through a yawn as I lean my head on Corentin's shoulder.

His steps slow as he wraps his arm around my waist and turns me until my chest is pressed into his. Of their own accord, my eyes flutter shut as he leans in and captures my lips in a sweet, lingering kiss.

When I peel my heavy lids open, I find him peering over my head rather than at me. From my left, Tillman steps closer and wraps his hand around the back of my neck, turning my head until his lips are locked on mine. The firm but gentle embrace is over just as swiftly as it started, and Draken closes in on the other side of me.

I was ready for the fiery intensity that's all things him, but he surprises me with the softest, calmest of kisses he's ever given to me. His shuddering breath leaves chill bumps across my skin when he buries his face in my neck for a quick second, then steps away.

"We'll see you in a little while, princess," Corentin says softly as the chill of Caspian consumes my back.

He gives me no time to ask any questions as his shadows engulf me, whisking me away from the rest of my Nexus. When he pulls his darkness away, hot water pelts down on his head from my shower head and the block he's been holding in place so firmly slides away.

The instincts in me scream to go to him, wash it away, make it better. The need is so strong, my hands shake, but I hold my feet still and take him in from head to toe. This is the first moment I've had to truly observe him since we left him at that volcano to find the doctor. The others made sure to always be near me, and it helped alleviate both their and my worries.

Not my dark and damaged protector, though.

He's been holding it all in for my sake that entire time. Now it's crashing down right in front of me. Tillman told me Cas had himself under control. He looked in his eyes, but he was looking for the wrong thing. I see it clearly.

Yes, my man and monster are one and the same.

But the demons...They aren't a part of the duo.

They're intruders.

"Cas," I say quietly, lifting my hand to cup his cheek, but pause my movements when his eye twitches. "Come back to me. I'm right here."

Slowly, I slink forward another step, standing close enough there's barely a breath between us, but not touching him. Yet.

"I'll meet you in the dark, Cas," I whisper, then surround us in my shadows.

My black veil blocks out all the light and the two of us stand under the spray of cascading water, breathing heavily. The tension around him begins to lessen, which immediately makes mine leak out of me as well.

"I'm back," he grits out.

"Not entirely. Tell me what happened."

His breath fans my eyelashes as he finally makes a move and pulls my body flush to his. The erratic beat of his heart thuds below my hand and my fingers run circles around his moon until it begins to level out.

"Those rooms the hostages were in looked like the one I was in. Cold stone and the empty promise of a death that seemed too far away. I didn't come across a single hostage that had a shred of hope left in their eyes." He takes a deep breath, and I wait him out, knowing he isn't done. "That lab. I never saw the one they had at the structure I was held in, but all I could think about is how he probably had one just like it. Recording every change in me as the days passed by. How I fucking begged for them to stop."

His black eyes, heavy breathing, and trembling hands warn me of his next move before he even makes it.

Calling my water element forth, I command it around his fist, protecting and blocking his knuckles from the tile behind my head. I saw the punch coming, and I refuse to allow him to hurt himself.

I order the elusive element to surround him, bring him closer to me. My earth flows through my hands and I strip away our shirts so he can feel my skin on his when he crowds me closer to the wall.

"Her," he whispers. "That bitch is still out there, believing she can do whatever she pleases to me. Believing she has some right or claim to me. I am not hers to claim. My soul is already owned."

I breathe through the possessive rage that rises in me like lava. This isn't about me or my feelings right now, but I can't help the fury that consumes me when I think about Silvia. How I want more than anything to end her for what she's done to my man. My Nexus member. I wish her ass had been there so I could've thrown her in the magma pit along with her best friend.

"Who owns your soul?"

I meant for it to be a soft question. I wanted my voice to come across as sweet, light, so I could pull him the rest of the way over the edge.

Instead, it was a fierce, possessive growl that just shoved us both into the abyss below.

My mind barely has time to process what's happening when a cold dagger is placed at the waistband of my pants. In a move as swift as smoke, he has my pants shredded and torn from my body.

His cold hands clamp on my thighs, and my legs automatically wrap around his waist as he crashes me into the wall with his lips plastered to mine.

In my mind, somewhere deep in the back of it, I know I should give myself over completely to him so he can let his darkness bleed out, but I can't. My possessive need to claim him, mark him as mine, all mine, won't allow it.

I deepen the kiss while grinding against him and my nails that have sharpened of their own accord pierce his shoulders, drawing a hiss from his lips when he breaks away from me.

"Naughty little Primary," he breathes, slamming my hands above my head with his shadows.

"Who. Owns. Your. Soul?"

A dark, twisted smirk crosses his face when he grips my hips tightly, pinning me completely against the wall. My body shivers as his hard cock lines up with my pussy and I bite my lip to hold in my whimper.

"You do, Willow Vito. Every blackened, broken piece is yours. As are the threads of light that now weave themselves through it. It's all yours."

In one brutal thrust, he slams into me so fully, I feel him in my gut. That line between pain and pleasure blurs and I cry out his name, begging for more.

And fuck does he answer my plea wholeheartedly.

With every punishing pump of his hips, his darkness bleeds out all over me. My skin absorbs it, loves it, then shoves it back at him full force until he's panting my name like I'm his dying wish.

His unforgiving grip is surely leaving bruises on my hips, and I hope there's a perfect impression of his fingers inside of Draken's seared handprint. Despite the fact those blemishes will heal, it makes me fucking feral thinking about two of my men's marks on my body.

The touch of his shadows crawls across my skin, teasing my clit in slow circles, keeping my release just out of reach. He places me on the edge of oblivion, then snatches me back, just so I'll feel as consumed with him as he does me.

I dig my heels into his ass cheeks and try to slam myself down on him harder, deeper, fuck faster. Anything. Everything.

"You'll come on my cock when I say you can, Primary. Be good or I'll restrain all of you," he grits out.

The strain in his voice tells me how close to the edge he is too, but he's holding back, forcing me to wait as well.

I try to savor it. I really do.

I don't break out of his shadows' restraints like I know I could, nor do I hit him with a bout of lust that I know could bring him to his knees, but fuck me, I'm ready to come. I want to come so hard I see stars and drag him down with me.

My moans grow louder as I swallow down the begging about to fall from my mouth and just relish in the feeling of him fucking me how he sees fit.

It's dizzying.

"Fuck, you're a tempting little goddess. It's so impossible to resist," he groans before snatching me off the wall and slamming me against another one.

Except this one isn't tile.

This one is all fire and muscle and my shadow trapped arms wrap around his neck.

"You called, little wanderer?" Draken purrs in my ear.

His lips trail down my neck. Kissing, sucking, biting all the way to my shoulder, and when his hands reach around to twist my nipples between his fingers and thumbs, I beg.

"Cas, please."

"You should feel how this greedy little pussy is strangling me, dragon," he taunts.

"Is that right? Shadow man not letting you come all over his cock, sweetness?"

"No, he's not."

A mixture between a moan and a cry of frustration leaves me, causing Cas to chuckle darkly and Draken to groan low. Both make my skin shiver and the pressure in my belly intensifies.

"Tell him how this greedy little pussy is his and you need his cock filling you up. Use those dirty thoughts you have and show him the goddess you are."

Oh. Fuck. Me.

"This greedy pussy is yours, Cas. You own it. Bury your cock so deep inside of me, I feel you fill me up." I pant shyly, but he hears me and his eyes sear through mine.

"Fuck," he grunts and if I didn't think his punishing pace could become more, I was dead wrong.

His shadows finally provide the pressure I need on my clit, and I scream, seeing nothing but darkness as my orgasm rips through me viciously. My back bows and Draken's strong arms wrap around me, holding me up while my pussy clamps Cas's cock in a death grip, sucking his release right out of him.

Breathing hard, he leans against me until the two of our bodies force Draken's to lean on the wall and hold us up.

"I could live inside of you, Primary. Fuck, you're my home," Cas says quietly as he lays a kiss on my throat, my jaw, cheek, and finally my lips.

"Who's greedy now?" I ask teasingly, and his smirk stretches across my lips.

When he finally slides his dick out of me, Draken passes me fully over to him, laying a kiss on my forehead. A moment passes between the two of them that I don't fully understand, but with an appreciative nod and a tight smile from Cas, Draken leaves us to get cleaned.

My dark protector washes and massages my body until I can barely hold my eyes open, while quietly murmuring how proud he is of me for not burying the things that happened today down. I tell him I'm just as proud of him as he is of me.

Stepping out of the warm shower, the air hits me, making me shiver for a split second before he pulls the water from my body and hair. Just as my lids lose their battle with staying open, he leans in close and whispers.

"I'll always be greedy for you, Primary. I love you. We love you beyond measure."

"I love you. All of you."

The sugary roasted aroma drags me from the dead of sleep, and I swear, like a bloodhound, I sit up in the bed, sniffing around without ever opening my eyes.

Four low chuckles draw a smile to my face and with an incredibly unladylike yawn, I stretch my arms above my head, then peel my lids open. The bright light from the sun beaming in from the balcony causes me to rapidly blink, then throw the rest of the covers off me.

"It is far too bright outside to still be midmorning," I say frantically, trying my hardest to get untangled from the sheets.

"Whoa, princess, take it easy." Corentin laughs, stopping my panicked movements with his hands on my shoulders. "You needed to sleep in."

"No, I needed to meet Oakly for breakfast," I argue.

All their laughing ceases and they each look at me so softly, I panic even more.

What the hell are those looks for?

"What's wrong? What happened?"

"Nothing happened, little warrior, she's fine. She's just still sleeping as well. Ry called and let me know a couple of hours ago. Said he'd get her to call or message you when she wakes up," Tillman supplies helpfully, no doubt sensing the rising freak-out.

My breath whooshes out of me, and I sling myself back onto the bed.

Damn, it takes a lot of energy to get that worked up as soon as your eyes open.

"So I take it you don't want your coffee?" Corentin asks sarcastically.

"Of course I do," I say, popping right back up. "Sorry, I just freaked out there for a second. I didn't want her to think I was standing her up or choosing sleep over seeing her."

Again, their eyes soften, and when Caspian offers me his hand to help me out of bed, I take it graciously.

The adrenaline of yesterday has worn off now, but everything else that I woke up feeling hits me like a ton of bricks. I see better now why the multiple times some shit like this has happened to me, Oakly's threatened to kill me. Our bond feels like it's on edge and if I don't lay my eyes on her to make sure she's okay, I'm going to flip out.

The guilt that always sits below my surface instantly floods me.

Crazy shit has happened to me a couple times now and it's not just my men who experience the wide range of emotions in the aftermath. It's them, Oakly, and Gaster who feel it on literally a soul level. Not to mention everyone else who cares for me.

The thought quickly sobers me.

"None of that, Primary. Shit happens, and it always will until we end this. Check on your bond and mental link. She's fine," Caspian says confidently as he sits me in a seat out on the balcony and Corentin places my coffee in front of me.

Nodding, I do as he says and focus on the thread that connects me to Oakly, as well as our mental link. I don't pull on either, just in case she really is still sleeping. I don't want to wake her.

I'm selfishly happy, though, when I feel her consciousness and I blow out a breath of relief.

Mentally. By accident, of course.

Her laugh rings through my head and a smile takes over my face. It's her normal giddy tone and her bond sings in my chest with her true happy spirit this morning. That settles the worry I'd been feeling the second I woke up and thought I missed our breakfast.

"Someone woke up in a good mood," I say.

"Well, someone has four men who know exactly how to wake a girl up."

"Oh, gross, Oak. Too much information before coffee."

Elementra, she's as bad as Draken.

I can't help but laugh out loud at her and the tension in my men's shoulders relaxes. They don't have to hear—well, Tillman may have—to know that the two of us are talking.

"Got that brought to me in bed as well. May have to get kidnapped more often if this is the pampering I'm going to get."

My eyes narrow dangerously and if she were in front of me, my look would strike her ass down.

"Too soon for the dark humor. Too freaking soon."

"My bad." She snorts, but I see it for what it is. Little shit is trying to shove it down and bury it with jokes.

"So lunch instead of breakfast? I can't believe they let us sleep this long."

"I woke up once when it was still dark out and my body was like hell no, bitch, back to sleep you go. Apparently, Jamie tried to wake me up so he could do a thorough check, but I wouldn't budge."

"I bet so. You needed the rest. So lunch?" I ask again since she didn't answer me.

The silence on the other end paired with the longing I feel pulsing in my chest gives me my answer. She wants to stay cuddled up with her men. Understandably.

"Ahhh, I see. Someone wants to stay in and be a pampered princess today," I tease so she knows I'm not upset.

"Well, they do know how to pamper me. You're okay with that?" she asks quietly.

"Umm, of course. I completely understand wanting to be wrapped up in your men's arms for the day."

"Tomorrow then. We'll make a girls' day out of it and make the men go to work." She chuckles and I shake my head at her.

"Sounds good. Check in with me today when you're not busy," I say with a little saucy tone.

"I'll check in during water breaks. Love youuuu," she singsongs and I groan.

"Gross. Love you more."

Her laugh fades from my mind and I close my eyes, cherishing the sound. Elementra knows I wouldn't know what to do without her.

"So what's the plan, little wanderer?" Draken asks.

"She's going to stay in with her guys today. We're going to spend tomorrow together."

"You plan on introducing her to Momma Vito?" he asks.

"Yeah. Maybe we'll make it an all-girls day and hang out with Tanith as well."

"Mom has a meeting in the morning with a few of the academy headmasters and I'll be joining her, but we should be done by lunch," Corentin says.

"Oh, about what?" I ask nosily.

"Well, the number one objective is she plans on checking for marks. Not that we think any of the headmasters are betraying us. They've been vetted extensively, but time and time again, loyalties have been compromised. If it proves they're all good, she'll be discussing increasing security, strengthening their wards, and she wants me to give them a breakdown of the attack on our academy. Even though we'll leave out the part about how it was a targeted attack, how the Mastery handled their formation, gathered and held the students hostage, and what they're doing to the hostages is all information the headmasters should be made aware of."

"You two aren't going alone, right?" I ask immediately. The thought of just him and Aurora checking for marks and possibly exposing one alone worries me. Despite realistically knowing, unless every headmaster is corrupt, then they can handle themselves.

"No, Tillman will be coming so he can check their minds. That'll be how we see if they wear a mark and all my dads will be joining, plus a small team of E.F. members."

"Okay, good. Speaking of the academy. We have three days until classes resume," I say, open-ended.

It feels a little surreal to me after everything that's happened. I haven't been to the academy since we rescued Keeper. We have so many other things going on, I sort of forgot I was a student.

"Are you reading my mind this morning, princess?" he asks teasingly.

"No, was that what you were bringing up next?"

"Yeah. We've got a few things to discuss."

"Uh-oh, that doesn't sound good," I taunt. Whatever he has to discuss isn't the end of the realm level discussion judging by his relaxed posture and nonchalance.

Rolling his eyes, he takes a sip of his coffee first, then sets it down and laces his fingers. I may have spoken to soon on the seriousness of the topic. "I think you've far surpassed any of the classes the academy will provide you with. I don't see any point in you continuing enrollment."

My eyes widen, and my hand quits reaching out for my own mug as I take in his words. Part of me completely agrees, whereas the other part feels like I'm getting kicked out of school.

I whip my head over to Tillman when he snorts and shakes his head at me, and I cock my eyebrow at him.

"You're not getting kicked out, little warrior. The paperwork would be filed that you've completed all levels of training, but seriously, all you did before the mission was study with Gaster, work with Vince, and train with the E.F. You were basically already done with classes."

"I mean, yeah, I get that. I guess I was just caught off guard. What would I do then and what about Draken?" I ask. If I'm not taking any classes, there's surely no reason he needs to.

My dragon man throws his head back, laughing, causing both Corentin and Tillman to grumble under their breaths, but this is obviously something they all have already thought about.

"Draken's going to be done as well, against my better judgment. He's picked up a class that he's going to help instruct," Corentin says with a huff.

"You what?" I turn to face Draken fully, the surprise evident in my tone, face, everything, and he shoots me a wink.

"Corentin's making it sound more important than it really is. I'm going to assist Vince with Layton's one-on-one classes. He's going to meet with the two of us every day, as long as our Nexus doesn't have other shit going on, until he gains better control over his shifts. Then he can move into a normal shifter class. We're going to take him to the academy the day after tomorrow to get a tour just like we did with you."

My heart.

I see him trying to downplay this, but it's incredibly sweet and not only that, this is a responsibility and role none of us ever would've thought Draken would willingly take on. Yeah, he helps Tillman with the E.F.

members, but that's training, fighting. This is molding a young mind and helping him develop into the best shifter he can be.

"I'm so proud of you."

I blow him a kiss when his cheeks flush and I've got to admit, it does something to me being able to make one of my men blush.

"Okay, so what's the plan for me?" I ask, turning my attention back to Corentin.

"I wanted your opinion on this, but I think it's wise you still spend your mornings with Gaster and Oakly, but Keeper and Tanith will be included in that now. As long as they're stuck here, they should learn everything they can, and I think they'll be beneficial to you. The time with them can be dedicated for you to learn and do as much research as you can on everything. Your bloodline, the five families, the history of Elementra, dream walking. Anything you think you need to put your mind to. If you need to come here and use the amplifier room during the day or whatever you may need here, you're not on a schedule that would interfere with that. Plus, Cas or Draken can come with you.

"Also, you still need to train. We need to continue training as a group. I think Oakly and her Nexus should join us. She needs to learn the capabilities of what a true completed Nexus can do. So our mornings are going to look a little different when classes start back up. Other than that, you'll just be fluid, like Cas."

Huh.

Bringing my coffee to my lips, I hum over the rim as I try to paint a picture in my mind of what my days will look like. Honestly, not much different than they did prior to this decision.

With the obvious exceptions and additions, nothing drastic will change. Plus, I think it'll take some pressure off me. I like the thought of dedicated time to focus on the issues at hand rather than letting them continue to rotate through my mind on repeat. Granted, that probably won't significantly change because I fixate, but it'll help.

I'll never complain about time spent with Gaster and Oakly, but it's exciting to think about adding Tanith and Keeper to the equation. I have so much to learn from Tanith, and Keeper has a realm of knowledge in his own right.

I like it.

"Sounds perfect to me, your highness," I say, grinning and shooting him a wink, but I see one more issue on his tongue. One I don't want to decide yet. "We'll play it by ear on where we'll stay. I'm not ready to decide."

He smiles softly, understandingly. He feels it too. When I look at the other three, they do as well. Even though Cas hasn't ventured into his room much other than to shower, he's scoured my book collection, eavesdropped into the amplifier room, and ghosted through all the walls. I know he loves it here too. The decision feels impossible.

"Okay, princess. We'll decide later," he says, leaning over to lay a quick kiss on my hand.

Later.

Eighteen

Draken

"Wake up, dragon."

My eyes fly open, yet I can't move, and Caspian doesn't even give me a minute to get my wings about me before moving me through the fucking shadows.

We materialize in the hallway our rooms are on, in front of a pissy-ass-looking Tillman, but before I can grumble or bitch about my rude awakening, he's shoving my shirt, pants, and some shoes against my chest.

I'm already unstable from being surprised and his heavy-ass hand knocks me even more off balance till I'm falling into the wall.

"Be quiet, for fuck's sake. Get dressed." Caspian hisses.

"You two stop manhandling me. What the fuck is going on?" I whisper-shout.

He rolls his eyes, ignoring me, and turns back to an even more impatient-looking Tillman.

What the fuck has happened now?

"Recon, Cas. I'm fucking serious. The two of you have no backup right now besides the three there. No funny business," he says sternly, shooting us both serious looks that I don't understand at all before walking back toward the bedroom.

"Hurry up," Cas commands and this time I growl in warning. "Stop that shit before you ruin my fun."

Once a-fucking-gain, he snatches me up and whisks us through the walls until we're outside the ward of the south wing. If not for his grip on my arm, I would've busted my ass from how I'm hopping around, trying to put my shoe on. Wordlessly, he continues to drag me until we're outside.

He's yet to tell me what's going on, but obviously, I'm down.

A little warning isn't too much to ask for, though.

"Ready?" he asks.

"Hell, I don't know, Cas. What's going on?"

He turns back toward the doors with a devious, shit-eating smirk on his face, and my beast ruffles himself out in my chest. My body alights with the giddiness of whatever it is that he has planned.

Fuck yeah. He's up to trouble.

"We're going hunting," he says cryptically and my little heart jumps with joy. I swear I'm so excited I could fucking squeal, but that doesn't really explain the secrecy.

"And Tillman couldn't know because..."

"About thirty minutes ago, he received a phone call that he had to leave the room to answer, so I followed him. Obviously. How you and the Primary can sleep through shit like that is concerning, by the way," he says as his eyebrows draw down and he scans me from head to toe as if he's looking for some sort of issue. I throw my hands in the air and then cross my arms, silently telling him to get the fuck on with it. He rolls his eyes but continues, "The team that he put on Oakly's parents' house called and said they've returned home. He told them to stand watch for a couple hours to make sure no one else showed up. I volunteered us to join them."

"Volunteered us to join them, but we're really..." I trail off, wiggling my brows, hoping I've got the right line of thinking. There's no way he just pulled me from bed, away from my little wanderer to hide in the shadows.

"Exactly, dragon, now you got it. Couldn't let Tillman know that. He wouldn't have let us go. Then the Primary would've woken up and wanted to go, or not let us go. Or worse, Corentin, then we'd have to wait around for a sound plan. It just seemed like a headache all the way around."

"Then what are we waiting for?"

We share bloodthirsty little smirks with one another before he grips my shoulder and pulls us through a transport. I don't like keeping secrets from Willow, like at all, but this doesn't too much feel like a secret. I mean, she'll know what we did as soon as she wakes up. She may be a little mad that we didn't invite her along, but her beauty rest is far more important.

This is also going to be such a fun surprise for Nikoli, Ry, San, and Jamie. The little tidbits Willow has shared without putting Oakly's feelings out there for us haven't alluded to much, so I don't know how she'll feel about knowing her parents have been caught. She's struggling with this level of betrayal. Fucking understandably. So her men can break this news when we get them back to the dungeons.

Palace prison. What the hell ever.

We pop in a couple feet behind the E.F. members and I'm a little disappointed we didn't startle them. They look like they were expecting us, so Tillman must have warned them.

"Any movement?" Cas asks.

"They're awake, sir. They came in and..." The E.F. guy trails off, looking a little uneasy sharing the news with us.

"And what?"

"Just started cooking. From what we've observed, they're acting completely normal. Leader Tillman was hoping to see, I don't know, maybe a sign of distraught, coercion, regret. He instructed us to watch their behavior, see if they acted upset, irrational, but for people who just sold their daughter, they're carrying on with a mundane routine."

My beast heats my chest, and I hold in the smoke that wants to come out of my nostrils. Not that I seriously expected them to act like they felt bad for what they did to Oakly, but at least shed a fucking tear. Be asleep, something. Making breakfast, flipping fucking pancakes—as little wanderer calls them. Are you serious?

"So they're in the kitchen?" I ask.

"Yes, sir. All five of them."

"Good. You all stay here, keep watch. We're going to eavesdrop from inside," Cas says nonchalantly.

"Leader Tillman said no one's to move in yet." The dumbass, well, truly he's pretty smart to be following orders, but incredibly stupid to question a man who literally manipulates the darkness.

"He told *you* that. Not me."

"What the hell do the two of you think you're doing?"

"Busted, shadow man," I whisper.

We both turn around slowly. Me wearing a smirk, Caspian looking like he's annoyed his plans keep getting interrupted.

"Ry. Coincidence seeing you here," I say happily.

"Cut the shit, Draken. T called me and told me he sent you two for recon. It didn't sound like recon plans just then," he says seriously, crossing his arms over his chest. Like a fucking mirror of Tillman.

Spoilsport.

"You cut the shit. You coming or not? Fuck, I should've just come alone." Cas sighs, pinching the bridge of his nose.

"Fuck yes, I'm coming. This is my Paterna-Nexus we're capturing," he says with a serious scowl, and I smile at him darkly.

Knew the ol' second-in-command had a rebellious side to him.

Without further ado, 'cause Cas is out of patience at this point, he wraps the two of us in his shadows, and we move through the darkness into the house.

Instead of popping right into the kitchen, we skirt the walls of the foyer, and my eyes trace the very boring decor. There's not a thing in this room that would even hint that Oakly lived here not that long ago. There's no color. The place is washed in creams and whites. It looks as though they attempted to make it as posh as possible but missed the mark and it just looks cheap.

"What's the plan?" Ry whispers.

Plan...good question.

"We don't typically operate under plans," I whisper back.

"What?"

"We just show up, fuck shit up, and get out. We don't require all the step-by-step you're used to. This isn't a high-stakes mission where there're hundreds of lives involved. We're capturing some piece of shits who sold my little wanderer's sister, your Primary. They come the easy or the hard way," I say, shrugging. It's really that simple.

"No wonder Tillman doesn't send you two with teams," he says, shaking his head as if it's a bad thing.

"Yeah, because extras get in the way and ask stupid shit like what's the plan. Can we move now?" Caspian asks with a tilt to his lip.

Look at how teasing and sweet he's being.

Fucking the shit out of Willow in that shower did a wonder on his mood.

"Fine, but no funny business. Take down and out," Ry orders, to which we just snort at him.

Moving us through the shadows, Caspian holds us in place in a darkened corner of the kitchen as we watch Oakly's parents. Her mom and one of her dads stand at the stove, seriously fucking cooking, while the other three men sit around the small table off to the side, talking.

So relaxed. So nonchalant. As if they didn't sell their daughter to the Mastery to have her powers taken and ultimately killed.

Vile.

Commanding my flame out, I set the food in the pan on fire and smile as Oakly's mom shrieks. I honestly didn't mean for her hair to catch on fire. It was perfect timing and a coincidence that she leaned in to taste test the food at the exact moment I commanded my flame out.

The man beside her shoots his earth element both at Oakly's mom and the ruined food, attempting to cover the blue fire in sand, but it's pointless. As if his element could ever compete with mine.

Ry, the sly dog, sees the other three scum about to step in to help and quicker than they can stand, he has them wrapped up in vines, tied to their chairs. Right before I know my flames are getting ready to sear through her skull, I call them back to me.

Caspian shoots his shadows out and ties Oakly's mom together to the other man, then covers everyone's mouths with a strip of shadow to silence their pathetic screaming.

It's always the same reaction. The loud, petrified wailing where their lives flash before their eyes for a moment, then they settle down when they realize they didn't actually die.

I wish someone did something original.

"Hello, fuckers. I mean Folders." I cheer when we step out of the cover of darkness and I perch my ass on their kitchen countertop. "You two just scoot on over, join the others."

The assholes look past me and Caspian as if we're nobodies, but when their gazes land on Ry, I swear they all piss themselves. Their faces instantly pale, Oakly's mom starts trembling, and her dads fall statue-still.

Idiots.

If they only knew, out of the three of us, he's by far the most levelheaded.

"You heard him," Caspian says, but he's already flinging them across the room to their new seats.

Once everyone is situated, the guys take a side each of mine and stand stoically, staring our little kidnappees down. Crazy how their roles have reversed so quickly.

"Why?" Ry asks sternly.

No other explanation is needed. It's a loaded question.

Caspian removes the shadows blocking their mouths, but no one jumps at the opportunity to answer Ry, so I send out a fireball for each of them. Holding it about two inches from their faces. It takes no time at all for them to start begging for it to stop.

Weak.

"What have you done? Where is my daughter?" Oakly's mom screeches.

"What have *I* done? You're the one who sold her off and almost had her killed," Ry growls, taking a step closer to her.

"She wouldn't have died. She just no longer would've possessed her magic." One of her dads tsks as if we're all fools.

"Is that what they told you? And you believed them? You're a healer, are you not?" Caspian asks, glaring at the mom. His cold, dead tone finally draws a reaction out of them, and they turn their heads to him slowly. "Well?"

"We have nothing to say," Oakly's dad, I think the biological one, says sternly.

"We'll do this one of two ways, and this is me being gracious enough to give you options. One, you can tell me what you know. Or two, we drag you to the dungeons, and my best friend rips it from your minds before me and my brothers tear you apart piece by piece."

Oh, I like a murderous Ry.

The Folders don't share the same sentiments. Their eyes nearly bulge out of their heads and Oakly's mom whimpers like that's the worst thing she's ever heard. Very rich for a bitch who's done what she has.

"We were introduced to the Mastery at the last Everglow family party," she supplies helpfully.

"Marika, shut up," another of her Nexus barks.

"No. I'm not willing to die for this."

That's pitiful. Ol' Marika believes that's not the only outcome for her.

"Kellie Everglow told me all about them and the vision they have for the future of Elementra. It was a no-brainer to join the society. The plans they have in place for those of us with great power are exactly what this realm needs. Those of us with power should be treated with the utmost respect, not as if we are on the same level as...as commoners."

Commoners? What the fuck is this? The dawn of Elementra.

"All we had to do was pledge ourselves to the Everglows, claim Pyrathia as our territory, make Oakly give herself over to the Mastery, and we'd be brought into the fold. With Oakly being as deviant as she has been in her coming years, reaching the age of Primaries, we felt that she no longer deserved her gifts. It's not like she's putting it to good use anyway. Archivist. My daughter. She could've at least joined the E.F. and brought honor to our name since she wasn't willing to have an arranged Nexus." She sneers, glaring at Ry as if what she just said doesn't fucking contradict itself. Ry is almost at the top of the E.F., which automatically elevates Oakly on the respect totem pole.

No, this bitch just wanted to be able to control her daughter completely and was pissed the hell off that Oakly wouldn't give in.

"Gima or Silvia or any of the other promising girls would've done extraordinary gaining a gift as good as Oakly's." One of her dads sighs, but that comment has the three of us tensing.

"What do you mean?" I growl.

"When we expressed our concerns over Oakly's defiance, the Everglows took our concerns back to our leader. His solution was to take her magic, gift, and element from her. Give them to someone more worthy. They explained the process and of course we agreed. She was supposed to be handed over the night we called her home for dinner, but she dropped the horrific news she'd already bonded. We thought that would be the end of our time in the Mastery, but it turned out to please the Summum-Master. It made the most sense to give another Primary the already strengthened gift. Then once one of them would've bonded the men, another boost would have occurred," her mom states as if that's obvious and grand fucking news, but I just continue to stare at Caspian. I see it in his mind he's already working it out. Just like I am.

"Sounds an awful lot like the Summum-Master is trying to create Primaries that have more than one gift."

"Yeah. An awful lot like our Primary," he replies darkly before turning back to Oakly's piece of shit excuses for parents.

"But why? For a society who hates females, why make them more powerful?"

"They'll be his and their chosen Nexuses to control. Remember what Franklin said about Willow not being able to hurt any of them once she's bonded? His self-made bond is one way."

Smoke blows from my nostrils before I can stop it, and I can't even find the gasps falling from these sorry-ass people funny in this moment. I hate absolutely everything that makes me think back to anything related to her kidnapping.

"I understand that, but it still doesn't make sense. Why not give the men extra gifts? Why only the Primaries?" I ask through my anger.

"That I don't know, dragon. Either he's trying to replicate our Primary now that he got a taste of the power she packs or we're missing something."

We're definitely missing something.

"Well, looks like I won't be killing you all at your kitchen table after all," Caspian groans like nothing about our little trip has gone according to his bloody plans.

All five of the disgusting fuckers in front of us breathe a sigh of relief that's opposite to his of aggravation, and he snaps his head up, glaring at each of them. I do actually laugh at that because he looks personally offended.

"We're going to need a room bigger than your favorite one," I supply helpfully when I hop off the counter.

"Figured as much. Room three will do," he grumbles as he stomps around the table and slaps his hand down on two of the dads. Ry takes Oakly's mom, who won't quit crying and asking what's happening, plus another male. And I get stuck with the last one, who hasn't spoken, just cried to himself peacefully.

Popping into the dungeon, Marissa...Marsha...whatever her fucking name is, instantly starts wailing like a dying animal and I cringe as the noise makes my ears ring.

Fuck, she will not hold up well under torture.

"Let's leave them be," Ry says after he finishes strapping them down to the chairs with the magical cuffs.

"What?" Cas asks, whipping around to look at him.

"It's not my decision how we handle this outside of questioning and Tillman looking in their minds," he says begrudgingly.

I snicker at the sneer on Caspian's face and the groan that leaves him. Poor thing's whole plan of kidnapping and torturing has been thrown to the wayside and he's pissy about it.

And they call me the psycho one.

"Come on, Cas. There will be plenty more traitors where they come from." I clap him on the shoulder as we turn our backs on the sniffling bunch.

That doesn't please him like I thought it would and he shrugs my hand off him as he stomps to the door, me and Ry hot on his heels. As soon as he slings the door open, though, he halts, and I nearly crash into his back.

"No, dragon, now we've been busted."

"You two...oh hell...three, have got to be kidding me," my little wanderer says, crossing her arms and staring us down.

Corentin and Tillman stand behind her, smug fucking smirks across their faces like they can't wait to hear the tongue-lashing we're about to get. Both are in white shirts and sweatpants as though they rolled out of bed on her command, and I can't help it as my gaze tracks down her body. She's wrapped in her robe, matching pajama set underneath. Her wild curls are pulled on top of her head, and the pissed off look on her face just makes her even more sexy.

Fuck that, the two of us aren't going down on our own.

"Tillman knew we were going and agreed to it," I say quickly, shooting her an innocent look.

Which works because she snaps her neck around to stare at him while he glares at me.

"I told you both to stay with the recon team and watch."

"Oh, don't even try. You knew what Caspian had planned or you wouldn't have called Ry right away. You would've waited until this morning when you had more word, then formed another team to go in," I argue, not letting his big ass get out of this.

"I'm upset with all of you. What if the Mastery had shown up, or it was a setup? There were too many unknowns for you three to go alone."

"Hey, I was sleeping with you the whole time. I had no clue," Corentin says, his smile turning into a scowl.

"Okay, so I'm not upset with Corentin."

"Listen, trouble, I get it. We'd be fucking livid if you and Oakly pulled this. But I couldn't risk them disappearing or the Mastery hiding them. What if we hadn't apprehended them and then this morning, they packed their shit and left? Oakly wouldn't get the justice she deserves, and she'd be looking over her shoulder, constantly wondering if they're just going to show up and take her," Ry says firmly but softly. Pleading with her to hear him out.

I don't think she's really mad anyways. If she were, there'd be far more cussing and yelling, or fuck, even worse, silence and tears. Right now, her bond is just on high alert and all the wrongs that could've happened are running through her mind.

She lets out a long sigh, dropping her crossed arms, and then strides between me and Cas. "I know it was the right thing to do, but I need a break from rescue missions for a while. Next time just wake us all up and we'll go, no questions asked. Together."

"Okay, Primary."

"Whatever you say, little wanderer."

"Thank you," she says, snuggling into us before turning to Ry. "And you. You will be the one to tell her that her parents are in the dungeons. I'm not doing it."

"Palace prison," Corentin quietly corrects, then quickly holds his hands up when she narrows her eyes on him.

"I will, I promise. I'll tell her before your date today," Ry easily agrees.

"Okay then. So what did they say? Did they try to apologize or were they regretful? What happened?" she fires off as we start making our way down the hall toward outside.

The three of us share a loaded look. None of us want to tell her the truth. Just because the Folders believed their daughter wouldn't die from this experiment, doesn't mean that justifies any of their actions.

Ry's the one who bites the bullet and tells the others everything. Not only is the fury obvious on Willow's face with each word he says, I can practically feel her dragon's growl within my chest. Her beast is just as protective of Oakly as she is, and when she came out in a blaze of glory in that volcano, I was fucking mesmerized.

There're no limits we won't go for the ones we love.

"They're fucking idiots. How could they remotely believe that bullshit? It's a given that this would kill her, kill anyone who gets everything that makes us, well us, stolen from them."

"Well, you bunch are up early. Who's pissed my Adored off as soon as she woke up?" my—Keeper says as he comes around the corner of the exit to the dungeons.

"Shit, you scared the hell out of me. What are you doing up so early?" Willow asks, pressing her hand to her chest.

It's cool and freaky as shit that he can move so silently. Even with our advanced hearing, she nor I can pick up his movements without him wanting us to.

"I'm always up early. Vampires don't require the amount of sleep that you all do," he says.

"Yeah, I definitely didn't get that trait from you. I need my beauty rest." I catch myself as soon as the words are out of my mouth, but it's too late and they're out there now.

He smiles proudly at me and nods without further acknowledging what I said. "You most likely get that from Tanith. If she doesn't get enough rest, she's incredibly cranky and more feisty than usual."

"Same," Willow says, causing us all to chuckle, and it breaks up my awkwardness.

"Switching topics completely here, but I haven't had a chance to bring it up to you, Keeper. I need to ask you about the ritual the Summum-Master performs to steal the gifts. You had mentioned that it was a concoction of things that he did to create it. Have you seen it performed? Also, the family that's betraying us led Oakly's parents to believe she wouldn't die from this, only be left without any of her blessings. We already know that's bullshit based on everything Darstein said, but can you confirm it?" Tillman asks, bringing everyone right back into serious moods.

"That's far from the truth. I heard whispers about it countless times, but only seen it happen once. The individual who loses their gifts most certainly perishes. Actually, in the instance I watched, both individuals passed, and the Summum-Master absorbed the gift. This was many, many years ago, and I have no doubt he's strengthened the acceptance rate of transferring the power."

"Do you remember what happened?" Willow asks.

"I do. It was like nothing I'd ever seen, nor did it feel like anything I'd ever felt. The energy wasn't right with the magic he was using. It was as though the relic he uses was attempting to fight him off. Many relics are sentient and know when they are being used improperly.

"The Summum-Master and the scientist knew this was an experiment going wrong and they were still trying to force it. Ale brought the man who was infected to the forest in a rush, complaining to the Summum-Master the infection was taking root far faster than he assumed it would. So the Summum-Master went to the nonmagical realm and returned within minutes. It was as though he had the other waiting for his call because they didn't fight back or anything, just laid down as he told him to.

"With a dagger much like the one used to mark people, he sliced both of his palms, then a hand each of the men's, and began chanting. Not in the language of old from here or my realm. I'm not sure where the dialect originated, but the more he said, the relic he placed between them began to glow. When it was as bright as a Star gem, he aligned his sliced hand over the infected man's cut, and his other directly to the relic.

"You could see the lifeforce pulling from the man. It was as though his soul was being snatched from his body. I'll never forget the sound of his last breath. His throat gurgled, chest wheezed painstakingly so, as if it was one last plea, then he fell still.

"Moving that same hand that was covered in both their blood, he joined it with the man who was intended to receive the gift. Never taking his other off the relic. That man at first just inhaled sharply, but it didn't take long for the screaming and thrashing to start. Ale had to sit on him to hold him down not to break the Summum-Master's connection.

"Ale tried yelling at him, telling him it wasn't going to work, to pull the gift back, but the Summum-Master just stopped his chanting and said, if he can't withstand it, he's not worthy. Well, he couldn't withstand it. After shaking so violently, I could feel it through the earth and into my shoes, the man fell still as well.

"The Summum-Master placed his bloody hand directly on the relic, and a burst of power surged from it, into him. I thought, well, hoped really, he was going to die as well, but he was obviously strong enough to accept what had been stolen."

The faraway gaze in Keeper's ruby eyes makes this feel like a haunting nightmare he's replayed repeatedly in his mind. The anger, regret, and sadness pulse off him. I couldn't imagine watching that and not doing anything.

Not that I'm accusing him of not doing anything. I'm sure he tried multiple times to stop shit that happened in that forest. With a cord that could cut your head off implanted in your neck, though, what really can you do?

"What did the relic look like?" my little wander asks softly.

"A small glass globe that sat within a bronze casing. It's nothing more than a ball that could sit in your palms, but it's powerful. Incredibly so."

His sobering tone hits home for all of us.

It's gut-wrenching to realize how close Oakly was to experiencing this and it also makes me think of another perspective that makes my stomach turn inside out.

It's very possible, more so probable, Willow was never going to be on the giving end of this ritual, but what about the receiving? If the Summum-Master is trying to pump up Primaries, she's the strongest and could really be a weapon if she was given three, four, hell, however many more gifts.

"I'd be him," she whispers, looking at me with glossy eyes.

Shit. Thought that too loudly.

"But that's not the case, nor will it ever be. Never will you or Oakly be placed in those situations again. I'm prepared to lock you both away and guard you until this is all over," I say firmly.

Fuck, I wish she'd let me do just that.

She smiles at me tenderly and brings my hand up to her lips to lay sweet kisses on. "We both know I can't do that, but the offer is still endearing."

Endearing...I'm being so serious.

"I got to get back to the room before Oakly wakes up. I'll see you all in a few," Ry says, rubbing the back of his neck. He looks like ten different shades of shit. I didn't think about how hearing that, knowing what the process actually entails, would make him feel.

"Thank you for telling us all this, Keeper. It's a big help," Willow says. It's hitting her hard as well.

"Of course, Adored. I vowed to you I would help any way I could, and I always will."

Cutting his eyes to me, I don't turn away from the affection reflected at me. I nod, acknowledging him, because at the end of the day, he is helping. Tremendously. And he puts my little wanderer first.

If he keeps it up, she's not going to let him go, and I'll just have to accept him fully then.

Nineteen

Willow

"Look at you glowing this morning," I tease as soon as my eyes land on Oakly when she walks into the south wing foyer.

She laughs, skipping toward me while her men surround her and mine behind me groan and whisper-shout my name. It's the truth, though. She looks stunning this morning, and if you had been there to witness the state she was in merely two days ago, you'd never believe it.

"I got *plenty* of rest." She winks, then wraps her arms around me.

My gaze softens on her men when they give her about a foot of distance and their shoulders relax. It'd seem I'm getting the more cheerful side.

Ry's features contort into guilt when I meet his eyes and I roll mine, knowing by that look alone he most certainly didn't tell her about his little early morning excursion yet.

"She was crying in the shower. I couldn't bring myself to tell her yet."

His thoughts ring loud for either Tillman or me, but I pick them up regardless and tighten my hold on Oakly. I know my best friend enough to know she's trying to pretend none of this happened.

"Chef's cooked us up a feast. You hungry?"

"Starving. Oh my goodness, I can't believe I finally get to see your infamous south wing," she says excitedly.

"Breakfast then a tour. Or you want it the other way?"

"Breakfast first. I need coffee."

Same, girl.

With quick kisses to each of our men, they leave us with orders to reach out if we need them. I'm not one hundred percent certain what they have planned for the day, other than Corentin, Tillman, and Aurora's meetings with the academies, but I can take a wild guess.

"The ward is going to sting a little this first time. The guys said it didn't shock them, just pulled on their skin," I warn as we approach the shimmering barrier.

"But not suck me down a killer rainbow, right?" she asks, causing me to snort.

"No, that was just a little side adventure for Gaster and me."

With a confident nod, I link my arm in hers and walk us through, commanding the ward to let her enter. Surprisingly and thankfully, we make it through like it was nothing and she's giddy about it on the other side.

"I knew I was loved the most. It didn't even pull. I'm going to rub that all in their—oh, holy shit," she breathes when she takes in the sight of my lounge in front of her.

The early morning rays make the walls of light purple shimmer and the glittering leaves on my willow tree shine bright in their green and silver glory. Her eyes eat up the rows upon rows of books and she can't seem to decide where it is she wants to look at the longest.

"I think I changed my mind. I want a tour first," she whispers as she takes a timid step forward. "Shit, Willow, the energy coming off this room is breathtaking."

"It's something, that's for sure," I say low, smiling at her awestruck look. "Well, go snoop, then we'll move on to the next."

Snoop she does.

There isn't an inch of my lounge that she doesn't investigate and the belly flop she does on my sectional has me dying in laughter. I thought I'd have to drag her out of here, but just one little poke about seeing the rest has her nearly sprinting down the hall.

We briefly poke our heads into the kitchen, and I tell Chef we're taking a quick tour, then we'll be ready to eat. He shoos us out of his domain with a chuckle at Oakly's groaning over the smell and gives us honey buttered croissants to appease us for now.

She has the same reaction that we did to the breakfast room and quickly claims the seat that will be hers going forward. Unlike us, though, she insists on seeing every guest room on the next floor.

Reaching our floor, I grow nervous in my excitement to show her the amplifier room as well as my bedroom. I've already warned her that the bedroom is the same as the one in the mansion, but she's ready to see the balcony. We pass the guys' bedrooms wordlessly because she knows I won't show her those. Even though she's my sister in all ways besides blood—well, I guess that isn't completely true now—she still knows I'm far too territorial to let her in their spaces.

"Is this it? The mysterious and dangerous amplifier room? Fuck yeah, it is, I can feel the power radiating even out here."

"It is. I can't go all the way in with you 'cause it'll suck me into my mind, but I'll stand at the door."

She doesn't wait another second before slinging the door open, then gasps at the room. It's a shocker when you first see it, but the aura calms you almost immediately when you step in.

I lock my mind up tight as I lean against the frame and watch her run her hands over damn near every surface. I lose just a slip of my leash on my control, though, when her ass starts dancing in front of the reflective walls.

Suddenly, images of her begin playing across the mirrors like a slideshow.

The day we met and had our awakening. Us rolling around on the carpet at her lake house, drunk and laughing. Her covered from head to toe in blood as she appeared at the ward when I was being rescued. Her body falling through the air toward the magma as I dove after her.

Finally, it shows the two of us, dressed in matching floor-length gowns, with our heads thrown back in laughter. The difference in our dresses is mine is a shimmering violet that matches my eyes and her hair with silver lace, while hers is black, with the same violet lace.

I just discussed these dresses with Aurora. This is what I pictured us wearing at the Spring Ball. Although the guys are treating this upcoming event as a mission, I still wanted it to be special.

For all of us.

Pulling myself from the doorway and stepping back into the hall, I squeeze my eyes closed to get my mind back under control. I should've known better than to get so close to that room with her in there. Now she's seen both good and bad times, plus another that's to come.

"You okay, Willy?" she asks quietly, coming out of the room and shutting the door.

"I'm fine. I didn't solidify my block well enough. That room...it's powerful. I'm sorry you had to see some of that."

"You don't have to apologize. It's okay. But those gowns...we've never worn those before," she says with a mischievous pitch to her tone, and I shake my head, leading her down the hall to my room.

"They were just some silly gown ideas I ran by Aurora for the Spring Ball. I thought it would be fun for us to match."

"I think they're perfect," she says softly, and I squeeze her hand. She's trying to push the same enthusiastic tone she had earlier, but it's diminished substantially.

The light enters back into her eyes slightly as we reach my bedroom, and she chuckles at the familiarity. Of course she has to confirm that the bathroom is the exact same and the closet is just as full.

"Do you want to eat on the balcony or in the breakfast room?"

"Your fancy new balcony, of course," she says, pushing the French doors open wide.

She takes a huge inhale with her arms spread wide, soaking up the sun, and I plop myself down on the couch to message Chef and my guys the change of breakfast locations.

"Ugh, this is so nice. I'd drink my coffee outside every morning if I had a balcony like this."

"Well, you do have an earth elemental Nexus member who's more than capable of building you one. Not to mention, his best friend, and your best friend are both more than capable as well."

"Are you crazy? I can't just start changing aspects of the palace."

Of her own wing?

She most certainly can. I've already asked Corentin and Aurora.

"I think everyone would be okay with it. It's not like it's a bad change. Everyone would enjoy it. Maybe we'll talk the guys into building us a connecting balcony so we can meet out there together and have coffee."

"Yes, I love that. Fuck yeah, you ask them."

Will do.

Pushing myself up, I head back through my room to open the door for Chef and Mrs. Grace, then thank them profusely as they take our huge assortment out to the table on the balcony. My smile slips just a second when I catch Oakly staring off into space, lost in her thoughts that quickly, but when Mrs. Grace places a cup of coffee in front of her, she's back to grinning and giving her thanks.

I'm stuck in the middle of the battle waging inside of me currently. I want to get her to talk about it, not let her bury it down like my guys have done for me, but at the same time, I don't want to push her. She's trying hard to put on a brave face and I'm so proud of her, but I don't want her to suffer in silence when I'm all ears.

"Dig in," I say cheerily.

I stay all smiles and giggles, listening to her talk about everything under the sun, except what she's feeling. Her mouth is moving a mile a minute, trying to outrace the thoughts, but I don't interrupt.

"Have you gone for your morning flight yet?" I ask Tanith.

"No. The infuriating vampire is working out with the boys. As though their little stretches are more important than me spreading my wings."

I hold in my snort, but mentally, I'm dying. She's so damn sassy when she doesn't get her way.

"Care to take Oakly and me up?" I ask, then backtrack because that may have been rude. *"Sorry to just flat out ask, Tanith. I didn't even consider if you fly people other than Keeper without inviting them yourself."*

"No offense, young one. Other people, most certainly not. But you are family, as is she. I will come pick you both up."

"Hey," I say, reaching across the table to lay my hand on Oakly's to stop her babbling. "Want to go on an adventure?"

Her eyes draw down and a devilish little smirk crosses her face. "What are you thinking?"

"Follow me," I order instead of answering.

Walking to the railing around the balcony, I lift us up on a ball of my air and she squeals when our feet land on the edge. I can sense how close Tanith is to approaching, so I lace my fingers through Oakly's.

"Willow, what the—"

"Hold on."

Tugging her with me, I jump over the side.

Commanding out a burst of my air, I slow our descent as Tanith swoops down and we land easily on her back. With a roar to rival mine or Draken's, she takes off through the sky, while Oakly shrieks.

"Are you fucking crazy? A warning, Willow."

"Oh, where would the fun be in that?"

"I was prepared for you, young Seeker. No need to fret."

Oakly flinches on my side and her grip on my hand becomes punishing. Her gaze bounces between Tanith and me, but I don't bother hiding my smirk from her.

Tanith has accepted her into the fold.

"She just spoke to me."

"Yeah, I know."

"Oh my fucks, she loves me."

"Family of my Adored is family to me. You're very loved, Oakly. By many."

My poor best friend shivers, and her face completely shuts down. The denial to Tanith's very true statement is sitting right there on her tongue. It's consuming every thought that tries to surface.

Wrapping my arm around her shoulder, I pull her closer to me. She's stiff and tense, reluctant to accept my affection, but I don't relent on my grip, and she gives in.

Then she shatters.

Hard, heartbreaking sobs tear through her as she pours her all out in the endless stretch of blue and white. The ground would surely shake if we weren't hundreds of feet in the air and I'm surprised the sky doesn't thunder in response to her pain.

I stay strong for her. Biting my tongue to the point it hurts so I can hold my tears at bay, but it's gut-wrenching to feel her fall apart in my arms. It makes me both murderous and heartbroken.

Tanith and I don't butt in or try to soothe away her sorrow. I knew this would happen once we got up here and I'm positive Tanith did as well. That's why she said what she said. Between her sweet, heartfelt comment and the peaceful bliss that soaring brings, it's nearly impossible not to let your feelings go. The concoction is like the realm's most gentle hug.

"How do you feel?" I ask quietly when she finally sits up off my shoulder and wipes her face.

A long sigh falls from her lips as she stares blankly through the clouds. "That day at Rebel Castle, when Gaster and I were teaching you our gifts, I was too ashamed to agree with him, at least out loud, that I question everything Elementra does when it comes to you. I've always known and believed you're just supposed to trust in her, but since you got here, nothing makes sense, yet it makes perfect sense in the end. It's so confusing, but I'm so grateful for it because things that need to change are changing. But times like your kidnapping, and now this with me, I just can't wrap my head around it. Why do things like this happen, Willow? Why does she allow it?"

Her head turns to me and the slow stream of tears flowing from her eyes, paired with the desperate desire for an answer nearly slings me off Tanith's back. Fuck, it's a question I've asked so many times. CC's asked. My guys. Everyone I know I'm sure has asked.

It wasn't until that moment in Pyra that I finally figured it out.

And it isn't until this moment, staring into my sister's shattering eyes, that I know my assumption to be true.

"I spent the whole time you were in the healing wing and all day yesterday thinking about that," I whisper, blowing out a harsh breath as

I cocoon us in a bubble of air, while keeping my mind open to Tanith. "There was a moment when we were rescuing you that Elementra came to me, quickly, just long enough to tell me to make my decision. I didn't even have to think about my decision. It was as easy as breathing to know what I was going to do."

"What do you mean?"

Holding her gaze, I fight with myself about what to do or say next. What will seeing what happened do to her? Will it help or hurt? Should she even know? Her men nor I have told her anything that's happened from the time the drug really took over her mind to the time she woke up. It's been obvious that she hasn't been ready.

"I need to know, Oak, honestly, how much do you want to know?"

Her face morphs into a multitude of emotions over the span of maybe three seconds. From grief, to anger, to vengefulness, to relief. It's all there.

"All of it."

I give her a tight smile, not questioning her decision, and I lace our fingers together, then pull her and Tanith into my memories.

Starting where I first saw Jamie and Nikoli outside the wing, I quickly move us through the motions of what all transpired to me getting through to her, to us arriving at Pyra.

I skip the part of us watching what was happening to Ry and San, because she doesn't need to see that, but I do show us pulling them into the shadows and making our way to her.

From there, I let it all play out as is. I don't hide a single second from her.

The influx of emotions passing between the two of us is astronomical. The wide range of my feelings at every turn was overwhelming enough at the time, but adding hers into the mix now is almost unbearable.

A smile does break out across my face when I feel her pride for me in the moment I killed Gima. An event I'm sure my men have been waiting and expecting to come up as if I'm ashamed of what I did, but I'm not. That couldn't be further from the truth. I accept what I did wholeheartedly. She was an evil monster dressed in spoiled rich bitch dresses.

It's a whirlwind from then on, navigating the absolute chaos that ensued while we tried to figure out a cure for her. I make sure to focus on her men's effort, their love, devotion, and unwavering determination to be with her one way or another. When she finally snaps open her eyes, I switch course. Her confusion is stark, and she tries to withdraw herself from my mind, but I hold on to her and show her a brief snippet of CC's and my conversation in the amplifier room.

I replay the moment I accuse him and Elementra of abandoning me and how he explains they aren't abandoning me, but they can't make the decisions for me any longer. Then, even though she knows this information, I show when I was being tortured and he explained for her to step in, it would bring about the destruction of the realm. Then I switch it again, to show her Jamie, explaining to me why it was critical that I was drained of my magic. How he could give me his, but I have nothing to give back to Elementra.

It's a confusing mixture of information, I know, but as soon as I can explain what I believe to be the truth, she'll understand.

She blinks rapidly when I cut the string in our minds and a puzzled look crosses her features. I wait her out, though, seeing if there's anything she wants to say before I explain.

"My...my parents did that to me. They were willing to let me die," she chokes out. She knew all along, but she needed to admit it out loud.

"I'm not trying to defend them, because fuck them for real, but they didn't believe you would die. They did have every intention of allowing the Summum-Master to take your magic, gift, and element and give it to either Gima or Silvia."

She flinches, looking at me with disbelieving eyes. "What? How do you know that?"

"Because your parents are locked in the dungeons. They were captured this morning," I say honestly.

"How...who...that was quick."

I quickly tell her how Tillman immediately sent a team to stake out her house as soon as we left Pyra, and they've been waiting there for their return.

Then I throw the guys under the bus.

"Sneaky bastard. I didn't even know he got out of bed."

"I didn't notice the guys either. Granted, usually, I can, but typically only if they're feeling some sort of negative emotion. I was cuddled up with a clueless as me Corentin, and Tillman came right back to bed, so I was none the wiser. Needless to say, Caspian and Draken were giddy at the prospect of going to retrieve them. Ry caught them. Then joined."

Her snort, followed by a blushing smile, is short-lived as she whispers, "I don't know what to do about them. Part of me wants them dead because what they did to me was so cruel, even by their standards. I understand I wasn't the perfect daughter in their eyes, but nothing is wrong with me. I just don't want to live by the higher society standard."

"You're completely right. Nothing is wrong with you. And you are perfect. Perfect to me, your men, our family, our real, chosen family. Nothing that happened is in any way, shape, or form your fault. Your parents made their own decisions."

She wipes away her tears with the back of her hands before lacing her fingers together and looking down at them. "The other part wants them to live. Live out their punishment locked away forever. Death seems like an easy out for them, and they'll never learn the error of their ways. They'll just die believing they were right to do these things."

"I know the choice well. It'll be a tough decision," I mumble softly.

"Decisions. They seem to be the primary theme of everything going on," she says knowingly.

"They are. Elementra knows, millennia in advance, what's to come, and she begins making her preparations. She lays the best possible paths forward without stepping across the line of balance. It's taken me, fuck, I don't know, Oak, countless puzzle piece by this point to put it all together, but there's one thing she can't always control. And those are people's decisions.

"If she were to make every decision for everyone, it'd cross the thin line of balance. So everyone has choices to make on their own. From there, those choices present the consequences. The consequences determine whether she continues to serve you."

"Continues to serve you?"

"Yeah. Elementra serves us as much as we serve her. It's the foundation of the bonds, the magic, the power, her love, of everything. It's the give and take relationship that she's perfected. The people, namely for us in this generation, it's the Mastery who has taken but is no longer giving back, so therefore, she no longer serves them. Their power is now corrupt, and she can't, mostly won't, recycle their tainted power back to us. With that, though, she's lost the ability to push any decision onto them. They've forfeited their privilege of having a relationship with her.

"Their decisions have consequences that sometimes will affect us unjustly, but in those moments, we have decisions as well. She will always guarantee I have what I need to come out on top of the consequences caused by others because of the decisions I make. We can question her all we want. Fuck, she knows I question her daily, but I continue to serve her. I make the choices that are for the betterment of the realm. And in return, she serves me. She's already blessed me beyond my wildest imagination."

I release a deep breath and rub my thumb across Oakly's hand. She's most certainly one of those blessings I'm referring to.

This realization started festering in my mind the moment Elementra told me Gima had made her decision. Regardless of if she lived or died that day, I knew in my heart she was no longer a part of our magic system.

"Holy shit," Oakly mumbles.

"I know."

"No, I mean, yes, everything you just told me is very eye-opening and I'm going to digest it, but just taking it in, if all that is true, the Summum-Master would've been one of those, hell, maybe even the first to lose his relationship and he's figured that out."

My head twitches at the startling realization of what she's saying. Faster than my mind can comprehend, everything starts playing out for what it is.

"Shit. That's why he started stealing gifts. Why he had to travel to other realms to gather other magical shit. Oh my fuck, why the asshole relies on my blood so much. He's trying to recreate his own magic system because

Elementra's withdrawn hers and he's still as powerful and strong as he is because he continues to take from people who are blessed by her. Shit."

My shoulders slouch as the flurry of words falls from my mouth just as fast as they race across my brain. Oakly's still staring at me wide-eyed but with a huge smile across her face that slows my erratic heart.

"You're so damn smart, Mrs. Master Archivist. I don't know what the hell I'd do without you."

"Same goes for you, Willy. Thank you," she says with tears welling in her eyes and I know that thank you is loaded with more than just the compliment I gave her.

The light shining in her eyes is so bright I see the reflection of myself when I fall into them. I see the broken pieces of my best friend mending themselves back together, and I know, after this flight, she's going to be herself again. But better, stronger, and freer.

"Very good, filia mea. I'm so proud of you."

"As am I, Adored. You are wise beyond your own belief."

"That she is, Golden one."

My laugh at the two of them is a watery one and I lean my head against Oakly's, where she parks it on my shoulder. I savor this moment as the love from her bond and CC's pulses through me and my tie—that I still don't understand—from Tanith has my dragon purring softly.

"Well, Seeker, are you ready to meet the Matriarch? She just arrived back at the palace," Tanith says slyly.

"Oh shit. I forgot about that," Oakly says, popping up fast as lightning. "No, I'm not ready. I look a whole-ass hot mess. My eyes are swollen, hair's a disaster."

"Nonsense. Those are ridiculous concerns. My lord says she's waiting for us to return, so we shall," Tanith says with a small laugh, then turns us around on the drop of a dime.

And Oakly's jaw drops just as fast.

"Looks like it's time for you to meet my mother-in-law."

"Fuck me. I should've stayed outside with the guys. I'm gonna puke."

"You're being crazy. Plus, they just came to give us quick kisses and check on us. If you had stayed with them, you would've had to go work out."

"Damn it, you're right, but still, this is petrifying. She's breathtaking. Literally, I can't breathe."

I smile warmly as Aurora crosses her foyer to us and yeah, I admit, she's stunning. She looks like an angel gliding through the rays of light, but regardless, Oakly's nervousness is for nothing. Aurora is by far the easiest person in the realm to get along with.

Well, as long as you're not threatening her family.

"I'm so happy to see you, girls. Uh, Oakly, it's amazing to finally meet you," Aurora says, wrapping Oakly in a hug that takes her by surprise. "Thank you so much for coming and having a girls' day with me."

Just like the day Gaster called her his granddaughter, she looks seconds from passing out and I hide my snickering behind my hand.

"She just thanked me. What the hell do I say?"

"I don't know, Oakly, maybe something like, it's wonderful to meet you, thank you for having me, you're beautiful. Any of that would do."

"I'm wonderful to meet. I mean, beautiful...I, shit," Oakly stutters, slapping her hand to her forehead, and I die laughing.

Aurora starts as well but quickly covers it with a cough, then smiles fondly at her. "Don't be nervous, please. You're family. Family should always feel comfortable."

Her magic washes across the room and Oakly practically falls into her open arms. It is a heady dose of happiness and even though I could block it out, I don't. There's no sense in blocking out a surge of ecstatic hormones.

"It's so nice to finally meet you. Willow's told me so much about you and yes, I've been incredibly nervous, but I'm also stupid excited. This is freaking amazing."

"Stupid excited? Freaking amazing? Are you kidding me?"

"It's her gift. You left yourself completely open and she's pumping you full of her happiness." I laugh.

"You may want to dial it back a bit, Aurora, or she's going to be a chatterbox," I tease.

"Oh, sorry, my girl. I'm just so thrilled. I went from having no daughters to two in such a short amount of time. All my dreams are coming true," she says sweetly, and both Oakly and I melt.

When you go from not receiving this type of affection to being overwhelmed with it, it's emotional.

"Okay, come on, you two. I've got the kitchens bringing coffee, Gaster dropped off pastries, and my whole afternoon cleared."

Linking her arms through ours, she steers us past a number of rooms, her office, and out through her patio doors where everything she just claimed to have waiting is spread out across the table. Plus, Tanith is sunbathing in her gardens.

It doesn't take long for the boost in excitement to wear off for Oakly and she eases back into her normal level of happiness. Once that occurs, the conversations start to flow seamlessly.

"I've never seen someone get so sick in my life. Granted, I should've known better than to let her drink that much. We can get ill here from too much drugs or alcohol, but I just figured by that point her stomach would've toughened up from being in the realm for a month." Oakly picks, recounting the embarrassing night I spent bound to her toilet.

"I still get ill from transporting too much. Not as bad as that night drinking, but I don't think it's going to go away."

"Ugh, I thank Elementra the only time in my life I've been that ill was during my pregnancy with Corentin. My goodness, that was awful. It lasted months but eased up. I was rejoicing that it was over, then I swear the second Tilly became pregnant with Tillme, it started all over again right along with her. As if we just couldn't do anything without the other," Aurora says and the sweet smile stays plastered to her face, but I sense the sadness lurking below.

"What was it like having siblings? From the stories I've heard and CC's still obvious shenanigans, it seems like it would've been a blast," Oakly asks.

I've wondered the same sometimes but usually shut it down. If I had a sibling growing up, they would've endured what I had to and that would've been a miserable existence. I'm thankful my siblings, blood and bond, came later in life.

"Wild but magical. We never had to worry about being alone or making friends. It was already built between us. The three of us were always up to something. Trouble mostly, let me tell you. Our mother made life very uncolorful, let's put it that way, but Orien always found the magic in everything. Our favorite game was hide-and-seek, and we surely passed that on to our boys. Unlike them, though, we weren't allowed to do it outside. We were limited to the central wing." She smiles softly, no doubt falling into the past.

"Thinking back about it now, it's so funny. Tilly and I always made Orien be the finder. Which in hindsight, no wonder we always lost. He had the gift of sight. We'd hide all over the wing and he'd find us in a split second, but on days when our mother had been particularly harsh or something happened, our favorite spot to hide would be under his bed. We didn't know it then, of course, we thought for sure we outsmarted him but no, on those days, he was letting us win, just trying to cheer us up. Anytime we needed a good cheering up, Tilly and I would hide under his bed."

Her musical laugh drifts all around us and we join in on the happy memory. I, too, have those fond moments. Hide-and-seek was certainly a favorite among the original Vito siblings because CC brought it to my life as well. We hid all over that forest until I created a clearing.

Just as I go to tell her about my own little hide-and-seek victories, a tickling across my mind halts me. I feel the words, the memory trying to push itself through, and I coax it gently. Encouraging it on.

My sweet, sweet Aurora. She's going to have a field day to find out I was hiding in plain sight, just down the hall from her for years and years.

My chair crashes against the ground as I spring from my seat, panting. The reluctance to the words was because they weren't my own. They were just a blip of a sentence thrown in with a hell of a lot of truth bombs that were dropped on me the day CC's memories came through.

"Willow, what's wrong?" Aurora asks, concerned. Both her and Oakly stand from their chairs rapidly and stare at me as if we're about to be attacked.

"That big little shit," I mumble.

"What?" they both ask.

"CC. He's been playing the ultimate game of damn hide-and-seek." I huff before turning fully to Aurora. "Where's his bedroom? Where you'd hide under his bed?"

"In the central wing, right down the hall from my room."

"Will you take me there, please?"

At her nod, she scurries ahead, with me and Oakly hot on her heels. Whatever we're about to find has my adrenaline pumping and my curious little heart doing cartwheels.

After a flight of stairs and numerous lefts and rights, we finally approach a door like any other, except it's so much different. This is the strongest I've felt CC's presence outside of the south wing.

"It's...nothing's really changed since he was a boy. Even after he moved into the south wing, we weren't willing to change a thing," Aurora says almost to herself as she turns the knob gently.

The only issue with that is, he never moved into the south wing.

I hold my breath as the room comes into view, and my eyes search every surface. It's nothing like you'd except a teenage boy's room to be like. It's neat, orderly, a bed perfectly made, and bookshelves that also serve as a headboard.

"What is it we're looking for, Willow?" Aurora asks.

"I'm not sure yet," I say as I continue to scan the room. That is until my eyes fall on the very out of place, not matching rug stretched out under the bed. "What's your favorite color? And Tilly's?" I ask.

"Mine is yellow. Tilly's was green," she says and I smile.

The chaotic green and yellow rug under the bed tells me all I need to know. All my most favorite gifts were given to me in some shade of purple. Colors were a personal touch he put on everything.

"Under the bed," I whisper.

Moving to the foot of the bed, using my air, I lift the whole thing up and move it to the other side of the room, nearly knocking Oakly and Aurora over since they weren't paying any attention.

A belly-deep laugh bursts out of me when I gaze down at the note on the rug and the two of them come to stand beside me.

"Oh, that asshole," Aurora whispers, bending down to pick it up.

I WON.

That's all it says, and Aurora laughs until there're streams of tears rolling down her cheeks. Both happy and sad.

"He seriously just wanted to leave me a note telling me he won hide-and-seek?" she asks.

"No, I don't think so," I mumble as I still feel his power pulsing through the room.

Looking down at the rug, its triangular-shaped pattern makes me dizzy as I stare at it for too long. My eyes begin to blur and beg for me to blink, but that's when I see it.

Arrows pointing upward.

Again, calling my air element out, I use the wind to roll the rug up and squeal in excitement.

"It's a secret room," Oakly and I shriek at the same time.

"Orien, you sly creature," Aurora murmurs.

Impatience and curiosity override all my senses as we gaze down at the small door carved into the floor and I reach for the grooved handle. A shock shoots up my arm and I snatch my hand back, screeching.

"What the fuck?" I cry out, gripping my hand.

"When will you learn, Willy?" Oakly snickers and I shoot her a deadly glare.

"Fair warning, everyone. It's going to shock the shit out of you."

They laugh at me, then gently lay their hands to the handle as well, taking the electrocution with ease and grace.

We watch a shimmering web skitter across the surface of the door, then gasp as we hear multiple locks begin to unclick. The sound of metal sliding against metal echoes around the room and I swear none of us breathe until the room falls silent once more.

"After you, Aurora. You're the one who lost the game," I whisper as if speaking too loud will disrupt something.

"Funny. You act just like him sometimes, you know?"

Yeah, I know.

Releasing a deep breath, she once again grips the handle, and my heart thunders in my chest as the creaking sound of hinges filters through my ears. A light illuminates a staircase for her to follow down as soon as the door fully opens, and me and Oakly glance at one another with her first step.

"This is so cool. I feel like an E.F. spy."

"Yeah, well, there's no telling the booby traps he has placed down here," I tell her with a devilish smirk that has hers melting away.

As soon as Aurora leaves enough room for me to take a couple steps behind her, I follow right along, leaving Oakly to pick her own jaw up off the floor.

From the top, the staircase seemed so much longer than what it actually is, and only after twelve steps, I'm freezing at the bottom beside Aurora as Oakly slams into my back.

"Shit, why did you quit—oh my."

The massive room is like Gaster's office but on steroids.

The walls are lined with books on not only the first floor but the second as well. Years upon years of information is piled into this room and the smell of wood and mint is potent. I swear if knowledge had a scent, this room is saturated in it.

There's a small kitchenette that has a kettle on the stove ready to go and three mugs are set out on the small table in the center. A never-ending fireplace burns softly, lighting the room in a dim glow, and my eyes water on the small, made bed.

A door that's partially cracked on the other side of the room draws my attention, and my feet move faster than my mind. I can't hold the waterworks back as I sling the door open wide and Aurora gasps behind me. His closet is full of his clothes and my nose fills with the smell of him.

He lived here. This was his room.

"Willow, Aurora, you should come see this," Oakly calls out and the two of us hastily wipe our eyes before hustling back out the closet to her.

Standing at the small table, she's holding an envelope in her shaking hand and she gulps as she turns it over repeatedly, checking the front and back.

"There's one for each of us. Even me," she says quietly.

The two of us nearly fall over ourselves as we rush to join her at the table, but we both freeze when we peer down at our names.

"Orien," Aurora breathes as she picks hers up and rips it right open, not wasting another minute to get the closure she needs.

Turning to Oakly, she gives me a confident nod before doing the same.

I still peer down at mine, running my fingers around the pointed edges. Every time I receive a note from him, something changes. Something big usually, but I swallow down that fear and face it head-on.

Filia mea,

Remember when our games of hide-and-seek turned into scavenger hunts?

Well, some of the answers you seek will be found here, the south wing, and various other places.

Continue the path you're on, my sweet girl, but just know, you're no longer on it alone. Everyone and everything you will need is now in your life. Together, you will conquer it all.

CC xoxo.

Bringing the letter to my nose, I inhale sharply, breathing in the scent of him before smiling against the parchment. I can picture him now, sitting at this table, writing these letters to us.

"Shit!" Oakly screams, followed by a loud bang against the table that has me whipping my eyes to her. "A book just fell out of my letter!"

"We can see that," Aurora says, laughing and crying as she wipes away the tears and folds her letter up close to her heart. I'm not going to ask her to tell me what it says. I believe if it gave her any guidance or information I needed to know, she'd tell me. Other than that, that's her letter.

For her eyes only.

"What does it say, Oak?" I ask.

Clearing her throat and tearing her gaze away from the massive encyclopedia-like book, she peers back down at her parchment.

"Dear Oakly,

This isn't how I wish we had met, but alas, I come bearing a gift to make up for my poor manners.

The book you just dropped on my table has never had eyes on it from anyone in this realm, other than myself. It is a collection of sorts that I've worked on over the years that I believe will come in handy to you. Not even the old man has seen this. He's surely going to be prepared to fight you for it.

I figured, though, the realm's—"

She stops reading, gasping for breath as sobs begin to wrack her chest, but when I step closer to her, she waves me off.

"I figured, though, the realm's most renowned Master Archivist deserved the first glance.

Read it. Memorize it.

As a matter of fact, ask your Absorber for the Recollection Spell. He's stingy with that ancient knowledge.

You're going to do amazing things, Oakly Mercie.

Don't let anyone make you believe differently.

CC xoxo."

Laying the letter down, she starts flipping through the pages rapidly, and her breathing quickens. Faster than I can follow, she starts spouting off facts and stats from every page and her face continues to grow brighter.

"This is crazy. The Nexus Mark, the Pyrathian Origin stone. What..." She trails off as she becomes fixated on the page she's on.

"What is it?" I ask.

"Well, the first, you know the Nexus Mark. It's a rune. The Pyrathian Origin stone is a relic. It's claimed to have come from the first layer of the decimated side. From Pyra's first ever eruption. The others...I haven't a clue. Relics, runes, artifacts, all kinds of stuff I've never even heard of."

Blood rushes to my ears and my body breaks out in a fever. Oakly's so occupied with the book, she doesn't even realize I'm having a moment.

It can't be.

"Wh-What did you say?"

"You heard me—" Her eyes flash up to me, and she startles at my pale face. "Willow, what's wrong?"

My mouth gapes open and I can't even get the words out, so instead, I send Trex's conversation to her and Aurora's mind.

Tracking. Relics. Artifacts. Runes. My blood supply. The ritual.

"Oh, Elementra," she breathes, running her hands around the rim of her new book. "We have a lot of training and studying to do, Willy."

"Yeah, Oak," I choke. "Yeah, we do."

Twenty

Corentin

"I'm a tad shocked to sense all this excitement coming from you."

Peering down at where my princess is tucked into my side, I shake my head and smile at her.

She's so nosy.

That beautiful gaze goes from soft and sweet to narrowed in the blink of an eye and Tillman snorts beside us.

"See, it's both of you. You're both nosy," I say.

"It's not nosy when it's just broadcast out in the open for me to feel or hear," Willow sasses.

"Of course, princess."

"So..."

A chuckle escapes me and her teasing laugh wraps around my heart as her arms lace their way around my waist. I don't mind her eavesdropping, nosiness, whatever we want to call it. I've just found that I like teasing her. I love the pink her cheeks turn when I make her blush from something other than arousal.

I know I can make her skin pinken from the palm of my hand or a darkened look, but to make her flush at something funny or playful I said is completely different.

The whole feeling itself is something I've never experienced.

Me? Corentin Vito, teasing. No.

Realm's most controlling headmaster, oldest and sternest of the heirs.

Yes.

For my princess, though, I'll be it all.

I want it all. Her laughs, her playfulness, her moans. I need it all. So for her, I'll tease, taunt, and joke until her cheeks are pink from laughing so much.

Then I'll spank the other ones to make them match.

"Corentin..." she breathes.

"See what you get, little warrior," Tillman mocks and the two of us send our low chuckles through to her, making her squirm.

"Draken's almost done talking Layton's parents heads off and Gaster, Keeper, and Tanith should be arriving at the academy any minute now, but to address your comment, princess, I am excited. It may not seem this way here lately, but I do love being headmaster. It's not always so chaotic, and that's when I really get to get important work for the academy and students done. Taking Layton today for a tour is a perfect example of that. Very rarely do we get kids his age with the ability and potential he has. This is going to make a huge difference in his life. For the better. This is the best part of my job," I tell her honestly.

I remember her tour like it was yesterday.

That was one of the best days of my life, and I'll never forget it.

Granted, I was still being a hard-ass, but on the inside, my body was thrumming with the awakening of our bond, and I wanted nothing more than for her to have an amazing experience. I didn't miss a moment of any of her reactions. The awestruck wonder that came across her face when she took her first look at the academy will be imprinted on my mind forever.

"Then let's get a move on so we can show it all to him and get him situated," she says softly, squeezing her arms around me tighter. *"Come on, dragon. You can talk more with them when we get there. Let's go."*

"Okay, Fank family, we can talk more at the academy. We'll have to walk you in through the wards, so hold on to me and the big guy," Draken says, rubbing his hands together excitedly.

Sira, Layton, and two of his dads join Tillman, while the other three move toward Draken. Each of them looks nervous, understandably, but hopefully once they see where their son will be, they'll grow less anxious.

Willow stays with me, and I obscure her sight of Sira touching Tillman, although I don't think it would cause her to growl this time. Plus, as Cas presses into her back, she shivers and we share a look, plenty pleased with her being smushed between us.

I'm surprised he's here, although I guess I shouldn't be when the being he's most obsessed with is between us. He's been consumed over our uncle's room since yesterday, but she got him to come to bed and come with us today without an argument.

Our mischievous grins swiftly turn into frowns when Willow announces, "Okay, on me."

Caspian quickly covers his laugh with a cough and then looks at me with that fucking twinkle in his eye. He's going to make me say something.

Asshole.

"Princess, maybe—"

"No, I know what you're going to say. I can do this. I don't like doing it, but I have to get over it. Oakly's training on long distance tracking is starting ASAP and I at least need to know how to transport more than just me before then."

Her unwavering tone settles any rebuttal I had ready. She wants to know and is determined to do it, so that's that. Who am I to stop her from learning, and if this is what she wants, I'll be the one to teach her.

"Okay then, princess. Pinpoint the spots we're touching you and send your magic there," I instruct and when I feel the caress of her magic across my palm, I carry on, "Perfect. Now in your mind, clearly picture the front of the academy. Right where I took you the first time. Once you have it clear in your mind, open the transport, but don't forget to pull our magic with you."

I leave my instructions short, quick, and to the point. She's already read everything she can on transporting herself and others. It's just the matter of doing it now. The only reason I bothered saying anything was to give her a moment to settle her nerves and ground herself.

"Ready?" she asks, blowing out a breath.

"Ready, princess."

"Ready, Primary."

Cas and I speak at the same time, giving each other confident nods. One of us will step in if we need to, but that won't be the case. She can do anything she puts her mind to.

The darkness steals my sight and the entire essence of her surrounds us. The roasted, sweet coffee scent of her invades my lungs and her magic wraps around me like a blanket on a breezy day. I've never felt this engulfed by a transport.

Just a blip in time later, the sun's piercing my eyes, and I'm left staring at Vito Academy in all its beauty. The sight beside me, though, is far more gorgeous.

"Open your eyes, Primary," Caspian whispers.

An elated laugh bursts free from her as she peeks out of one eye, then jumps up and down, squealing. She launches herself at me and I easily catch her, spinning her around and stealing a kiss from her soft lips.

Passing her over to Cas, she wraps her legs around his waist and cheers, "I did it! Oh my God, that was exhilarating. It felt so much easier with the two of you with me. It didn't feel nearly as unsettling as it does when I do it alone."

Her excitement is contagious, drawing the attention of her other two men, and Cas doesn't twitch or sneer about his face being smushed between her hands or her lips crashed against his. He embraces it fully and falls into the affection she's pouring all over him.

"Good shit, little wanderer. Knew you'd do it. You can transport me back with you when we leave," Draken purrs, pulling her into his chest before attacking her mouth.

We all roll our eyes at his over-the-top public display of affection, but we don't dare say anything. It's got to be a shifter thing because Willow eats that shit up. She loves for everyone to see him claiming her so possessively.

Tillman doesn't speak out loud, but whatever he says in her mind, only to her, has her eyes shining bright. They flutter closed expectantly when he grips the back of her neck and tilts her head back, sealing his lips to hers.

Fuck, how times have changed so much.

"This place is...I'm going to get so freaking lost," Layton says, almost to himself, but loud enough we all turn to look at him.

"Nah, you'll be fine. We're going to give you a good tour, and you'll have an escort with you this whole first year," Draken tells him, slinging his arm over the kid's shoulder.

"Oh, I like that idea. So he won't ever be alone?" Sira asks.

"Not until he's eighteen, and even after that, he'll still have supervision. He's the youngest in the academy and will be for quite some time or until we can locate his Nexus brothers," I say mindlessly as I type away on my communicator to inform Geo we've arrived.

"My...what?" Layton asks, confused, and I peer up from my phone to see not only his confusion but his parents' as well.

Glancing over at Draken, the sly smirk on his lips tells me he didn't inform them like I asked him to, and I just gave the kid, plus his parents, a shocker.

"He already likes me but is petrified of you. Figured you needed some brownie points," he says, reading my face like a book.

Holding in my sigh, I plaster on a small smile and explain, "I thought it'd be in your best interest since you're not going through the steps of lower and mid-level academies, that we visit those and see if you find your Nexus. Schooling at this level will be much easier with your brothers by your side. Not only that, Nexuses, for the most part, are paired equally. If you have a rare gift, there's a likelihood your brothers do as well. Of course, if you don't want to do that, you most certainly don't have to."

An eager smile crosses his face as he looks at his four dads, and his gaze settles on his mom. He's playing through his mind what that would be like for him. Every boy, man, does it. Well, with a few exceptions.

"I want to do that. Thank you, Headmaster Corentin," he says, grinning from ear to ear.

"Just Corentin, kid. Well, when it's just all of us," I tack on as an afterthought. I'll be damned if the rest of the students around here started calling me just Corentin. "Come on, we've got a lot to see."

Turning back to the academy, a loud, warning roar sounds overhead, and we all shield the sun from our eyes with our hands as we gaze up at Tanith soaring above us.

A booming roar answers from around the corner of the castle and out bounds a massive-ass fucking lion.

I swear, it's like he has a sixth sense to other animals.

The second Tanith's claws touch down, Vince, in his shifted form, runs right up to her as though he has no fear in the world. He presses his chest to the ground with his tail wagging like crazy in the air behind him, then completely ignoring Gaster's yelling, he pounces.

Not in an attacking sort of way, definitely a playful one. He rubs his coat all over her, every inch he can reach and every gentle twitch of her wing, he paws at her. She huffs a couple times, gently flicking him away, but he doesn't give it up.

A swish of her tail draws all his attention, and he bounds toward it, tackling it like a damn kitten playing with a toy. He's lucky he didn't spear himself on one of her spikes.

"Uh-oh," Draken says low before chuckling to himself.

"Uh-oh, what?" Tillman asks.

"He's gone full beast. I've never seen Vince lose control before." Draken continues laughing as we all stare at Vince in shock.

I've never seen it either.

Damn, this is going to be embarrassing for him.

A warning rumble, paired with a ring of smoke blows out of Tanith's nostrils and she whips her head around to where Vince is...Fuck me, he's licking her tail.

I've found by observing Tanith since she's arrived, for a dragon, she can control many facial expressions that are honestly easy to interpret. Right now, she's glaring at Vince like he is the vilest creature she's ever seen.

She finally has enough and with a powerful flick of her tail, Vince comes tumbling down the gravel way, stopping only mere feet away from us. Thankfully, that little hit knocks some sense into him, and he shakes his coat out, all majestic. As if he has a paw to stand on now that we've seen what he just did.

Shifting back into his human form, the mortification is obvious.

"A fucking dragon. A real dragon, not a shifter," he says, bewildered.

"Well, little pussycat, that's one way to introduce yourself. I'd give her some space for now, or you'll be cooked right up," Keeper says with a bloodthirsty smile that shows off his long, white fangs.

Fuck me.

"You brought a real dragon and the vampire here?" Vince asks, whipping his head toward me so fast, I'm surprised it didn't snap off, and again, I glare at Draken. This was information that was supposed to be relayed.

"I had a feeling something like this was going to happen. Enjoy the moment, boss man, it's hilarious."

"Draken, that could've turned out very differently," Tillman scolds.

"Nah, I warned Tanith. She knew a lion was going to be coming. She flew over the training fields first just to give him time to shift and run all the way up here. She was excited for his reaction till he decided to defile her tail."

Pinching the bridge of my nose, my mouth twitches involuntarily, and I try hard to hold my laugh in. I nearly choke on the air that's forcing its way up, especially when Draken's loud laugh bursts from him.

The second Tillman's deep rumble bubbles out, it's a losing game for the rest of us. Poor Vince stands, huffing with his hands on his hips as the entire group falls apart.

Even the Fank family joins in, and honestly, it probably settles their nerves seeing Vince like this. They were intimidated to learn their son was going to be taken care of and mentored by a Nemean lion. Which made no sense since they treat Draken like he hung the sun.

Clearing my voice, but not bothering to hide my smile, I say, "Vince, this is Keeper, and his bonded dragon that you so gracefully just licked, is Tanith."

"I'm sorry about that, really. I haven't lost control over my animal in, I don't even know, almost two decades. I believe having a beast as formidable as her just called to his baser instincts and I wasn't prepared for it. He never did that with Draken or Willow," Vince says in a nervous ramble, sticking his hand out for Keeper to shake.

"Draken's told me about you and your knowledge of shifters. It's impressive, but your beast probably senses the human side in my son and his beloved, whereas Tanith is all creature with the intelligence to rival any in this realm and my own. It will not be me who needs to accept your apology but her. She has a mind of her own," Keeper says with a mischievous grin, and I'm positive he's setting Vince up to get eaten or maybe burned.

"Let's meet the man of the hour, give Tanith sometime to...cool down until you apologize," I suggest, putting my hand on his shoulder to steer him the other way when he looks back at the pissed off golden dragon. "I apologize for the dramatic introduction, but this is Vince Callico. Vince, this is Layton Fank and his parents, Sira, Langston, Sim, Joe, and Dani Fank."

"Please do not take that display as my usual show of control. My lion and I are typically very much on the same page," Vince says, embarrassed.

"That was so cool. You weren't even scared," Layton says, glancing at Vince the same way he does at Draken. Awestruck.

"Yes, well, my counterpart may not have been worried, but I'm about to piss myself, so this is a perfect example of the balance our other halves bring."

I give Vince a second to give a more proper introduction to Layton's parents and he explains what's to be expected in their upcoming months together. The more he talks about the nitty-gritty of what he'll be teaching, the mortified side of his embarrassment fades, leaving the typical, high-energized enthusiasm that comes from him when he gets an opportunity to work with a rare shifter.

Right before my eyes, it eases the turmoil we've seen in Layton's parents since we had the original discussion that Layton had to come to an academy. The kid's smile continues to grow, and each time he looks at his parents for validation in his excitement, they reciprocate it. Whether it's a mix of a show and sincerity, I'm not sure, but it puts his worries to rest.

"Lead the way, Draken. We've got a lot to do this afternoon," I say.

"I thought all we had planned was this?" Willow asks.

"This will take the majority of our time, but this afternoon we're having a family meeting."

"Mom's dragging us all together, huh? Great," Caspian drawls with an eye roll.

"Not Mom. Me," I say.

Willow and my brothers all whip their heads toward me questioningly, but I don't let my mask crack. We'll discuss everything we need to when we leave the academy. For now, we need to focus on this kid and his future.

The future we'll be able to provide for him once we wrap up this shit show of a war in our realm.

Twenty-two...

Twenty-two people sit around my parents' table. Including me.

That's how much our family has grown in the time my princess has been here and although she's anxious, has been since I announced we were having a family meeting, she's grinning from ear to ear. Her gaze bounces across each Nexus, ours, my parents', the Mercies', and Lyker's, plus Keeper and Gaster with such tenderness and so much love, it's heartwarming.

That's the whole point of this meeting.

We've got to make some changes, put plans in place so our family, all families across the realm, can relax, enjoy their lives without the threat consistently hanging over their heads.

Me suggesting major changes. Never thought I'd see the day.

And actually feel...be okay with it.

Having Layton's tour of the academy first before this meeting was more of a help than I realized it would be. As we walked through every building, every square inch, the new training gym, where he'd be staying in Vince's new house. Every occurrence was a small, subtle change that loosened me up and fortified what I'm going to bring up in a moment, is the right thing to do.

It's even more solidified in my mind now as I gaze at every person in this room. We all have our roles to play and if we play them properly, we can make irrevocable strides in the direction we need to be going.

"Corentin, my boy, you called this meeting. We've eaten, talked, teased, so let's get on with it or Aurora and Willow are going to lose the fragile amount of patience they have," Gaster teases, looking between the two of them, grinning as they glare at him.

"It's not a lack of patience, thank you very much, Gaster. It's anticipation of whatever he's about to say. You know how hard it is to know I could just dive into his mind to find out, but I don't?" Willow sasses right back.

"Exactly. I can feel his assuredness and apprehension. It's got me on the edge of my seat," my mom tacks on.

"I get it. It's nothing bad, so everyone can ease up on the worry, but I do want to address some things I believe are important," I say, gaining everyone's attention.

Normally, I'd lace my fingers in front of me, to ground myself and keep the small glow of light beneath my fingertips concealed, but instead, I unbutton my jacket and lean back.

Willow's hand slides into mine from beside me, where she's perched in Tillman's lap, and I bring it to my lips, sending her a burst of my love through to her bond. Some of this is going to come as a shock to her because I didn't discuss it with her first, but I believe she'll see where I'm coming from.

Turning my focus on my mom, I soften my eyes. She's going to hate this. "We need to move the Spring Ball out."

Just as I suspected, she startles and gazes between my dads, her mouth falling open and closed.

"The Spring Ball has been the same day for, for..."

"Two thousand years," Gaster, San, and Caspian all answer at once.

"I'm aware, Mom. It's been a Vito family tradition since our family took power, but it's a few weeks out, and I can't shake the feeling that we're not ready for it. If there's one thing I've learned here lately, you can't ignore any inklings. It's going to benefit us more by pushing it out, gain as much information as we can before we have a castle full of possible traitors," I state firmly.

Willow's disappointment slices me momentarily before her complete, unwavering agreement stitches me right back up.

"Corentin's right. Things fall in place when they're supposed to and if this is a feeling he can't shake, then we aren't supposed to shake it," she states confidently, squeezing my hand harder.

"Okay then," my mom whispers, a little teary-eyed over the broken tradition, but she clears her throat and rights herself. "When do you think we should host it?"

"The last day of spring for the Central. That gives us six weeks total to learn as much as we can and make as many moves as we need to."

I emphasize spring for the Central because it lasts longer here than anywhere else. Because of the four territories meeting here, the seasons change very differently than anywhere else.

"That's only three weeks more, angel. It'll be fine," Dyce says softly, reaching over to grip Mom's hand.

"Send a decree tomorrow changing the day of the ball and announce we've found our true Primary," Caspian says, and we all turn toward him.

"You all asked me—"

"I know, we asked you to wait, but this news will lighten any grievances people have over a fucking party. Not only that, but it's also going to put the Mastery in a bad spot. If anything were to happen again to Willow, the realm will now know the Mastery made a move against the awaiting Matriarch. That'll make them reconsider everything they do," he says begrudgingly, looking at Willow for her opinion.

"Princess?" I prompt when she stays quiet.

"I agree. It's something we all wanted to wait to do, but I think it's for the best now. It's no longer a secret to the Mastery that I'm here and who I am. Including that I'll be introduced to the realm during the ball may also draw the second family further into the light. We'll see their reaction to me firsthand when they have to meet me," she says and our pride for her blows across my chest.

Each of my brothers, including me, smiles at her fondly. I don't think she has any idea how much she's truly grown.

"Okay. I'll send the decree tomorrow. What's next?" Mom asks.

Turning my head to Tillman, he nods, and I know he's on board with my next decision. It was a passing conversation the two of us had, but now a full-fledged plan has formed in my mind.

"Lyker, I have a large request of you."

His serious face never flinches or changes, but I catch the softening in his gaze when his eyes turn to Willow. "I'll do whatever you need of me."

He says that now.

"I want to send you all the wolf shifters in the E.F. I need you to train them properly. Also, any wolf in your pack who wants to be part of the fight. Previous E.F. members or not. Tillman and I have discussed it. We'll grant you authority to authorize them as active E.F. members. They'll receive the training and all other resources as if they went through the academy."

His mask crumbles into a pile of confusion as he looks between Tillman and me. I knew this would be a shock, but not only that, a huge responsibility to place on him on top of his responsibilities as Alpha.

"Why?"

"Wolves are the fastest, most well-organized land shifters in Elementra. The pack dynamic gives them unimaginable strengths, but it's no secret they're some of the hardest to train. Simply because of the dynamic of your beast. Their animal craves an alpha, and although the human side can identify Tillman, Ry, any of us as their superiors, their beast does not. Of course there're exceptions to the rule. You, Rhett, his brothers, you all don't rely on that relationship, but you lot are few and far between.

"The members we have, have ridiculous potential, but we don't have the resources to provide them with what they need. Draken and Willow possess the dominance of alphas, and could easily fill that role, but that would just be a disservice to the shifters. When this war is over, there will always be wolf shifters, but neither Willow nor Draken want to have to lead them every day. They need a permanent place to grow and thrive."

He observes me for a long moment. Most of what I just said, he already knows. Who am I to teach him about his own gift, but it needed to be laid out like that so he could see where I'm coming from and where I'm going with this.

"You want me to open a wolf shifter academy," he concludes.

Smart, smart wolf.

"Precisely. We'll support you fully every step of the way. You won't do anything alone, and we'll provide everything you need for it."

"I love the idea, I do. It was always a dream of my dad's to have a school for wolf shifters. He—and I agree now that I'm older—always felt the wolves wouldn't get such a bad rap if they had their own place to learn. But I'm not sure how the pack is going to feel about me clearing land to build a shifter academy right in their backdoors. They're still healing from the betrayal of the last Alpha allowing a multitude of species to train in their lands," he says, but I was ready for that. I considered how it would make his pack feel.

From my coat pocket, I pull out an envelope and pass it over to him, then wait for him to read through it.

"What is this?" he asks quietly.

"The unclaimed land outside the pack lands where your childhood home is. Apparently, it wasn't unclaimed. The paperwork had just been hidden. The land you believed to be unclaimed is actually in the name of Alpha Lyker Quinn. Your childhood home's land was left to be reregistered in the name of the children of Iris Quinn, Lyker and Willow."

I thought I was losing my mind yesterday when that envelope appeared in my office desk drawer. I've been through the desk so many times, I knew I'd never missed it. But once Willow called for us to see they'd found my uncle's secret room, I knew their discovery unlocked mine.

"This was the surprise you said you had for me," Willow whispers.

"Yeah. I hope it's a good surprise."

"It's great, it really is, but...it really says children, as in plural and my name. I was included?"

"Yeah, princess. Take a look for yourself."

"May I?" she asks Lyker softly, to which his confused features turn tender, and he slides her the page.

Down the parchment, it reads just as it did the day Willow's mom filled it out, but at the bottom, a clause was included that the land would pass to her children in the event of her death.

Willow covers her watery smile with her hand as she says thank you and passes the paper back to Lyker. Her heart is beating so fast I can feel it through her fingers that lace tightly again with mine. Hopefully, now any worry about whether her mom wanted her to have that house alongside Lyker will vanish.

"That's a perfect place for an academy," Lyker finally says, smiling proudly.

"I swear to you, we'll do this with you. You won't bear all this responsibility alone," I tell him seriously.

"I know. Tillman will have to come show his scary face every now and then. Remind everyone who the boss is."

"Scary? I got the prettiest face out of all of us," he teases, causing everyone to laugh at the obvious shit talking. His stern glare is one of the scariest looks I've seen.

The laughter breaks up the tension that was building in the room and everyone falls much more relaxed, even though I'm not done. Those two issues, though, were the biggest.

"What's next on the agenda? I'm ready for dessert," Oakly says, reaching across the table to battle Draken for the last handfuls of pastries.

She wins, by the way.

"Well, now that you've drawn attention to yourself, you are," I say and she nearly chokes on said dessert she just shoved in her mouth.

When Jamie quits pounding on her back, staring at her as if she's going to fall apart, they both turn to glare at me.

"Me?"

"You. I don't believe you should continue at the academy."

Her evil, narrowed eyes shatter and her face crumbles instantly, but I quickly hold my hand up for her to let me continue before she has a meltdown.

"I'm not kicking you out. Just like Willow, I think it's in your best interest to be finished with your studies. Let's be honest here, Oakly, you're already the top of your class academically, as a first year. The time you've spent with Gaster, Willow, and San has propelled you far past even the fourth years. There's nothing left that the academy can teach you. You're needed elsewhere now."

"But what about my Archivist Aid? Final test? Certificate of Completion? I can't just be done. I don't have anything to prove it," she says frantically.

I can't help but smirk at her. I really appreciate the fact she wants to prove herself, do things the way they're supposed to be done, but certain situations call for certain measures.

Also, I think sometimes she forgets who her sister truly is. If she hasn't figured out already or if she's simply forgotten that she has a place at the palace alongside all of us by now, I'll let her figure it out in her own time.

"All will be awarded to you properly. You'll receive a Certificate of Completion for the academy, E.F. training, and Archivist Aid. All signed off by me, my mom, and Gaster."

She looks at her men dumbfounded as if she just can't wrap her head around this. Gaster gives her an encouraging nod. My mom gives her a warm, reassuring smile, but when her look falls to Willow, my princess squeals.

"Why the hell do you look so lost?"

"This is real?" she asks quietly.

"Fuck yes, it's real! You're done with the academy," Willow shrieks, causing the whole table to erupt into cheers.

Which causes Oakly to cry.

"Stop all that, *Perfecta Anima.* You know better than anyone you deserve it," Cas says, but it's missing its usual coldness.

Oakly snorts, wiping her face clean. "You're right, asshole. I definitely do."

Cas rolls his eyes, but the two of them still smile, and that seems to light my princess up with happiness. The bridge that's been gapped between the two of them makes her overjoyed and I'm so happy to see my brother moving past issues, not even caused by Oakly, but regardless, he's taking baby steps starting with her.

"Last topic," I say, quieting everyone once more. "I was going over reports this morning. With the exception of Willow's kidnapping and Oakly's, Ry's, and San's, the Mastery hasn't attacked anyone since then. Nowhere in the realm has reported anything from them."

"What do you think is going on?" my mom asks.

"They're gearing up."

Tillman, Caspian, Draken, Ry, San, Nikoli, Lyker, Lennox, Kyan, Zane, my dads, Roye, and Dyce, even Keeper all say the exact answer I figured. Their years of experience, and Keeper's years of being kept prisoner, told them immediately what the lack of attacks are hinting at.

"So what's your plan, son?" Roye asks.

"We prepare. Starting tomorrow, everyone's schedules will have to change up to focus on their strengths and work on weaknesses. Every morning, apart from your Nexus for now, Lyker, we'll have Nexus training here. Following that, Draken, Tillman, Ry, Jamie, and me will report to the academy. Willow, Gaster, Oakly, Cas, San, and Keeper, you all..." I trail off just slightly. Fuck, I'm not too happy about this, but it's how it must be for now.

"You all will be here. Studying, researching, digging through any bit of information you can. The new book Oakly received, the amplifier room, figuring out the Summum-Master's identity, finding Willow's blood supply, Trex's brothers. All these things have to be taken care of. Ideally, we find Willow's blood supply and the second family betraying us before the Spring Ball. The afternoons can be spent at the academy where you'll work on combat, long-distance tracking, and whatever other areas need to be worked on."

The thought of Willow being separated from me for half of the day every day is a kick to the balls. I hate it, regardless of the fact we can easily transport to one another whenever we want. I'd feel better with her being wherever I am.

"That's a big change from what we discussed," Willow mumbles, her displeasure evident in her bond and tone.

"I know, princess, and I'm sorry. I'm sorry for springing all of this on you and if there's anything you disagree with, I'm all ears. This doesn't have to be the end-all plan," I say softly, kissing each of her knuckles as I hold her sad gaze.

"No, it's all perfect, unfortunately. It's what needs to be done and this way, with a schedule and plan in place, it will get done."

Tillman pulls her closer to his chest, whispering sweet nothings to her mind and easing the worry from her brow. She mindlessly rubs her hip, both receiving and sending comfort from Draken. The shadows that dance around her wrist soothingly are braided, hers and his.

When her thumb runs across my finger, I can't help but smile down at my ring that she caresses. The ring she put so much effort, love, and pieces of herself into. Countless times I've caught myself turning it in circles since she slid it in place, rubbing its smooth surface instinctively. All of us have done it.

Wherever we go, we'll always have a piece of her.

Twenty-One

Willow

"You Primaries believe you can take on all of us? On the Mercie Nexus's first day of training?" Dyce's challenging tone draws a snort from Oakly, Aurora, and me.

The twelve men standing solidly in front of us all look amused at Aurora's offer of boys versus girls to end our first training together this morning.

It wasn't a surprise to me at all, but she and her Nexus were floored to see Oakly and her guys pick up on the true Nexus mingling—as I'm calling it—so fast. Nikoli and Oakly got it right their first time with their water elements, and it only took a few tries for her to get it right with all her men.

I had told her all about what the training was and what it required, and I lent her the book, so there's no doubt she spent the night reading up on it in preparation for this morning.

"The lot of you really don't believe we can take you?" I ask, gazing around at their overly confident smirks.

"This is different than E.F. training, trouble, where you and Oakly can take down six men. The twelve of us have trained the three of you in some form or fashion. We know every move you'll make," Ry says.

"He doesn't know every move I can make."

"Oakly."

She giggles and his eyes whip to her, confused and believing she's laughing at his words. She's too sly to tell him the truth and just winks at the glare he's shooting her.

"I think it's a brilliant idea and I have a way in which we can make it fair," Gaster says enthusiastically, grinning from ear to ear at the three of us, and Keeper shakes his head beside him knowingly.

Well, I know who Gaster has his money on.

"Let's hear it then, old man. If the Primaries want to try their luck, who are we to stop them?" Caspian says sarcastically, causing the guys to chuckle darkly and us to glare.

"A Forcefield Ring. Theo can draw out a large circular formation and once one of you boys or *ladies* is knocked out of the ring, you can't enter back in. It'll only be him that will have to be truthful about whether he gets knocked out, and obviously we'll be able to see if that happens. This way, you can't just continue to attack. Metaphorically speaking, you'll be out."

The horde of Nexus members look at each other to weigh their opinions in that scenario, while us girls are game. We were ready for this face-off without this fairness added.

"Fine, but we need rules," Corentin declares, and Aurora scoffs.

"No rules, son. Gifts, elements, magic, it's all fine. You men just get ready for this ass whopping we're about to deliver."

Oakly and I practically keel over laughing. Her voice was so sweet and soft. Nothing like the threat she's letting linger in the air. Her Nexus stares at her heatedly and my men all groan in disgust. Of course Oakly and I swoon because it's so romantic.

"Our men better still look at us like that in two hundred years."

"If they know what's good for them, they will," I snark with a tilt to my lip as I gaze at my Nexus.

"It's settled then. Come on, Theo, I'll walk the barrier with you. Everyone else get prepared," Gaster orders, clapping his hands in mischievous excitement.

The three of us turn from our guys and I lace my fingers with Aurora's so I can open my mind to both her and Oakly so she can hear our words. While simultaneously, I attempt to block Tillman out, although I know he won't try to eavesdrop. I feel his eagerness to see what we'll do.

"So what's the plan?" Oakly asks.

"Willow, I believe you should be the middle point. With all four elements at your disposal, you'll have the greatest advantage. My men are going to try to attack from behind me, so keep your eyes peeled there."

"My guys are going to attempt to hit from all angles. That's their attack formation," I say.

"Ry likes to hit head-on, so mine will be coming from the front," Oakly tacks on.

See, these men may have trained us, but we've been watching them as well.

"So, Oakly, right side, front and back. Aurora, left. I'll take middle and behind," I say, and they both give me nods as we take our positions.

The men all line up in the exact formations as we assumed they would, creating a circle all the way around us.

My men are spread out, Tillman ahead of me, Draken to my left, Corentin to my right, and I feel Caspian's eyes on my back. Without being able to see him, I assume he's positioned himself between his dads, like Tillman's positioned himself between Oakly's Nexus. They're spread out enough around the circle we're completely surrounded, and I have half a mind to just send out a big-ass blast of air, knocking them all out of the circle together.

"On my count, everyone," Gaster yells, "One..."

Shit.

"Wai—"

My sight decides that this is the perfect time to send me a vision and blurry images begin to race across my mind. Every strike, every move, every counter, and every step that needs to be taken at this moment to ensure the three of us are the victors.

"Three."

Gaster's voice pulls me out of the vision, and I rapidly lay my hands on Aurora's and Oakly's shoulders as I send out a ring of waves to hold the guys back for a second.

"Aurora midmorning, wrap a vine around Jamie's ankle and drag him out of the circle. Oakly midday, Roye's going to try to get you in a dirt mound. I'll deflect with my air. You get him in a globe of water and roll his ass out."

My waves come crashing down around us, soaking the bottom of our pants, but with a quick whip of my wind, I dry up all the water, while simultaneously, I send that burst of air up to block Roye's earth.

In perfect synchrony, Aurora and Oakly follow my directions, sending the first two men out of the ring.

Then there were ten.

The first strikes take the rest of the men by surprise and they each pause their attacks, breathing heavily as they reevaluate what they assumed was going to be an easy takedown.

Aurora's magic washes over me and Oakly, and we both take deep breaths as the calm focus she bathes us in settles across our minds.

Standing in the middle of them, with their backs turned toward me, I lay my hands back on Aurora's shoulder so her mind stays open to me and call my dragon's sight forth. Letting the violet take over my senses, I breathe slowly.

The maneuvers the men are preparing to cast out filter across my mind seconds before they actually leave their fingertips. By the time they command whatever they plan to send our way, I've already relayed the information to the other two and they're ready for it.

The sensation of Tillman beating on the barrier of my mind draws my attention to where he's making his way closer to me and I grab Oakly's hand in mine, lacing our fingers together.

Her gasp is loud, sudden, but she instinctively commands her element to obey, and I take control of the water flowing through her.

It looks like my Nexus isn't the only bond I can connect with.

Like a geyser shooting from our connected hands, the brutal stream of water hits not only him but Ry straight on. Their stone-covered boots drag across the floor, tearing the hardwood up, and they cast an earth wall between them and the water.

Pushing even more of our element out, the earth wall collides with the two of them, sending them right over the forcefield line.

The three commanders are down.

Growls roar around the circle and I whip around as Draken and Dyce, in their partially shifted forms, run head-on toward Aurora with fire-blazed hands.

"Aurora, I need to command them out. Hit me with something."

Lacing her hand with mine, my shoulders straighten of their own accord, my violet eyes glow, and confidence on a whole other level blooms across my chest. Instead of a ground-quaking roar, a low, commanding purr leaves my lips.

Draken and Dyce hit a knee with their heads bowed to us, and together, our earth elements sweep them up on a wave of sand.

The two most fearsome shifters I've ever had the privilege of meeting go rolling over the line with growls and sand falling from their lips.

Six down. Six to go.

Repeatedly, we twirl around our three women stronghold as if we were having a dance party in the middle of a room. Our bodies sway smoothly in sync with each other, and my hand always finds one of them as if I'm being passed between two dance partners.

Before I know it, Oakly is sending San and Nikoli surfing out of the ring. Despite Nikoli's attempt to command her water with his own, he's too late. On my other side, Aurora has Theo and Neil lassoed together, faces smushed to one another's. She snatches her vines back, and like a spin top toy, the two men go spiraling out of the line.

That means two.

In this calm, Aurora and Oakly breathe heavily, searching around us for my two men who currently can't be seen by the naked eye. The tension and anticipation build so high around us as our gazes scan the seemingly empty space, it's electrifying.

Tickling up my spine calls my shadows out and a gentle breeze that has my chin tilting up brings light to my fingertips. That cold chill that makes me shiver in the best of ways is warmed by a subtle heat on my front.

The God of Light and God of Dark believe they've caught their Goddess.

"Sorry, boys."

Turning sideways, I shoot my palms out.

A stream of light pours from one and shadows as dark as night from the other.

My light surrounds Caspian in halos, snatching his cover of darkness away from him, and my air cocoons him in a bubble. My shadows take over Corentin's form, making him as fluid as they are.

"Out," I command.

The brothers go soaring over the line, and as soon as they cross the threshold, I pull my gifts back to me, smiling in triumph.

There's a beat of tense silence as the three of us stare our men down.

"That's my girls. I knew it." Gaster breaks out in rambunctious cheering as he jumps up and down. Keeper's laugh echoes around the room a split second later as he applauds and whistles as loud as Gaster cries out.

All our men turn to the two of them, and me, Oakly, and Aurora giggle, wrapping our arms around each other while we celebrate our victory.

"Did you have any faith in us whatsoever?" Draken asks Gaster.

"Not for a second, my boy. I knew those girls were going to hand you a beating to be remembered."

With shakes of their heads, our men begin walking toward us and we break apart, meeting them halfway. I'm surrounded in seconds, and the pride vibrating from each of them makes my cheeks hurt from the smile crossing my face.

"You were phenomenal, princess," Corentin says, laying a soft kiss to my forehead.

"She cheated," Tillman says teasingly and I narrow my eyes on him. "Visions before you battle us is unfair advantage, little warrior."

"I don't dictate when they come," I sass in defense.

"I'm aware," he says, gripping the back of my neck. "That's an amazing advantage, Will, and I'm so proud of you for taking it," he whispers against my lips.

The hunger for me pumping between his bond to mine is almost overwhelming. I've felt Tillman's pride plenty of times now, but this...this is fucking heady.

My eyes are dilated as he breaks away from me and I shove my dragon down because all she wants is to pounce on him. Our ghost doesn't give us a chance, though, as I'm wrapped in shadows and twirled around like a ballerina.

"Dangerous little Primary. You didn't pull a single punch," he says low as he leans down to my ear.

"Of course I didn't. I wanted us to win," I breathe.

"Good girl."

My body trembles in his hands, and his dark chuckle engulfs me as I'm passed off to my dragon man. You'd think for a beast so dominant, he'd be a little upset at being forced to submit, but instead, he's hungry smiles with devilish eyes.

"If you wanted me on my knees for you, little wanderer, all you had to do was say so. I'll gladly bow to you and worship you the way you deserve to be," he purrs and I melt.

Fuck.

Nothing in the realm can compare to sparring the way we just did, then have each of them look at me like I'm something so spectacular. There's not a shred of anger, resentment, or anything with a negative connotation in relation to how they feel about the Primaries' victory.

If anything, they're the opposite. As if us winning makes each of them feel better, more confident, and determined.

The blaring sounds of Tillman's and Corentin's timekeepers startle me, and I flinch in Draken's arms. The thrill of this training distracted me from the reality of what the rest of my day will look like now that it's over.

The sting in my nose is instant, and I suck in a deep breath. Regulating my now pounding heart is even harder as the guys close in on me, but I force it to calm.

"Everything's going to be okay, princess. We'll meet at the mansion for lunch, then you'll transport back with us. And if you need any of us in the time between then, we can be here in seconds," Corentin says softly.

"I know. I'm just being emotional. I'll be fine once I'm knee deep in research and my mind's distracted."

"The Amplifier room, Primary. If you're having mini visions of what's about to happen minutes in the future, you'll be spending the morning there. Honing that in," Caspian commands behind me.

Well, damn it. No dipping my toes in on this new routine.

I'm being tossed right on in.

"Why has this spell been concealed from my knowledge and why have the two of you kept it from me?" Caspian growls darkly, cornering San and Gaster.

To say he's not taking being informed about the Recollection spell very well is an understatement.

Keeper snickers as he walks up to us with two mugs of coffee in his hand, one for me, the other for himself. Caspian's deadly glare does nothing but make him laugh harder as he walks away to explore CC's room.

San rolls his eyes and crosses his arms. It takes a good bit to ruffle the walking library, and him not telling Caspian a tidbit of the knowledge he holds in his mind is the least of his concerns. Gaster, on the other hand, looks guilty, and I'm a second away from stabbing Caspian in the ass with my shadows for making him feel bad.

"There're reasons why certain spells have basically been wiped from the books, Caspian. It's a powerful spell that doesn't need to be in everyone's hands," San states boredly.

"But it should be in yours and not mine? You already have a gift that remembers everything you fucking read."

"Calm down, Cas. They're going to teach it to you now, so all's okay," I say softly, trying to hide my smirk behind his back.

"All is not okay, thank you very much, Primary. You didn't tell me either. I want a legitimate answer. Now." He huffs.

I shake my head and look at Gaster with pleading eyes, begging him to give Cas a reason that is worth his while so he can get over this. It's not usually my darkest of men who gets so worked up over things. That's typically Draken, but this surely has him bent out of shape.

"Some things are better to forget, Caspian. This spell is one that wraps completely around the mind, and when you activate it, it remembers any and everything that transpires until you deactivate it. Even once deactivated, you still have your own consciousness that can recall the events that take place. Until now..." Gaster trails off, looking between the two of us before sighing. "Until now, my boy, this was not a spell I thought would be in your best interest to know. I do believe you can agree with me on that."

Caspian's dark eyes gaze down at me, and I watch as the anger bleeds away. We both know there're things he's both done and experienced that I'm sure he recalls fragments of but doesn't need or want to remember it all. With a spell like this around his mind before now, he would've kept it activated all the time. We both know that, and we know that would've done more harm than good.

"Fine, yes, I agree. But that's no longer the case, and you'll be teaching it to me now." Caspian compromises and Gaster deflates.

"Yes, I believe you're ready now."

"Great, so me and Oakly will hit the books while you all do that. I'll worry about this spell another time," I say as I try to mosey out from underneath his arm.

"Not so fast," he and Gaster order.

Groaning, I turn back to them with the most innocent smile I can muster.

It doesn't work on either of them.

"I know what you experienced the last time in the Amplifier room was rough, child, but you can do it. It was obviously needed for it to be that hard on you your first time, but this time will be different. You're more prepared. Now, San taught Oakly the spell last night, so she is ready to go. Oakly, take your *fancy* new book and go with Willow. Stay outside her door in case she needs you, and us four will do what we need to in here." Gaster decides, leaving no room for argument from me.

Pressing up on my toes, I give Caspian a kiss on his cheek, then turn away, chugging down the piping hot coffee to distract my mind.

Yes, I'm nervous about going in there again. The last time, I got some half-ass vision that made me feel like I was burning from the inside out and never once did it allude to the fact that's what my best friend, sister, would be experiencing. Never mind the other confusing shit I saw about the Summum-Master.

"Come on, if you need me to come to your rescue, I'll bust down the door," Oakly says as she hip bumps me before climbing the stairs to leave CC's room.

"I very well might need you to." I sigh, linking her arm with mine when we step out into the bedroom. "So how much of it have you already read?"

"Well, when San taught me the spell, I skimmed through the Elementra bits since I was already familiar with them. It's kind of a crazy sensation. With the spell activated, it feels like it's literally being written across my brain permanently, then it just fades into my knowledge. It's hard to explain," she says, and I hum as I cover us in my shadows.

Like the trooper she is, or maybe because of our bond, she doesn't sway, get dizzy, or need a minute to collect herself when my shadows release us in front of the south wing ward and we walk through.

Since her kidnapping, both Caspian and I have realized we can travel much farther in our shadows now. We don't even have to be completely covered in darkness or move through walls to get to where we need to go.

Although I'm far more confident in transporting people now that I've done it a couple of times, it feels so much more natural to me to move myself and others through the shadows.

"That sounds a lot like the communal knowledge Tanith explained to me and Draken. I think we have a touch of it, small things we just know, but she makes it seem like information on the brain, waiting to be called on."

She snorts, nodding along. "Exactly, it's just there now. I'll never forget it and it'll come as soon as I need it to."

Blowing out a harsh breath as we hit my hallway, I squeeze her hand. "You'll use the spell wisely. I know it. CC wouldn't have mentioned it if he didn't already know you were meant for it. This spell will benefit you for the rest of your long, long, *long* life."

"Is it cheating, though?" she asks quietly.

"What? What do you mean cheating?"

"Well, being a Master Archivist requires you to rely on your own intelligence. I feel like having this spell is a crutch for me to remember things I should remember on my own."

"Oakly, that's ridiculous. Gaster uses the same spell. When you live to be as old as him—which I assume is fucking ancient—then can you imagine how hard it would be to remember things you learned two thousand years ago? No, it's not a crutch. If anything, it's best practice for your line of work. In my opinion, a Master Archivist should use whatever tools are provided to her so she has the answers and knowledge whenever she needs it."

"Pot meet cauldron," she says as we come to stand in front of the door of the Amplifier room. "CC's given us both other-realmly gifts. Between this wing, this whole palace, and what Elementra's blessed us with, we've got plenty of tools at our disposal. We need to use them wisely."

"See, you're already so smart." I grin down at my feet rather than at her as I shake my hands out.

She's right. Time to get to work.

"If you need me, call for me. I'll barrel on in there," she says, giving me a little push forward before she sits on the ground with her book.

"Yeah, yeah, I know. Happy reading," I grumble.

Taking a deep breath, I push the door open and walk on in before I convince myself otherwise. The power of the room is already calling to me, but I lock everything up until I can get in and get comfortable.

I haven't even made it across the room to my platform and the reflective walls are making ripples like the first raindrop disturbing a calm puddle.

Still, I lock my barrier up and caress each crystal that circles the dais. My hands linger on the Angel Aura Amethyst. The pure connection and protection to Elementra herself surge into my palms from the four massive spires and I get lost in the stunning purple shades.

Just gazing at them, they're striking in beauty. The varying light and dark tones of the purple gives them depth, and at first glance, the only thing anyone would think is how stunning they are. Then, like I'm doing now, they'd lay their hand on one and realize how incredibly powerful this crystal is.

Fitting.

Lowering myself to the ground, I lean my back against the crystal and release a steady breath. The last thing I want is to be invaded with the burning pain I felt last time. I'll stay pressed as closely as I can to my crystal until I know no shit like that will be happening again.

You can do this, Willow.

You can control what comes through.

Breathe.

"I wish I could tell you it was as simple as that, filia mea, but sadly, it's not. You can, however, tell it what you want to see. Sometimes you get an answer. Sometimes you do not."

I close my eyes and relish the warming of my bond that comes with CC's voice. I've had to face the hard truth lately, well, really, when Tanith fussed at me, that he did and is still doing everything he can for me, even from the beyond. I can let my emotions overrule me every time he comes to me. Or...I can accept the fact that his and Elementra's hands are tied, and they've done everything they could to keep me safe and get me here.

"Tell it what I want to see...okay. So set my intentions and tell it to show me something?"

"Tell it exactly what you want to it to show you. Do not give it options. The sight is not like the other gifts that will work seamlessly with you as you know. You must be firm with it, and even then, it's stubborn on the best of days."

Snorting, I smile softly. *"Sounds familiar."*

"That it does, filia mea, that it does."

His presence leaves me once again, and I sigh.

This is another hard truth that's plagued my mind since Oakly's rescue. I'll never be able to just have a casual conversation with the man who was more of a father to me that my own for a large part of my life. I'll never be able to just call him up in my mind or otherwise and tell him about my day or ask him about his. The only time I'll be able to hear his voice is when there's something I need to know.

I'm so grateful for that, and I'll cherish the information he gives me, but damn, what I wouldn't give for one more teasing conversation, inside joke, training session. Anything really.

Gripping the blanket beneath me tightly, I regulate my breathing once again and clear my mind of those sad thoughts. I focus on what he just told me to do, and I ground myself in the belief that I'll be able to.

Peering at my wobbling reflection in the mirror, I nod to myself. Start with something easier but just as important.

Show me the families betraying us.

The second I lower my block, the sight takes hold.

Gathered around a table, five females pass around a parchment, talking frantically amongst themselves as a swarm of men behind them speak in much quieter voices. Çounting them out quickly, there're twenty.

The five families.

"I just can't believe this. Why are we pushing out a ball because the heirs have met their so called Primary? It makes no sense at all." One of the females scoffs, tossing the parchment to the woman beside her.

"It's tradition to announce when a royal has met their true Primary, Kellie. You know this as well as I do. And knowing Aurora, she'll want time to plan something grander for the girl," another answers.

Kellie...Kellie...why do I know that name.

Shit.

Everglow. Gima's mom.

"Well, it's a little showy if you ask me." Kellie hisses.

"Why? Is it because you had high hopes for your daughter to be paired with the boys? How is her retreat going anyways?" one of the men asks. His deep tone is laced in disgust and everyone in the room senses it as they fall into tense silence.

"Enough. It's been decreed. Let's carry on with the meeting," another man barks and everyone shifts around nervously. "We called this meeting today..."

No, no, fuck, wait.

With all the power of the gift I possess, I snatch on to the fragments of the vision, but it doesn't matter. The sight kicks me out just as easily as it allowed me in, and I growl as I come to fully.

Staring once again at my reflection rather than that crowded table.

Huffing, I run my fingers through my bangs and untangle the bunched-up blanket in my lap.

As annoyed as I am, technically, the sight did show me exactly what I asked for, just not exactly what I wanted to see. I'm going to take the wins where I can get them, though, and at least now, I've seen all their faces. I can even put a name and face to Gima's traitorous-ass mom.

It's easy to assume the four men who were standing behind her, including the one who said they called the meeting, is her Nexus.

And I know good and damn well Aurora didn't organize a meeting. And seeing as she wasn't there, she has no clue that they planned this little get-together.

So two wins.

I know all the faces of the five. And I know those assholes are having secret meetings.

Talking it out with myself transforms my thought process from that being a failed attempt at controlling the sight, to a small taste of what I could really do if I kept at this.

Okay, let's try this again.

Building up my magic, I think clearly about the biggest obstacle we're facing and how much it would help to know who we're truly up against. If we knew his name or could see his face, we could figure out where this vendetta came from, what his capabilities truly are, and so much more. We could start working on tearing him down before we even get our hands on him.

Show me who the Summum-Master is.

For a brief, blip moment, a figure cloaked in all black crouches and shakes so violently, their limbs tremble through their covering. Repeatedly, they beg to be spared.

Their body continues to vibrate to the point they become nothing more than a hazy form.

After countless seconds of nothing but a distorted picture, finally a...

Elementra.

I suck in a startled breath as that same pixelated picture that I saw the first time I came in here begins to take shape and a lump forms in my throat as I watch the chaos and destruction he brings.

The Summum-Master dances around, shooting power out of his body with the ferocity of a volcanic eruption. Every way he turns, he cuts down another body with nothing more than a flick of his wrist.

There's something different about him this time, though.

He's...more.

There's something about the gifts he's wielding to kill what I'm assuming is our people. It doesn't flow naturally through him as our blessed gifts do, and even those I've seen wield the stolen power move more fluidly than he is right now.

Regardless, whatever it is. It's deadly.

Blood. Bodies. Destruction.

It's everywhere. Everything.

As he turns around, his cloak flaring out behind him, the scene completely changes, leaving us eyeing the two young men standing in front of him.

Oh, Elementra.

I know one of them. The other's identity is easy to guess.

"The illusion will fortify your glamour completely. No one will be able to bring it down."

"Good. Looks like your brother lives another day."

With that dark threat, the Summum-Master turns once again. This time, I see the all familiar blurry face that keeps his identity his most well-kept secret.

Gasping, I fall to the side, catching myself between the Angel Aura crystal and the Blue Calagate. The sudden rush of my mind being my own once again makes everything around me spin and I crawl across the room to get to the door.

Fuck me, I can't wait till this little side effect stops.

Searching in the darkness for the handle, as soon as the cold metal touches my fingertips, I snatch it down and pull the door wide to break the connection.

I nearly eat carpet as I fall out into the hallway in a heap, and the groan that leaves me ricochets down the long stretch almost loud enough to cover up Oakly's shriek.

"Willow, what the fuck? Are you okay?"

"Fuck me, those visions are so much more intense than when they come randomly."

"That's because you're attempting to force it. Which is what you'll have to do to gain any control over it, but that's beside the point. What the hell? Answer me if you're okay or not."

"Fine. Just need a healing vial and a minute."

Huffing, she latches onto my wrist and the little shit that she is whisks us through a transport back to CC's room.

It's one hundred percent her fault, and I don't feel even a touch bad when I throw up all over her shoes.

"Shit. Gaster, Caspian, someone get her a healing vial," Oakly yells as if I'm on the verge of dying.

"Primary," Caspian says, panicked, as he kneels at my side immediately and lifts me into his lap.

"Oakly's freaking out. I'm fine. The vision made me dizzy, then she transported me here," I groan, squeezing my eyes shut from the sudden movement.

"Oh, okay, blame it on me, huh? You're the one who fell out the damn door barely able to catch her breath." She fusses.

"Here, child, drink. My, I didn't believe this time would be just as bad. I really didn't."

"It wouldn't have been if I didn't force out two visions. Got a little cocky after the first one." I sigh as the liquid miracle works its magic as soon as it slides down my throat.

"Two? You got multiple to come forth?" Caspian asks quietly, respecting the fact my head is still pounding and everyone else is practically yelling.

"Yeah. And I learned some things. Is it almost lunch yet?"

"We'll take an early one if need be, Primary."

"Let's do that. Call the others, please. Tell them to have Codi and Trex meet us at the mansion as well."

Other than it's the right thing to do...

I finally know why it's so important that we find their brothers.

Twenty-Two

Tillman

"Got to say, sir, I'm feeling pretty privileged being personally invited and escorted to the Vito mansion," Codi says from behind me.

Standing from my crouch in the grass, I wipe the dirt from my hands and take another look out over the sea of green that stretches across the back lawn. It didn't need any upkeep. It's still flourishing as ever, but nonetheless, I pushed my element out across it.

Call it habit, maybe homesickness, whichever.

"You can call me Tillman here, Codi, and the invite was Willow's doing. She needs to talk to you two," I say, attempting to carry a lighter tone.

Caspian, over our mental link about twenty minutes ago, informed Corentin, Draken, and me, we were having an earlier lunch because Will needed to show us something and to get Codi and Trex. It was easy to assume it was because she saw something about their brothers, but Caspian wouldn't give anything up and before the asshole cut the link, said he had to get back to taking care of her. If not for her mentally telling me she was fine, and the Amplifier room made her ill, I'd have transported back to the palace, whopped his ass, then took care of her myself.

I kept my cool and sent Ry and Nikoli to go get the two of them while the three of us came on here.

I'm still waiting for my little warrior to arrive, but rumbling overhead has us all looking up to see Tanith soaring over us with Keeper and Gaster on her back, so she'll be here any second.

Fucking crazy how normal it is to just see a vampire flying on a dragon's back nowadays.

"Well, that's either a good thing or a fucking awful thing," Trex says as he gazes into the sky before resuming his stare out over the vast expanse of forest in front of us.

"Probably a little of both. You're looking less dead," I say as we start heading to where Corentin, Draken, Ry, and Nikoli are all waiting around the patio table.

"Feel it. My lips are back to being sealed, unfortunately, but I no longer feel the Summum-Master's fingernails in my brain. I'll call it a plus for now."

Grunting in agreement, my steps pick up their pace when finally, the others arrive, and my eyes lock on to where Caspian's practically holding Willow up.

The rest of the realm ceases to exist as the three of us crowd around her. Her face is pale as paper, she's wobbly on her feet, and the grim look on Caspian's face has the hair on the back of my neck rising.

"I'm fine. I'm really not as bad as Cas is making me look. I just need another healing vial and some food. The double vision really kicked my ass, then Oakly transported me to CC's room unexpectedly. Give me just a few minutes and I'll be okay."

"As bad as I'm making you look? Primary, she brought you into that room laid out on the ground, throwing up, and it took you ten minutes to stand. Don't act like it's me doing anything." Caspian frowns down at the guilty look across her face. That look alone tells us that she does feel as bad as she, in fact, looks.

Instinctively, we all reach out a hand and lay it somewhere on her, and she sighs deeply, slouching into Cas's chest. We give her a moment to soak it all in, then Corentin pulls out a healing vial from his pocket for her.

Won't catch him without one ever again.

She gratefully chugs it down and smiles up at him like he just gave her a priceless jewel and me, Draken, and Caspian share a smirk.

"Thank you. Let's—what's wrong?" she asks, panicked, looking beside me.

Turning my head, Trex is gazing at her with a mixture of curiosity and a stern scowl that if he doesn't wipe off in a second, Draken's going to do it for him judging by the rumbling in his chest.

"What were you doing to cause this reaction?" he asks.

"Having a vision. Well, two back-to-back."

"And your visions do this? Make you this ill?

"No, not typically. Not when they come on their own. I was in my Amplifier room this time, though. I was going to explain that to you in a minute. Why are you looking at me like that? You're freaking me out."

"May I?" he asks instead, holding his hand out, pointing to her head.

Despite my hesitation, as well as my brothers', Willow nods confidently like she doesn't have a care in the world, and Trex, with all his death wishes, rolls his eyes at us.

She sucks in a sharp breath, followed by a deep exhale the moment his finger touches her forehead. The color of her skin brightens, her eyes lose their tired droop, and the straightening in her back is nearly instantaneous. I don't know where to look, at her or him, but I want an answer.

"What the hell is going on?" I ask.

"Your hypothalamus was lit up like a Star gem. It was working overtime. Just to clarify, you don't typically have physical reactions when you have a vision?" he asks, completely focused on Willow.

"No, never, except for in there. The last time, I felt like I was burning from the inside out. It felt incredibly real, and I barely made it to the door to break the connection to the room."

"Assuming based on the name of this room, it's supposed to intensify your visions, correct? Or at least force them forward?"

"Yes to both."

"Let's take a seat and get Willow something to drink. You can explain what's going on to all of us, Trex, without all these damn questions," Corentin says, finally growing frustrated.

Lacing his hand with Willow's, he walks her a few feet over to the others and sits her right in his lap. Not a second later, Mrs. Grace is bursting out the back doors with a pitcher of coffee, water, a kettle of tea, and Chef is following right behind with two trays of food.

I try to be helpful and fix Will a cup of coffee for after her water, but Corentin literally knocks my hand away with a fierce glare that screams don't you fucking dare.

Chuckling, holding my hands up in surrender, I lean back in my chair and look at Trex to carry on with his explanation. He's much calmer now that he's done whatever he did to her, but if there's something going on in her mind, I need to know about it.

"Last question and I swear I can give you an answer after this," Trex says as we all look at him. "How do you and your magic feel before you go into that room?"

Will startles and looks at him as though he's lost his mind. I'd chuckle at the twitch in her nose and the glare in her eyes if I didn't want that answer as well. If this were a one-off occurrence, then this would be different. But this is the second time now that she's come out of that room in both mental and physical distress. If he has an answer to fix that, we need it.

"Why?"

"Because I need to know. Honest answers only. No bullshitting," he says when he sees she's about to downplay her answer.

Blowing out a breath, she readjusts herself on Corentin's lap and her face grows more serious. "Nervous, scared, excited, determined...all of it. The whole point of that room is to help me get better with my sight. I've come to accept I won't ever control it completely like I do my other gifts because of its nature to need to be able to tell me things on seconds notice, but I am supposed to grow to the point where I can call on it and it'll respond. It's both thrilling and intimidating. It's hard to think straight before I go in there."

He nods along like that makes perfect sense, and it does. That room is an other-realmly experience, and we all want it to do its purpose for her. But without these fucking side effects would be nice.

"Whenever you use a tool to amplify your gift, it disrupts your natural magic and mind, even if it doesn't feel that way. Combine that with the flood of emotions you're experiencing, and you're making your body, mind, and magic vulnerable to imbalance. You might not notice it, though. You probably enter the room, calm your nerves, and proceed, but you're doing things out of order.

"Most of us understand that our minds heavily influence our magic. Emotions often cause our magic to surge, and those emotions are driven by our thoughts and external factors. But few realize the full extent of the mind's role. I'm more knowledgeable about the brain than most, and I can tell you—it's responding to everything. It sees the amplification as a threat.

"When you go in anxious or afraid, your brain scrambles to fix the situation. Even when you think you're calm, your brain isn't. So when you jump into a vision with unbalanced magic and mental strength, you're left vulnerable, both mentally and physically."

Willow's mouth gapes open, an argument, confusion, and acceptance all sitting there on the edge of her tongue. Without addressing Trex just yet, she turns her head to Gaster.

"He didn't experience any of these physical side effects?"

"No, but at the same time, child, he had years to perfect his calm, balanced nature. He had to. He didn't have a Nexus to help with that. Also, unlike you, he only had the gift of sight. He didn't have to worry about balancing six other gifts and all four elements," he says softly with tender eyes.

That seems to put things in a different perspective for her and her tense muscles relax back into Corentin. "I walk in with my magic, gifts, everything locked up because if not, as soon as I'm in, I'll be sucked into a vision. I sit down in the middle of the room, clear my thoughts, set my intentions, and release my magic, while calling forth the sight."

"You need to work on being balanced with everything before you go in. Let your mind, magic, and gifts know what it is you're going to be doing. It may seem strange talking to yourself, but everything within you listens to what you tell it. If you go in there with the mindset that this is overwhelming or this sucks, that's exactly what you're going to get. You need to go in clear-headed and determined, with everything already open and on the same page," Trex tells her, and I gain a little respect at the gentle coaching coming from him.

He's not being his typical assholish self and seems genuinely concerned with helping her get this right. Granted, it still could have a little self-serving motivation behind it, but he's willing to teach her something she needs to know.

"So what did you do to her just now?" Draken asks the burning question I know all four of us were waiting for an answer on.

"I sent a signal to her hypothalamus, letting it know everything in her body is fine. It's a part of the brain that controls multiple different things. Hormones, body temperature, appetite, sleep cycles, emotions, behaviors. You fucking name it. It was in overdrive trying to figure out a problem it couldn't find. It didn't know what to make function or force to stop functioning. That's also why the healing vial wasn't working. There was nothing to heal."

"But she's fine now?" Corentin asks.

"Should be. Ask her."

There went that small glimpse of the nondickish attitude. Fuck, I hope getting his brothers back causes him to chill out a bit. We're stuck with him for a while, no doubt, and eventually, one of us is going to punch him.

"He's right. I feel perfectly fine now," Willow says, but it's unconvincing.

She picks up on our doubts but doesn't show that outwardly.

"How the hell am I supposed to balance everything in me before going in there? I struggle to balance myself before I even open the door," she says in our minds quietly.

"You're bonded to the most balanced person in the realm, princess," Corentin says, smirking over at me.

"Mostly," I tack on.

Her beautiful wide eyes whip to mine and hope shines through their depths, piercing me right in the heart. Her unwavering belief in me nearly knocks my breath away and I clench my fist against my thighs to keep myself from pulling her into my lap.

"We'll work on it this afternoon, little warrior," I promise.

This isn't just a simple act of calming herself and balancing her emotions. What Trex is explaining is on a much deeper level that involves balancing everything within her. I would've already worked on this with her if I thought she truly needed the help, but she has an insane ability, in my opinion, to do it on her own. Of course, like any of us, she loses her cool every now and again, but she's always able to rein it in quickly.

I've never noticed, even on a bond level, everything in her not being balanced. She always feels level if her emotions aren't heightened, but I guess this room brings something out in her that we need to work on.

"Thank you," she says and blows me a kiss.

"So what did you see that caused this today? I assume we can know since we got invited here," Codi says after a moment of everyone taking some bites of food and starting easy conversations.

We chuckle as Willow grunts like the question surprised her, and she hurriedly takes a large gulp of coffee, then wipes the corners of her mouth.

How in the world she drinks coffee all day and doesn't jitter out of her skin is still a mystery to me.

"I could take it by IV injection and would still want more," she says, grinning over at me.

"I'm going to show you rather than tell you. There's importance to both visions."

Wiping her hands off and sitting up straight in Corentin's lap, she waits for everyone's go-head before latching onto our minds. I hold in my groan at the gentle caress of her magic flowing through me because I'm sure our guests don't want to know how fucking amazing it feels to have your Primary's gift rub against your own.

Closing her eyes, her mind floods ours and she skips right to her visions rather than what she does when she walks in. I'm caught off guard when the first thing we see is the five families gathered around.

I can identify each Primary in that room and the men are recognizable although some, to my annoyance, I can't put the names I know to the faces. This is definitely Corentin's area of expertise and since it's been so long since I've been around the lot of them, I'm no help with anything here.

Except for the fact that it's glaringly clear they're having a meeting without Aunt Rory and I'm proud my little warrior picked up on that sly tidbit as well.

Moving on, she skips to the next, and her shift in mood, thought process, everything changes as soon as the unidentifiable image shifts from the quivering person to the Summum-Master. This is the moment she lost the tranquility she thought she felt, and the sensations start in her body.

The confusion in a few of the people at our table, namely Oakly's Nexus, is evident in how the connection all of us are sharing shudders slightly. It's just a small vibration of what they're feeling, but I can pinpoint it.

I don't feel that same. I know when I see a powerful Illusionist and the most powerful one I've ever met, known, loved, is no longer with me, so that only leaves one I can identify.

As soon as Willow cuts my connection to her, I turn to observe Trex and I'm taken aback by the shattered look in his eyes. I was expecting to see something, but he looks on the verge of throwing up, possibly crying.

"That...he was only eighteen, maybe nineteen at most then. There's no doubt he's had to strengthen it."

"Wait, that was..." Oakly says, trailing off as she puts it together first.

"Yeah. Xander, our brother. I told you all, his illusions are on another level. If he's concealing the Summum-Master's identity, no one will be able to break that illusion but him, and that's what appears to be happening." He grits his teeth and squeezes his eyes shut. The anger in him bleeds out all over the table, and Codi reaches his hand out, gripping his shoulder.

"We're going to find them. I'll keep trying to get through to him."

"How have you been trying?" Willow asks Codi.

"Really, just trying to think about him constantly, putting myself in deep sleeps at night to see if he can come through. Nothing's happened yet, but I'll keep trying."

"We'll continue to look for ways to track or reach them as well. I need to let my mom know about this secret meeting of the five. Her decree is set to go out today, so it hasn't happened yet," Corentin says, pulling out his communicator and kissing Will on the top of the head before placing her back in his seat while he steps away.

"We've assumed the Summum-Master is a Fortifier based on what Keeper told us and I believe that vision confirms it, Primary. I'd hate to refer to a Fortifier as weak because their gift is honestly astonishing, but most of the time, without a form of defensive gift, they are lower on the power scale. So that black cloaked figure you saw, I think is the Summum-Master before he became the Summum-Master," Caspian says with a faraway tone. His water twirls through his fingers as his shadows circle around him. He's deep in his mind, trying to piece it all together.

"I thought the same thing, but I was more concerned about that weird feeling of his power. It didn't feel...I don't know, Elementrian, Elementr-ish. You know what I mean," Will says.

"That's because it wasn't, child," Gaster says quietly.

His pale face and glazed eyes silence everyone at the table as we take in the state of shock he's currently in. He shakes himself out, but the seriousness that takes over his features makes us all hold our breaths and wait. Even Corentin notices and ends his call.

"When I was in the Valorian Veil, there was a being there that many feared. He's one of the original Gods of the realm and his power was vicious, to say the least, if that's how he wanted to wield it. The time I told you I sensed the realm was on a path to war, you remember?" he asks Willow gently, and she nods. "It was because I witnessed his gift. His name is Kirabaddon and he's the God of Obliteration. I watched him lay his hand to the temple of the God of Boundaries and decimate it with one touch. In the Veil, an act like that is an act of war. That was his gift the Summum-Master was wielding."

"But that's impossible. He doesn't have that capability from what we've seen and the portal to that realm is closed," Nikoli says.

"It's not impossible," Willow whispers. A lone tear escapes her eye and she's quick to wipe it away, then sniffles. "It's not impossible to get into the Valorian Veil with my supply of blood."

A muttering of fucks echoes around the table and I reach out to grip Will's elbow, pulling her into my lap. There's a rush of guilt washing through her as though she believes she is at fault for this, and I can't stand the weight it's bearing down on my chest. Nothing about any of this is her fault.

"Don't blame yourself for this, little warrior. Any of it. You had no choice when your blood was stolen from you, and you have no control over what he does with it until we locate it," I tell her softly but sternly.

She doesn't respond, but instead, closes her eyes and lays her forehead to mine. I wrap my hand around the back of her neck, holding her to me, and I keep my breathing level until she mimics the steady flow.

"Caspian, Gaster, San, expand your searches to all known locations of the portals. We know the main five but find any mentions of secret or well-hidden ones. We need a count for as many or as little as you can find by the end of today. Tillman, be thinking about who you want to assign to those portals so we can post lookouts at each one for the time being. Princess..." Corentin softens his tone and kneels down in front of us, gripping her hands. "It's time to open your Mom's book."

A shuddering breath falls from her lips and her fingers flinch against his, but nonetheless, she nods and cups his cheek.

Turning her hand out, he kisses the inside of her palm, then the bracelet we all made her as she strokes the ring around his finger. "Three weeks tops. For the next three weeks, we continue our training, research, everything. The guards will keep post at each one for the time being, then we will go ourselves to check and make sure they're definitely closed. Yes, I know he has enough blood to open his own portal, but I don't believe he will take that route first. It would expend far too much of his resources. After we confirm they're still closed, we'll track your blood right then. This is now a full-scale mission and we'll treat and operate as such."

"Okay," she breathes.

That's the plan.

"We'll meet you all at the south wing. We need to make a stop first, then we'll be in my room if you need us," I tell the guys as they surround us in the gym.

After lunch, we carried on with the original plans of combat training this afternoon. For many reasons. One, Will was in her head about the visions and everything that came after. She needed an outlet, and I needed a way for her to calm her mind before we jumped into what we're getting ready to do.

The guys give me a nod, then pass Willow around, drinking down her giggles and soaking up her affection. The training this afternoon helped get some of the more negative emotions out of the way and she's ready to start her next training lesson.

Becoming balanced on her own.

"So where are we stopping?" she asks, smiling up at me.

"You'll see, little warrior."

Opening a transport, I whisk us away to a place she holds so dear to her heart.

When the darkness releases us, we step out into my greatest piece of work. The room we spent so many years planning, preparing, then perfecting once we met the woman who was going to make us one.

She happily hums and races around her bedroom in the mansion, checking and touching everything as if it may have changed or maybe it's just because she needed to see and feel it all again. Her disappointment that we didn't even come into the house at lunch was evident when we transported to the academy, so I knew this needed to be done.

When she scurries into her closet, followed swiftly to her bathroom, I chuckle and make my way to her desk. The object I need has been sitting here, waiting for us to retrieve it.

"Oh, Tillman, I'm so—Oh—" she stops mid-sentence and step when she rushes from the bathroom and sees me holding her box.

I run my hands over the smooth wood and let the now returned memory of that moment infiltrate my mind. My uncle was right in assuming I was questioning why I wanted this to be so precise. I had no clue at the time, but it felt so important, and I needed it to be perfect.

I smile down at my little warrior when she gently places her hand on top of mine while the other traces the rim of her box.

"It's so perfect. It's amazing to me you had never seen my tree, but the color of the box and the bark are nearly identical. I was convinced that someone had carved the wood to make this from it," she whispers.

"Call it instincts maybe, I'm not sure, but I just knew."

She hums and when she tries to take the box and place it back on her desk, I hold on to it.

"It's coming with us, little warrior."

"But...you know."

"I do. I think we've all had an inkling to where we'd be staying for the foreseeable future, but none of us wanted to admit it. It's a big change. This has been our home for over a decade. We've stayed very minimally at the palace since we started at the academy, and this is the only home you've known since being here. But it isn't going anywhere, Will. It'll always be here for us. We just don't need to be here for now."

Her eyes well with tears and I step closer to her, bringing her into my chest with my free arm. She has an attachment to this place just as we do, and she feels like she's saying goodbye, but that's not the case.

"This has been so impossible for me to just decide. I feel like I'm giving up so many amazing memories by not being here every day. Fuck, it's crazy to be so emotional and indecisive over something like this." She huffs.

"It's not crazy at all and you're not giving anything up. This place is ours, little warrior, and it always will be. I mean that very literally. It's our Nexus's now, and we never have to part with it. This has always been a vacation home of sorts to all the Vito generations before us. We were the first to decide to stay here permanently, make it our own, and Aunt Rory gifted it to us for good after Draken's first year. Nothing about this mansion will ever change again if you don't want it to and we're only a transport away if you want to stay here for a night.

"You, me, hell, even the guys, we all feel that we're supposed to be in the south wing right now. Why exactly, I don't know. Could be secrets we still need to figure out, our own growth we need to work on, any number of reasons, but regardless of those, it's time you accept the decision and put this war within yourself to rest."

It didn't dawn on me until Trex was explaining what was going on with her and her visions, that this hit me. It's something I've had to overcome as well. Small things like this that linger in the back of your mind, distracting you randomly, are so much better off being put to rest. Little things add up after a while, and once you set yourself free by accepting your decision, the weight becomes so much less.

"I love it so much here." She sighs, gazing around at the room lovingly. "But I know you're right. I think I've told myself if we came back here, we'd somehow escape our troubles for a little while, but that's not true. They'd just follow."

"They would, but one day, that's exactly what this place can be for us. An escape from reality where our Nexus can just be. Peacefully. It's not going anywhere. And neither are we."

Her small smile and glossy eyes turn up to me, and my heart thuds with the appreciation I see reflected at me. "Let's go home."

Laying my lips to her forehead, I pull us through a transport and deposit us in the middle of my new room in the south wing. The ambiance here is exactly what she needs. It's exactly what I need for what I have planned.

Strolling over to my desk, I gently set her box down beside my family pictures and release a nervous breath. Now that it's decided we aren't going anywhere, it's time I rebalanced myself. Find that inner peace I've barely had a grasp on since we've been here.

With the frame in my hand, I turn back to her but then pause.

Standing in the middle of the room, barefoot and glowing now that she's got that emotional decision out of the way, she giggles lightly as the moss carpet tickles her toes. The light coming in through the window casts a halo of light around her and I swear, this is the most stunning I've ever seen her.

"Whatcha got?" she asks, peeking through her bangs as I take a step closer.

Lacing my fingers with hers, I sit us down on the floor with her nestled between my legs and bury my face in her hair, taking deep breaths until my racing heart slows itself down.

Linking my arms around her until I can hold the picture frame in front of us both, I point. "This is one of my fathers, Ian. You've heard Aunt Rory talk about him. He was an Illusionist. The strongest one I've ever met in my life. This is Hudsen. He could manipulate electricity. An Electro. Sean, he was a Plantist. Think of being able to grow, control, and flourish any vegetation known, even those not of this realm. This is Wesling. I think it's a little obvious, but he was a giant. And of course, my mom. Matilda, or as everyone who's ever known her calls her, Tilly. She was a Shield. The best one to ever walk this realm. I don't say that because she was my mom. Her reach was the largest one ever recorded, ranging up to twenty-eight people at one time."

"She's beautiful, Tillman."

"She is. I've been told my whole life I look just like her." I smile at the small snort that escapes her.

"You do favor her a lot, but I see each of them in you. Wesling's height came through strong." She chuckles, leaning further into my chest.

"I have a little piece of each of them, but the piece I've strived to hold onto the hardest was my mom's balance. You've heard the horror stories of our grandma Drudy. Well, of her three kids, Mom was the most neglected. I don't just mean the physical, what my grandma would've called discipline, but mentally, emotionally, she was completely ignored as if she didn't exist.

"That rejection fueled my mom's motivation to be the best at everything she did. Despite my grandma's shitty treatment, she wanted her approval, bad. Desperately. So she worked hard, nonstop, and eventually became the fiercest E.F. member this realm has ever seen.

"Typically, the commander over the entire E.F. is a member of the Ruling Nexus, but the rumors and talk about Mom's success forced our grandfather, who held the position, to succeed it to her. He made it a grand thing. Put on a show that it was in the best interest of the realm, for the ruling family, everything." I sigh, shaking my head.

I was much older, long after she passed, that Uncle Orien and Aunt Rory told me this whole story. Mom had given me bits and pieces of the truth, but they spilled all the beans once I was old enough to truly understand.

"He didn't mean it, did he?"

"No, he didn't. After the ceremony, my grandma and her Nexus called all of them together. Uncle Orien, Aunt Rory, her Nexus, and my mom. Told my mom she was a disgrace for accepting this position and it was a test, to see what she would do, and she failed. They forced her to take the post at the academy. They gave her instructions to find and appoint an E.F. Leader and they would oversee the palace members."

"Wait, one of your dads, he was E.F. Leader like you are."

I chuckle at her quick thinking and good memory, then grip her hips to keep her from turning to look at me.

"You're beating me to the best part of the story, little warrior."

"Oh shit, sorry. Please continue."

"Mom was much, much older to be finding her Nexus, but my grandparents didn't care enough to try to arrange her one early on like Aunt Rory. They were content with whenever because they didn't care, so by this point, my mom was in her thirties, Nexus-less, and didn't give a fuck to find one. The only pleasant example she'd ever seen of one was Aunt Rory's and they were still in their honeymoon phase.

"But lo and behold, she sent out the notice to the Nexuses around all the stations of the E.F. Leader Trials, and here came my dads, coming to compete. Approaching their forties, mind you, and Primary-less. The first time in nearly ten years that anyone had ever got her off her feet and pinned her in training was against Wesling. And her first awakening happened."

A hot tear hits my arm, and I tilt Willow's chin to look at her, but she quickly turns away, wiping them away before I can. "Gah, why is that so damn romantic?" She groans, something between a laugh and a sob.

I can't help but laugh as she carries on, and I pull her as close to me as possible. "They were romantic. All the time. It was like Aunt Rory and my uncles multiplied by two. My dads had a long road with breaking through to my mom. Not that she wasn't ecstatic that she had a true Nexus, but she didn't know how to be affectionate. She'd only been that way with her siblings. But they never gave up and together, they helped her heal from the damage my grandparents had caused. Like everything in my mom's life, she had to become the best at regulating her emotions, staying calm, collected, balanced. She mastered it, so she could protect herself, her men, and eventually...me."

I swallow the lump forming in my throat. I never knew any other side to my mom beside the affectionate, loving, caring one. A side that apparently was very absent from her personality until she met my dads. It kills me sometimes to think about how she was treated.

Who does that to their children?

"A lot of parents, unfortunately," Will whispers and I kiss the top of her head.

"My parents, they..." I blow out a harsh breath, getting choked up over memories I rarely let surface. "There's something I want you to see, little warrior."

When she tries to turn to face me again, I let her.

The calm demeanor rolling over her is an emotional state I'm desperate to feel. And maybe after this, I'll find it again.

"The memory I want you to watch is at the front of my mind. You probably saw bits of this when our souls connected, but if it was like anything I experienced, it was more blips in time rather than full stories."

"Yeah, I saw it all, what felt like every moment of your life, but only snippets," she agrees, and I nod.

"Watch this one, little warrior."

Closing my eyes, I let her take us away.

"Go away," I shout.

Every step I take has my walls shaking. Both the physical ones that confine me to my room and the ones that are crumbling in my mind.

"Open the door, son, please," my dad Sean calls.

"No. Unless you're here to tell me I can come with you all, I'm not leaving this room."

"That decision will be made depending on how the next few minutes go."

His easygoing voice halts my stomping, and I stare at the door in disbelief. I don't believe there's ever been a day he's lied to me, or ever gotten mad. I think his gift as a Plantist makes him more levelheaded. Always having to make sure you keep the realm's plants alive, never allowing them to die or go extinct gives you an appreciation for patience.

Something I severely lack even on my best days despite trying to prove to everyone else otherwise.

Today, though, my fuse is even shorter than normal.

Slinging my door open, I glare at my dad in newfound anger. It's bullshit they're not letting me go with them to rescue Caspian. It's even bigger bullshit Aunt Rory gave in to Corentin so easily under the stipulation he stayed by my mom.

I can kick ass far harder than he can.

"That anger, son, is going to destroy a forest one day. Then where will the animals and vegetation live?"

I swear if my element were fire, there'd be smoke coming out of my nose.

"Are you going to let me go or not?" I grit the question out between clenched teeth.

"Come with me."

Silently, we march—my dad walks normally—down the hall of the east wing. Every step has the picture frames vibrating and me sneering with every laugh that falls from his lips.

Exiting the wing, my other three dads are sitting in a circle in the grass, surrounding my mom. They're all quiet and pay us no attention as we walk up.

"Sit with me, Tillme," Mom says softly, patting the grass beside her.

Huffing, I do as she asks and drop down with the force of an earthquake. The ground may even shake a little and my mom blows out a steady breath.

"I'm sorry for upsetting you so badly," she says quietly.

Guilt tries to force its way through my rage, but I swallow it down. She's always so understanding, so gentle, sweet, but right now, I'm angry at her, and I don't find any of this fair.

"I don't understand why Corentin gets to go and I don't. We've had the same amount of training, preparation. We've been on the same number of small-scale missions. He's no more or less prepared than I am."

"I never said any of that to be the case of why I said you couldn't go, Tillman. My decision was solely based on the way you react to things, son. This is a high-stakes mission. One that could mean life or death, and in those situations, you cannot lose your cool or it could mean losing someone you love."

"Then what can I do to prove to you I can do that? I'll do anything," I beg.

"Just sit with me, Tillme. Sit and listen to me. Close your eyes and focus on my words. Can we try that first?" she asks so low, I have to strain to hear.

Darkness presses in as I do what she asked and I close my eyes, but I still sense everything around me and inside my mind. The steady buzz of the earth, the rustling leaves, the thoughts of my dads surrounding us, although I try to ignore them. Each one is whispering reassurances and relaxing words to me, trying to calm my mind, but really, it's just too much. Between the low tones, the outside noises, and the anger buzzing in my ears, it's overwhelming.

"Breathe, son. It's just us. We're all here with you. Breath with me," my dad Ian says quietly.

Taking a deep breath, I follow the breathing technique until our inhales and exhales sync up, and my racing heart slows.

"You have to find inner balance, my boy. In the moments that feel too much, too overwhelming, sad, angering, bitter. Those are the moments when your reactions mean the most. If you let the actions or words of others always bother you to this level of anger, you're never going to be able to encompass the greatness lingering inside of you."

The pressure building behind my eyes continues to get harder to fight back, but I try my best not to let the tears fall. I try to do what she says daily, but it's days like today, when too many emotions hit me at once. It's hard to balance them.

First, I was overjoyed to hear they believe they found Cas, then I was heartbroken to hear he's at a location they assume to be some sort of lab, then I was pissed they told me I couldn't go.

It was swift changes that I couldn't settle all at once.

"I don't know how," I say quietly, and although I can't see them, the vibrations in the ground tell me they're all shifting closer to me.

"Take another deep breath, then follow this pattern," Wesling says, and I follow. "In through your nose, out through your mouth. Breathe in, hold it, and let it out slowly. Do that until your mind silences."

In through my nose, out through my mouth.

Repeatedly, I do as I'm told until silence.

"Good, Tillman. Now feel the ground beneath you. Not its power, not your power, just the strength of it. It's always there, carrying you, no matter what," Mom murmurs.

I focus on the earth and push the pounding of my element in my chest to the back of my mind. If given the chance, it'll come out and call to its source.

After a few moments, the cool dirt calms the fever in my blood and my fingers wiggle around playfully in the soil. I focus on the way it feels constant, solid, yet, despite how strong, almost indestructible it is, it gives so much life.

It's nurturing, comforting. I feel the thrumming energy it puts off flowing through my veins.

"That's it, my boy. Good job, continue to focus on that balanced peace it brings," my mom whispers not to break my concentration.

Pulling my fingers from the ground, I lay my palm flat on the grass, and instead of trying to mold it or bend it to my own will, I let it hold me up. I let it take away my frustration, my anger, my overwhelming thoughts and the constant noises, and I allow its blissful balance to consume me.

"Very good. Your will is always going to be your greatest asset, but you must know when to wield it. When is the right time, what is the right thing to do, who will be affected by the choices I make. You must balance yourself, your magic, your gift, your element, everything before you make those decisions. Accept the things you can't control or change, and the things that you can, accept it fully and own it. Be so sure of yourself that everyone else has no other

choice but to be sure of you as well. If you do that, son, then you can always be confident in anything you do."

Breathing out, I finally let my tears fall.

"I will, Momma. I promise. I'm sorry for yelling at you. All of you. It's just...he's my best friend, my brother. I need to be there for him. He needs me."

"I know, and I'm sorry for making my decision based on your reaction without considering that you and Corentin are struggling. This hasn't been easy for either of you, and in times of worry like we're facing, it's easy to forget the feelings of everyone involved. I know you're more than capable of joining us. I let my fear of what could happen cloud my judgment first without thinking it through. I'm still learning, just like you're still learning, baby—in a realm that slows down for no one. But I'm so proud of you, Tillme, and I always will be."

Twenty-Three

Willow

Fading out of that memory is like tearing myself away from the realm's most comforting embrace.

Tilly's patience and understanding as a mother and Primary is unmatched, and now knowing more of what she went through prior to even Tillman's existence is just a testament to how she chose to grow as a person.

Fuck, I am so incredibly blessed to know such an amazing woman.

Even if I can't know her directly.

Blinking my watery eyes open, they collide with shimmering emeralds and the shine to them makes my heart clench painfully.

Teenage Tillman is nothing like the man sitting before me now. Never have the guys made comments about him being unbalanced or impatient. Nosy, always eavesdropping and calling people out, yes—but all I've ever heard is how my gentle giant has an impenetrable will and more patience and understanding in his pinky than most have in their lifetimes.

"Are you okay?" I ask quietly.

"I will be, little warrior. Once I get it all off my chest, I'll find what I'm looking for once again," he says, wiping the stray tears from my cheeks.

"That day...Talk about being torn and unbalanced. I was riddled with guilt, anger, sadness, happiness. I simply didn't know what to feel. Part of me was so happy, thankful Caspian was okay and we got him back. The other part was consumed by grief. I wanted to die right along with them," he mumbles and closes his eyes.

His grief spears me right in the chest and I nearly choke on the lump in my throat. I've said it before and I'll say it again. Tillman, out of all my men, can control and compose his emotions the best out of the four of them. But right now, I can barely breathe through what he's pushing out.

It's all-consuming, mournful, and if I didn't know any better, I'd swear to you we both were about to perish from it.

Holding on to his hands, I surge our bond with my love and pride for him. The amount of strength it takes a person to get over a travesty such as this is no small feat. And fuck, am I so thankful to have him here with me.

"The only thing that kept me sane in the coming days, hell, really hours, was that last lesson she gave me. I held onto every word like it was my lifeline, and in some cases it was. When we returned..." He pauses, taking a couple deep breaths, and instinctively, my body begins to mimic the rise and fall of his chest. "I've never spoken to anyone about what transpired when we got back here after that mission."

"And you don't have to now if you don't want to," I tell him sincerely.

"No, I do want you to know, but I have to be honest, Will, you know the ending. It's not a happy middle."

I can only imagine. I've never dared to ask, although of course my mind has thought about it. I remember what I felt keenly when he told me what happens with a true Primary, who's fully bonded, dies.

"I know it's not, but I want you to talk to me about anything you need to. I don't care how sad or happy it may be. I'm right here and I've got you."

Calling out my earth element, I wrap a vine around my wrist and his, keeping the two of us tethered together.

We're stronger when we're together.

"I'll never forget the look on Aunt Rory's face and how she reacted when we arrived back at the palace. At first, I heard her cries of happiness when she saw Sean, who was out front, carrying Caspian in his arms, but when she started asking for my mom, Ian and Hudsen, who were concealing us, parted. It was like all the happiness was sucked out of the realm when she saw my mom in Wesling's arms. I'll never forget the wail that came out of her. It used to haunt my nightmares. Whatever Uncle Roye said to her when he picked her up snapped her out of it, and her eyes moved to mine.

"Whatever she saw when she looked at me seemed to break her apart a little bit more, but she held strong. Started barking orders at the palace staff to go get the healers for Cas. She made my uncles take him to his room while she had my dads take my mom to theirs and very calmly, she told me to stay in the foyer and she'd be back out to get me. At that point, I had shut down. I wasn't calm and balanced. I was...nothing. I don't even know how long it was before she came and got me and took me to my parents' room. I was so confused until she opened the door and reality slapped me in my face.

"It wasn't until I walked in, saw my mom in her favorite dress cuddled up in the arms of my dads, who were now changed into her favorite outfits of theirs, that I realized in a short few hours, maybe, I'd be saying goodbye to them all. Aunt Rory told me to say my goodbyes, but I couldn't. I refused. I told her I wasn't going anywhere. She didn't force me out, but she did ask me to reconsider. I wouldn't. I took my mom's words that she'd said earlier and held firm. I accepted that I was going to stay with them until the very end."

I try so hard to stay strong and hold my tears at bay, but I fail. It was heartbreaking the first time he told me what happened, but now hearing he stayed with them the entire time until it happened slices my heart in two.

He was so strong. They all had to be far too strong for teenage boys.

"Those were the longest, yet fastest eleven hours of my life. I made my dads talk to me until the minute they couldn't speak anymore. I wanted to hear every story, every piece of advice they could share with me. Once the last words they could muster passed through their lips, I resorted to reading their minds. I wanted, needed, to know everything they were thinking about in those last few moments. Every thought was about me and her. How they couldn't wait to be with her again, but they hated they were leaving me behind.

"After they passed, I went searching for Aunt Rory, only to find her and all my uncles on a pallet on the floor outside her room. I didn't say a word. I just crawled on the blanket with her. She was up and down the whole night, bouncing between checking on Cas, Corentin, and me. At some point, Uncle Roye carried me to my room, where I spent the next four days locked in there, crying to myself. I refused to go see Caspian or Corentin, so I had no clue the condition either of them was in before I finally got tired of my four walls and went to stare at Corentin's with him.

"The days following, Aunt Rory let me help her plan their entire Ceremony of Remembrance. When my mom was put in the ground last, I lost it again, but that was the last time I allowed it. I held onto her lesson firmly from that moment on. I told myself, okay, you grieved for a week, there's nothing you can change or control anymore, so you have to accept it and let it go. It wasn't that easy at first, but it's been fine for a while, until now."

He takes a long deep breath after that and I stay quiet just in case he isn't finished. I want him to get it all out, talk about it, and be free from any burden he may be feeling. Grief and mourning the loss of a loved one is something that will never ever go away, and it takes a monumental amount of time for it to grow easier, so whatever's disturbed his ease, I want to help him through it.

"What's changed that's brought it all back up again?" I ask gently after a long stretch of silence.

When he looks up to meet my eyes with a small smirk on his lips, I gasp.

"Me? I did this?" I ask, horrified.

"Not you directly, little warrior, but everything going on around us. Being back at the palace, the south wing, the palace E.F. members, being called Tillme. These are all things I've avoided for the better part of a decade, but the situation surrounding us has put me right back in the middle of it, stirring up things I haven't felt in some time. In no way, shape, or form is it your fault. I just believe that it was a push I needed but never would've gotten if not for you. I needed to be honest with my grief, what I went through, and I wouldn't have with anyone other than you.

"A lot happened leading up to this. Draken and Keeper being united. You and Lyker. Hearing you talk about your mom, even just the bits and pieces you know, has made me realize I don't even allow people or myself to speak about my parents. It's like unconsciously, I knew that if I allowed their stories to be told, I would've had to handle my grief better. And my soul wasn't ready for that yet. It didn't have the balance it needed to get through it. Now I do. I have you."

My body crashes into his and my arms wrap around his neck as I hold him close. He's been my strength since even before I knew I was his Primary. In his own silent way back then, he was holding me up and encouraging me on. I'll do it for him now, loudly and proudly. I'll be his strength, his mountain, his shoulder, whatever he needs me to be.

I'll hold him up just as he's always done me.

"You do have me, and you always will. I'll forever be your backbone, your strength, your balance. I'll be it all because that's what you are for me. You'll never suffer in silence or alone, ever again." I swear.

The air that whooshes out of him may be weightless, but the way his body slumps into mine is like thousands of pounds have been lifted off him. His entire body shudders against mine, and I hold him tighter, letting whatever he needs to release come into me so I can expel it for him.

One of his arms loops around my waist and he runs slow circles over my spine, while the other hangs down beside him. I thought he was laying it there for a prop, but then I lightly feel his hand moving in the same pattern along the moss-covered floor that he's doing on my back.

He's searching for the tether to the earth.

Like we just watched in his memory.

Slowly, I retract my arms from around his neck and crawl out of his lap until I'm sitting crisscross in front of him. He looks at me curiously until I lay my palms flat on the ground beside his.

"What do I do?" I ask.

Gracing me with a rare, full-fledged smile, his eyes shine with readiness and he transforms before me into the steadfast leader he is. Apart from the stern glare the E.F. members would receive.

"Close your eyes, little warrior."

My lids fall shut to his command and my breathing instinctively tries to quicken when his hand presses to my chest.

"Breathe with me, follow my lead. In through your nose, out through your mouth."

Again, my body obeys him easily. I feel his heartbeat through the palm of his hand, strong and steady, and focusing on that solid thud, my breathing follows his tempo as well.

Long inhale.

Long exhale.

Repeatedly, we regulate our breathing in silence, and his presence in my mind lingers like a quiet companion, letting me get comfortable before giving me my next instructions.

"Feel the ground beneath your hand. Run your fingers through the moss. I want you to recall the times the earth has brought you good times."

The cool moss tickles between my fingers and I let the softness lull me into a peaceful state.

Twisting some of the delicate texture together, the feel of the strands growing thicker reminds me of when I was laid out like a starfish in front of Gaster's cottage after I created the dimension spell. I may have been wiped out, but twirling that grass around my fingers kept me grounded and elated by the fact I achieved what he set out for me. The power beneath the soil pounded against my back, replenishing me before my men got there to finish the job.

That same power thudded beneath my feet as I ran down the running trail from the guys when Tillman told me to run, and they were going to catch me. I even got distracted by a beautiful flower that I hadn't seen out there before.

More and more meaningful times come to mind, and a smile permanently tattoos itself on my face as I recall every time I've either wielded the element and it's brought me peace, or it just simply was there and grounded me. Like the many times I've just lain in the grass and let its strength hold me up.

"Good, Will. Now call your element out. Let it softly surround you in whatever comes to mind."

My earth element flows through me, soft yet so strong.

When it glides out of my hands, ivy wraps around me in a gentle hug, and little blossoms of flowers spread out between the leaves.

"Now call forth your mind transference gift."

Without a second thought, comment, or question, I call the gift to me and Tillman's mind practically lays itself bare. The prideful praises, the sweet whispers, the gentle nudging and coaching. I hear it all.

"Very good, little warrior. Now we're going to do this with every element and gift. Start with your air."

And with every element and gift, I do just that, letting the peace and happiness each one has brought me flow through my blood.

My air dances around us in a playful breeze, while I shine like the sun cresting the trees in the early morning.

My water, the typically elusive element, rains down on us softly from a cloud of my shadows.

My fire dries and heats my chilled body just before scales replace skin in my partial shift. My dragon purrs softly and my violet eyes pick up on the light in the room that the darkness behind my lids conceals.

I don't have to see to know the added brightness is Tillman's aura radiating around him. I nearly feel it caressing my face.

Casting the metaphorical line of my magic out, I wrap it around each of my men, who are spread about in the palace, or well, I assumed they'd be spread out, but no. I don't have to physically track them to know where they are. *Lazing in my lounge.*

This entire experience feels cleansing.

As each element and gift came out to surround me, then went back in, a layer of worry and stress fell away. So much so, there're happy tears falling from my eyes as though my body just didn't know where else to expel the release.

"One more, Will."

Breathing, the way he just taught me to, I call forth the ficklest of all my gifts.

Flashes in my mind come and go just as fast. Not of moments far into the future or times that have already passed, but minutes from now. If I wasn't certain and could feel the thrum of the gift, I would've assumed I conjured the scene on my own.

My body feels weightless in this moment as everything that resides inside of me settles in gently and for the first time in I don't know how long, my mind silences the rambling thoughts, the to-do lists, the what-ifs, or anything else that has kept it in overdrive for however long it's been. For now, it's just peaceful...balanced.

"Open your eyes, little warrior."

My soaked lids blink away the water and my gaze collides with the gorgeous sight in front of me. No wonder my dragon's vision could see the light shining. Tillman's practically glowing as though he's the one who can bend light.

"Thank you so much."

"There's nothing I wouldn't do or help you with. I'd mold mountains into whatever you wanted them to be even though I know you could do it all on your own. There's nothing you can't do, Willow."

Uncrossing my legs, I crawl into his lap. My arms link their way around his neck again as my legs straddle his and I run my fingers lightly down his spine, mimicking the feeling of him doing it to me.

The steady rise and fall of his chest inhibit me from the constant feel of his body pressed to mine and on each exhale, I mourn the loss of his touch. I shimmy as close to him as I can get and tuck my face into the crook of his neck and shoulder.

The sudden jump in his pulse twitches against my cheek, beckoning me to calm its now erratic beat. The soft hum that leaves his throat causes my lips to linger and my eyes to fly open.

He likes that.

I lay kisses slowly across his golden skin and shiver as his grip around my waist flexes. The more times I lay my lips to him, the harder I feel him growing underneath me, and I can't help but grind myself against him.

Just as I go to shift my hips again, faster than I can flutter my eyes, he has our positions flipped and his massive body covers mine.

"Looking for a reward, are you, little warrior?" he asks hungrily.

I don't even try to repress the groan that leaves me when he kisses me tenderly, then moves to my jaw, then my neck. Every new touch heats my skin and sends jolts of desire shooting through me as his tongue lightly licks every place his lips touch.

It's as if he has to map out the same path I made across his pulse.

"What if I was trying to reward you?"

"You think I deserve a reward?"

"Yes." I moan, arching into him as he sucks on my neck.

"How did you plan on rewarding me?" he asks, and I feel his teeth graze my skin from his smile.

Fuck. I want to say it out loud, I really do, but damn, dirty talk still chokes me up. It's so much easier when Draken tells me what to say.

"Did you want my cock in your mouth, little warrior, is that what it was?"

"Yes."

"Tell me that," he orders.

Biting my lip, I mentally whisper, *"I wanted your cock in my mouth."*

His groan vibrates through my whole body, and he shifts his hips, grinding his dick against me.

"As much as I'd love to fuck your tight little throat and watch you choke me down, it's been far too long since I've tasted your pussy on my tongue. So I'll take that as my reward."

Fucking please.

He chuckles darkly and with a glide of his hands between the valley of my breast, down my belly, and my legs, my clothes crumble into nothing more than particles.

My body blazes as his eyes heat, staring down at my naked body and bare pussy. The caress of his element comes back out and I'm prepared to be tied up however he sees fit, but instead, two small pillows form underneath me, lifting my hips higher in the air.

It's my gaze's turn to burn when I'm graced with the sight of how perfectly his dick lines up with me in this position.

"Spread them," he commands, running his fingers softly up my ankles.

And damn does my body obey.

My legs fall apart, and he dives down like a man starved, causing my legs to wrap around his head. Ropes loop their way around my thighs, spreading them right back apart for him and the shit nearly pulls me off my pillows.

My hand flies to his chestnut curls while the other grips the moss beneath me to hold me steady, but the fucking view I see when I get myself balanced might as well have me free-falling off a cliff.

I can't even close my eyes from the pleasure because I'm too consumed watching him devour me. I can see it all. Every stroke of his tongue, the desire on his face, his hard cock.

It's all there for my viewing pleasure.

All that calm, centered balance we both felt goes flying right out the window as his tongue rotates, working over my clit and plunging inside of me. If he keeps up this maddening mix, I'm going to reach my peak multiple times over before finally achieving the release that's on the edge, waiting not so patiently.

"Tillman, please. I need you inside of me."

The deep groan that leaves his mouth has my pussy clenching around fucking nothing, but the guttural moan that leaves me has him answering my plea.

Like the master of pleasure he is, he sinks two of his fingers inside of me, while never stopping his tortuous circles around my clit. But when I watch his other hand travel down to his cock and stroke it in sync with his fingers, I can't help the two things that go through my mind.

One, he's so fucking amazing at this. If I had more patience with coming, I'd want him to feast on me all day.

Two, his cock is mine, as well as his pleasure.

Possessive? Yes. In this moment, do I give a single fuck? No.

"Your pleasure belongs to me."

Something between a moan, purr, and growl comes out of me, and the ravenous smile that comes over his face has me both clenching around him and shaking from anticipation.

"Is that right, little warrior?"

His eyes never leave mine and my nipples grow so incredibly painful watching him slowly lick me, I almost forget what he's asking about.

"Yes," I cry out, both answering his question and because he presses the pad of his tongue harder against me.

Without missing a beat, his thumb replaces his tongue, and he slams his cock inside of me faster than I saw him raise his head, and all the air in my lungs gets sucked out.

His hands grip my hips, holding me down as he fucks me recklessly and I release the moss that's clutched in my fist. My nails dig into his forearms, holding on for dear life as he gives me exactly what I asked for and owns every inch of inside of me.

That beautiful burn that starts in my lower belly and spreads through every drop of my blood heats up almost unbearably. All I can manage is to pant his name over and over to let him know I'm about to detonate.

"Are you going to let me have my pleasure after you come, little warrior?"

"Fuck. Yes." I gasp.

"Then choke my cock so I can fuck this tight pussy full of my cum."

Yeah, I explode.

It's not even stars I see as my orgasm rips through me, it's just blindly white light, and I swear if this were the way I was meant to go, I'd sit my ass happily in the beyond.

"Good fucking girl." He hisses through gritted teeth.

I didn't think it was possible for him to get deeper than he already is, but with ease, he lifts my hips a little more and buries himself further inside of me.

His arms tremble as he pulls almost all the way out, then slams back into me one last time.

Everything around us shakes as he comes undone.

His head bows while he catches his breath for a second and his strong fingers flex on my hips before he lifts me off my pillows and lays himself where I just was. With no complaint from me, I happily lie spread out across his chest, gripping his dick every time it twitches.

"Well, that's one way to get yourself balanced, princess." Corentin's teasing tone flutters in from the doorway, and I turn my head to see him leaning against the frame with a smirk on his lips.

"It's usually your brother who likes to spy, your highness."

"I'm here, Primary, don't you worry," Caspian says as he appears in the doorway right along with Corentin.

"Fuck me, some privacy," Tillman barks halfheartedly.

"What's the point in that? We've seen everything in this room plenty of times," Draken says, crashing through the other two.

After giving me a quick kiss, he flops into Tillman's hammock as if this is his room and everything's completely normal. Granted, it doesn't bother me a bit, but I'm pretty sure they bust in like this on purpose to fuck with whoever I'm with.

"The point is—"

"The point is, we've been outside the room since the little Primary sent a burst of lust out to all of us. That was the privacy we afforded the two of you rather than busting in and joining," Caspian says slyly.

Whoops.

I definitely didn't block our bonds or even attempt to after I felt so balanced. My body, mind, everything felt far too peaceful to try to switch anything up.

I shoot Cas a smile as Tillman's element covers us in clothes and he sits us up on the floor. Like I said, it doesn't bother me at all that they busted right on in here, but I appreciate that they do respect my alone time with each of them.

Even when Draken came into the shower when I sent him a mate's message, he knew me and Cas were having a moment and that I reached out by accident. It's important to each of them to have me to themselves every now and then, so they respect each other more than enough to make it happen without expecting anything from me in return.

"On another note, you feel calmer, little wanderer. Aside from the amazing sex you just had, do you feel better?"

Snorting, I smile over at him and the little twinkle in his eye. "Yeah, I do. Tillman taught me exactly what to do, and in those few moments, I felt so settled. My sight even answered and gave me a little vision."

"Hell yeah. So is this something you need to do daily?" he asks with a wiggle of his brows.

"Yes, she needs to balance herself every day until it starts to feel more natural and comes on its own. Plus, anytime before she goes into the Amplifier room," Tillman answers him quite literally, although I do agree.

I'm down for what Draken's suggesting too, though.

Twenty-Four

Caspian

"Do not cut yourself again," I say low, warning my Primary when I see her once again reach for her mother's blasted book.

For two weeks now, we've been holed up in my uncle's room, or the south wing. Researching, reading, doing everything we can to get ready to leave in a week to check on the portals and hunt down her stash of blood.

The thirteen out of the fourteen days we've spent doing that, my Primary has cut her palms and smeared her blood across the cover of that book numerous times, in every pattern she can imagine.

Nothing has worked.

I'm over it and I won't be watching her do it again.

While my brothers are handling everything they have to handle while we're in here, I'm the one who deals with the disappointment, the outrage, and the confusion every single time it doesn't work for her.

Granted, I will always be here to support her and I'm more than capable of dealing with it on my own, but I hate to see her beating herself up over it. I'm not allowing her to do it to herself again today.

Today, she will have a good fucking day.

If I thought torturing Oakly's parents would make her happy, that's where I'd take her.

"That wouldn't make me happy," she says sternly, eyeing her *Perfecta Anima*—who really drew the line about torture—then she cuts that glare back to me. "I have to continue trying, Caspian. We have a week, one, singular, until we go check on the portals, and I don't know what the fuck I'm supposed to check. No other book in here has provided the answers either, so it has to be in here."

She shakes the bound leather at me as if that'll sway what I just said.

It won't.

If she keeps it up, I'm going to take it and hide it.

Her eyes widen in shock before narrowing once more and the sassy little creature puts her hands on her hips, daring me to try.

"I won't be falling for your whims and attempt at seducing me, Primary. We both know I'd get plenty of pleasure pinning you down while I take that book from you."

Her cheeks blush a shade of crimson that could rival the vampire's eyes and I lick my thumb, then flip my page, ignoring the lust now pumping in my chest.

Naughty, distracting little thing.

"Tell me what you've learned about the five families," I say, closing the book in my hand so I can focus on her, and she can focus on something other than her mom's book.

Huffing, she stomps over to me and plops down in my lap, leaning back until my shadows pull us as close together as possible. She should know better by now that her sassy attitude does nothing but bring out my sarcastic side. We can go around and around all day for all I care.

"I'm not trying to be sassy. I'm just frustrated. I've read through the book Aurora gave me, multiple times now, and it all fits together, plus explains being a true Primary perfectly. I don't understand why this isn't working." She sighs, completely relaxing into me. "Maybe I'm not supposed to read what's in it, or this isn't another little tidbit that's been left for me. Maybe it was my mom's diary and Lyker just found it. No hidden message or anything in there I need to know."

The disappointment in her tone this time is for a completely different reason. She wants to get into the book just to have a piece of her mom. She was hoping to get a little closer to the woman she never got to know.

"Or hear me out, it's not time for you to get in the book. Just because Corentin said it was time, doesn't make it so. You of all people should know everything happens when it's supposed to," I say softly into her hair.

I hate giving anyone false hope. Especially her.

My words feel like the truth, though, as they flow freely with barely any thought given to them. No matter how fucking ugly, trying, hard, and catastrophic it may be on the way there, everything surrounding us happens just when it's meant to.

She hums softly, nestling even deeper into me. "I hope you're right."

"I know I am. Now, the five families. Go."

"Ugh, fine. The obvious traitors, the Everglows of Pyrathia. The council Primary is Kellie Everglow. I swear I remember all the men's names for all five Nexuses, but I couldn't care less to say them all right now, although I did take special interest in Gean Everglow, Gima's father."

My chest rumbles with laughter at the disdain in her tone. I'm sure she did take an interest in the man who was promising his daughter and the bitch who raped me, Nexuses made of us and her best friend's men.

"Next, the Drover family of Terian. They seem like a rowdy bunch, and I was shocked to learn that the entire Nexus is a mixture of shifters. I mean, nothing wrong with that, but I had it in my head they were like Layton's parents, where they all were different reptile shifters, not completely different species. And Tris, the Primary, being a bunny with a Nexus full of predators and a son for a predator was even more surprising. I don't believe they're the ones betraying us, though. I think if they were, they would've been involved with the Terravile ordeal."

Sound reasoning but not disqualifying anyone yet.

"Don't let the bunny fool you. She's highly trained, strong earth element, and has a mean tongue when she wants to use it," I tell her.

"I got that from my vision. She spoke softly to Kellie, but her eyes showed no sign of submission or weakness."

"How about the Central?"

"The Gale family. They're the closest with Aurora and her men because of location and Vicki, the Primary, is close to hers and Tilly's ages, only a few years older. I don't believe it's real friendship from the way Aurora spoke. Just more convenience and it was pushed on her by her mom. They've never had any children, but they still have fifty years, give or take. Also, according to Corentin's detailed notes and Aurora, Vicki likes to talk. So much so, her men don't. No secret is safe with her."

"She gets on my last nerve. I haven't seen her in years, but even when I was younger, I couldn't stand to be in a room with her very long." I chuff.

Catty chatterbox that one is.

"Corentin said the same, but he pretty much said that about all of them, so I sweep them all into the same pile. Aside from the obvious."

"The Aeradora family?" I ask, although I know she knows. She's studied plenty on them all, especially since her vision, but this is a helpful distraction for her.

"The Alewoods. They raised some red flags for me. Namely, Corentin claiming the Primary, Aaren, has an air element that could compete with his. I know that's not the case anymore, but still, that's a strong element. Also, I felt a deeper level of secrecy from their notes. How they wouldn't send their son to Vito, how at meetings they only speak if addressed directly, never offering any solutions to anything or giving any input whatsoever. I don't know if it's a level of secrecy or arrogance, but either way, they were off-putting to me."

I'll move them up on the list.

"Finally, the Teals, or I guess Tealwaters since they changed their name themselves. They give me bad feelings too. Mostly because they believe the water element is above the others, but also, I found it disturbing that in Aurora's notes, she mentioned she's never seen the three men who don't possess water elements, ever use theirs. The only reports are the ones from her spies who have followed them. Not just right now but over her ruling. That's insane to me. And for their young daughter's sake, I hope like hell she emerges with a water element."

Even though I possess the same element, it's incredibly difficult for me to wrap my mind around the notion that it's the most valuable, most important of all four.

The elements work in perfect harmony together. Without one, the entire way of our existence would fail.

I don't understand how that's hard for people to understand.

"Do you have any questions on any of them?" I ask.

"Not on any of them in particular, but I did notice a pattern or I guess similarity that I didn't understand and that was the Nexus departure that all the five families took at some point in time. Is that like a vacation?" she asks and I snort.

"If you want to refer to the first year of your child's life as a vacation, then sure, Primary." *I don't believe I'd consider it that.* "Each Nexus when they have their child is relieved of their council duty for a year. The only reason they would need to be brought in during that time is if something realm-ending happened. They all had their kids prior to shit really hitting the fan around here."

"That makes—Wait, the Gale family don't have any children."

"No, they don't. Vicki requested a year off when her parents died suddenly. That was some forty-odd years ago, so knowing what we know now, they were probably murdered by the Mastery. Mom of course felt bad for her and had only been ruling a few years, so she didn't want to come across as someone lacking compassion like her mom. So she granted her leave under the stipulation that one of her men came to the monthly meetings in her place."

None of us were even born at that point, but according to my mom, my uncle began hounding her about taking better notes and paying more attention to the people she's surrounded by.

I have no fucking doubt he already knew by that point which two families would betray us, and he was trying to get her to open her eyes before such a time happened. She'll even admit that her first ten or so years ruling, she tried everything she could to look and come across as completely opposite to her mother, but she took Uncle Orien's words to heart.

She slowly but surely got into the ruling mindset. Realizing that spies were a necessity even against those you thought you could trust and that knowing both their strengths and weaknesses would be an asset.

"That was nice of Aurora and the right thing to do. Sometimes rules such as that need to be bent, depending on the circumstance, but beside the point, I still haven't a clue which of them could be betraying us. Corentin, well, all of you, have such disdain for each of the families, and I see why. It's blatantly clear. Well, other than the Drovers. I really just think they're a rough bunch because of their shifter nature. But I know we can't excuse them yet. Unless something just falls into our lap, I don't think we'll know who the second family is until the Spring Ball and we can speak to all of them, hear which man's voice matches the one we heard in Layton's memories."

"I do believe you're right about that, Primary, and if I'm being completely honest, knowing the identity of the second family is so far down on my list of fucks to give at this point. Is it something we still need to know? Absolutely. But Mom and my dads are aware and taking precautions. They're careful with allowing them at the palace, they have spies tailing them everywhere, and they mind their words when speaking. This next meeting coming up, Mom has all intentions of acting as though the realm is in perfect alignment. So as far as I'm concerned, as long as you know everything we do about them, that's as far as you worry about them for now," I tell her.

Her to-do list grows by the week and the five families are a nuisance that won't be going away until we figure out the second family, and even then, I don't believe at this point they're as big of an asset to the Summum-Master as we had assumed.

His biggest weapon is her blood, the ability to move realms, and the hundreds of soldiers, according to Keeper, who are marked. That doesn't include the ones who aren't marked but are still fucking stupid enough to join the Mastery.

Her worrying about a family who only gives a fuck about social hierarchy and betraying the realm is a waste of her valuable time.

She blows out a forceful breath of air, and I smirk at the flapping of her lips. Her frustration still slithers across my skin, and I don't believe it'll go away until she gets out of this standstill that she feels like she's in.

"Would you like to try the Amplifier room today? You haven't been in there for two days," I ask semi gently.

Over the last two weeks, it seems the room that was supposed to be a tool to better her, has rebelled. Even with the guiding balance that Tillman taught her, that she practices daily, the room shows her one vision, and one vision only.

The Summum-Master destroying everything.

She's broadcast it to us multiple times, in hopes we'd see something she missed that would lead to another vision if she pointed it out, but we see exactly what she does.

Two days ago, she declared a break from the room, stating that the vision isn't going to change unless he's stopped from moving through the realms. That the outcome is set unless we interfere, and she isn't wasting time in there anymore for now. If there's something she really needs to see, it'll come to her.

"No, I wouldn't. What I want is to be doing something productive. Not go around and around with no results."

"Maybe a calming tonic would help, child. Or you and Oakly can practice on your tracking now rather than this afternoon. I believe you've got it down now," Gaster says, smiling at her encouragingly.

"Hell yeah, I think she has it down. She's tracking like a pro already. Vince hiding yesterday didn't stand a chance against her," Oakly tacks on.

"If neither of those opinions appeases you, Adored, Tanith is driving me mental. You could fly her to the academy and leave her there with Draken so I can have a moment of peace."

Willow and I both snort as he shakes his head and plugs his ears as if that'll keep the dragon out of his mind. I admit, I like the feisty little golden beast a lot. Now that she'll finally speak to me, Corentin, and Tillman. She said she had to test our patience and worth for her Adored.

I told her it didn't really matter what she thought because the Primary is mine. All she said was, you pass. Ever since then, she likes to give me little nuggets of knowledge.

"What I'd really like is to just sleep for twenty-four hours straight. Maybe then, my mind would dream up some shit that could help us or at least tell me what to do."

The hums of their conversation, the snickering, and all the other noises in the room become nothing more than a distant murmur in my ears. Her words play on repeat in my head as the thought that was sparked from something she said tries to creep its way through the mounds of information in my brain.

My sudden narrowing of focus has the libraries' worth of books I've read since gaining access to this room flipping across my mind's eye.

"Fuck," I breathe, hopping up out of the seat and bounding over to the stairs that lead up to the loft of books on the second floor.

"Caspian," my Primary shrieks, and through my single-minded focus, I remind myself to apologize for dropping her on her ass just now.

Come on, you sneaky little bastard, where are you?

My eyes and fingers skim the books at rapid speeds.

The one I'm looking for, I merely glanced through it because it was irrelevant to anything we needed. Or so I thought. It was more of a recipe book, and who the fuck am I to be brewing up tonics or elixirs. That's Gaster's domain and he obviously passed a little of that to my uncle because his handwriting was in it. Changing up some of the ingredients and measurements.

There's one tonic in particular I recall flipping past and it's exactly what we need.

"Gotcha," I hum as I finally spot the decorative spine.

After pulling it off the shelve, I fly through the pages until I get to the tonic we're going to need for this crazy-ass idea I've conjured up.

The Dream Tonic.

Using my finger as a bookmark, I make my way back down the small staircase and come face-to-face with everyone. Who are looking at me as though I've lost my mind completely.

"Get to Uncle Orien's room," I say through our link.

"What's wrong?" Corentin asks.

"Either Caspian just found something amazing or he's cracked," Willow tacks on, I thought sarcastically really, until I look at her very concerned eyes.

"I'm sorry for slinging you off my lap. I got caught up in a thought," I whisper as I wrap her in my shadows and pull her to my chest.

"So you're okay?" she asks softly.

"Fine, Primary, better than fine. I believe I have a plan."

That concern washes away to unrestrained curiosity, and I smirk down at her before laying a kiss to the corner of her mouth.

One of two things are about to happen.

One, she's going to be completely on board with this or she's going to call me crazy. Well, she may do both. We'll see.

"What's going on?" Corentin asks as soon as he, Tillman, and Draken stampede down the stairs into our uncle's room.

Their eyes widen with worry as they gaze at Willow wrapped in my shadows, and they're on us in seconds.

"Everything's fine. Caspian has a plan for something," she says, rubbing her hands across them, calming their frantic thoughts.

All eyes turn to me and with a wave of my hand, I instruct everyone to take a seat, but I snatch my Primary back when the dragon tries to take her from me. He relents with a growl and takes a seat beside the vampire, who smiles at him as though he's so proud of him for that little warning noise.

"Here, read this to the room," I instruct, opening the book to the recipe and passing it to Willow.

She cocks a brow at me for a second, then looks down at the words. Clearing her voice, she begins, "The Dream Tonic. The drinker of this tonic can be pulled into a vivid, controlled dream state, where they can create a reality of their own making. Dreams induced by the tonic feel lucid, sensations may feel intense, and the reality they weaved may be completely foreign to anything they've ever seen. The effects last for hours, allowing the dreamer to explore or bask in the beauty of a crafted dreamscape of their most wanted desires."

She pauses, looking back up at me with confusion marring her beautiful face.

"Keep reading. Read my uncle's insert."

Her breathing shudders out of her as she runs her fingers down the page, passing the recipe, to where he wrote his notes.

"After many trials and errors with this little fickle tonic, I've found the results that heed what I wish of them. Firstly, don't mix the tonic in with sleeping tea as the recipe calls for. I've learned I have no control over the crazy shit that comes to my mind that way, like the other night when I was almost eaten by a giant." She snorts, then chuckles, as do we all before she clears her throat again and carries on. "Also don't drink it straight. I woke thirteen hours later, completely unaware if I was back to reality or not. Mixing it with a calming tea, such as chamomile or peppermint has worked best in my favor.

"Second, create the tonic per use, not batch. That's why the measurements have decreased. By doing this, I can set my intentions on a single individual while brewing the tonic. Thirdly, I've found it best if I go to sleep with an object of said individual's. This allows my magic to connect with theirs." She flips the page, searching for more of his words, but that's where it ends. It's enough for me.

"Cas, I still don't understand."

"Holy shit," Tillman mumbles, and I shoot him a glare for reading my mind. He doesn't get to announce my brilliant idea.

I sneer at him when his lip tilts up, and these are moments I wish the gigantic asshole would be more like the Primary and respect boundaries.

"This is your way to connect with the Dreamwalker, little Primary," I say quickly.

"What?" the entire room, aside from Tillman, asks.

"You'll brew and drink the dream tonic. I'll walk you through all the steps following. I have them mapped out in my mind," I tell her confidently when I see the doubt creeping in.

"I have no doubt you do, but I don't see how it'll work. Also, I don't have an object of his. I don't even know where he is."

"We don't need an object. We have his brothers."

Her head whips up to mine lightning fast and her mouth falls open as the rest of the room falls silent, I'm sure still trying to figure the schematics out. It's a bit more complicated than just taking this tonic, I'll admit, but I have complete faith in her and the wild plan running through my mind.

"Shit..." she breathes. "Okay. What do we do?"

"Go get the mind reader and sleeper. Then you're going to take a little nap."

"Then let's go," she says excitedly.

"Wait a second, princess. Cas, I need the entire plan you have laid out," Corentin declares, standing and crossing his arms.

"You'll get it as soon as we get to them. It'll be best if everyone hears it at one time anyway. There're some kinks that have to be worked out," I tell him with a sly smile.

"Fine, let's go then," he grunts, lacing his fingers with Willow's, dragging her toward the stairs. Draken, Tillman, and I laugh at his hasty retreat now that he's shitten 'cause he doesn't know every detail, but nonetheless we keep our teasing internal.

"Here, Caspian, while you all go inform them, I'll gather the ingredients for the tonic. Where would you like me to meet you?" Gaster volunteers, holding his hand out for the book.

"Three tonics and the mansion," I say.

Everyone turns to look at me, but I don't explain further for now.

"Okay then. I'll be there soon," he says, then transports out.

"Oakly, if you'd like to be there for this, you and San can go get the others from the academy, then meet us at the mansion," Tillman says.

She nods at him, lacing her fingers through San's before blowing Willow a quick kiss, and leaves the room as well.

"You wanna go get Tanith and fly over?" Draken asks Keeper and I hold in my eye roll.

Not sure why everyone we know needs to be there, but whatever.

"We'll meet you there, son," Keeper says, clapping Draken on the shoulder, then speeding from the room. The dragon doesn't cringe like he normally does when the vampire calls him that, and my little Primary smiles softly.

"You came up with this brilliant plan. Don't know why you didn't think everyone would want to witness it," Tillman remarks as our Nexus surrounds Willow.

"Fuck off. Ready, Primary?"

"Ready."

The five of us transport to where Trex and Codi have been placed in a Nexus house at the palace compound. With the lessening side effects of his mark, they asked if they could leave the healing wing, and Tillman allowed it under the condition that at any sign of trouble with Trex's mind, he'd return immediately and not try to brush it off.

As soon as we step out in front of their house, we find the two of them already outside, fucking off with their elements.

"Well, this is either a lovely or fucking awful surprise. Which is it today?" the mind reader asks sarcastically.

"Hopefully lovely. Caspian's found a way for us to reach Dec. We need you to come with us so he can explain what needs to be done."

Both drop their smirks and elements, no questions asked, and step up to us.

"Wish every time I told someone to do something, they just did it."

"He's talking about you, little wanderer."

"I do what I'm told. All the time," she argues in faux outrage.

"Okay, Primary."

"I can think of a couple times I've done exactly what I've been told to do, with no complaint from anyone."

She accompanies that little snark with broadcasting an image of her on her knees in front of all of us. I hang my head, holding in my grunt as the others mutter a fuck through our minds.

Naughty little Primary.

Fuck, I love it.

Clearing his throat, Corentin's the first to compose himself, of course, and he addresses the confusion on Codi's and Trex's faces. "We're heading to the mansion. Caspian's going to explain everything there," he says, holding his arm out for them to take so we can transport out.

Moving through the fabric of Elementra gives me enough time to get myself back in check and I mentally remind myself to get payback on the Primary when this experiment is said and done. I believe I'm going to recruit the dragon's help. He's whispered in my mind all the things he wants to do as a group to her, and some of the ideas really walk the line of torture and pleasure.

We'll see.

When we step out into the back lawn, we're the first to arrive, but that only lasts long enough for us to pull the patio chairs out before Oakly and her Nexus are popping in.

"Gaster's not here yet?" Oakly asks.

Willow turns in the direction of his cottage and shakes her head. "No. He's still there gathering what he needs."

"Look at you just casually tracking someone," she cheers, shooting Willow a huge smile.

"Figured the more I do it, the easier it'll be. And apparently, I'll be napping during our lesson today."

Turning to me, I nod, letting her know that's more than likely true. I'm not completely sure the extent of how long she'll need to stay asleep for this to work, but that's what the sleeper is here for.

It isn't much longer and the *coming in for a landing* warning roar sounds above our heads.

Keeper slides down the side of Tanith's wing, and she gives him a little flick, sending him flying feet in the air. He just chuckles, gracefully landing on his feet and stepping in stride toward us.

"She's a mischievous thing."

We all turn to face Gaster, who, like a damn ghost, just pops in at the end of the table silently with a tray of ingredients in his hands. Tillman and Willow share a look that we all catch before bursting out laughing, leaving us all staring at them in confusion.

"What's funny?" Draken asks.

"Nothing. Cas, take it away," the Primary says, wiping the tears from her eyes.

I narrow mine on them but let it go for now.

Jumping straight in to explaining the Dream tonic to Codi and Trex, they listen with unwavering concentration and determination to make this work no matter what. Their eagerness will either help or hinder, but I haven't even gotten to the important bits before Codi cuts me off.

Which is a hindrance.

"So if I'm catching on to what you haven't said yet, I assume you want me to put her to sleep. That way she's connected to Dec in a way," he says.

"Yes, but not only that," I say, glaring at him to shut the hell up. Then I look between all three of them, Codi, Trex, and Willow, softening my gaze for her. "I want Willow to wrap her magic around your minds and you all go to sleep. You'll put Willow and Trex to sleep first, then you'll join them. I believe by her pulling you both into her mind while she's dreaming, it'll create a stronger connection to him, and he won't be able to ignore it. She may even be able to pull you directly into her dream, or at least that's what I'm hoping for by you both taking a tonic. If that doesn't work, your presence will still be felt in hers, and I think Dec will respond."

The two men's eyes grow comically large, but Willow nods mindlessly, working out what she needs to do and what she believes she's capable of doing.

"If the goal is for me to pull them in with me, we'll need to weave the same reality, and each make our own tonic with Dec being the center intention. I think, like I pull everyone into my memories, it's going to have to work the same. But I won't be for certain until we're asleep. Plus, how are we supposed to keep the connection between the three of us strong once we're asleep?" she asks.

I grit my teeth because I thought of that as well, and I fucking hate it.

"Touch," I grunt out and the immediate rejection of that notion from her in my chest eases the displeasure I'm feeling.

"The three of you can lie down in a triangular formation, with your heads touching. Nothing intimate, and it'll probably best serve you in that position as well with the amount of mind power you'll be using." Gaster offers, and the compromise seems to help the tension in all of us.

Breathing the way Tillman taught her, she settles herself down and a wave of calm rolls through her.

"You'll have to open yourself to me, Willow. I wouldn't usually be able to put you to sleep," Codi says.

"I will. Keeper will me wrapping my mind around Trex's mess with anything?"

"No, all should be fine, but if not, I'm here to help," he says, shooting Trex a wink.

"If all that is settled then," Gaster says, glancing around the entire table for confirmation. "Okay then. Let's get to brewing. Very good job, Caspian, my boy."

Yeah. Now let's just hope this shit works so my Primary can get some fucking peace.

Twenty-Five

Willow

I love the tranquil feeling that brewing something brings.

It allows my mind to be silent and focus solely on the task in front of me, and in this case, Dec. I'm able to put him at the forefront of my thoughts and really push the best intentions out possible to finding him.

Despite knowing his hatred for me, I know it's misguided and hopefully soon enough, it'll be nonexistent.

Unlike anything else I've ever brewed, the Dream tonic doesn't require any fermenting. All it takes is a few minutes of seeping and stirring, and it'll be ready to go. It also doesn't resemble anything I'm familiar with either.

It's brewed directly into our intended tea, which Gaster suggested chamomile, so that's what we went with. Two ingredients are liquids that just blend right on in, and the third is a flower called the Nightbloom that is supposed to soak, then we eat it before drinking our tea. One liquid is called moon water—which is actually rain collected at night. The other is nectar extracted from lavender.

It honestly smells sweet and delicious. If I didn't know what it was, I'd drink it down no questions asked just from its aroma.

At the sound of someone's timekeeper, I'm pulled from my concentration and pour my little concoction in the mug Gaster placed in front of me as Codi and Trex do the same.

I'm absolutely tickled with Gaster because he went all out for this like it's a party. In minutes after we decided we were doing this, he basically crafted an entire kitchen outside for us to make our drinks individually, while also setting up a comfy pallet out in the lawn for us to lie on.

The guys were furious about that and wanted to destroy it, but Gaster put his foot down, explaining we have no clue how long I'll be asleep for, and he refuses to allow me to just lie on the ground for hours. The guys still weren't convinced, so he suggested we all go lie in my bed.

That swiftly changed their minds.

"Ready?" Trex asks me as we walk through the grass.

"I think so. You?"

He blows out a shaky breath before smiling tightly. "Ready, yes, but trying not to get my hopes up."

"I understand, but this is going to work. We just have to believe that," I tell him as we make it to where the guys are waiting in front of my spot.

Each of them is on edge at this point and I smile at them, hoping to alleviate some of their possessive-ass issues right now. If they want to frown at someone, it should be Caspian. It was his idea.

I can't talk. I'd flip the fuck out.

Let me just stir the pot before I take my nap.

Then when I wake up, they'll be all kinds of obsessed with me.

"Well, do I get a kiss before I take a nap with two other men or what?"

Although they move as one to surround me, Draken breaks first.

Growling, he crowds me into Caspian. Corentin, my gentleman, takes the mug from my hand right as Draken attacks. His lips crash into mine, and he holds me possessively by the back of my neck as he devours every inch of my mouth. Letting everyone who can see know exactly who I belong to.

When he tears his mouth from mine, I know my eyes dilate at the beast lurking below his cobalt blues.

I'm spun to the side faster than I can pounce on my dragon man, and my gentle giant lifts me off my feet, laying his forehead to mine.

"You're playing a dangerous game, little warrior."

"Do you think I'll win?"

He snorts, laying soft kisses on my already swollen lips. *"I know you will."*

Setting me back on my feet, I don't even have time to catch my balance before shadows are tugging me to their master.

"You know better than to taunt a monster."

"Not when that monster is mine."

The hum in his throat is the only warning I receive before he bites my lip, then slips his tongue in my mouth when I gasp. Every stroke is dark, demanding, and all for me. He consumes me so completely, I forget there're people around.

The promising darkness in his eyes when he pulls back from me makes my breath hitch and the devilish smirk on his face tells me I'm in for it when I wake up.

Turning to the last of my men, his stern mask is what I expected to see, but the soft features that greet me give me butterflies.

One-handed as he's still holding my mug in his other, he presses his index finger below my chin and tilts it up until my eyes are locked onto his. The burning amber in the middle of them heats my belly like a straight shot of whiskey.

"Princess."

"Your highness."

"Be good. No trouble in dreamland."

"No promises."

His knowing smile is contagious, and when he slowly leans in, my eyes automatically close.

"You're going to wear my handprint on your ass for a week for that little comment, baby," he whispers against my lips after giving me one of the softest kisses I've ever received.

I blink through the whiplash, while he practically preens at the red shade my face is surely turning.

Clearing my throat, I gather myself back together after my teasing backfired tremendously. Despite obviously knowing it's four against one, I still tend to get a little big for my breeches.

Corentin offers me his arm, leading me the few feet to my spot, and helps me sit before passing me my mug. Fuck, how that man can be so damn dominant, then do the sweetest things like this is mindboggling.

"Okay, so one more time. We're going to drink, eat the flower, give it five minutes. Willow, you wrap around our minds, then, Codi, you put us to sleep," Trex says, going over the plan for the umpteenth time.

"Right. The reality we're weaving is this back lawn. We're all familiar with this," I add and they both grunt in agreement. "Then cheers, boys," I say, tapping my mug to theirs.

It's cooled down enough now that I chug it back easily, and it, in fact, does taste as sweet as it smells. I'm a little weirded out about just eating a flower, but I push it out of my mind and pop the little blue petals into my mouth.

The guys all stare at me like they're waiting for something drastic to happen, but after a minute, they relax their shoulders.

Until the three of us lie down.

"Nope, don't fucking like this one bit," Draken growls.

"I agree. Get up, Primary. I've changed my mind."

"Cas, this was your idea. A great one at that. Their heads are touching my head. It'll all be fine."

"Exactly, this is your fucking fault," Draken says, turning his menacing stare to Caspian.

"Yeah, well, I didn't originally think they'd be lying in a fucking makeshift bed together."

Sighing, I close my eyes and tune them out while they bicker back and forth. It's Draken's dragon that's pushing him like this, and Caspian's feeding off the madness. Not that Tillman or Corentin are doing any better, but they're not outwardly going to argue or attempt to stop me at this point.

When things that resemble the northern lights start flashing in my mind and my body begins to tingle, I mumble quietly, "Ready?"

"Ready," Trex and Codi answer just as softly.

Sending my magic out, I lace it through their minds and magic, making sure they're tethered to me.

"Do you want a countdown?" Codi asks.

"Yes, please."

"Five...four..."

"Sleep tight, little warrior."

"Three...two..."

"We love you, princess."

"One."

The sensation of my entire body growing heavy to the point I couldn't lift my limbs if I wanted to washes through me and the surrounding sounds become distant white noise. Like a dimmer on a light switch, my awareness begins to fade and quicker than I can count backward, I enter darkness.

Blinking my eyes open slowly, the most beautiful lilac sun shines above me and I stretch my arms out above my head, pulling my cover with me so I can hide my face. I nestle down deeper into my pillow, chasing my precious sleep again when a yawn escapes me. My body hums happily when I decide that's exactly what I'm going to do, but my mind won't allow it.

But I'm so comfortable...

Gasping, I sit straight up.

Panic surges through me as my mind catches up and clarity returns to me and for a long moment, I breathe through confusion and astonishment. I frantically glance around at the reality my mind's created, and the tension in my chest settles when I see the familiar space.

My fingers tangle in the blanket on top of me and I stare down at it as I try to slow the racing beat of my heart. The fabric feels so real, exactly as it did in my consciousness, and when I bring it to my nose, I startle as the smell engulfs my senses.

Shit, this is so real.

Turning in my spot, the entire pallet that was made for us is laid out around me. Even the mugs are sitting beside where our forms were lying. The only thing missing is the two men who were lying on those pillows.

The whole back lawn and tree line look just as they do in my normal reality, except here, the colors are so different.

Everything is a shade of purple.

That checks out.

"Trex...Codi..." I shout as I push myself to my feet.

No reply comes from either of them, not that I thought it would be that simple to pull them with me, but it was wishful thinking.

Taking my first step, I nearly fall to my knees because of how unnatural it feels to be up moving around. It's as though I'm walking along the springiest trampoline, and I have to plant my feet firmly to hold myself steady. It's an out-of-body experience and I shake my arms out until the motion feels more normal.

Okay, let's try it with no dream shoes.

As soon as I bend down to unstrap the sandals I'm wearing, they disappear into thin air, leaving me standing barefoot in the grass.

Well, fuck, okay then. Be careful what I think up in dreamworld.

Oh, Elementra, this isn't the time for any intrusive or impulsive thoughts if things happen the moment I think it.

Slamming my eyes shut, I dig my toes into the earth and take a deep breath as the sensation of the cold dirt feels so familiar, normal. Nowhere in the instructions did it make it seem like we weren't going to be able to walk and whatnot like we usually could.

Granted, I have had some weird dreams before where my body was in slow motion and no matter how hard I tried, I couldn't force myself to punch Donald faster. This is just like that.

All right, feet, get moving. We've got shit to do.

Nodding to myself, with more caution than a second ago, I take a small step.

Then another. And another.

I walk a couple feet here and there until I'm practically pacing, but that's how much effort it takes to make my body cooperate.

"Trex...Codi..." I call out again as I slowly start walking toward the tree line.

Their magical signatures and mental awareness are in my mind, but no one is here. Just me and my echoing voice.

Shivering, my hands instinctively rub up and down my arms, chasing away the goose bumps, and the little raised clusters take me by surprise. My fingers follow the path of my standing hair follicles until I reach the inside of my bicep, and I pinch.

"Shit," I shriek, desperately trying to rub away the pain.

Unlike my own dream walking, I'm neither incorporeal nor protected from not feeling things. So that one hundred percent hurt.

Great. I can barely force my legs to work properly and now I'll feel it if I face-plant.

Glancing back in front of me, I find the reason for my shivering standing feet in front of me and I hold in my startled flinch. The anger radiating off him is so strong, it's causing my lush purple forest to darken. Every slow step he takes colors the foliage beneath his shoes black.

"It worked," I breathe.

"What have you done?"

"Dec, listen to me—"

"Where. Is. He?" he shouts, punctuating each pissed off word.

"I can explain everything, just listen."

He doesn't listen.

In fact, he bellows out, and I stumble back a couple steps from the devastation mixed in with his rage. I don't know if it's because he senses but doesn't see Trex or what, but he just snapped.

"Trex!" I shout and his name leaving my lips has Dec's eyes whipping to mine.

Shit.

When he starts charging toward me, I turn on my heels and run back toward the pallet. The last thing I want to do is hurt him or use any of my magic on him. Then he'll never trust me.

Like a baby fawn who hasn't the first fucking clue how to run, I barely make it halfway there before the weight of a freight train crashes into the back of me and the wind gets knocked out of my lungs as we crash into the ground.

Instinctively, I try to shove him with my air and wrap him in vines, but no element responds to me.

Fuck, looks like it's good old-fashion hand-to-hand.

Tillman's training instantly floods my mind as the weight of Dec against my back is crushing and his arm digs into my stomach, making it a struggle to draw in any air.

I widen my legs and plant my toes firmly into the ground so I can lift my hips, and he presses his chest into me harder to stop my wiggling. I make enough room underneath me to slip my hands free from where they're pinned between my body and the ground, then rapidly throw my elbow into his ribs twice. The second I feel his hold let up, I wrap my hand around his wrist, and plant my feet more firmly.

With more power than I'm sure he was expecting, I buck my hips up and turn my body sharply, rolling him off me.

His back slams to the ground and a huff of air gets forced out of his lungs, but I don't waste any time as I push up off the ground and run once again.

Mentally, I command my legs to fucking work, while simultaneously trying my hardest to tug Trex and Codi to me from wherever in this dreamscape they're at.

I sense him coming up behind me once again, but this time I'm ready. As his pounding feet give me an idea of how close he is, I spin on my heel to face him.

"Stop and listen to me before you get hurt," I command forcefully, but with no magic or power behind it, it's just a pleading shout.

His eyes narrow on me even more, and I soften mine, even raise my hands in no offense to show him I'm not a threat, but that seems to only piss him off more.

The air around us grows so thick, it's almost impossible to draw in any. The misguided hatred rolling off him makes it toxic.

His limbs tremble with either his fury or adrenaline. Which, I'm not sure, but regardless, they're both only going to lead to one thing. I open my mouth to try to explain again, but in the blink of an eye, he attacks.

He lunges forward with his fists flying at me like he has all intentions of breaking bones and drawing blood.

With a swift sidestep and a raise of my hand, I deflect the first punch just enough to send it past my ear. "Dec, stop, I'm not going to fight you. I'm here to help."

My words are met with a snarl before he fucking unleashes an onslaught of attacks—each filled with more desperation than the last. Every punch I dodge or deflect riles him up even more and they come quicker, sharper, harder. I can't even attempt to say anything else because I'm too focused on not getting my face bashed in.

The precise maneuvers—the obvious training he's been receiving—soon give way to much more vicious attacks and techniques, and when he reaches out to grab a handful of my hair, I jump back.

"Fucking listen to me! Trex is safe and we're looking for you." I pant out, but my words go ignored. He's lost to his fury.

My hands, elbows, thighs take a beating from hell as I continue to block him, and my lungs beg me to take a deeper breath. Every fucking move takes every drop of my concentration in this Elementra-forsaken dream world. I have to focus on every move he makes, while simultaneously commanding my body to work like it's supposed to, follow the muscle memorized training.

Growing tired and impatient, I miscalculate his next strike and the graze of a knuckle across my cheek and the immediate pain that registers through my face color my vision red.

Gripping his wrist on the next swing, I pivot my body into his and flip his ass on his back, then pounce.

My knee presses into his chest, bearing down on the edge of his throat, and I have half a mind to beat the fuck out of him for all that, but Trex's and Codi's awareness skitters across my brain, keeping me pissed but less murderous.

His fists connect with my ribs and I grab his wrists, slamming them down above his head, putting all my body weight into it.

"If you don't fucking listen to me, I'm going to knock your teeth down your throat," I growl.

"I don't want to hear shit you have to say. Because of you, my brother's going to be dead soon."

"Your brothers, plural, asshole, are fine. Safe, protected, and looking for you. I'm starting to wonder why, though. Hotheaded shithead. Who attacks without listening to what someone has to say?" I grit out angrily, slamming his arms down again as he tries to wiggle free.

"You're a liar," he sneers, narrowing his eyes at me.

I'm the liar? Are you freaking serious?

Just as I go to talk shit back, an inkling scurries across my mind, and my fingers flinch around his arms.

Holy shit.

"No, Dec, you're the liar. You've been lying for fourteen years about not eating Trex's blackened berry pie on his birthday," I say softly.

The slightest bit of shock crosses his features, but before he responds, I'm being lifted off his chest.

"Willow," Codi and Trex say together.

Trex places me on my feet and passes me to Codi, who protectively pushes me behind him. If my men could see this, they'd be proud, but I just snort because where the fuck were they the last however long.

Peeking around Codi, I watch Dec scramble to his feet. His gaze bounces between Trex, Codi, and me in disbelief. I'm sure the defensive stances in front of me are throwing him all the way off since I'm such an evil person who's trying to get his brother killed.

"Dec," Trex says slowly, holding his hands up in front of him.

"This...this isn't real."

"Technically, no, it's a dream, but it's as real as we've got right now."

A cool drip slides down my cheek, and I know good and fucking well I'm not crying right now, so I lift my fingers to wipe it away. When I see dark purple smeared across my hand, I mutter out a slew of curses, knowing it's actually blood. I felt it earlier when I was leaning over Dec, but I thought it was sweat.

Guess I can do everything in this dream, except use my elements, magic, or make my legs work right.

My foul mouth draws everyone's attention to me, and I raise my bloody middle finger to Dec as Codi steps closer to me.

"Well, shit. It doesn't matter now that we've found him. He's dead. We're all dead," he says frantically, turning to look at Trex, who also curses and bows his head.

"Why are you with her? How are you here?" Dec asks Trex, stunned.

Without answering, Trex pulls him into a hug, and I swear right before my eyes, the hate-filled gaze he's held this whole time bleeds out of him. He sags in his brother's arms, wrapping his own around him for stability.

"You've got it all wrong, Dec. I don't even know what you believe, but when Willow told me you hated her from your first dream together, I didn't want to believe it, but it's a little obvious now. And you're wrong," Trex says gently as he pulls them apart and grips his shoulders.

He doesn't give his brother a moment to say anything else before the word vomit of everything that's happened since my kidnapping falls out. He doesn't miss a beat, laying everything he can talk about out on the table for his brother to know and understand. I don't show it outwardly, but I'm a little satisfied when Dec sends me a guilty look.

It's short-lived, though, when his gaze turns to wonder at the mention of Codi.

"I've dreamed about you," Dec says.

"I've heard," Codi says, nodding awkwardly.

Dec doesn't take any offense to the obvious nervousness lingering around Codi, and I assume since we're in a dream not reality, the bond for them won't snap in place. It doesn't stop Dec from pulling him into a hug that shocks Codi, and I stumble back a few steps to give them some space.

They eventually break apart with one of those manly hug pats guys do, then Dec turns to me. "I didn't know," he whispers.

"Yeah, I know. But honestly, you would've thought being kept hostage by that psychopath would've made you think twice before believing anything he's told you about me," I say softly.

"It should've, but with the story he told about you destroying the compound, killing Max, and taking Trex, it was very believable. He told us that he was going to melt his brain if you didn't return him, and that only you would be to blame."

"Well, firstly, I didn't kill Max, my father-in-law did, but the other stuff is all true, except it being my fault. He did try to melt his brain, and it was stopped," I say firmly. "Is that why you came into my dream, or did he make you?"

"He—" Dec grunts, gripping his head, and I close my eyes in frustration.

Even in their sleep, they get no peace or reprieve from him.

"Are you and Xander still being kept together?" I ask, changing the subject of the Summum-Master.

"Yeah, we're together."

"Where are you guys? We're coming for you. You tell us, and as soon as we wake from this, we'll come," Trex says, his words colored in determination.

Dec shakes his head sadly, clenching his fists to his sides. "I can't say. Whatever rift you all have caused in the realm has made him paranoid. He tugs on my rune daily. X as well."

"We've taken down several structures by this point. Took back the Terravile pack, broke Keeper, the vampire, out of the forest, killed some of his top Masters, and the latest ordeal, we captured, then my Nexus member killed the scientist, Darstein," I say factually.

"You what?" he asks lowly as though he doesn't believe it.

"Now we're—"

"Wait a second," I say, cutting Trex off. "We can't tell him what we're doing. What if he tells the Summum-Master or someone gets it out of his head?"

Trex looks heartbroken at the prospect of me accusing his brother of being loyal to the Summum-Master, but that's not what I'm implying. He doesn't have much of a choice in his loyalty or have any control over who has access to his mind at any time. We've been planning for way too long to lose the ability to track down my blood right here a week from it.

"I know I've made a really piss-poor first impression, and I'm deeply sorry for that. I have every intention of making that up to you now, as well as informing Xander of everything as well. The next time you see me, meet him, I swear to you, it won't be like this. Ever again. The truth came from my brother's mouth, and I have complete faith in him. There's no loyalty between X, me, and the Summum-Master and no one checks on us, really. It's the same people. They never change, never leave. I put that on my life and my brothers," he says seriously, never breaking his eye contact from mine.

Subtly blowing out my breath, I look him over from head to toe. That same feeling in my gut that I had about Trex in that shitty situation I was in fills me when I look at Dec.

He's just a victim of his circumstance as well.

"I'm sorry for making that sound like I thought you were on the Mastery's side. I meant that I've met a couple people now who have been forced into this, and they don't have a choice on what they can or can't keep secret, but..." I pause, searching inside myself once more before making my decision. "We're going to track and destroy my blood supply. Whatever the Summum-Master intends to do with it will bring destruction to Elementra."

A range of emotions, from disbelief to relief, crosses his face. He glances at each of us slowly, and I have no clue what's running through his mind, but a slow smile begins to spread across his lips.

"If you—"

Small trembles below our feet interrupt his words, and he tilts his head up to the sky as the three of us look around in confusion.

Suddenly, the foundation of this dream reality that I've woven shakes more violently, sending me falling into Codi's side. The water from the pool a few hundred or so feet away shoots into the air like a fountain, the mansion begins to crumble, and all the trees in the forest start uprooting.

A crack in the earth splits right between us, sending Dec jumping backward, and Trex crashes into me and Codi.

"What the hell is happening?" I shout.

Dec glances around us with calm written across his features as though he's experienced this a million times.

"You're waking up," he hollers.

"What? How? We've barely been here thirty minutes."

He shakes his head at me. "Time moves very differently in the realm of dreams."

Shit.

"We'll do this again. We'll come back and figure out a plan without messing with your rune." Trex swears.

Again, a smile creeps across Dec's face. He's just as calm and steady as though he's in his element. "No need, brother. If you find her blood, you'll find us."

We stare in stunned silence as the earth continues to shift and separate us further from Dec. A cloud of black fog edges up behind him and a chill at my back has me peering over my shoulder, witnessing the same darkness closing in around us.

My panicked gaze whips back to where he stands on the brink of the now massive sinkhole. He offers me a small nod, and with a smile to Trex and Codi, he waves bye as the darkness swallows him whole.

The three of us share a look, letting the realization of his last words settle in, and I hold their gazes as the black fog sucks them in.

Leaving me alone.

What the fuck do I do?

The darkness grows closer, circling me, but it never fully engulfs me. Reaching out to run my fingers through it, it fades and splits open to present a path for me to walk. Right back to my pallet.

Okay then. The way out is the same way I got in.

Wish any other time I asked myself questions, the answer would come that easily.

The soft blanket beckons me in, and I sit, watching as what I assume to be my awareness takes over my dreamscape. As I snuggle down, a drawn-out, seemingly never-ending yawn pours out of me, and the longer it lasts, the less clarity I have.

My head hits the pillow in sync with my eyes scanning the darkness one last time.

Then there's nothing.

□

My eyes fly open and slam back shut just as fast. The blinding bright sun of Elementra is vastly different from the subtle lilac sky I created and with no fog to dim the shine, my lids refuse to lift.

Turning my face to the side sends a wave of dizziness through me, and the other two heads that are connected to mine flinch at my movement.

"Fuck. He was right there." Trex's groggy voice pulls a groan from my throat and the godawful feeling of being drunk makes my head swim.

"Will someone get me a healing vial, please? The two of them probably need one as well."

Quiet murmurings ring in my ears, and I breathe through my mouth, fighting back the nausea crawling through my stomach. Each of my men's presence flutters through my chest, but I can't focus on that right now or I'm going to be sick.

"Here, princess. I'm going to sit your head up a little," Corentin, my hero, whispers.

With one hand, he holds my head tenderly as the other pours one vial, then another in my mouth and I take every drop thankfully. The sweet liquid makes me hum in both appreciation for it being given to me, and with how fast it works.

Gaster is healing vial craft master, I swear.

The back of my lids changes from red to black as someone so graciously blocks out the sun and I blink a few times to straighten out my sight. It's no surprise when they finally open on my command, I come face-to-face with my men all kneeling around me.

"Are you okay?" Tillman asks.

"Much better now. I didn't know the tonic would make us feel so drunk and groggy."

"And it worked? He came to your dream?" Caspian asks stoically, and I arch a brow around at all four of them, but no one gives anything away.

"Yeah to both and I was able to pull Trex and Codi in there. Eventually."

"Okay then," Corentin says flatly, and confusion colors my face, but he doesn't look at me. He nods behind me.

"Okay then...what does—"

I don't get to finish my question before shadows swarm me and my men, whisking us through the walls of the mansion in seconds.

We're spat out in the middle of my bedroom, but unlike my men, who step away from me, I find my feet tethered to the floor by vines and my arms strung up by shadows.

"What in the realm is going on with you four?" I ask, glaring at them as they stand together in a line, glaring right back at me.

"Who the fuck did that to you?"

I startle at the venom in Corentin's voice. It's not aimed at me, but the shaky tremor and anger behind it cause my brain to malfunction, and I have no clue what he's talking about.

"Who did what?"

Despite my soft voice trying to rebuild the small thread of control I see him holding onto, it doesn't work. He's on me faster than my eyes or gift can track.

Gripping my chin in his hand, he turns my head to the side and with his other, he runs his finger across my cheekbone.

"Just because it's healed up now doesn't mean we didn't have to watch that little cut bleed for an hour with no way to check on you or know what was going on. Which one did it, Willow? Now," he whispers, completely contradicting the demand evident in his question.

He kisses my cheek where the mark I got must have come through to the real world and my breathing stalls in my chest.

Fuck me. This isn't going to be good.

"Let's just take a minute to cool off, okay? It wasn't as bad as it may or may not have looked. It was a misunderstanding, and I handled myself just fine."

"There's not going to be a misunderstanding when I eat that whole fucking Nexus, Willow," Draken growls, stepping up beside Corentin.

The murder in his blazing cobalt eyes has my dragon shaking her body out in excitement and I have to shove her and her damn purr back down before she encourages him.

Turning to my most levelheaded of men, my mouth gapes open, then shuts right the hell back when I see the look in Tillman's emerald eyes.

Shit.

"Tillman, call Ry off. Trex nor Codi did anything. You know that, you all know that. If you let me explain or, hell, I'll show you, you'll see everything was okay. Please," I plead, knowing good and well Tillman's probably told Ry to take them both to the dungeons or some shit.

"Fine. But he's on standby if I don't like what I see," Tillman agrees after staring into the depths of my begging gaze.

Opening my mind, I lock it around theirs without giving them a warning or a minute to change their minds. If I don't prove fast that this all went down before Dec knew anything, it's going to be ugly for Trex and Codi. Dec still may get the shit beat out of him when we find him, but I'll worry about that then.

The dream is easy to show in just a few seconds, and I blow out a breath of relief as the murderous tension in the room dissolves a slight bit.

I can work it the rest of the way out.

"See everything's okay," I say softly as soon as I cut them out of my mind.

"We have different definitions of okay, Primary," Caspian says coldly.

"Okay, enough is enough. I get it. I got nicked in the face and I'm sorry it worried all of you, but it's done. I handled myself just fine as you saw, and everything got worked out. Just, everyone, calm down."

A tsk falls from Corentin's lips as he turns my head back to face him and the dark smirk he's wearing makes me press my thighs together.

I don't exactly know what I said that just provoked him, but I do love it when his mask crumbles.

"You don't get to tell us when enough is enough, princess. Weren't you the one who busted into my office and threatened to rip my assistant's throat out if she took another step toward me?"

A growl passes through my throat faster than I can stop it. It's out there now, though. They all heard it, so all I can do is own it. "Yes, but she was trying to touch what's mine."

"And someone *did* touch what's mine. After that, you needed to suck my cock to remind me who I belong to. You don't think we all feel that possessive need? Sexual touch or not, another man had his hands on you with ill intentions. You don't think we all want to bury our faces and cocks so deep in you, there's no mistake who you belong to, who's allowed to touch you?"

Oh, dear sweet Elementra.

"I do belong to you, all of you," I choke out through my suffocation from the intense looks and dark, delicious intentions floating around the room.

"Yes, you do. And we're going to make that very clear."

The highness before me drops to his knees and bows his head until his face is buried in my pussy. The vines around my ankles spread my legs for him, while the shadows lift me up, giving him complete access to eat me out like a buffet.

The rest don't give me a second to even gasp before they pounce.

Tillman takes my nipple fully into his mouth, causing me to cry out when he bites down lightly on it, but the sound is cut short when electricity shoots through my nerve endings from the chilled lips that capture mine.

Caspian doesn't take it easy, sweet, or soft as he swallows down my moans. He demands them from me and takes them however he wants.

"That mouth's gone and done it now, Primary. There won't be ass spankings or edging. The dragon's convinced us all you should endure the ultimate pleasure. I can't wait to see how many orgasms it takes to make you tell us enough is enough again."

Without another word, instead, with a dark promising chuckle, he dips his head down and latches onto my other nipple, pulling a cry of pleasure from my throat. When I throw my head back, it collides with a wall of muscle.

"Don't worry, sweetness, I've given them a few of my tips and tricks on how to make you come the fastest. What I really wanted was a competition to see who could make you come the most, but I think they knew it was a given I'd win," Draken whispers in my ear before laying kisses up and down my neck.

The stimulations are already too much.

Four against one is never a fair battle, and right now, my men are working together to lay waste to me. I'll be lucky if I even know what realm I'm in by the time they're done with me.

Draken's hand slides down my back, and his blazing heat lights my spine on fire, causing my ass to arch into him, but Corentin snatches me back to him by my hips.

"Fuck, princess, your pussy tastes so good. Don't try to take it from me again."

"Oh fuck," I moan.

His words drive me absolutely mad and a burning starts in my belly from something other than Draken's hand.

"Almost there, little wanderer. I feel the tremble in your skin. Curl them fingers inside that tight little pussy, Core. She'll come apart so beautifully," he groans into my neck.

Fuck me, do that, please.

Corentin plunges two fingers deep inside me, curling them just the way I love, fucking crave, and damn if I don't come on the spot.

His name bellows from my mouth and my other three men hold me up even though I'm firmly suspended in the air for their feasting pleasure. The slow, soft kisses he continues to lay on my clit has me squirming, trying to escape his magical tongue. I can't take any more right now.

"It's funny you think he's the only one eating your pussy," Tillman mocks in my mind, and my eyes fly open.

"Tillman," I breathe.

"Don't worry, little warrior, I'm gonna take care of you."

He and Corentin switch spots seamlessly, as though they're planning this out mentally without involving me. Draken and Caspian laugh at my whimper.

The side of me that is lust drunk off these men right now is completely on board with being eaten out until I pass out. The other side is, in fact, fearful I'm going to pass out from too many orgasms.

"Caspian can keep you hydrated. You just worry about coming on my tongue. I'll have you there in no time. Much faster than Corentin."

"Draken said there wasn't a competition," I groan as he slowly starts to lower his body in front of me.

"We agreed on no competition for the most orgasms. No one said anything about the fastest."

His knees hit the ground and his mouth is on me.

As is everyone else's.

That little reprieve I got, they all backed off to mere teasing, toying with my nipples, running their hands up and down my sides, over the curve of my ass, but now all bets are back on.

Tillman pulls out every one of my favorites. The perfect pressure of the pad of his tongue on my clit. The exact curl of his finger inside of me. The vile, dirty praises he sings in my mind. They all add up to sending me right over the edge faster than I could prepare myself for.

My head lulls back on Draken's chest and he lays sweet kisses up my neck and my throat until he can catch my lips with his. When he pulls away from me, he turns my head back forward, facing me off with my dark and damaged protector.

Who looks more like a predator currently.

"What will it be, Primary? You need a little break? Want me to take it nice and slow?"

Yes. No.

The challenge in his devilish smirk sends my body and mind into a tailspin. Fuck, I could use at least five minutes to regroup, but I know if I asked for that, their game would be over and I'm not truly ready for this to end.

Not by a long shot.

"Do your worst. Or your best. Whichever way you want to look at it."

"Fuck, I love that sassy-ass mouth," Corentin mutters from beside me, laying his lips on my shoulder, but I don't dare take my eyes off the man in front of me.

"As you wish, Primary."

His clothes vanish in a cloud of shadows, and Draken from behind me, grips my thighs and pries them even farther apart. I'm practically being presented to Caspian as an offering.

The leashes of shadows that have held my arms hostage this entire ordeal drag them forward where they loop around his neck for support as he crashes into me.

His lips are on mine, with his tongue fighting for control. His thumb finds its way to my extremely sensitive clit and his cock pounds into me. This overabundance of ecstasy is all my fault, though.

As he warned...

I know better than to taunt a monster.

Well, no, I don't. He's mine and my body, heart, and soul were made perfect for him. All of them.

I can take whatever they give me. Ten times over.

"Caspian." I gasp as my ass fills with his gift. No warning, nothing.

The sudden fullness has a deep moan pulling from my throat, and I swear my eyes go crossed.

"Got to get you ready for the dragon, naughty little Primary."

My eyes widen and my dragon purrs a sultry sound in my chest, thoroughly looking forward to that.

Again, with no warning whatsoever, my vines are released from my legs, and I'm whisked through the shadows for a brief second. When we reappear, I find myself looking down at Caspian.

His eyes are hooded, and small hisses fall through his lips as my hips begin to move of their own accord. Just like Corentin taught me, I grind myself down, begging for both more and less friction.

I'm so damn worked up, sensitive, and still turned on, my body doesn't know what it wants at this point.

"That's it, get yourself off on my cock," Caspian orders, gripping my hips, making me go faster.

"Fuck, fuck, fuck."

"Good job, little warrior, just like that. Take what you want," Tillman murmurs beside me.

And finally, I do decide enough is enough.

I want my men. All of them.

When this orgasm rips through me, I unleash my power. My earth element coats the room, undressing the still clothed men around me. My dragon summons Draken's and with a resounding purr, he presses his chest to my back, holding his hand out to Cas.

Liquid flows from his fingers into Draken's palm, and I stare, half mesmerized, half don't give a fuck, as the water grows thicker. I already know exactly what he's preparing to do, so I lean myself forward, poking my ass in the air. Provoking him on.

"Fuck, this is going to be amazing," he mutters as he lines himself up at my asshole.

It's far easier this time around now that Cas has prepared me plenty and after he takes a few cautions pumps, I push myself back, hissing as he slips past my wall of muscle.

"Damn it, little wanderer. Always so impatient for me."

"Fuck me," I command.

I need them to pound into me. I need to make them come undone. I need this overwhelming feeling of too much and not enough to be over.

And they do just that.

A couple strokes in, the two of them have a perfect rhythm going, and I'm a wanton mess between them, but I still need the other two on my sides.

Wrapping my shadows around them, they crawl toward me, slamming their mouths to whatever part of my body they can touch, but I need more than that.

"Stand up for me."

Both do it with no hesitation, and I turn my head to Corentin first, sucking his cock down my throat without giving him any sort of warning.

His hips buck, forcing himself further into my mouth, and I gag around him, but I don't stop. I don't slow down.

Commanding my shadows and water element to merge, I wrap Tillman's dick up and lavish him with the same attention I'm giving to Corentin, while being fucked to oblivion.

If these men thought for a second that I didn't or don't decide when enough is enough, they're wrong.

My lustful haze takes full control over me, and I rotate between which of my men gets my mouth while the other gets my gift and element. My name is a prayer being muttered from four different voices and it boosts my ego to unspeakable heights while I take them all like the goddess they call me.

As my final—this is the last fucking one—orgasm approaches, I know it's going to do me in. I can't take it anymore. The burning heat starts at my toes, traveling through me faster than a wildfire, and I come off Corentin's dick with a loud, wet pop as it reaches my lower belly.

"Come," I command, sending everything I feel, everything I have felt over the last however long, straight down their bonds.

Hot cum splatters across my chest as grunts and mutters of 'fuck' echo around the room. I scream out as Caspian and Draken empty themselves inside of me and when I feel their dicks stop twitching, I collapse.

"You okay, little wanderer?" Draken asks as he kisses his way down my spine.

"You all killed me. I'm dead. Death by too much sex," I mumble against Cas's chest.

"If you're dead, Primary, you're by far the most incredible, beautiful, and fucking badass ghost I've ever met."

I snort and smile stupidly at Cas's words, laying my lips to his heart and closing my eyes as they pull out of me.

"Let's get you a healing vial, then you can get some good sleep, princess, we'll take care of you," Corentin whispers softly across my temple as he pulls me into his arms and starts carrying me to the bathroom.

The whiplash from these men, I swear.

Crazy-ass, psycho, jealous, possessive men.

I hope I dream of them when I go to sleep like he told me to.

Twenty-Six

Corentin

She's going to pace a hole in my carpet.

Willow's footsteps are silent as she goes from one end of my office at the academy to the other. She runs her fingers slowly over the back of my couch every time she passes it, and as she makes her full circle, she lays her hand on the window. Leaving an impression on the glass with every touch.

"Princess, either come sit on my lap or on the couch. Your wandering in this circle is making me dizzy and I can't focus on my work," I command, holding in my smirk when she scowls at me.

"How can you be so calm right now?" she asks, placing those soft hands on her hips.

Laying down my pen, I swivel my chair to face her and beckon her over with a curl of my finger. I see the refusal on her face, but with a tilt of my lip, she huffs and makes her way to me.

As soon as she sits, the tension that's rolling through her slithers across my skin and I press my lips to her temple, attempting to calm its rapid beat.

"I'm calm because I have full faith in them. Caspian and Draken may live for the thrill of a fight, but they're smart, resourceful, and would never do something stupid enough to jeopardize coming home to you. They also took the Bane of Essence. Keeper is the literal ruler of their home realm and can command the vampires with a glare. It's very normal and natural for you to be anxious, but they're fine."

We decided that it'd be wise to go check on the portal in the Forsaken Forest. Although we already know it's open, and the Summum-Master can come and go as he pleases with a couple of drops of blood, there's been no report whatsoever from our recons that anyone has gone in or out of the forest. Since it's been weeks of nothing, we thought it best to see what's been going on inside since we got Keeper out.

With only four days left before we check the others and track down Willow's blood, it's better to be over prepared rather than under.

The original plan was to send Keeper in with a small team, but Draken quickly stated he'd be going with him, followed by Caspian declaring if Draken was going, he was going. So it went from a small E.F. recon mission, to a side quest for half our Nexus.

"You're right." Willow sighs, leaning into me more. "It's just worrisome. I haven't wanted to talk in our mental link because I don't want to distract them, but by their bonds, they're perfectly fine."

"See. And they're due back in just a few. Let me fix you a cup of coffee. You can snuggle up on the couch and read or relax, whatever you want until then."

Swooping her up into my arms, she throws her head back, laughing as I clench the back of her thighs repeatedly, tickling her all the way to the couch. She nearly flies out of my arms to get away from me, but I set her down and seal my lips to hers.

I linger, letting the remainder of her worry bleed out into me. When that happy little hum vibrates in the back of her throat, I give her a few pecks before making my way over to the kettle.

Four sugar cubes.

Six splashes of honeyed cream.

And my secret ingredient...an incredibly small pinch of allspice to enhance the roasted, earthy coffee grinds.

The guys think they could make her coffee perfectly, but they're wrong because I hide that little flavor that so many turn their noses up to. If you used too much of it, yeah, the strong undertones would ruin the whole drink, but the minuscule I put in is just right.

Some would find it weird that I keep a small stash hidden with me all the time, but I don't give a fuck. Never know when my princess may want a coffee pick me up.

She deeply inhales the aroma as soon as I pass the mug over to her and sighs happily around the rim. I give her a quick kiss on the forehead and march back to my seat with a smug grin plastered to my face that she can't see.

I hold in the groan that wants to escape me as I look down at the paperwork scattered across my desk. My room at the palace has spoiled me beyond belief when it comes to taking care of the administrative side of my role. There's no sense in spending hours of my day working on things such as this when I can have it done in minutes.

Biting the dagger since we've got to be here when the others return anyways, I take a peek over at Willow, who's already zoned into her book on true Primaries, again, then I center my attention on my own work.

The buzzing of my communicator steals my focus as soon as I gather it, and I side-eye it, planning on ignoring it, but the name I see causes me to pause.

"Gean Everglow is calling me," I announce, grabbing the device and staring at it.

"What?" Willow whisper-yells as if he'll hear her, jumping from the couch. "Are you going to answer it?"

Nodding, I place my finger to my lips.

"Headmaster Vito," I answer on speaker with my scholarly tone rather than the relaxed pitch my Nexus and family get to hear.

"Corentin, how are you today?"

I grit my teeth at the lax way he says my name. He's always addressed me and my brother as if we're below him rather than show us the respect we deserve. I've always brushed it off so I don't cause my mom any problems, but now that I know what I know, it pisses me off beyond fucking belief.

Fucking scum.

"It's Headmaster Vito, Councilman Everglow."

The silence on the other end is telling but not surprising. Gima got her holier than everyone attitude honest. Her mother and father believe they are Elementra's gift to us all, and the rotten Genko berry didn't fall far from the bush.

"Of course."

"What can I do for you today?" I ask smugly.

"Just wanted to give you my proper congratulations. We've been quite busy over the last few weeks since we received the decree about the Spring Ball. The Matriarch's announcement was a shock, to say the least, but a happy one."

"I appreciate that. We're all excited and overjoyed by Elementra's blessing of a true Primary," I say, casting my gaze over at Willow.

"Ah, yes, a bountiful blessing. For her to be a true Primary to the Vito heirs, she must be quite a powerful female," he says, and the phishing for information on Willow is apparent in his *compliment*.

"What do you think he wants to know?"

"I'm not sure, princess. I don't believe there's anything I could say that they don't already know. The Summum-Master is plenty aware of your level of power."

"That she is. She's impressive, to say the least."

"If the rumors are true, I'd have to believe that. It's been said she's a shifter, dragon, just like the one in your Nexus. Does her beast have the same vicious tendencies?"

This motherfucker.

Willow's eyes flash purple before settling back to her lethal silver and I smile because truthfully, her dragon could or would be a thousand times more vicious if need be over us.

"I'm not sure what you're trying to insinuate with your question, *Gean*, but I'll remind you, you're not speaking to a friend. Mind your words when speaking about my Primary or my brothers."

My words are firm and steady. There's no hint of anger or aggression in my tone, just unapologetic facts. I'm not some subordinate that he can speak freely with, and if he can't manage to remember that with this conversation, I'll gladly remind him when I wipe his entire family out for betraying our realm.

"No insinuation, just concerned curiosity. We all remember what happened when your brother emerged. It's best to prepare the people for who their future ruler may be."

May...I don't like that wording.

"No need to worry yourself with such things. It'll be Gima who will need to fuss about those problems in the future. How is she, by the way? The staff and her peers are missing her around the academy."

Willow covers her mouth with her hand, and her eyes widen when she looks at me in utter shock. No, I'm not usually one to stoop to pettiness, but I couldn't give a fuck about this man. His sideways-ass ways of saying things in this pointless conversation are pissing me off.

I've already figured out the entire reason for this call and it's not going to make any difference.

"She's doing fine. Her mother has her on a study retreat, so she's keeping up with what she should. I must be going now, Headmaster, duty calls. I do appreciate the conversation. Please tell your Primary I look forward to meeting her at the Spring Ball." With that, he hangs up, not giving me a chance to say anything else.

Willow and I share a loaded look, and I shake my head at that ridiculousness.

"What in the hell was that all about?"

"That, princess, was social and political scheming at its finest. He's holding the meeting between the five to discredit your name and make you out to be someone worth worrying about."

"What?" she asks, outraged.

"That is the elite and the five for you. I could predict how the entirety of that meeting will go now. The Everglows, and whoever the other family is betraying us, will talk about how you're a threat to the realm, just as they did when we found Draken. They'll attempt to rally the other three families behind them in this stance, then they'll bring their concerns to my mom. It'll be the five of them against her, and she'll do one of two things.

"One, she'll shut the shit down immediately, just as she had to do with Draken, or two, which as much as it pisses me off to say, may be the better pick. She'll pretend to take their concerns into consideration. It'll set the Everglows and the others up into believing they're roping her in. They'll outwardly appear more comfortable, condescending."

Willow looks at me in pure disgust, and it's not aimed at me, but at everything I just explained.

"That is the stupidest shit I've ever heard. I mean, I've read your notes, Aurora's, and whatever else I could, so I get that they're petty, very social status centered, to a dangerous level, but they're really like that? They'll try to convince the realm I'm a rabid beast? For what?"

"Yes, they're really like that. It's like early academy all over again, but with deadly adults." I sigh, holding my hand out for her to take so I can pull her between my legs before I tell her this next part. "If this was before we knew as much about the Mastery as we do, I'd say they were doing it to gain leverage over you. Think of it as a way to control you and your behaviors. If they have you by a leash, they can keep you in line. But...now that we know what we know, it's—"

"If I were to die or disappear, the realm wouldn't be in an uproar. They'd already fear me, and it'd seem like a blessing. Then there'd possibly be another realm trial because we all would die. They'd never let Aurora continue ruling. They'd overthrow her." She finishes for me.

I hate the sadness I hear in her voice, and I pull her down completely on my lap. She lays her head on my shoulder as the unfairness of this weighs her down.

"We're not going to let it come to that. Elementra willing, there will never be another realm trial, nor will one ever be needed. For generations to come, we'll teach them integrity, compassion, and what it means to care for a realm and the people they love. It won't ever be like it was two thousand years ago, princess."

She nods and exhales harshly, but it's the contemplative look on her face that really catches my attention. Something about what I said has just sparked something in her mind.

"What is it, princess?"

"I don't know, Core. There's something I'm missing, and I feel like it's on the tip of my brain, but I can't figure it out. Something either happened before the realm trials or after. The records Cas and Gaster were so concerned with that we found in CC's room didn't show many revelations about the families that entered. All the lines were accounted for, no surviving relatives or Nexus members seeking revenge, but something happened between that generation and Drudy's that sparked the Summum-Master's grand plan."

"I know. I think—"

"Can you two come to the dungeons or are you doing freaky shit in the office again?" Draken asks, cutting off my words.

"You'd know if we were doing that, Draken." Willow snorts.

"What's going on in the dun—palace prison?" I ask, rolling my eyes as Willow laughs. It's a prison, not a dungeon. There's a difference...usually.

"We brought a little spy back with us. Need Tman or little wanderer to do some digging."

Willow hops off my lap with quickness and I stand right behind her. Whatever spy they've captured, we need whatever is in their mind.

"Ready?" I ask her.

"Ready."

Wrapping her in my arms, I transport us straight to the door of Cas's favorite room and at the same time, Tillman pops in beside us.

"Well, that was quick," he says, shooting us a wink.

"He's getting worse. If his nonsense is rubbing off on you now, I'm screwed," I say, shaking my head and buttoning my jacket. It's going to be the four of them against me with their jokes and teasing nonstop.

"Nah, life's just getting sweeter. Laugh a little, Core," he says, swinging Willow out of my arms and kissing her like it's been days not hours since he's seen her. *Hopeless romantic.*

And I do laugh plenty. I've laughed every single day for weeks, as a matter of fact.

Since my princess gave me a piece of her soul.

They all just enjoy riling me up and then laughing about it.

"After you, your highness. We have a spy's mind to pick apart."

That they do.

Pulling my shoulders back, I push the door open and walk into the tortu—interrogation room, but my steps halt, causing Willow to slam into my back. Instinctively, I swing my arm around, gripping her before she falls.

"A vampire? You all stole a vampire out of the forest?"

Caspian, Draken, and Keeper turn to me with the most innocent fucking smiles on their faces as they stand around the snarling vampire they have strapped to the chair. By the color of his eyes, I can tell he's completely sane, but he's pissed to be in the position he's in.

"I don't think it's considered stealing, brother. We've brought him in for questioning and then he'll be returned," Caspian says so nonchalantly, I pinch the bridge of my nose.

"I thought when you said spy, you meant like a Mastery member. What are we going to get from...I don't know his name," Willow says, cocking her head to the side, observing the vampire in fascination.

"Ah, my dear, Adored, this here is Renic. He's a scared little Baccum who has an impressive ability to sneak around undetected. Many of the vampires, even with their enhanced hearing and speed, can't keep up with him. He likes to spy on all the others and the Mastery members. Selling what he knows for the price of blood. That's incredibly valuable in the forest. I believe he's the one who..." Keeper pauses as his eyes flash crimson before he shakes his head and sneers at Renic. "He'll know things. Whether they're helpful or not, I'm not sure."

A wave of sadness hits me in my chest, but just as fast as I felt it, it's gone. When I peer over at Willow, her eyes stay trained on Keeper with a softness I don't understand, then they glare down at the captive creature.

"Well, then let's see, shall we."

Strolling up to him like she doesn't have a care in the realm, before any of us can stop her or just step up to help, Willow slams her palm against his forehead. He immediately bellows out in pain, and I'm surprised by the forceful use of her power, but obviously, she knows something about this vampire that the rest of us don't.

Minutes stretch by as he grunts, snarls, and shakes beneath her palm, but she doesn't relent. She rips out whatever information she deems important, and by the time it's taking her to do this, she's looking years back.

Finally, stumbling away from him, heaving, Keeper grips her by the elbow to steady her and she mutters, "Fuck." It's softly spoken at first, but then her voice rises as she shrieks, "Fuck."

That burst of outrage is paired with dread, anger, guilt, all kinds of emotions I can't decode fast enough. Anger I understand. I'm sure this vampire has seen some shit, but the others are completely lost on myself and my brothers.

"What did you see, little wanderer?" Draken asks, standing in front of her to block her sight of the vampire.

Her chest rises and falls heavily as she stares into his eyes, then they turn to Keeper and soften. "The answer to the question you've been wondering is yes. He used to lurk outside your perimeter."

For as long as I've known him—which I get hasn't been long—much like Draken, he's a very cheery person. He's extremely grateful for the second chance at life, but right now, every feature on his face crumbles before filling with fury.

"Thank you for getting me that answer, Adored."

"You're welcome. Let's give Keeper a moment, then we can meet in the foyer, and I'll tell you what I found out," she says as she turns around and looks at me, Tillman, and Caspian.

"I do not need a moment."

Keeper growls, and faster than my eyes can follow but loud enough my ears can hear, the sound of bones breaking and skin tearing echoes around the room. Willow's eyes close gently and her body shudders, but she stops walking, waiting for Keeper to finish.

"What the hell? What is going on, Primary?"

"It's not my story to tell...yet."

Her lids flutter open, and guilt swells in her eyes along with water. I don't believe the guilt has anything to do with the vampire's death, though, more so being the one who had to tell Keeper whatever her cryptic message means.

"Draken, would you please use your flames?" Keeper asks quietly.

"Yeah, of course."

His blue flames obey his call, lighting Renic's body on fire, and the smell of burning hair flows through the room. That pungent stench is enough to make my nose twitch, and I use my air to circulate the reek out the door. It minimally helps, but soon enough, there's nothing but ash on the floor.

"Is there anything prudent I need to hear?" Keeper asks as he comes to stand in front of Willow.

"Nothing we can't catch you up on."

Nodding, he pulls her into his arms for a hug that they both seem to need, and the four of us just stare curiously.

Dying on the inside to know what the hell is happening.

"Do not feel burdened by telling me that. That is a truth I've searched for, for many years without any proof. Thank you, Adored," he whispers into her hair before striding toward the door otherwise wordlessly.

"Where's he going?" Draken asks with concern lacing his question.

"To Tanith. He just needs a few minutes to calm down," she says lightly, holding her hand out for him to take.

He accepts it easily, but his face is twisted in confusion and his eyes bounce from between her and the door Keeper just exited. I'm sure more than any of us, he wants to know what just caused that.

"Then let's go hear what you learned, little warrior," Tillman says steadily. The strain in his shoulders tells me he's not reading her mind like he desperately wants to, and she knows it too, by the small smile she offers him.

"Cas," I say, giving him the go-ahead to move us.

Instead of the foyer, he whisks us through the shadows until we're in what we've deemed Willow's lounge. It's most certainly her space, handcrafted to perfection with everything she ever wanted in a room just for her to relax.

We all plop down on the couch heavily, and the tense, confused silence stretches on. There's a weight sitting on Willow that I can feel all over my body and my brothers nor I know what to do in this moment. This isn't something she's told us about, which means she can't. For now, if I picked up on her 'yet' correctly.

"The Summum-Master has been going to the nonmagical realm over the last few weeks. He must be using some sort of concealment to not be noticed by the recon teams hiding out," Willow finally says, breaking the rigid hush in the room. "Renic has been watching him bring in men. It's obviously nonmagical men, seeing as he leaves alone but returns with someone. The last man he arrived back with was the scientist, Drin. He didn't look more powerful or any different, but who fucking knows with that cloak and illusion covering his face. But he's still stealing gifts."

Fuck.

I lock down the rage attempting to crawl up my throat and spew through my lips. I had a hunch the news had something to do with the Summum-Master, but I wasn't prepared to hear he's brought in another scientist. Not any old scientist, but the fucker who drew her blood from the time she was a child.

We've been asking ourselves how or if he was still going to be able to perform the ritual without a skilled scientist there to brew and administer the infection, then aid him with the ritual. Just because we knew about Drin, we figured since he's been stuck in the nonmagical realm for fuck knows how long, he wouldn't have the knowledge Ale or Darstein did on the infection or ritual to transfer the gifts.

Assumptions. We've been making far too many of them lately and they're posing to be no help.

Based on her vision of the Summum-Master, we've also assumed we'd have time to stop him from moving to the Valorian Veil by destroying her blood supply.

That possibility is still there, but it just got a lot more dangerous and needs to happen sooner rather than later.

If he's moving men in to power them up, he'll be powering himself next.

"This doesn't change the plans. As of today's reports," Tillman waits, looking at me, and I nod, knowing what he wants to know, "All the main portals are still closed, so he isn't traveling that way. From what we gathered from shit in Uncle Orien's room, if he was going through the nonmagical realm to access other portals there, it's time-consuming and he'd be gone longer than what you're telling us. So for now, we stick to our plan.

"Does it suck he's stealing gifts? Fuck yes, absolutely, but we have no way of tracking down every possible concealed structure, and that hastily made decision will cost us lives. You're the only person I know who can tear the concealments down, little warrior, and you can't be all over the realm at once. I'll form teams of scouts, call in our Master Geographers and find the most secluded areas in Elementra to send teams to watch for activity. Once we destroy your blood and retrieve Codi's brothers, we will make offensive moves and start hitting possible locations. Does that answer the majority of what's running through everyone's heads?"

We all nod.

I'm already making a list of the top Geographers I know and where they are. We can get them in here today, and they can begin mapping out the best possible locations. I'll ask Gaster to lead this up. With his already extensive knowledge, he can aid and lead them on what we want better than even we can.

"I've got to figure out this portal situation. I need to close the one to the nonmagical realm. If Keeper can confirm from the vampires that the Summum-Master is currently in Elementra, I need to keep it that way." Willow blows out a heavy breath, her disappointment spreading through the room.

"Everything you need to know or do will come with time, little warrior. Stop doubting yourself and believe that," Tillman tells her firmly.

She nods wordlessly and falls back more fully into both Draken and Caspian. Neither try to move her or manhandle her. They just look at her with worry written across their faces.

At every turn, my princess feels like she's being outsmarted, but I don't believe that for a second.

Unfortunately, I believe this is the reprieve before the shit show.

Twenty-Seven

Willow

Two days.

That's all the time I have left and there still isn't an answer in sight.

Figuratively and literally.

There's been a dull ache spreading through my chest for days now. My disappointment in myself, my mom's book, CC's and Elementra's absences, it's all starting to physically weigh me down.

I catch myself more often than not blinking but not seeing anything because my mind is just swirling. I can't stop the thoughts, the overwhelming feeling of failure as the time continues to count down until we leave, and I don't know the first thing about the extent of what my blood can do nor do I have any more control over the sight.

"Caspian's not going to like that." Oakly tsks at me, and I startle at the sudden sound, my dry eyes blinking.

Looking down, my finger is still partially shifted from where I intended to try again to get in Mom's book, but then I zoned out. Consumed with thoughts on how it's not going to work again.

Peering over at Oakly, she's staring at me with her brow arched and her beloved book in her lap. I've barely been able to glance in it. She keeps that thing well protected, but she does like to show me her most interesting finds.

Interesting is putting it lightly.

It's astonishing.

"Hence why the two of us are in my lounge while he, Gaster, San, and Keeper are in CC's room."

"You don't think he's going to feel or know you've once again carved up your palm? He told you no more." She chuckles and I glare at her.

"Whose side are you on?"

"Your side, obviously. *Hence* why I'm warning you away from doing it. He threatened to hide the book from you until this was all over and not a part of me believes he was bullshitting you."

I roll my eyes at her stupid-ass sound reasoning. Am I going to listen to her? No. My time is ticking, and I've got to figure this shit out. I know this book holds valuable information in it one way or another.

Everyone else around me is making amazing strides in everything they're responsible for handling as we prepare to check the portals and hunt down my blood. Not only that but keeping up with their other day-to-day shit too.

It's just me who's falling behind and I'm tired of that feeling.

"I can tell you aren't going to—Oh holy fuck," she screeches, sitting up straight and dropping her book.

"What? What?" I scream in a panic, looking for her paper cut or a spider, whatever the fuck freaked her out.

"I think I found it. Oh, my Elementra, I think I found the relic."

"The whole damn book is relics, Oakly. Give me more than that."

I don't mean for it to be so frantically demanding, but her bond is shocking my chest like I stuck my finger to an electrical outlet. She's radiating so strongly right now, I can barely think straight.

"The relic for the fucking ritual. I think this is it."

She flips the book around to show me, and the entire right side of the page is the image of a small ball. The crystal clear globe in the middle is surrounded protectively by a wielded bronze casing, and it sits on top of a four-footed bronze display stand.

My eyes widen as the description Keeper gave us comes barreling to the front of my mind and my heart pounds in sync with the thud of Oakly's bond.

This has to be it.

The Gods' Binding.

The Gods.

"It's from the Valorian Veil," I whisper. I don't have to see any other information to know that. The name of the relic spells it out.

She quickly flips the book back around to her and begins skimming over the next page silently as I sit here tapping my foot, waiting for her to speak.

"Willy, this has to be it. According to this, the relic was used as a method of binding the Gods' power as a form of punishment when found guilty of neglectful use of their powers. I got to take this to Gaster and get Keeper to confirm this is it," she says low, hopping up from her seat, and I follow suit, but she shoots me a look.

"No, ma'am. I know it's been a rough few days, but you're trying to procrastinate because you don't want to continue failing. You're not failing, by the way. Some roadblocks have been put in front of you, but you're going to figure it out. Stay, study, meditate, talk to CC even if he won't respond. Do something that'll get your mind right and I'll be back."

I deflate as she gives me a little finger wave and transports out faster than I can argue. I could obviously follow her anyways, but I don't. She's right and her words cause frustrated tears to spring in my eyes.

It's not just that, though. With her gone, the room feels so empty, lonely.

I never feel lonely even when I ask for alone time from the guys, but today is hitting me harder than usual. This feeling doesn't have anything to do with them. It's all me and the wave of grief that my inability to make any progress has brought forth. It intensifies when I gaze over at my willow tree and memories start fluttering across my mind.

He'd know what to do. He always did.

Talk to him. That's all I can do, even if he doesn't answer.

Scooping up my mom's book, I make my way around the couch and drop down at the trunk of my tree. I lean my head back against the steady, familiar bark and breathe through the longing, begging the tears to stop.

"You know, if you were here, you'd be laughing or mocking me right now. You'd say some inspirational shit that would both piss me off and make me feel better. You'd pick me up, dust me off, and wipe away these stupid, pointless tears. You'd tell me it was just my frustration leaving my body and it's okay to cry. No one will hurt or punish me for crying.

"How many times do you think we sat against my tree in the clearing, and you had to hold me while I broke down? Probably more times than I can recall, even with my memories. Whether it was something Franklin did, or I had a bad day at school, or I just couldn't get something right that you were trying to teach me. You were always there for me. Fuck...you were the best. I'm not asking you to make any decision or tell me exactly what to do. I just need you to be here now."

My sigh is sad, small, and I aggressively wipe away my tears. It's an irrational feeling, I know, but I can't help as a surge of anger bubbles through me. I feel abandoned. By Elementra, by CC, by my mom. I've tried to be understanding, take each thing thrown at me and carry on, but this full stop, radio silence, is hard.

I've gone years now without my memories of him, then they're returned, and I get told he's going to be here for me, but when I need guidance navigating unfamiliar territory, I get nothing.

I don't need him to make decisions for me. I just need my...

My dad. He was my dad.

And he knew my mom, even if it was just a little. He could talk me through this. Tell me a little about her so I could figure this out on my own.

In my heart, I know her book was left behind for Lyker to find and give to me. I can't accept it was the one and only coincidence I've ever experienced in Elementra. It had to be left for me.

Honestly, I believe a part of me was desperately thinking I'd get a small taste of what it would be like to have them both in my life together.

Her book, his guidance. Both helping me along the way.

I want my dad and...I need my momma.

My heart cracks open with my internal confession.

I need him. I need her.

I've needed them my entire existence and now that I've had a glimpse into their lives, I want even more. Holding this piece of bound leather that I know belonged to her, in a room he created just for me, I need it opened so I can hold a piece of them close to my heart.

Wiping my tear-drenched face, I take a deep breath, inhaling the faint scent of his room that lingers on my clothes, and I press my nose against the cover and wonder if this is what she smelled like. *Rain.*

Not just any rain, though.

Not a booming thunderstorm that floods the land, but a steady, gentle rainfall on an early spring day. Where the weather may or may not reach seventy, and it's best you grab a coat to keep you comfortable just in case.

The peaceful picture I'm falling into has me trapped. I can't open my eyes to break away from the serenity and my mind refuses to loosen its hold.

It tightens its grip on my entire body.

All my thoughts, feelings, emotions flee me and a mind that's not my own takes control.

"Willow, what in the realm are you doing out here with no coat on?" I fuss as soon as my eyes land on the small shivering form under the tree.

This blasted realm's winter lasts far longer than Elementra's and although it's early spring, add in this rain and wind, it's freezing. To me.

Tear-drenched eyes cast up to me and the ring of violet in the haunted silver tugs at my heart painfully.

He's hurt my baby girl again.

Sinking to the ground with her, her cold, wet body shakes violently against my chest, and I command an air bubble to surround us. I pull the blanket that I store in the trunk of the tree out and wrap it around her, swearing to myself as soon as she emerges, I'll show her how to do this.

"What happened, my sweet girl?"

"I skipped school and got caught." She hiccups and I hold in my shocked flinch.

Skipped school? She's never done such a thing.

"Why would you do that? You know you can't do things like that or you'll get in trouble," I say gently, not wanting to upset her even more, but also, she needs to know, she can't do things like this.

"It's mommy and me day again."

Ah.

This would've been the third year she's been in school and has had to endure being the only child who doesn't have a mother show up. When she was six, it was confusing but exciting. A couple moms included her in the activities, and she had a good time.

But last year, her questions became more consistent, and she wanted to experience it fully. I explained to her, much more gently than her fuck of a father did, that it just wasn't going to happen. She tried to put on a brave face, said it was okay and she hoped that the moms would play with her as well, but that teacher ended up taking her to a room alone to watch a movie.

She cried for days afterward. She realized she was being isolated, and she felt it in the depths of her soul.

This year, though, hell, I don't know. I guess something about eight just makes children stronger.

Her brother was the same.

"I'm so very sorry, Willow. If your mom could be here, she would."

"Obviously not." She sniffles.

A lump forms in my throat at the heartache in her tone. There's so much I wish I could say, so much I wish I could do. There's only one thing in this moment that I believe would help, but I just don't know if she's ready.

Looking down at the distant, sad look on her face, I know I'm wrong. She's ready. It is me who isn't. My sweet girl has aged a lifetime in the past two years.

Her age may only be eight, but her mind is much older, unfortunately.

"Would you like to watch a movie?" I ask.

"No."

I snort at the sharp rejection. "This isn't your ordinary story or a movie you've ever seen before, though."

Got her.

That little head pops off my chest and she narrows those eyes on me, searching for the trap. Curious as ever even in the face of sadness. I'll see to it she never loses that wonder.

"What kind of movie? What's it about?"

Smiling, I tuck a piece of her wet hair behind her ear. "It's a movie that's in my mind. One I've replayed many times."

"How will I see it if it's in your mind?"

"If you let me show you, it'll answer your questions."

"Is it funny?"

"Not really."

"Eww, romantic?"

"Absolutely not."

"Happy? Sad?"

"A little of both, my girl," I say softly.

"Will it make me cry again?"

"Very possibly, but I'll be here to wipe away your tears."

Her face softens and she looks at me as though I am her world. I guess right now, I am, as she is mine. I hope what she sees doesn't change the way she views me.

"Well, what do you say?"

She glances around me, watching the rain through the gaps in the branches.

Poking her little hand through my air bubble, she catches a few drops that run off the leaves of her tree and rubs the water between her fingers.

"Yeah, today's a movie kind of day."

"Then get comfortable and close your eyes."

She nestles in, leaning her back to my chest, and tucks the blanket around her tightly. When she laces her fingers together on her tummy, I smirk down at her. "Ready?"

"Ready."

At her nod, I take us back in time.

Standing at the edge of Iris's ward, I glance over at the cave that I walked her through so, so many years ago. My, how not a thing has changed. At least on this side. I'm curious to see what she's done on the inside of this Elementra-blessed protection.

Releasing a breath, I walk through the ward, hoping her men don't come out preparing to attack. No one should be able to pass through, but I'm not just anyone.

A small cottage comes into view as soon as I'm through, and I smile at the quaintness of it. No one would ever look at this design and believe that the strongest woman to walk this realm lives within those walls.

Holding the present I brought in front of me, I walk a couple feet, then pause. The vibrations slithering over my skin let me know that the Nexus inside has just been alerted to my presence, so it'd be best I wait right here for them to come out.

It's no surprise to me that Iris is the first to crash through the door, gifts blazing, with her men hot on her heels. I smile as the formidable bunch halts to a stop, glaring at me.

"Dangerous game you're playing there, old friend," Iris sasses, placing her hands on her hips as her men snort and shake their heads at me.

"Old? Two hundred and sixteen has never looked so good, thank you very much," I say, using her words against her. Just, you know, add a couple years.

She snickers, looking at her men affectionately. That's the day she met them. They were waiting for her outside that cave, where I made them stay while I waited for her to come out of the portal.

"Well, come on in, I've got the kettle on," she says, but I shake my head softly.

"I cannot stay long, unfortunately, but I need a word, if you don't mind."

They all grow somber and I hate that I have that effect on people. I'm like the deliverer of bad news. Many don't get excited and stay excited to see me.

"Of course," she says, smiling at me tightly.

Each of her men gives her a kiss and wave me goodbye, but before they can walk back inside, I call out, "Congratulations, by the way, guys."

I smirk and wink at their confused stares. They don't push, knowing the rules, but they'll find out soon enough.

"What do you have there?" Iris asks as she guides me over to a bench she has built beneath her trees.

"I love what you've done with this place," I say rather than answering, just to annoy her.

She groans, rolling her eyes. "You love dragging out my suspense. As much as I love your company, what little of it I receive, I know you're here to share something with me. Get on with it."

My toothy smile fades to nothing more than a pinched grin as I look at her with sincerity in my gaze. "Please do not be mad at me."

Her playful features melt away, and I bite my tongue as her saddening eyes remind me so much of the girl's.

"I won't be. I understand you're the messenger, CC. I won't hold you to fault for anything."

"Thank you...Tell me, what is it you've wished for the most in this life, Iris?"

Her face shudders, but she doesn't shy away or hide the hurt on her face. "To be a mother. To have and be able to raise a child with my loving Nexus. I know I will be a mother, but my dragonfly won't have me."

I close my eyes tightly at the nickname.

The girl will most certainly fly.

"Why is it you ask, CC?"

Clearing my throat, I pass over the gift I brought her. "Here." She looks down at it warily, then back at me with a raised brow. "It's not going to bite. Just open in."

She grins and then does as I asked, chuckling as she takes in the stained-glass picture. "Oh my. This is her form, isn't it?" she says quietly, running her finger across the girl's dragon form. She doesn't like to speak much about her, so I've never truly been able to grasp her true feelings, but she's far from a jaded person, so all I can make are assumptions. "You got Sedric's coloring a little off, though. He's going to ask why you made him so dark."

"Is the color of your woven bonds not a sleek black?"

"How did you...Yeah, it is," she answers rather than finishing her question.

"Your wolf is silver as is your thread. Sedric's wolf and bond are midnight blue. Kelso, with his ability to speak to animals, I assume gives off a dark green. Allton and his metal manipulation is more than likely a reddish, maybe burgundy color, something darker, and Esben's extraordinary healing I can see as yellow. Mix them all together, you get the largest and strongest, sleek black wolf."

"I don't...I don't understand the message you're trying to give me," she says quietly, looking down once again at the picture and then at me.

"Those are your children. Both of them."

Her face startles as she stares at me in disbelief, but I hold her gaze and show the seriousness of my words through my eyes as I watch hers begin to well.

"Oh, Elementra..." She gasps, laying her fingers to her lips. "When?"

"Now. Your scent will begin to change within the week."

"Fuck," she cries as tears begin to stream down her face. "How could this happen?"

"Well—"

"I don't need a literal answer," she snaps, and I shut my mouth. "I mean, how could Elementra do this when we already know what is to happen? I already know my role as well as Willow's. How could she allow me to bring another child into this realm, knowing I will have to abandon them?"

"Because you have begged for the girl not to be alone as well as your want to experience motherhood. She is answering your prayers. The wolf has a story of his own. One you will know soon enough," I say as tenderly as I can.

There have been many times I have asked Elementra similar questions. The answers always come eventually.

"His...it's a boy."

"It is."

She closes her eyes and sighs gently before sobs begin to tear through her body. I let her get it all out as I sit here quietly, being her shoulder to cry on. I knew this would be difficult for her to hear, but it was something I had to tell her.

"Will they ever forgive me, CC?"

"Yes, they will. You will be the apple of your son's eye and the girl will grow to love, respect, and cherish the pieces of you she gets."

"Stop referring to my daughter as the girl, CC. I've let it slide for hundreds of years now. Her name is Willow. Say it." She growls at me, and I grit my teeth.

It's hard for me to say.

Saying it makes what she is to me a reality I've yet to accept or tell Iris about it. I don't know how she will take it. She's always drawn a hard line with me anytime I've tried to bring her up or anything I've seen. I know she has seen much of her life as well, but she will not go into detail about her. I don't know if my truth will help or hurt her. I don't want to further upset her with what the future holds for her daughter.

Our daughter.

Not born from blood, but from a bond.

"Elementra is blessing us with a Guardria bond."

The words spew out of my mouth forcefully, and I grunt as Elementra herself doesn't give me an opinion but to deliver the truth. Regardless of if I was ready or not. I guess this is her way of saying too fucking bad.

"You...you and Willow will have a Guardria bond? How long have you known? How will it manifest?" she asks with wide eyes.

"Iris..."

Gasping, she nearly drops the picture as she turns fully to face me. "Father, daughter. CC, tell me if I'm right."

Closing my eyes and looking down at my laced fingers that bear white knuckles, I nod once.

"Yes. For the time I have with her, that will be the bond we share. I've known for sure for fifty years."

The silence that stretches between the two of us is heavy. It sullies the atmosphere of this beautiful escape she's created. My continued secrecy has that effect no matter how I go about it.

It's out there now, though, and I don't know what's running through her mind. Many don't understand the strength behind a Guardria bond, but Iris is well informed and smart. She knows I won't be able to reject this entirely and I don't know if she will accept that I have a relationship that strong with the daughter she won't get to share any experiences with.

I've known for one hundred and eighty-six years, Willow would mean something to me, but it wasn't confirmed what until fifty years ago. It was the day Iris told me what she planned to name her. That same night, I had my first vision of our awakening.

In the fifty years since, I've seen Iris three times. Never once have I brought it up.

The overabundance of joy at the prospect that I will be able to love a child like my own and bless her with the same love Gaster has blessed me with has battled with the deep despair that I feel when I think about how I will also have to give my life for this realm. Another part of me feels like I am somehow stealing Iris's future and role from her.

"Look at me."

Blowing out a harsh breath, I turn my head up to do as she asked. I'm prepared for the anger and bitterness. I'll understand it.

"Love her with your entire being. Make her feel worthy, special, beautiful. Put the broken pieces she's going to have from her father back together. Show her what a childhood is supposed to look like. What it feels like to be free. Be her father, CC. Filia mea nunc est filia tua"

"What does that mean?" I ask, choking back the emotions clogging my throat.

I didn't expect tons of weight to lift free from me with her words. I've been petrified to tell her this truth and here she is, giving me her blessing.

"My daughter is now your daughter. Call her filia mea as much and as often as you can. Remind her she is loved. She is a blessing."

Her stern gaze leaves no room for argument and her command, although I know she's not meaning to, flows across my senses. The shattering in the depths of her silver pools causes mine to water. Not being able to bestow the endearment on her daughter herself is breaking her.

I see it. I feel it.

Obviously, it's Elema Lingua Vetus, but I've never heard those words before. There isn't anything in the language I don't know, which leads me to believe, if these are words no longer in our vocabulary, there's significance to why.

This moment feels larger than her asking me to address Willow by a nickname. It feels like she is blessing me with an honor far beyond my own comprehension or worthiness.

"I will. I promise," I swear and she nods, forcefully wiping away a stray tear.

"One more thing," she says as she swirls her hand in the air, opening a pocket dimension in front of me. "When the time comes and I must go, I've enchanted this so when my signature leaves this realm, it will appear in the house. Please make sure she gets it."

Passing me over a book, I trace the Nexus mark on the front cover. Such a powerful sigil that so few have ever and will ever understand.

Opening it to the first page, I run my hand down the blank cream parchment and the vibration of her enchantment and concealment tingles through my fingertips.

"How will she know to reveal it?"

Holding her hand out for it, I pass it over with no hesitation and watch, memorizing every move she makes so when my time comes, I know what to do. She shifts her index finger into a claw, and she presses it to her other one until a small trail of blood begins to run down her hand.

"Watch and listen closely. She needs to move the points counterclockwise and say what I say, okay?"

"Okay."

"Air, Earth, Water, Fire so bright,

Four elements, pure and right.

Remember these with joy and cheer,

The elements become one, the world becomes clear."

I repeat the enchantment in my mind at least a dozen times, as fast as I can until I know it's permanently imprinted on my mind.

It makes complete sense.

Knowing what Iris and Willow are, it fits perfectly.

"Got it?" she asks.

"I got it."

"I'm sorry for requesting so much of you. I know you already have the weight of the realm on your shoulders and I'm adding more to it. I'm sorry I won't be here to care for them. Either of them."

"Iris, do not look at it that way. You're not requesting anything of me that I wouldn't want to do. I'm sorry for keeping the truth from you for so long, but I didn't feel worthy enough for this blessing. I too am going to have to leave her. I've known when my time comes for a long, long time. I felt like I was stealing something from you, that is rightfully yours. You do deserve to be a mother," I admit quietly.

"You're stealing nothing. You're granting me a peace I never saw coming. Because of you, I know my daughter, my children will be okay."

"They will be. I swear it."

She smiles softly at me as she places her book back in her pocket dimension and closes it up. When she leans back against the bench, we both sigh at the same time. A small chuckle falls out of both of us as we notice her men standing on the porch, watching us keenly. Not for jealous reasons, or at least I hope not. More so protective because they felt her get upset.

"Should I tell them now or let it be a surprise?"

"A surprise. Make sure to wait until Kelso steps away from the stove before you say it." I smirk. I've already seen the excitement unfold.

"Do you know his name?"

"I do."

"Will you tell me?"

"No," I snort at her immediate growl. "The little wolf's name comes with a story to be told. You'll know soon enough. Have patience, old friend."

Standing, I offer her my hand to help her up and I throw my head back, laughing when she slaps it away. "Do not treat me like I'm fragile," she growls.

"Fragile, no. Hormonal already, yes," I tease and jump out of the way of her oncoming claw.

"Not funny. Damn, everything makes a lot more sense now. I threw a whole flower pot at Esben yesterday." She says it with a fond smile on her face like it's a precious memory and I look at her, a little petrified.

"Did you miss?"

"No. I never miss."

Laughing together, I walk her to her stoop where her men instantly surround her, checking her over from head to toe, and I do smile fondly at the display of affection. They're about to get ten times worse.

"Sure you don't have time for tea after all that?"

"I wish, old friend."

"Next time then," she says, waving me off as she climbs the steps to go inside.

"Next time," I murmur sadly.

I hate to know that the next time I see my friend, I will be sending her off on her final journey.

Blinking my eyes open, Willow is statue-still in my lap and I have to adjust my hold to check and make sure she's breathing. She is, but she's unnaturally calm and I immediately begin worrying I never should've shown her that.

"Willow."

"She's the most beautiful girl I've ever seen," she whispers.

"You take after her."

She slowly pushes herself up and turns around so she can face me fully. Those shattered silver eyes are so familiar, it's breathtaking.

"I'll never meet her in person, will I?"

"No, my sweet girl, you won't," I say as softly as I possibly can.

"Do you think she's watching over me wherever she is?"

"I know for a fact she is. She's in a place we call the beyond. It's where the most special and the strongest of our kind go."

"One day, I'd like to go there and visit her."

My heart clenches so hard, it steals my breath, and I have to force my lungs to take in air. I hope and pray she never ends up in the beyond. Despite that it's a paradise for those of us who perish before our time, I never want her time to end.

"One day, Elementra will show you her."

"And you'll give me my book? I'd like to read it now."

"You will as soon as the time is right, my girl."

I haven't the heart to tell her the book hasn't appeared yet. I'm the only one who can pass the barrier of Iris's ward, and I've checked multiple times. Finally, Elementra told me to stop, and it would show when it should.

She cocks her head to the side, and her calculating look quickly turns to devastation. I'm not sure why, or if maybe the reality of what she just watched is settling in and it's upset her tremendously.

"I'm sorry, Willow, maybe it wasn't the right time to show you that," I say, pulling her closer to me and hugging her tightly.

The Memoria stone around my neck heats at my command and just as I go to call for her memories to come to me, she speaks. Well, more so shrieks.

"You don't want me either, just like my father." She bursts into a fit of tears, attempting to shove away from me as hard as she can, and I'm completely caught off guard.

"Whoa, whoa, hey! What's that about? What are you talking about?" I ask, shushing her softly and moving the hair from out of her eyes.

"You've never called me your daughter or feely maya. She told you to and you never have." She sobs.

My eyes widen at the true hurt ripping through her right now. It's so strong, my soul is screaming at me to make it better this second. I didn't think she'd pick up on that so keenly. I really thought she'd be more focused on her mom.

"Hey, look at me, please."

She shakes her head forcefully, refusing to budge, but I try again.

"Please."

Sniffling and wiping a snotty nose across my shirt, she brushes the strands of hair from her face that I missed and looks at me with a trembling lip as I look down at the boogers on my shirt, smirking.

"You are my daughter, Willow, in all ways but blood. I haven't ever called you filia mea because I wanted you to know what it meant before I did. Once you give someone a title such as that, there's no taking it back. I wanted you to trust me, to realize how much you truly mean to me, how much I love you, and how proud I am of you.

"I wanted to earn those things in your eyes, and I wanted you to have the awareness," I say softly, tapping her temple, "to truly understand what all

that means. Just because we share a bond doesn't mean I'm entitled to your heart or your love. No one is. You choose when, how, and where to give that piece of yourself to someone else."

"And I don't have to if I don't want to?" Her small little voice makes my throat close.

I'm the adult here and I'd never make her feel bad for her feelings, but goodness if she were to tell me right now she doesn't love me, I'd go back to the palace and cry myself to sleep. This child has my whole heart.

"No, you don't."

"I don't love my father. My other one," she whispers so quietly it's as if she's afraid she might be overheard, but the word other plays in my head repeatedly.

"He isn't the realm's greatest dad. He does things that fathers aren't supposed to do and I'm so sorry for that," I say carefully. I'm always careful to watch what I say about him. The last thing I want to do is say what I really feel, and she go back and repeat it.

"I think you're the realm's greatest dad."

Dad...she just said dad.

Stay calm.

"I think you're the realm's greatest daughter."

Her sad frown morphs into the largest and brightest smile I've ever seen. It's like the sun has made a home within her and now it's trying to burst free.

Shit.

That's exactly what's happening.

She's glowing.

That's not supposed to be happening yet.

The coloring, just as fast as it started, begins to fade and I exhale slowly not to alert her to anything. I guess the range of emotions set something off.

Fuck, she's going to be a force of nature.

Poor Vito boys.

"Is it okay if I still call you CC?" Her question catches me off guard, and I give her a funny look that she giggles at.

"What else would you call me?" I ask, laughing as I tickle her when she pulls my arm hair for no reason at all other than to do something with her hands.

"Now that you've called me your daughter, that makes you my father. But I don't like the way father sounds in my brain. You're just my CC."

She says it so nonchalantly like it's a fact that she's always known and it's time I got with the program. This sweet girl has no clue she just caused my heart to explode. I've waited years for this moment.

I've thought about it countless times how I was going to show her the conversation between her mother and me. I had always planned some grand gesture with presents, pictures, food, the whole kit and caboodle, but there's a right time for everything.

And today, on this early spring day with the gentle rainfall, and her feeling so down, was the perfect moment.

"One day, you'll know so much more, but I want you to know now that your mother loved you, and I'm so grateful she gave me her blessing to call you and treat you as my daughter. Because that's what you are in my eyes. You're my daughter born from a bond instead of blood. And I love you, filia mea."

"I love you too, CC."

And that was the first time she ever said it back to me.

Twenty-Eight

Willow

The sobs that rip out of me when my mind becomes my own nearly split me in two.

My earth element bursts free with no command from me and wraps the branches of my tree around me in a cocoon. The woodsy smell mixed with a day of rain makes that entire memory settle into the compartments of my mind, finding their new home.

"CC," I cry out in my mind.

"I'm here, filia mea, and I always will be. See what your momma left you, my girl. You've both been waiting a long time for this."

Frantically, my eyes fly open, searching for the bound leather that I brought over here with me when I took this spot. My element frees me from its hug but bends my tree so much, I see no other part of my room as it conceals me. Just the shiny green leaves, the floor beneath me, and the black cover with the striking silver sigil engraved across.

Snatching it closer to me from where I apparently dropped it during the memory, I prick my finger and squeeze it to make my blood pool faster. As I lay my tip to the top point on the marking, another sob wracks my chest.

My lullaby.

She came up with half my lullaby.

CC the other.

I can't stop the tears, gasp, or hiccups no matter how hard I try. The shaking in my hands is so bad, I'm dripping blood all over my clothes, but my need to know outweighs it all.

"Air, Earth, Water, Fire so bright,

Four elements, pure and right.

Remember these with joy and cheer,

The elements become one, the world becomes clear."

Despite the fact it's a garbled, stuttering mess, magic sizzles through my hand and a light shock travels up my arm. I wholeheartedly welcome it. A laugh mixed with the downpour coming from me echoes around my isolated space and I slowly peel the cover back.

And wait.

And wait.

The longer I sit here staring and nothing happens, that elation I just felt starts to melt away, and I mentally beg for this not to be a joke. Please, Elementra, for all things, let this work for me.

Just as I go to fucking rage at the disappointment, a beautiful, black cursive script begins to draw itself out across the parchment.

Hello, my little dragonfly.

"Oh my God," I cry out loud, covering my mouth with my hand as I stare down at the book in amazement.

More and more words begin to show up and my eyes can't devour them fast enough. My heart is beating so fast, I'm surprised I can't see its rhythm through my skin.

"If you're reading this, baby girl, it means that it's your time.

Your time to learn who you are, who we are, our gift, and what that will mean for your future.

Before that begins to reveal to you, though, I just want you to know, Willow, I am so sorry. So, so sorry. To you and your brother. Nothing about any decision I ever made was made lightly or without the two of you at the forefront of my mind. If I could've, I would've chosen a thousand lifetimes to be with both of you.

I'm sorry that I never expressed my emotions and feelings about you to CC. I know if I had, he would've had more to share and explain. I never want you to think it was because I didn't want to talk about you or because of how you came to be. It was simply the fact that I had to keep you safe. Not that I didn't trust him with my true feelings. I didn't trust the realm. I didn't trust what could've been pulled from his mind. All the snippets of information we've had to leave for you, it was a risk I wasn't taking.

I feel bad for doing that to my old friend, but for you, your brother, there was no limit I wouldn't go to protect you.

CC worked very closely on ending the Mastery. He was in dangerous situations all the time, and he has kept that from you and his family for his whole life. You all may be aware now or at least assume it, but the fact of the matter is that back then, his knowledge was a threat to the Mastery, and he was in the trenches of the war. Right smack in the middle of it."

I breathe heavily as I read those words. They stick to me like glue and there's an inkling tickling my brain that I just can't grasp and pull out.

"CC, is that true?"

"My old friend is a snitch."

"Well, are you going to explain yourself?"

"Not at this time."

Groaning, I roll my watery eyes, then wipe them so I can focus on the words that continue to appear.

"Regardless of that, I want you to know, there's no other in the realm, aside from my own Nexus, I would have wanted to look after you. Knowing Franklin, I know you weren't protected from everything, but in my heart, I believe that CC gave you a piece of life you needed just as I asked him to."

He did. I promise he did.

I know she can't hear me, but I don't stop myself from mentally confirming it. He made life so much better. He took amazing care of me until he couldn't anymore.

"That leads me to my next point I'd like to discuss with you, and this is a difficult conversation, but you deserve the truth and much about your life to come.

Since my parents were on the run with me, I had to grow up far faster than many in Elementra. I didn't go to an academy. I didn't get to have other friends, just my parents. They did everything they could to prepare me for anything.

Then the day I emerged.

All the women in our family emerge at fourteen. It's always been unrecorded for our protection. Our Nexus members usually emerge earlier than most as well, except for yours. Yours emerged at fourteen to prepare for your coming. They had their own paths they had to pave before your arrival.

We knew and were ready for my emerging. Or so we thought. What we didn't expect was for Elementra to appear to me and tell me what the future of the realm held. What my future held. Her power coming through caused the entirety of mine to explode out far stronger than we thought possible.

I shifted into my wolf immediately and ran faster than the wind while she talked to me. My animal's mind was at the helm, running free, while I sat in the back and talked to Elementra. It didn't stay that heightened after she left me, but the consequences of that had started the timekeeper on my countdown.

I knew that day, everything, well, mostly everything, that was going to happen to me. That includes you."

Oh no.

Picking the book up off the floor from where I've basically hovered over it to read it, I lean back into the trunk of the tree so I can sit crisscross for this. I don't want to miss a thing, but I also feel like I need to be grounded to hear it. Whatever she writes, whatever she felt at the time, she has a right to those things.

Fuck, she was only fourteen, finding out pretty much her whole life.

"I convinced myself that since I knew it was going to happen, then I could accept it, not let it get to me and I would be fine until I could return to Elementra. Grit my teeth and bear it.

And that's what I did. I was fine while I was in the nonmagical realm.

Coming back home and meeting my men shattered my jaded reality.

The first time one of them touched me willingly, I panicked.

Our bond stepped in and calmed me, reassured me I was okay, and that helped, but my men took it upon themselves to shut down any more sexual attempts made by me. They wanted to reteach me what it meant to be loved.

I didn't know how to be touched tenderly, caressed, or wooed.

They had to reteach it all to me.

It took me many, many years to admit the fact that Franklin raped me. I'd trained my mind to believe it wasn't true because I knew what was to come and I didn't want you to know one day you weren't made from love.

You were and you weren't if that makes sense, but I wasn't going to have a way to show you that. You would only know him.

That's why it was so important to me to tell CC to show you as much love as he could. I knew it wouldn't prepare you romantically, but my mom's and dads' love held me together for the majority of those first twelve years.

It was around year ten, Franklin informed me that they were gone, and that seemed to shatter something inside of me. They were my hope, my heart, and I held onto the thought of them during the long nights.

I didn't know it would happen so soon. Their deaths made me angry, rageful, resentful. I'd run through in my mind what I thought was happening to them. If Franklin was draining me almost every day, they surely did the same to my mom. They probably made my dads watch. The thoughts and questions caused me to fight back, and I paid the price for it at every turn, but I didn't care.

I hated Franklin for all he had done to me, and I wanted to kill him. So many times did I want to unleash my strength and end his miserable existence. And I could have. I had a choice to make, though, as you well know, and I chose you.

Even as a young child, I knew I wanted to be a momma. Have a Nexus like my parents. I wanted men to shower me with affection and love the way my dads did my mom. So even at fourteen, I knew I wanted you.

I had loved you from the time Elementra showed me a little girl with silver and violet eyes that looked just like me. She told me your soul was in the beyond with her, asking a thousand questions, and I thought to myself, yeah, she's going to be mine.

"My, the questions I asked growing up. I needed an understanding of everything. You poor thing. You probably got a double dose of it being raised by CC. He asked more questions than even me."

Yeah, she's going to be mine.

Laying the book to my chest, I close my eyes as silent tears flow down my face. I let the claim I've desperately craved my entire life settle into the void in my heart that I thought I'd filled in with the family I've created and grown to love.

I knew a part of me would always be eager for her. I thought I'd done a good job of accepting the fact I'd never have her until I found out I had a brother, then I heard his sweet little voice call her momma. And then this book.

I've realized here lately, I want her badly. I want her love.

I'm getting it now. It's not conventional in any sense. But this was the way she was able to make sure I knew it.

Using my hands to wipe my face dry, then rubbing them down my thighs, I peel the book off my chest and pick up where I left off. If I get nothing else from this book but this note from her, I'll be okay.

I'll be better than okay.

"Elementra came to me a few more times throughout my life. Anytime there was a major change in the plans. Usually, her visits were accompanied by CC's either before or after. Sometimes there were years in between, but I knew that it would all line up.

When he came to visit me and informed me I was pregnant, I was around six months along when Elementra came to me. Told me the story of the wolf. It was my new path. My course had changed just a smidge with Lyker's upcoming arrival, and I had to begin making decisions for his future as well as yours.

The biggest decision was whether my men would accompany me on my return. There were two paths to that, and the only one that guaranteed Lyker's future was if they left him. Everything would've changed if they had stayed with him because they would've died eventually when I did, with

Lyker there to witness it. It would've started a devastating chain reaction for him. But I couldn't tell them that straight out.

So going against what I was told not to do, I only told Lyker one version of the story of the wolf. I'm sure Elementra knew, probably shook her head at me, but I had made my decision.

On the second return, they were my rocks.

Franklin was too consumed with himself and torturing us to concern himself with learning anything about my men. He'd torture them in front of me, he'd torture me in front of them, make us all watch, then lock us away in our cages every day. Separately.

But if he'd taken any time to know anything, he'd have easily found out that Allton and I could mend any metal. Those cages couldn't keep us apart and every day, after everything he'd done to me or them, we held each other close.

Day in and day out, Franklin would rape me, and I fell pregnant rather quickly, which was Elementra's interference. That shouldn't have been possible. He didn't touch me again after that, though. The deed was done, and he had no more use for me sexually. He found it vile to have sex with a pregnant woman, as he said, and I was beyond relieved.

So for the entirety of my pregnancy, I wasn't tortured or raped. Yes, he still drained my blood, but within the limits that Drin had told him was safe without harming you.

I spent those nine months in the arms of my loving men every chance I got. They'd rub my belly, talk to you, they staked their claim over you as though you were theirs. The first time they felt you kick was when Sedric was purring for me. You went crazy with your little legs, and they celebrated as if they'd just won a war.

I often referred to them as your fathers when I talked to you. They were in all things other than blood. They got to hold you before I did.

The morning you were born, Elementra came once again, but this time, not only to me but to my men. All she said was, 'It's time to come home.'

My contractions began picking up and my men couldn't take my pain anymore. They broke out of their cage and came to me. We knew what was coming and they refused to be without me.

Franklin found us or was more so told by Drin and he was furious.

My men easily could have killed him. I told them not to, but they could get a few swings in, although pointless.

Before they attacked, they each gave me a kiss and said they were going to meet our baby girl. I told them I'd see them soon.

They did beat the hell out of Franklin for a few minutes and I got a lot of satisfaction from watching, but when enough was enough, they stepped back and allowed his gift to overtake them.

Franklin was pissed, pumped from the boost in power flowing through him from the pain, and he ended them quickly. He left the room with instructions to Drin's aid to bring him the baby when it was born.

The second my soul split, my water broke.

I held you in my arms thirty minutes later.

Laying my forehead to yours, I tried to promise you the realm. I told you how much I loved you, and I hoped and prayed you got my strength. I named you Willow, and with a kiss to your little lips, my eyes closed.

And opened once again in the beyond."

My fingers trace the edges of the book, and my heart clenches in a way that's both familiar and unbearably foreign. I've felt the pain of grief before, but it's different mourning someone you didn't truly know, but love.

The parchment feels fragile as if it's holding not just ink and information but all the warmth and love of a life that never was shared. My trembling hands continue to glide softly over her words, careful not to get them wet or smear them.

Her handwriting is so smooth, so intimate, and it jumps off the page, tugging at something deep within me. It feels like she's speaking to me from the beyond, her voice a soft echo in my mind.

Wait...

I reread the last few paragraphs she's written again. My tears blur the words, but I push forward, trying to make sense of how this is possible. It's a story told that should have no possibility of being so.

Flipping the page, my eyes widen as more words begin to appear.

"Now you're a very smart girl. I know it because you have been blessed by so, so many and no daughter of mine would miss such a detail. So I know you're wondering how I wrote you my story when I was already gone."

A strangled laugh bubbles out of me as I smile down at the words. We must have been so similar for her to know that.

"Just as CC did—I'm pretty sure he stole the idea from me, by the way—I asked Elementra for a favor. It was my request that when I got to the beyond, I would be allowed to update my book for you. It's a snippet of my story that I wanted to share with you. She granted the request, even gave me a new method in which to rewrite it, on the condition that the information in this book reveals in the time it needs to.

That didn't settle with me well.

Like you, I wanted to know everything at one time. I hated the wait and I wanted instant gratification, but unfortunately, this isn't how these things work. Also, you, filia mea, are different than all the other women of our family. You will learn the knowledge in these pages differently than any before you and I'm so proud, happy that I get to walk this journey alongside you now. So nonetheless, I agreed. It's not a long wait, and I'm sure you've grown used to being patient."

No, no, I have not.

I snort at my mental argument. I have a feeling she was being sarcastic and that brings me a lot of joy. Her words are like a tender touch—a hug, a kiss on the forehead, a whispered 'I love you' that reaches me across an impossible distance. It's comforting and devastating all at once. I can almost feel her sitting beside me.

Wiping away another slow tear, I look back down at the new ink and my heart rate kicks up and I sit straight as a board.

"So without a further wait, my girl, you'll learn two major lessons. Each with their own little subsections you'll need to know. So here's the beginning of lesson one, handcrafted by me. Well, with Elementra's input.

Ultima unum. The Last One.

You will be the last to hold the ability that all the women of our line before you have been able to do. Manipulate the portals. There is so much more to your gift than this, but this is an ability you will not pass on and it's imperative to your current journey.

Starting strong with detecting the portals. Any and every one.

Repeat after me.

'Release to me the ties of time and space,

Deliver the information for me to embrace.'"

Without an ounce of hesitation or really any consideration, I call my magic forth and repeat her words.

The air in my lungs empties with my gasp, and I clutch my head as the words that are beginning to scribble out on the page are also scribbled across my mind. My eyes shift back and forth so fast, it's dizzying, and I have to look away from the book until the madness in my brain settles down.

The pages of the book flip repeatedly with no command from me or flick of my fingers, and as soon as it stops on an empty cream parchment, my mind stops moving as well.

"That's a nifty little gift you got from your dragon Nexus member, my girl. I'm a tad jealous I didn't get to learn this way.

Everything you need you should have in your mind now, but it's written here as well. I like the feeling of a book in my hand, and I figured maybe you would too, so I wanted it here for you if you ever felt like sitting down and reading.

Take a little break and process what you just learned. I'll be here, ready to discuss it and move on to the next mini lesson whenever you are.

I love you, filia mea.

Momma xoxo"

My body falls motionless, as do my tears finally, but my mind doesn't. Not with what feels like centuries' worth of information on the locations of the portals now settling in.

I can see the map of Elementra clearly as though I graphed it out myself.

In Aeradora, mixed within the massive Everest Trees, is one that the bark is cracked and breaking apart, but I can see it for what the large rectangular outline was. The twenty-five-foot doorway stood tall and shimmering green once before. The giants of Colosyree would pass in and out through there.

A swirling indigo pool, littered with sparkles now sits stagnant, dull, in a secret stream in the heart of Aquaria. Long ago, beings as beautiful and gorgeous as Aurora would step out of that water, glowing as though they always bathed in radiance. Not only beings that the nonmagical would consider angels but also demons. Shadows that almost match mine sit on top of the water like morning fog. That's the way to the Valorian Veil.

If you look closely enough, you can see a path carved out through the rocky, volcanic terrain of Pyrathia. Through those sharp turns, and possibly falling rocks, you'll come to what now just looks like an intricate stacking of stones. It used to be an archway adorned with glowing runes, leading you right into the heart of Mystara Hollow.

At the farthest end of Terian, where it borders Central territory, there's a huge cave mouth that looks home to the deadliest animals that may live in the forest. Its foreboding aura wards people away, but there's beauty in the structure of the cave. Prior to its gloomy appearance, the glow that the portal gave off from the back wall used to resemble light reflecting off gems. It created quite an art display.

The most astonishing thing about that cave is if it were only one hundred more feet inward, crossing the Central line, it would be in the Forsaken Forest. Where the residents who came out of the Essemist Keep portal now live.

Instead, they're trapped, one hundred feet from their way home, guarding the last of the portals.

Why it was such a shock to everyone when we found out from the Terravile elders that there was a portal in the Forsaken Forest is obvious now.

It's unrecognizable.

It used to be a lush, brilliant, and blooming forest, with animals, flowers, streams, everything. It was one of the most enchanting forests I've ever laid my eyes on in this entire realm. Those gnarled and twisted trees we saw when we went in have always been that way, but they had canopies that hung down to the ground, creating a secret escape and the most enticing place to explore or even relax.

Two things dawn on me as I metaphorically put my map up in my mind. Both realizations make me jump up, needing to find the guys, Gaster, Oakly, everyone.

Commanding my earth element to release the branches so I can be free of my hideaway, I race through the opening as soon as my tree stands back tall. I don't have to search far for my people, though. They're all standing in my lounge, waiting for me.

I can't contain the huge smile that crosses my face. It's so contradictory to the worried and concerned mask they all have written on their features.

Draken's eyes are the first to light when he looks down at what's in my hand. "You got your book open," he says excitedly.

"It's not just any old book or diary or anything I assumed it could've been," I breathe heavily as a laugh tumbles out of me. "It's my communal knowledge. She complied generations' worth of knowledge of who and what my family line is. She and Elementra handcrafted lessons for me to learn as we go."

His jaw falls toward the floor as he stares at me in astonishment. My gaze travels across the others and I chuckle at the mixture of responses I'm seeing.

There's a twitch on Caspian's lips that screams, told you so. It doesn't hide the shock in his whiskey eyes, though. Tillman's face is full of relief like he was battling not to reach out to me mentally while I was in there. Now that he knows everything's fine, his pride is starting to show.

Corentin is...huh.

Excited.

Studying his face, he's trying his hardest to keep a blank mask on, but I see right through it, and I burst out laughing. Crumbling that hard-ass exterior right down with the sound.

"You're really that excited to be finally getting my answers, huh?"

"You deserve them far more than I want them. But yes. It's driven me mad for months now not knowing how it's possible you do what you do, princess," he says with a smile to match my own.

I catch a glimpse of Gaster's tender look just before his long white beard begins shaking from laughter, joining the sounds of everyone else's. Oakly is beaming at me, and happiness for both of us surges from my bond to hers. We both had major wins in the learning department of our day.

I can't wait to tell them all everything.

"Oh shit, I forgot to tell you all what I was racing out here for. We don't have any recon teams on the main portals to the Valorian Veil or Essemist Keep. Just at the assumed ones, but both of those will actually lead to the nonmagical realm."

Well, that got everyone's attention.

Twenty-Nine

Draken

What a day.

I shake my head down at my communicator as I quickly shoot off a reply to Vince and one to Layton. We were right in the middle of a lesson when Willow's heartbreak speared through my chest.

The best I was able to growl out before transporting was 'I got to go.' I didn't get or really try to explain anything else, and so they've both messaged me, concerned.

Corentin, Tillman, and I all popped into Uncle Oreo's room at the same time, scanning the room for Willow. Oakly and Gaster were staring around, lookin' alarmed, and Caspian was pacing anxiously.

When Corentin went to storm from the room to find her, Cas stopped him. Told him to give her a minute, that she was trying again to get into her mom's book and to wait to see if she got it.

Us standing in there lasted all of ten minutes before his ass was the one to break first and shadow to the south wing. That was a torturous hour, waiting for her to emerge from the block her tree put up.

Since then, we've listened to the amazing story she had to share, followed by the plethora of information she now holds in her mind. It's the craziest shit I've ever heard, yet my dragon rumbled in my chest the entire time excitedly like he was witnessing his abilities unfold right in front of him.

Gaster and Keeper, since they're the only two who've actually passed through the portals, told her all about their experiences.

Gas-man explained that he never used the one she was describing to get to the Valorian Veil, so he offered her a chance to take a little peek in his mind to see which he did use. She squealed and lit up like a damn Star gem as soon as she recognized it as one her grandmother had opened. Her elated laugh fell after that when he explained he had no clue at the time which realm he was getting ready to travel to, but he was doing it for the thrill.

I thought it was hilarious. Willow did not. She said she's happy his mischievous days are over.

Her attention moved to Keeper after that, and he stated he used the main entrance. I guess in the Keep, there're also several portals and entry points to places, but he and Tanith exited through a cave here like the one Willow described. He didn't speak on it much after that. He got that faraway look in his eye. Willow immediately picked up on it and moved on. Or rather back onto the topic of her mom.

It's a breath of fresh air, honestly.

She's been glowing with more excitement in the last couple of hours than she has in the last few weeks.

I'm thrilled for her...

And jealous.

Sighing, beating myself up over the ridiculous envy I'm feeling, I slide my communicator into my pocket and lean back in my big-ass dragon chair. The paintings around my room make my beast purr happily in my chest, but my eyes and mind fixate on the one in the center of the bookshelves.

The majority of the people in this realm I consider as family are in that picture. There're even two additions that I'm slowly but surely bringing into the fold—well, really one. I've already claimed Tanith. She can't go anywhere.

And Keeper chips away at my resistance every single day.

Today was a big ol' knock off the ice around my heart toward him. It was like he knew something was wrong. He didn't say anything exactly straightforward, but when I left to come up here, get some space, clear my sad thoughts, he gripped my shoulder and said 'me too.'

Now I have no clue what that me too was directed at, but I've summarized it to two things.

One he misses his mom.

Or he misses mine. And that thought has had me spiraling.

I don't understand why he won't talk about her, but it's hypocritical of me at this point to get aggravated or upset with him over it because I refuse to bring her up as well. Their relationship is a mystery to me, and I don't want to tell him the truth and have him judge her. Or say anything bad about her.

I might kill him if he did.

A small snort escapes me when there's a knock at my door and I feel her standing there. I knew she'd been tapping against my bond, trying to figure out what was going on without invading all my privacy.

"Come in," I call out.

She opens the door and hastily makes her way through the frame before shutting it quickly. I arch a brow at her sneaky little movements and watch as she presses her ear to the wood to listen for noise in the hallway.

"What are you doing?" I ask, chuckling.

"I stole these for you. All of them so I was hauling ass before Gaster and Oakly noticed."

I throw my head back, laughing when she whips around with an entire bag of pastries clutched in her hand like they're a bag of jewels. The old man's been doubling his batches again now that I'm back to eating them, and she really did just steal every bit of them.

"Did anyone get any?" I ask.

"Nope, not even one. Oakly went to the bathroom when he brought them out, so I did a snatch and run."

We both laugh as she strolls across the room and plops down in my chair with me. She takes a pastry out of the bag and presses it to my lips, then grabs one for herself, and we groan at the same time.

"Damn, he's got this down pat. He sprinkles some shit in here to make them addicting, I swear," I say with a full mouth.

"Yeah, he'd never tell us. He'd say the secret ingredient is love."

Her mischievous giggle wraps around me like a hug and I pull her closer and bury my face in her hair.

My guilt about feeling jealous over her getting a piece of her mom that she one hundred percent deserves eats away at my heart. It's not the type of jealousy where I'm mad at her or feeling anything negative at all.

I just simply wish I had the same.

I feel like the realm's shittiest Nexus member for feeling this way.

"I need to talk to you," she says quietly as I assume my feelings right now drift into her.

"I'm sorry, Willow. I'm not trying to feel this way. It's such an asshole thing. That's why I came up here to give myself a minute to get over it," I tell her sincerely as I pull her completely onto my lap.

"You don't have any reason to apologize. At all. You don't think I felt this way about Corentin and Caspian a time or two?"

"You did?" I ask, shocked.

No, I've never thought that.

"Of course I have. Granted, I get neither of them act like or even say they need Aurora, but the way she's always been so caring, sweet, and there for them. Calling just to check on them and ask about their day. Yeah, I got jealous of it. I wanted that too."

I blow out a relieved breath and thank my fucking lucky stars. It still amazes me how she knows exactly what to say and when to say it, to make me feel better. It's something we both do often, but damn, it's a heady feeling every time.

I hope it always stays that way.

"It will. It'll probably get stronger as we go, but that isn't exactly what I wanted to talk to you about," she says, turning in my lap so she can look at me.

Her eyes can't lie. They've never been able to.

This is a big talk. Life-changing.

She nods slowly, and I mimic her. Whatever it is, is going to be fine, and I obviously need to hear it if she's doing this with just the two of us alone.

"Your mom was Keeper's beloved. His only beloved."

I startle at her words. That's not what I thought she was going to say. I don't know what I thought, really, but it sure as shit wasn't that.

"I'm sorry?" I ask, maybe say, I don't know.

"So..."

I listen as the story starts to unfold with her appearing in the forest on her little wander to the past and my heart feels like it's going to explode the more she talks.

The phantom feeling of that cold-ass forest causes chill bumps to break out across my arms, and a shiver races down my spine at her words. Hell, even my dragon ruffles himself out as her dark description of what she witnessed grows even darker.

"What do you mean a burlap sack?" I growl.

"All the women had sacks over their heads. He couldn't see the faces of any of them, but she stayed strong, and he picked her," she says softly, running her hand down my chest to settle my rumbling.

At my nod, she carries on. This is hard to hear, but I need to know now.

The soft smile that she has as she describes how my mom's voice was so gentle yet sassy when she smarted off to Keeper that first night pulls a watery laugh from me. I hear in my mind the exact tone she's talking about. She never spoke to me like that, but the ladies at the brothel got it, especially in the morning at the breakfast table.

I chuckle a little harder at the fact that they apparently argued quite a bit over food. Mom wasn't Chef by no means, but she kept me fed, every meal. Breakfast, lunch, and dinner.

Even so high she didn't know her own name, she always kept me fed.

Willow's eyes begin to water when she talks about their fight and how my mom ran. A mixture of fear and anger swells within me at the picture I paint in my mind. I've seen my little wanderer get bit by a vampire, so it's easy for me to just see the same thing happening, but to my mom. It's petrifying, heartbreaking, and makes me want to burn down the whole fucking forest.

There's a smidge of satisfaction in me knowing Keeper tore them all apart, but it doesn't come as a surprise to me. He's proven to be the type who when someone he cares about is hurt or in danger, he acts first.

It's something I've found I like the most about him.

I may not have accepted our relationship fully yet, but I know without a doubt that he'd protect me, her, my brothers, any of us if need be. I trust that completely.

"The Summum-Master said he'd heard, like the vampires were just strolling around the fucking forest gossiping?" I ask skeptically as she gets to the part about Keeper being summoned.

Gossiping seems like a pathetic fucking pastime for hundreds of years old vampires.

"I've assumed that up to this point, well, up to Renic," she says.

"The vampire we just captured?" I ask, but then it all clicks together for me. "He's the one who told the Summum-Master about their relationship."

"Yeah. The only other part I don't know the truth about is the comment about her scent changing. I don't know if that's a vampire bonding thing, or...they could smell that she was pregnant."

"But if they could smell that, he would've been able to, right?" My eyes widen with that thought. That answer will change it all.

I mean, I don't necessarily know how because it doesn't sound like he had much of a choice but to let her go or she'd get brought into the Mastery. But if he knew, he's done a hell of a job acting like he didn't.

"I don't know. He's going to have to answer that for you," she says gently, lacing her fingers through mine.

Yeah, I'll need that explained to me.

"I know what you've been fearing, and I understand. I'm not hurt, upset, or anything of the sort, Draken. It's a fear anyone who has experienced what we have would naturally fear, but I want to reassure you, you don't need to be afraid of that. I can prove it, if...you want to see this next part," she says, looking down at her thumb running circles on my hand.

Fuck, she always sees right through me. And calls me out just at the right time.

When her shattering eyes meet mine, a lump forms in my throat. Her showing me whatever comes next, I know I'm going to have to face two things that I really want to, but at the same time, as she said, I'm petrified too.

One, I'm going to have to see my mom. For years, I've painted the prettiest picture of her in my head. I don't want to sully it. I want to hold onto the childlike wonder I had of her.

Two...I'm going to have to see how Keeper truly felt about her.

I need the truth, but I don't. I do.

Fuck, this is about to be painful.

I nod slightly, and she mimics me, then lays her forehead to mine and throws us right into the past. In the middle of a bloodbath.

Keeper's tearing men apart left and right with no fucking care in the realm. No one that's in his vicinity is safe. He demolishes them as if it's nothing more than a walk in the forest.

The entire time, he screams in rage. It's so clearly written across every swipe of his dagger-like nails or in the tearing of body parts. I swear, I can sense his anger like it's my own.

Once he's finished, he breathes heavily, then zooms back through the forest and a sense of shock rushes through me when he bursts through the door of a home.

And I see her, my mom. Well, I can't see her fucking face because of that sack, but I know it's her. I'm so frozen in my own mind, I can't do anything but watch.

"Oh, Elementra. What happened?" she shrieks, jumping up from her seat and rushing to him like all she cares about is making sure he's okay. He pulls her in close, presses his face into her neck, and takes a deep breath.

I swear he and I exhale at the same time.

A shuddering breath that I can't control right now falls from me at the sound of her voice. Fuck, I've missed that sound. Her singing, her nighttime stories. Sometimes the words would slur, but they were still gentle and comforting.

"It's time for you to go," he says tenderly.

"What?" she asks, taken aback by his words.

"The others have told the Summum-Master about you, about us. He's showing keen interest now. You must go."

Her head shakes back and forth furiously, and she latches on to the burlap sack still hiding her face from us.

"Why...why can't I stay with you?" she asks, choked.

"Because he will use you against me. He will make you suffer, just to control me. I can't allow that to happen. I can't watch that happen because I won't be able to protect you from what he will do. My life is in his hands, and he will continue to hold whatever he can over me. That now includes you."

"Keeper. I don't want to leave you." She cries and my heart cracks open.

"I wish you didn't have to, beloved, but you must. You must live for yourself. For us. Please, do not fight me on this. It'll only make it harder."

Beloved...

Keeper wraps his hand around the back of her head and holds her against his chest. Her cries seem endless and the longer she pours her heart out, the more mine breaks.

Witnessing what my parents could've been is gut-wrenching.

Gently picking her up, her arms wrap around his neck, while her legs circle tightly around his waist, and they're off.

A decade feels like it passes as he just runs. It's as if he was trying to find a place so far in the forest, maybe they both could've escaped.

But the end of his line finally comes, and the dark ward comes into view.

"Do one thing for me before you go, beloved," he whispers when he sets her down.

"Anything."

"Take off the mask."

She trembles at the request but nods nonetheless and I hold my breath.

Her hands shake uncontrollably as she slowly pulls it off, and her midnight black hair is the first thing I recognize. I used to brush it and play with it. All the women at the brothel used to sit around and do each other's hair.

I thought I was supposed to as well.

"You're the most gorgeous creature I've ever seen," Keeper mumbles with wide ruby eyes, then leans forward to lay a kiss on her forehead. "Do not wait for me, my beloved, but know that one day, I will find you, and I will give you all of me."

"I'm already yours, Keeper, and I'll love you even after my last breath. There is no other."

She presses her lips to his fiercely. Through her tears, through her obvious hesitancy and want to stay, she kisses him like she knows this is goodbye forever.

And sadly, it is. When she drifts through the ward, he may not have known then, but I do. That's the last time he'll ever see her.

I'm glad he stayed there watching her until he couldn't see her any longer.

The soft glide of hands across my wet face pulls me the rest of the way out of my mind, and I kiss the tips of my little wanderer's fingers as they rest on my lips. I can't bring myself to open my eyes just yet. I just want to see my mom's face for another second.

Even heartbroken, she looked happy and healthy.

She was always beautiful to me, but she seemed truly in the best condition she was ever in, in that forest with him.

That fear that's kept my mind and heart at a distance from Keeper's settles with the knowledge that they were in love. They definitely attempted to fight it, probably even denied it to themselves every day, but you can't truly fight that kind of love. It happens fast and most times, unexpected.

When we found out what Franklin did to Willow's mom, I was horrified, disgusted, and obviously was ready to kill him. Unfortunately, when who Keeper was to me was revealed, that was the first accusation and assumption that came to my mind.

It wasn't logical. I know that now. The way he acts toward me, all of us, doesn't fit the characteristics of someone who'd do something so vile to a woman.

But nonetheless...I was afraid I was a cruel monster, made by one.

"Thank you for showing me," I murmur after I clear my throat.

"You don't have to thank me. You deserve the truth...So does he," she says softly and I finally peel my lids open.

"You think I should bring this up to him? Tell him what happened to her after this?" I ask, shocked.

I think it'll break him.

I know a man in love when I see one.

I am said man. So are my brothers.

"I do. You both have been avoiding talking about her, and I think talking about it will break this barrier between the two of you."

"Yeah, or it might just break the relationship we're starting to build."

"The relationship is being built on rocky terrain, dragon," she says lightly but matter-of-factly. "Keeper has gone all in with you, yes, but he's got some deep anger buried down, just as you had your fear. I don't think he's going to be able to get himself out of it without your help. He also may have answers you want."

The knowing look in her eye tells me everything. She truly believes this conversation needs to happen and I'm going to have to be the one to approach him about it. Tanith's already told me he isn't going to push, and this conversation would be just that. So I'm going to have to do it.

"I'll talk to him," I agree.

"Good. Sooner rather than later," she says, smiling.

"That can mean many things, little wanderer," I tease, and she rolls her eyes.

"I know, but the plans have changed. We're leaving tomorrow now. We need to make sure the main portal to the Valorian Veil is closed, and Corentin said we can't rush off today and haphazardly do this, but we have time to arrange to leave tomorrow."

"That's probably a good idea. If there's one thing we know, shit surely can change in a day," I say both seriously and cryptically.

She sees it for what it is, though.

I don't know how this conversation will change things, but it will, and it's best I do it before we all venture on another possibly dangerous mission.

"He's outside with Tanith. Moping, according to her."

"Damn, she can be mean sometimes." I chuckle.

"Feisty, blunt, yes. I wouldn't say mean, though."

We both laugh a little at that, and she runs her hand around the rim of my mating mark through my shirt as I sigh. The tender touch of her fingers and eyes as she gazes at exactly where she knows her teeth imprints are calms my rising nerves.

"Come on then, little wanderer. Let's get this over with," I say, standing us both up.

"I'll walk you to the garden, dragon, but that's as far as I go."

Damn. It was worth a shot.

"Everything's going to be okay. I think this will go a lot better than you think," she says, squeezing my hand as we make it down the hall.

Then her ass pulls a Caspian and whisks me through the shadows with no warning, and I grumble as she spits us back out right at the gardens.

"You said you'd walk me to the gardens."

She laughs, shaking her head at me before pressing up on her toes to give me a kiss on the cheek. "You're stalling. If I had let you walk all the way here, you'd have found a way to distract me."

Yes, yes, I would have.

I know, ridiculous.

Blowing out my breath, I lay my lips to her forehead. "I needed the push. Thank you."

"Anytime, Draken."

Her hand grips my arm as she turns to walk away, and her smile speaks a million words. If she believes this is going to go better than I think, then I'll just think it's going to be great.

Forcing my feet to work, I walk around the bend in the garden and chuckle as Tanith and Keeper come into view.

He most certainly is moping.

He's kicking at grass, pacing back and forth, and Tanith huffs, rolling her eyes every few steps he takes. I wonder if that's what I look like when I sulk.

Probably exactly like that.

"Oh, thank goodness, young lord. You're here to rescue me from this imprisonment," Tanith says and I hide my smirk behind my hand when Keeper whips around, glaring at her.

"Are you comparing my company to being locked away?"

"Obviously."

"Ungrateful dragon," he sneers and I do chuckle then. So does Tanith. "Draken, I thought you and your beloved were discussing our new plans for tomorrow?" he asks me, way nicer than he spoke to Tanith.

The reply to his question runs through my mind, and I tell myself to say we did, then start a conversation from there and easily lead into what I want to talk about, but that's not what my mouth does.

"She was your beloved. You loved her. Willow just showed me."

His whole body falls statue-still and he doesn't hide anything as his face crumbles. I mean, just flat out falls apart. Gone is the happy, cheery, teasing personality that I know I get from him, and in front of me stands a shell of that man.

"Oh, this would be my cue to leave," Tanith says, and with a few beats of her wings, she's gone, but me and Keeper never break eye contact.

"I wondered when the Adored would tell you. I'm surprised she waited as long as she did," he says mournfully.

"She's pretty proficient with timing. She always knows when it's the right time, or at least something tells her when. So...it's true? I mean, I kinda saw it with my own eyes, but I'd like to hear it."

He closes his eyes and his head bows low. "Yes, it's true."

"You didn't want it?"

"What? No, of course I did," he immediately says as his bright ruby eyes fly up to mine. "I was...I was just a fool, Draken. I should've released her from the forest the second I felt anything. I never should've let it last as long as it did."

"Don't do that. Don't say regretful shit like that with me standing here coming to you for answers. I won't be made to feel even more like a mistake, especially not by you. I've experienced it my whole life," I growl.

I don't mean to jump straight to being defensive, but the deed is done. I'm here in the flesh now. There's no changing that.

He's on me in the blink of an eye. I've grown used to tracking him, so I knew he was coming, and I don't move as he lays his hands on my shoulders. "That is not what I meant by any means, son. Nothing about you is a mistake. Not a thing. Not how you became and not what you've become. I have zero regrets, but I am riddled with guilt."

"Can you just explain it all to me?"

He stares into my eyes for a hot minute, and I let him see the want, need I have for these answers. I feel like a child begging for a scrap of anything he's willing to throw at me.

"The bond between Eryken..." he stops, shaking his body out as if it pains him to say her name. Honestly, it kinda hurts me to hear it.

"The bond between your mother and me was vastly different than with Tanith and me. Whereas in the Keep, it was an immediate feeling. Here, it was too late for me to notice. It was as though the way in which you all bond was merging with my nature. Everything about our relationship was like the two realms colliding. The bond took time, slowly developing as I've heard that it happens with awakenings, yet I felt protective over her the second I was a few feet in front of her.

"We fought, and we fought. Endlessly really. Then we talked, spent time together. I learned your mother was incredibly smart, had a voice that could lull me to sleep, she loved art, and had an imagination of a storyteller. It wasn't until after she was free, I realized, those were our challenges. We were matched in both strength and intelligence.

"I was so naïve not to see it or maybe I simply didn't want to, I'm not sure, but in my mind, I'd deemed it impossible. An actual bond hadn't snapped in place, so I firmly told myself it was my loneliness clouding these crazy feelings I was having. The first time I called her my beloved, it had slipped out, but it felt right. It was the first thing that felt right since I became imprisoned in that place. So I told myself, she could be that for now."

The way his eyes lit up when he spoke about the things he learned about her and the emotion in his voice now make my heart pound against my rib cage painfully. I don't want to tell him what became of her.

"Did you know she was pregnant? The comment about the scent," I choke out.

"No, I didn't. If I did, I would've hidden her so far into the forest, she never would've been found. I would've made every vow possible to keep her safe. The scent that the other vampires smelled was the bond and the pregnancy. It's not something I would've picked up on. That should've been another thing that told me the truth, but I refused to accept that.

"When a beloved is claimed, the smell of their blood changes, but not to their other half. They will always smell the same. Your mother always smelled like Estra fruit. A very popular delicacy from the Keep. She smelled like home." He pauses, taking a deep breath.

"Her scent would've started changing for them, warding them away from her. The pregnancy would've solidified that because they would've started catching her scent and mine, mingled. I would've known eventually. Once the taste of her blood changed."

He doesn't look at me when he says that, thankfully, 'cause I grimaced. "So if the bond never snapped in place, is there a possibility she wasn't your beloved?"

It's not that I'm doubting he loved her, it's very clear in every word, every expression, but I can't imagine what it feels like. If I had lost Willow before we bonded, I know a part of me would never be the same. There'd be a hole the size of this realm in my heart.

I don't want that for him.

He closes his eyes once more, and my body startles when a tear slides down his face. I want to take my question back. I want to rewind time by twenty-five seconds and never let the words come out of my mouth.

"The moment she crossed through the ward, our bond solidified. I couldn't do anything but stare as my entire life walked away from me because I told her to. She had to."

Fuck.

"I'm so sorry," I whisper. I don't know what else to say.

The devastation rolling off him is suffocating. It's pounding against my lungs like I'm reliving my own grief and now his.

"There's nothing you have to be sorry for. I am. I'm so sorry I wasn't there for the two of you. If I had been, she'd still—"

He can't finish the sentence, and I don't want him to either. It'll lead to me having to tell the story and fuck me, this is going to be so much harder than I thought.

"Start nice and slow, young lord. Tell him the happy things. Not all of them but start there and end there."

Peering out of my peripheral, Tanith is nestled in the tree line, watching us keenly. I was too caught up in his story to notice her spying.

"Thought you were giving us some space?"

"I could no longer ignore the call to come. He is in pain. But he must break before he can rebuild."

"Fuck me. I don't want to break him."

"I'm sorry, but you must."

I'm already telling the alternative story in my mind. The one I've crafted over the years. It's all a lie, all an escape from reality. That's the version I'm prepared to give him so I don't have to do what Tanith just told me to. But Willow's words ring in my mind.

The relationship is being built on rocky terrain, dragon.

We can rebuild.

"She got better at cooking. At least I suppose she did. It was all I knew, and it was edible," I say.

"Edible is the key word." He snorts, showing the barest amount of happiness at that.

"She liked to tell me stories. I always thought she just made them up as she went, but I think they were stories about the two of you, just with a twist to them. The main characters always fell in love and had a happy ending."

I don't stop talking. I tell him almost everything I can remember. I search into the depths of my mind, as far back as I can go, and let it all free. Years of memories that I haven't spoken about in all the time she's been gone, but I give it to him so he can share it with me.

Then, I break his heart.

"She was a sex worker and a drug addict who died of an overdose when I was four. Everything I just told you all happened in the brothel we lived in and she died in. They kicked me out that same day, and I lived on the street for over a month until a farmer adopted me and abused me until my gift emerged. Then I killed him, ate him, and came to live here with my brothers."

He stumbles back from me like I just rocked his jaw, more like his whole world and his eyes shift to blood red. The smile that was plastered on his face melts away as he shakes his head back and forth.

"No...no. You said she was a good mother."

"She was, in the way she knew how. But there was always something inside of her missing. Of course, as a child, I thought she was perfect. As a teenager, I hated her. Until recently, I accepted that she was a good mom in her own way. She did take care of me, clothe me, feed me, love me, but something was broken in her that could only be fixed with the bandage of a drug. I loved her very much, and it's taken me a long time to come to terms with it. Honestly, I never would have if not for Willow showing me how to look at things from other perspectives, but...I forgive her."

My body slouches with my confession and the weight of that truth lifts off me, making me feel twenty feet tall, but it seems to crush him. His body vibrates like it's taking every bit of his strength to keep from being buried beneath it.

The wind from his speed nearly knocks me to my ass. It's a burst of raw power and my eyes scan the surroundings, looking for him, but all I see is plants, scrubs, and dirt flying in the air. The roots being snatched from the ground sound like bones breaking as he annihilates the garden. Thank fuck no one is out here but us because he's completely lost it.

Tanith finally emerges from the tree line, rumbling, purring, doing everything she can to calm him down as he absolutely snaps, but nothing works.

"Go to him, Draken. Do not allow him to lose himself to his grief. If he does something horrid in this fit of rage, he will never forgive himself."

She starts up a hum in my mind and my eyes bug out of my head.

What the hell—

"How do you know that song?"

"Your mother taught it to him."

You're kidding me.

Turning back to him, I sprint to the garden and focus my eyes on finding and tracking him. It takes longer than it has lately, but as soon as I do, I throw a fireball in front of him to slow him down long enough so I can tackle him.

Our bodies hit the dirt with a deafening bang and a cloud of dust covers us as we roll. He tries to shove away from me, but my dragon flies forward, evening our strength.

Getting him pinned, I start humming.

Repeatedly, the little melody my mom used to sing to me vibrates through my throat and the grip he has on my biceps loosens as his eyes slowly shift back. When I think he's in control enough not to fuck anything else up, I get off him and offer him my hand. Never missing a beat of my song.

Standing tall, he quietly mumbles the last few lines of the chorus with me and as our notes end, he exhales sharply.

"I'm so sorry, son. I will be everything I can and more for you. I will make up for it all and be the father you deserve," he says, laying his forehead to mine.

"I'd like that a lot," I say, and a shock passes through me.

The same shock I felt in my dragon form, but this time, it warms my body, spreading everywhere until it settles within my blood.

"Congratulations, young lord. You've accepted your father's bestowing."

Thirty

Willow

Today's going to be great.

My breathing stays even as the air in my lungs empties through my mouth and my heart rate stays a calm, gentle rhythm. The sun is just now rising above the trees, and I tilt my head toward it, seeking its heat.

I, according to Tillman, was a little too excited for this mission and he instructed me to come simmer down. He's in full leader mode, and the rest of my men are preparing for battle. My apparent cheeriness was making them nervous.

I can't help it, though.

Unlike any other mission we've been on, I haven't had to keep any secrets from them. I don't have any gut-wrenching feelings telling me something is going to go wrong, nor have I been plagued with awful visions. I mean, aside from the one that'll happen if this does go wrong, but it won't.

I refuse to accept it.

Regardless, I guess I was being a little too optimistic for my men this morning, so I was ordered to come balance myself out.

I don't mind, though, because after I found my balance, I started running through everything on the portals and everything that's been discussed since then. I have all the faith in the realm now that I'll be able to detect if any of the portals have been open. I already know for a fact I'll be able to tell if any of the makeshift ones my mom, grandma, or any before them opened are still open.

Tracking those will require me to bleed into the ground, connecting myself to the fabric of Elementra. Almost like Oakly's imprint. The difference is I'll be sending and receiving a signal from each individual portal, and its vibration will tell me if it's closed, open, even if it's been recently used.

My body will pretty much turn into a radar.

Explaining to the guys this process last night did not go over well. The second they heard I had to cut myself, they were already shutting it down. I went ahead and told them then, any and everything to do with a portal will require me to bleed.

We pretty much knew this from Franklin's and the Summum-Master's obsession with it, but none of us, not even me, truly understood. What I learned opened my eyes to the reality that even getting a sense of the strength of a portal will take a drop of blood. Nothing can be done to them without it. That's why they've always been so adamant about having a stockpile.

Their extreme reactions came from knowing how much I hate getting my blood drawn. Their minds immediately flashed back to my kidnapping, and their consideration of my feelings melted my heart. I'll admit, I felt a little queasy at first, but realizing that I was in control—doing this to myself, not having it taken from me—helped ease my anxiety over having to cut my palms open, possibly often.

They grumbled for a good few minutes before Tillman finally accepted it and Gaster said enough, it was the way it was and that'll be that. His no-nonsense on my behalf will always make my heart happy.

Once they were all on board, Corentin had a plan in place, ready to go. Tillman decided to switch some things up and instead of taking multiple palace E.F. teams, it would just be our Nexus, Oakly's, Lyker's, Keeper,

Codi, and Trex. All the recon teams who are currently positioned at the portals will be on standby for his call if we need them after we track my blood.

Caspian tore everything apart to the bones. Every step of the plan, my new knowledge and how easy it is for me to access it in a split second, Oakly's and my ability to track my blood. He asked question after question until he was finally satisfied with the answers.

But there was one question he didn't ask, that I thought for sure he would. Instead, it was Draken who caught on to the fact I can't do my little radar checking on the main portals.

There was fire in Caspian's eye when Draken called him out for that. Twenty more minutes of grilling ensued after I informed them that the main portals are too ingrained in the fabric of Elementra. It would take far too much blood and energy for me to sense them farther away and even then I could only do one at a time. It's faster and safer for me to go there physically.

No one had any objections.

With one more round of my breathing technique, I stretch my arms above my head, then push up off the ground. My moment of settling myself and thinking through everything did, in fact, calm my excitement, but I'm just as confident today as I was when I first perched my ass in the dewy morning grass.

"About time, Willy. Thought you'd done come out here and fallen asleep," Oakly teases from a few feet behind me, causing me to jump.

"First of all, you just scared the shit out of me. I didn't even hear you coming. Second, I haven't done anything today to deserve the name-calling." I smirk.

"As a matter of fact, you did. All your damn giddiness has got them in there freaking out. I just got kicked out and told to come find you and make sure we're ready to track your blood."

"I don't know why my good mood freaked them out so bad. You'd have thought it'd do the opposite," I say, shaking my head.

"Not on mission day, apparently. They've grown used to the chaos. This is too calm for them. All the reports are too good, the realm still hasn't had any attacks, you aren't riddled with worry or the tense energy you carry when you keep secrets. They're thrown all the way off," she scoffs playfully.

"Well, in that case, we can stay out here, and when they've figured out everything they need to, they can come find us."

Not needing any more convincing to stay away from the command room, she plops herself down, laughing. I follow suit and grab her book of relics that she passes to me.

"Put this in your pocket dimension for me just in case we do come across some crazy-ass shit," she says.

"It's about time you make one of your own. It's like a purse that you never have to actually carry."

"Yeah, a purse that knocks you on your ass when you make it. You sound like Gaster. He's been harping on me about it too."

"Then after this mission, that's what you're doing." I chuckle as she throws a handful of grass at me.

I'm pretty sure a few pieces fall into my pocket dimension, but after going shoulder deep, not being able to feel for them, and her just laughing at me like it's hilarious, I give up.

"Okay, on a serious note, how do you feel about tracking today? Good, bad, scared, confident? Anything you want or need to go over?" she asks.

"I mean, I'm a little nervous but still feel pretty confident. I didn't until we tracked Vince by his blood, and getting that right helped because I have no connections to him, so I didn't feel like I was aided in any way."

"Yeah, that was a perfect track and imprint as well. I honestly think this is going to be even easier since it's your blood and we'll be doing it together. I've got complete faith in you," she says, tapping her shoulder to mine.

"Thanks. I really do have a good feeling about today. I'm not bull-shitting or hiding anything, I swear. I have no clue how getting the blood and destroying it is going to go, but you've been nonstop reading, remem-bering. We've trained as hard as we possibly can. I've got faith in everyone today."

"Good. I don't want to hear any more shit from those men then."

"And what shit are you referring to exactly?"

She squeals as Ry's voice sounds from behind us and I peer over my shoulder to see him and Tilman standing there with their arms crossed, staring down at us. I heard their approach but didn't say anything because I wanted them to hear what I was saying. I should've known she was going to talk shit, though.

"You men freaking out about today. You all don't know how to react to just a calm, cool, easy mission," she says as she climbs to her feet, giving me her hand and pulling me up.

"Nothing about any mission is easy. Especially adding you two in the mix," he says, glaring at both of us as we share a look.

"He may have a point," I say.

"Don't tell him that."

Tillman's stern look cracks and the minuscule twitch on his lip tells me he heard that. "Time to go. Ready, little warrior?" he asks before I can call him out.

"Been ready since I woke up."

As we make our way through the freshly restored gardens—compliments to Tillman—Ry and Oakly can't resist their playful bickering. Their banter echoes off the new flower beds and bushes while in my head, Tillman's amused voice chimes in, mocking them about their weird love language. I can't help but laugh, earning curious glances from the two lovebirds and everyone else who's waiting for us right outside the garden path.

"You do look as excited as they warned," Lyker says, cocking his head to the side before swallowing me up in a hug.

He was thrilled when I called him last night and told him I got into Mom's book. He's been so busy lately with getting everything ready to break ground on his new academy, we haven't seen each other. Just the daily messages or calls.

Being able to spend more time with him is one of the top things I'm looking forward to on my list when we get this shit over with. Talking through a communicator is all fine and dandy if it means I get to hear from him, but nothing beats spending quality time together. I want to stay at

Mom's house, visit his pack lands in detail now that it's not overrun, and just spend time with him, his brothers, and Aria.

"I've settled my excitement down as per their request. I just found something funny as soon as we walked up," I say, cutting my eyes over to Tillman.

"Well, show me this magic trick they were telling me about then, little dragon." He smirks, winking at me.

Little my ass.

My men surround me as soon as Lyker steps away and the nervousness that was ringing like an alarm through my chest from them earlier is still present. I don't believe it's going to fade, so I straighten my shoulders, let my smile slip away, and hope the seriousness in my expression will settle them.

"You ready, Primary?" Caspian asks.

"Yeah, I'm ready," I say firmly.

"Good, princess. Once you do this and verify all the individual portals created are closed, we'll move to the main portal in Pyrathia for Mystara Hollow. It's the hardest to maneuver and less likely to have any activity. From there, Aeradora for Colosyree, Aquaria for the Valorian Veil, ending at Terrian for Essemist Keep and so Keeper can check on the vampires right there and the nonmagical realm. Missing anything?" Corentin asks. We've been over it a thousand times since yesterday, but I still appreciate him checking with me.

"Nope, perfect, your highness."

I receive a kiss from each of my men, relishing the subtle shift in their moods. I know missions are nerve-wracking, and I'd never downplay that—just because I'm feeling confident today doesn't mean I'm not mentally prepared or in denial that something could go wrong. There's always the possibility and likelihood, but I'm not going to worry myself sick with nerves when I have no reason to this go around.

I slip off my shoes and walk away from the group, each step paired with a slow, steady breath. The earth hums beneath my feet, grounding me, and I focus on centering myself in its steady pulse, merging with Elementra's raw strength.

My knees sink into the wet grass on my final exhale, bolstering the connection I started with each step. I rub my palms down my thighs a couple times, then turn them upward, calling forth a shift in my index fingers.

I begin on my right palm, carefully tracing the mark of the Nexus. This time, I only need one layer instead of all five. With steady hands, I repeat the process on my left palm, then hold them together, feeling the warmth of blood pooling between my fingers.

As the river of red starts to drip through, I open the earth beneath me. It mixes with the soil, turning to thick mud as I focus, gripping tightly onto the fabric of the connection buried within. The threads of magic tug at my own, and I set it free.

"Passages through time and space, show me your travels through this blessed place."

With my hands pressed into the now damp earth, the ground trembles faintly as my magic spreads outward. Like a ripple in water, my blood forms invisible vines, snaking through the territories in all directions, seeking the portals scattered across the realm. Little throbs vibrate beneath my skin, reverberating through my bones, each one distinct, each one carrying its own unique frequency.

Then the first true pulse hits me.

It sends a buzz through my mind—a soft, gentle breeze. There's no huge punch of power or overwhelming flow of energy. It's just...there.

It's closed.

I allow myself just a fleeting moment to cherish it—the first time I've ever wielded the power that has only passed through the women in my family. The weight of that hums through me, but I quickly refocus as the next pulse comes.

Closed.

Closed.

Closed.

My body feels electrified. The thump of the earth beneath me flows with every beat, every vibration, as I map each portal's status across Elementra. The farther I push, the fainter the connections become, but the fabric of the realm remains ever present, its web of energy binding me to each closed portal.

As the vines of my blood reach the end of the territory's lines, they snake their way back to me, and the tie to Elementra slowly starts to recede. The connection breaking isn't a forceful one—I'm not shoved to the ground like when I closed my pocket dimension for the first time. It's a gentle, tender release.

"Very, very good, filia mea. That was perfect. One step closer."

The pride in CC's voice reverberates through my body, adding to the lingering small aftershocks of the portal's pulses. My skin shivers from both it and my water element flowing out to clean my hands off.

"Thank you for being here for this."

"I'll never miss the big things, filia mea."

A warm smile crosses my lips, and I push myself up to stand, commanding my air to dry the water from my pants around my knees. That small breeze seems to be the only circulating air around. My anxiously waiting Nexus and family behind me sucked it all up, holding it in while they waited for me to finish.

The glow on my face stays in place as I turn to face them. "They're all closed."

There's an explosion of excitement as I'm surrounded by my guys. Their feverish kisses and praises are heady and I snicker at how the roles have suddenly reversed. I'm as calm and focused as I've been all morning, while all of them are jumping with joy.

I'm ambushed with sweet smiles, tight hugs, and warm endearments by everyone else when my men give them room. It's emotional, thrilling, and settling all at once. Of all the things I'm able to do, that felt more natural than any of it. There was muscle memory within me, that's never been present before, guiding me, coaching me, and silently supporting me from the depths of my mind.

"Using the knowledge of those before you is a sensational experience, Adored."

"It is. I thought it was amazing to just know facts, but using my ability was something completely different just then. Certain portals I passed, I could

pinpoint if it was my mom or grandma who opened it. I didn't expect that to happen more than once or without me focusing on doing that."

"There are moments when I speak of the Keep's times long ago, and the elder of my flights' knowledge will come through. His energy is ancient and distinct, easy for me to identify. A sense of wisdom falls over me when it comes forward. With time, it wouldn't surprise me if you're able to feel many more generations before you, depending on how your communal knowledge continues to be fed to you."

I smile over at her, thanking her for her insight into this new and thrilling experience. I'm grateful that she's here to help me navigate this and she will be as well when Draken's fully comes forward. I know it will. I've already seen clues and picked up on the hints she's dropped.

I've noticed changes in him lately, not bad ones, but more so, my dragon man coming into his own. Yesterday, there wasn't much of a shred of the over-the-top energy jumping around him. He didn't avoid or joke his way out of tough conversations, and when all was said and done between him and Keeper, he was freer.

"That was phenomenal, child. You should've seen the energy encompassing you. It was blinding," Gaster says excitedly, bursting through the crowd.

"It felt otherworldly. I'm not sure how to even explain what it was like," I say, matching his smile.

"It was ethereal as though Elementra herself was surrounding you," he says, and an itch in the back of my mind starts up. I don't have time to tug on it as it settles away, and he continues, "Be careful in your travels and pay keen attention to details. I want to see it all when you return."

I laugh when he pulls me into a hug that's full of wonder and excitement. I can't help but hope when I'm however millennia old he is, things still get me going like they do him.

"Time to move out, little warrior. Anything we need to know?" Tillman asks as the four of them stand around me.

"No, not that I can think of," I say, shaking my head and latching onto each of them with a tendril of my shadows.

"Let me see your hands before we go, Primary," Caspian commands gently, and I turn them palm side up to show them.

"Has your healing increased somehow?" Corentin asks, bewildered, healing vial at the ready but not needed.

"No, it's the mark. I use it with intentions and when those have been fulfilled, it seals itself back up," I say as that tidbit comes forward.

To my shock, they have no follow-up questions. Actually, they seem relieved at the prospect of me not having to drink a healing vial at each stop, or that I'm going to be tearing my healed hands back up multiple times today.

I receive a nod and a smile from each of them, then the serious expressions return.

"First stop, Pyrathia," Tillman orders and all three Nexuses get ready, with Keeper joining us, and Codi and Trex going together.

For the first two transports, everyone knows where to go, so we won't be moving together. It's when we move to Aquaria for the Valorian Veil portal that I'll have to send an imprint.

Darkness closes in around me and I embrace its peace for the fleeting second before the heat of the territory slaps me in the face. Although it's not as bad as summers in the nonmagical realm, there's a world of difference between here and the heart of the Central.

At first glance, the landscape looks harsh and unforgiving—a span of jagged volcanic rock that seems to stretch as far as my eyes can see. But when I focus, just beyond the shifting shadows created by the towering rocks, a narrow path reveals itself.

The recon team isn't in front of the path but spread out in front of the imposing terrain, standing silent, steady, at the ready when we pop in, although they knew we were coming. Tillman doesn't outwardly show it, but his approval etches across my chest.

He passes his commands silently, and none of us speak with more than nods to them as we enter the tight trail.

I feel the energy of the portal already calling to me from the short distance it is away, but we take each step carefully to avoid the fallen stones and sharp rocks. This had to have been easier to maneuver and get through when this portal was open, or I don't see why any of the beings from Mystara Hollow would have wanted to make this trek.

"Shit," Draken breathes through my mind, and I lift my eyes from watching every step I take to see what he sees.

At the end of the path, my gaze settles on what appears to be a chaotic stack of stones, deceptive in its appearance. My eyes trace the stones deliberately placed with their edges worn by time, but they still hold the power they once did.

I can feel it—the hidden pulse beneath the rocks, beckoning me forward, and I answer the call with a few more steps.

My fingers outline the worn runes that are still visible but barely. You'd easily miss them if you weren't looking for them. They hum underneath my hand as if they know I can make them glow again.

With a deep breath, I carve the Nexus mark once again into my left palm, and my trembling hand lifts to lay against the stone. The buzz is immediate, heady, and I suck in a shocked gulp when the information assaults me.

"Closed. Has been for nine hundred and seventy-two years," I mumble to everyone who can hear me.

Gaster's and everyone else's approximations are pretty spot-on. A thousand years is just easier to say, and records indicate the same. Drudy Vito was a stickler for rules and harsh punishments, but apparently, admin and accurate records weren't a worry of hers.

I stare at my bloody handprint for the second it shows, then watch in astonishment as it fades into the stone, leaving no visible trace of me behind.

With nothing more than a confident nod to our group, we prepare to move through another transport. In and out. Silent and stealthy is how the entire mission will go until we reach the portal for Essemist Keep and prepare to track my blood.

This time, when the darkness releases us, fresh air and a cool breeze dries the sweat beading on my forehead. I take a large inhale, savoring the pure, clean air of Aeradora.

The trees stretch so high about me, I have no clue where they end and the sky begins.

It makes sense why this is where the giants would exist. There's plenty of room between each massive tree, and there's no overgrowth or foliage that makes the paths dense or hard to walk. It's gaping space that the wind travels through, creating its own symphony.

If the four E.F. members standing in front of a random tree didn't give it away, the broken bark, perfectly crackled in the shape of a rectangle, would. This particular tree is a few feet wider than the others, and the portal is shaped just like a door as if there's a knob somewhere that we'd just turn to open.

As I approach it, laying my bloodied hand on the smooth brown bark, my heart hums with an easy thud. There's a gentleness radiating off it that reminds me so much of Tillman, I can't help but cock my head over toward him. If I could just assume solely based on what I'm feeling, it's that his gentle, protective nature is more instinctual than we realize. I believe all the giants were like that. It's only their size and strength that makes them so intimidating.

"Closed. Nine hundred and thirty-three years ago."

I place myself beside Oakly this time, linking our fingers and pressing our shoulders together. Simultaneously, we'll send an imprint to everyone, even our Nexuses that will be transporting with us. This way, it's guaranteed if I slip up somehow, she'll still be able to get the information to Lyker's Nexus, Codi, and Trex.

"Deep breath. Pin the location, pass it to me, and then all of them. I'm right here with you," she softly instructs in my head.

Closing my eyes, I call to the location on the map in my mind and stick a pin in it as she said, then I share it with her. Like a beep on a metal detector, the imprint flows from me, and we're sucked into the fabric of the realm. Then we're gracefully released right at our location.

This portal isn't like the others.

The energy from it consumes me entirely. Everyone is busy getting their bearings, seeing where we are, while I'm on my knees, slicing my hand, ready to dive into the unmoving clear pool.

My hand gets sucked through the water and the sight sucks me in.

The vision unfolds like a storm ripping through the heavens.

Powerful figures clash with both weapons and gifts I've never seen, their movements swift, deadly, and realm quaking. In the midst of the chaos, the line is clearly divided.

This battle isn't just one of physical, magical strength but of wills colliding. Echoes of their roars and swords clashing thunder across the sky, rattling the stars themselves. I can feel it—the raw, primal force that exists in the realms of gods.

This is a glimpse of destruction, a war that could reshape the very fabric of existence.

I gasp, my chest heaving as though I've just surfaced from deep waters, and I fall back on my ass, scooting away from the edge of the portal. My head throbs with the booms of fighting gods, beings, their energy still buzzing in my veins.

This portal cannot be opened, not now, and not for many years to come.

Hands grip me under my arms, and I'm pulled to my feet as the lingering effects of that vision cloud my brain. It takes me a second to get myself together before I can gaze around at everyone staring at me with fear etched across their faces.

"What was that, little wanderer?" Draken asks quietly.

"Did you all see and feel something?"

"Felt. A ripple of energy pulsed through all of us when you stuck your hand in. Not good energy either," Caspian says, and by everyone, he means that. Not just my Nexus, our whole group experienced it.

I nod, catching my breath. "The realm is either about to have a war or is in the middle of one. The portal is closed for now, and it must stay that way. If their problems bleed everywhere else, it's going to be bad. For all the realms."

"How long has it been closed?" he asks.

"A thousand years," I mumble.

"And some change or...?" Corentin tacks on.

"A thousand years exactly."

My mind whirls around the possibilities. Gaster said they were already having issues when he left, so did Elementra know our problems would only become worse because of theirs? What if the Summum-Master stealing the gods' power from there is that what triggers this event? If so, is that what he was referring to when he said he'd rule this realm and any other he chooses?

Oh fuck.

That thought is even more petrifying knowing that the Valorian Veil is viewed right beneath Elementra's in terms of power and strength. Granted, that could be biased opinions of the scholars who wrote that, which means they could be even more powerful than us.

"Time to go. We got to check the portal to the Keep, then get to my blood supply," I say frantically, lining myself back up with Oakly.

No one argues or needs any more discussion. That taste of energy was enough to give us all a feeling of what more we could face if we don't guarantee his access to other realms is cut off.

This time, I don't need a pep talk, reassurance, or guidance as I latch onto the location of the portal and send everyone their signal. The calm I felt has been replaced with a desperate desire to find my blood and destroy it. The last thing I want is to drag this out, end up in a war with a whole other realm. I want to worry about my own home, not decimate others in a senseless war.

The cave mouth comes into sight, and it's just as hostile appearing in person as it was in my mind, but that doesn't slow our steps.

"It is closed. But while you verify, Adored, I'll check the vampires and see if there're any changes to the nonmagical portal," Keeper says grimly as we cross the threshold of the opening before zooming away.

I'm positive he's right based on the same low frequency of energy pulsing in the air, but just as the others, I check anyway.

The cool and damp wall at the back of the cave is cold against my hand, chilling the heat I've been feeling since being spat out of the vision. The energy is dejected here as though it's absorbing the emotions on the other side and pushing them out this way.

It makes my heart hurt thinking about an entire realm so saddened by the loss of their heir, but it pains me even more thinking about how we're going to have to let him go. One day soon, I'll have to open this portal so he and all the others trapped can go home.

I don't know what that will mean for us and our new blossoming relationships.

After fifty or so feet away from the cave entrance, Keeper reappears, joining us in stride as we give ourselves some distance to quickly regroup and get ready to track my blood. The anticipation is starting to kick up now and everyone feels it.

"The portal is still open as it has been, but the Summum-Master is in Elementra. The vampires haven't seen him since he brought Drin in," he informs us and we all nod.

"Put what we just learned as far out of your mind as possible, little warrior. We succeed in this, we won't have to fear him getting to that realm, and their problems will stay their own. Breathe. Focus on Oakly's and your task at hand. Stick to the plan. You'll be pulling our Nexus, Keeper, Codi, and Trex. Oakly will be taking her Nexus and Lyker's. Only focus on that," Tillman says confidently, gripping the back of my neck before laying his forehead to mine.

When he releases me, I can't help but cut a glance at my brother. I hate that he isn't coming through my imprint and transport, but at the same time, I'm humble enough to admit when someone is better at something than me, and Oakly most certainly is. I'd feel safer with him going with her, while I take the smaller group.

Each of my men gives me quick, passionate kisses, none too distracting but enough that their confidence in me blooms in my chest and relaxes the nerves I've finally started to feel.

"When we get wherever we're going, we'll observe and analyze before making a move. We'll decide from there on backup. Willow and Oakly, stay as close as possible if there's a delay in our arrival with you," Tillman orders once more and everyone moves in.

"Ready?" I ask Oakly.

"Yeah, you?"

"Nervous now."

"Oh, thank fuck, me too. I didn't know if we were still pretending not to be."

I smirk, thanking her for that recess from the seriousness as I shift my finger back into a claw. Her left hand stretches out, cupped, waiting for me to pool enough of my blood for her to use.

Once my palm is full, I carefully pour half into hers, the warmth of the liquid lingering between us as I hold the rest in my own. Our clean fingers interlace, and we squeeze tightly, grounding each other before tilting our heads back toward the sky.

"Track."

The command echoes in my mind as my blood surges back into my palm. I count down the seconds, tension building with every heartbeat, waiting for the signal. When it finally hits me—faint but undeniable—I grasp for it, wrapping my energy tightly around the line, refusing to let it slip away.

"Got it," I say.

"Got it."

We snatch—pulling ourselves through the fabric of the realm once more as our imprints pass to the others.

The phantom feel of Oakly's hand in mine seems to tighten as we tumble through existence. The strain on my skin sends panic rippling through me because it feels as though we've just transported through a ward that didn't want us to pass through.

I fear we've imprinted on the exact location of my blood, rather than close enough to know where but far enough away to get ourselves together again.

I prepare myself mentally for a fight as soon as we step out of this never-ending darkness, knowing we're going to be face-to-face with someone in enemy territory. But all those thoughts flee me when we're shoved out of the transport, hitting our knees with a bone-jarring thud.

As soon as I hit the ground my stomach bottoms out, and the sounds of my sickness echo loudly, mingling with Oakly's.

"What the fuck?" she groans, gripping her head in one hand, stomach in the other.

My vision blurs as tears from throwing up so forcefully blind me, but I reach my hand over, rubbing her back.

"The others?" I choke out.

The words pass my lips as a loud pop booms in front of us. Instead of the faint, almost undetectable sound of a transport, this one is deafening as our entire group is spat out unceremoniously.

I sway harshly as I try to get up to check on them, but they all rebound so much faster and easier than Oakly and me. Neither of us even gets to our feet before they're helping us up.

"Fuck, that was not in the plan. What happened?" Corentin asks, placing a healing vial to my lips as Jamie grips Oakly and me by the arms.

"We passed through a ward. Fuck, I don't—"

"Primary, I don't believe that was a ward," Caspian interrupts, low, cold.

The tone instantly draws my attention and makes the hair on the back of my neck stand up. His gaze isn't on me but behind me, and true fear takes hold as I see the alarmed gleam in his eye.

Slowly, with my heart pounding in my throat, I turn to face whatever it is that has my most fearless of men looking like that.

No.

"Elementra," I breathe.

The moment my eyes locked onto it, the realm seems to lurch sideways. My breath gets caught in my throat, and suddenly, everything else fades into the background. A sharp ringing fills my ears, growing louder with each passing second. It feels as though the air has been sucked from the forest, leaving me suspended in a suffocating silence.

"Willy." Oakly's soft voice penetrates the eerie emptiness of my mind, and the loving hands that grip me as I stumble hold me up. "Is that..."

"That's my willow tree."

About the author

Welcome to the land of delusion where I dive into realms where imagination reigns supreme and love knows no bounds. With every stroke of my pen, or tap on the keyboard, I'm creating worlds where magic thrives and destinies unfold.

I'm thrilled you've found me and I can't wait to continue bringing you an escape.

My WIP's are a mile long which fuels my coffee, writing/reading, and fictional men addiction. It's not really something I'm working on though, so expect some sweet, beautiful chaos to come your way soon.

All jokes and funnies aside, I truly hope you find some peace, bliss, and escape through my words. If one person feels something from the pages I write, then it's all worth it.

Always, happy reading!

Willa Rae, xoxo

Follow me for updates!

Willa's Wildling's Private Readers Group!

@WillaRae.author on

TikTok, Instagram, Facebook, Amazon

Made in United States
Troutdale, OR
01/11/2025